The Cursed One

Dani Healy

Dani Healy Fiction

Printed in the United States of America

Copyright © 2017 Dani Healy

Cover artwork by Kate Ford

Final edits by Mohammed Al Mohammed Al Sibahi

ISBN-10: 0-9987614-9-4

ISBN-13: 978-0-9987614-9-7

Dani Healy Fiction

DEDICATION

For Jamie, Chaylee, and Dexton.
I love you three to the moon and back.

CHAPTER 1

Avery Miller thought back to the fateful night that had brought her and Sebastian Taylor together. To this day, she still didn't understand exactly what happened six years ago on that cold October night. Halloween to be exact.

After trick-or-treating with her friends, twelve-year-old Avery decided to take a shortcut home through a plot of empty houses under construction just a couple of blocks away from her street.

Big mistake.

When she stepped off the sidewalk, away from the streetlamps and into the darkness, an overwhelming stench of copper engulfed her. The foul odor should have been her first clue that something wasn't quite right, but she was too young to know what that smell actually was. Shortly thereafter, she stumbled upon the body of that poor man. He was lying motionless in a growing pool of red liquid. Bloody footprints were scattered all around as if someone had tried to keep him from escaping while he bled to death. His bulging eyes were wide with terror as they stared blankly at her. Even after death, his hands were still latched around his throat, as if they were trying to stop the blood from pouring out of the huge gaping hole in his neck.

It was then that Avery heard a low rumbling growl. She tried to swallow the lump that abruptly formed in her throat as she willed her feet to move. Slowly and carefully, she began to back away as her gaze shifted upward. An immense black shape hovered just a few feet above the bloody remains. A dark, misty cloud surrounded this demon-like creature, emanating pure evil.

At first, Avery thought her eyes were playing tricks on her, until her startled gasp shifted the creature's attention in her direction. The fiery red of its eyes were like glowing lasers burning through the night.

The creature's elongated mouth opened slowly until it hung fully agape, revealing dozens of rows full of razor sharp teeth. A deafening screech emanated from its throat, sending ripples through the air straight toward Avery's frozen body. When the waves of energy hit, she temporarily lost her footing.

Fear completely engulfed her as she stumbled backward. Her throat suddenly felt dry, and her heart began to race out of control. This *thing* was now coming straight for her! She scrambled to her feet, dropping her 'Sleeping Beauty' pillowcase full of candy, and ran as fast as she could down the dimly lit street.

"SOMEONE HELP ME!" she screamed. "SOMEONE PLEASE HELP ME!"

Her heart was pounding so hard in her chest that she could feel it thudding loudly in her ears. Her lungs were starting to burn with each shallow breath that she took.

Don't stop running! Whatever you do, don't stop running!

The shrilling shrieks were right behind her now as a groan escaped her trembling lips. The angel wings of her costume seemed to be weighing her down. As she struggled to unhook them, the creature's claws slashed at her back, tearing and ripping the soft white feathers. The creature growled deep and throaty, then snarled as it reached out for her again.

Tears began to fill her eyes, blurring her vision. "PLEASE

DON'T KILL ME!" Her continuous cries echoed into the night.

When all hope seemed lost, that is when Sebastian entered her life. Suddenly, two hands grabbed hold of her shoulders, jerking her backward off the sidewalk. She let out a frightened squeal as she landed softly behind some azalea bushes that lined the road. Then the high-pitched shrieking came to an abrupt halt.

Her entire body shook violently as she struggled to catch her breath while tears streamed down her flushed cheeks. Frantically she looked around, expecting that horrifying creature to reappear at any minute. It took a few seconds for her brain to register that someone was holding onto her. A brief moment of panic shot through her body, until she looked up into those soft grey eyes.

A young boy, about her age, was staring at her with such an intense look of wonder on his face; as if he had just discovered some foreign artifact.

She threw her arms around his neck and cried into his shoulder. "Thank you so much! I was so scared! I thought it was going to kill me!"

"It's okay. You're safe now," he replied in a whisper.

<u>CHAPTER 2</u>

Six years later...

Avery, now eighteen, stood in front of Sebastian with her arms crossed defensively across her chest. He still looked at her in that wonderful unique way on occasion, but this very moment was not one of them.

She sighed. "You say that you want me to really know you, but you still won't give me a chance!"

"You wouldn't like what you see," Sebastian declared.

She rolled her eyes. "I already like what I see!"

He laughed, deep and hearty. "You see what *they* see." He gestured all around himself. "What everyone sees is a lie."

She took a timid step towards him. "If that's the case, then let me be the first to get past this so-called lie."

The desperation in her voice pierced his heart as he shook his head sadly. He couldn't bear to look at her anymore, so he quickly turned away. "I can't risk it," he whispered.

This is how things had always been. For the past six years, she would try to get close to him, but he would instantly put up his walls. No one knew Sebastian like Avery did. All the girls in school wanted him, and all the guys envied him. Yet he hated all the attention. Snooty glares from jealous girls were constantly given every time they entered the cafeteria together, laughing and smiling with their arms linked. Of course, that meant everyone thought they were a couple. Though unfortunately for Avery, that was only in her dreams.

Her happy expression faltered. "What could you possibly be hiding that's so bad? You know you can trust me, Bastian! After everything that's happened between us, I don't understand why you still won't let me in!"

Sebastian's shoulders rose and fell as he turned back around. His eyes landed on the necklace she wore…the one he gave her on her sixteenth birthday. "Can we change the subject, please?"

She gave the best pout she could muster as another sigh escaped her lips. "I guess I have no choice."

He had to look away again. It was as if those beautiful green eyes of hers could see right into his soul. "One day you'll find out the truth," he stated sadly. "And then you'll remove yourself from my life."

Avery felt herself getting flustered. "How many times do I have to tell you that you're wrong? I'm not going anywhere."

"I'm never wrong," he replied. "Not about this."

She scoffed and placed her hand on her hip for effect, though he wasn't even looking at her. "That's a bit cocky, don't you think?"

He shrugged. "Maybe so, but it's also true."

She pulled on his arm in an attempt to turn him around. "Please…" She swallowed hard.

The tone of her voice made his chest ache. He wanted to see the expression on her face, though he knew he would regret it later. Against his better judgment, he stole a glance in her direction. When their eyes met, he saw exactly what he knew he would. Love. Adoration. Yearning.

That is when she reached out for him. She cupped his face in her hands and studied him closely. His usually strong and masculine features began to look rugged and distressed.

Normally he would have pushed her away. And every fiber of his being was screaming at him to stop her, but he just couldn't bring himself to move. Not this time.

She could sense some discomfort boiling underneath his steely exterior, so she casually asked if he was alright.

He hesitated, taking a breath. He was enjoying the fact that she was touching him, but he knew that once this moment was over, he could never let it happen again. He placed his hand on top of hers and nuzzled his face against her palm. "I can't..." he whispered painfully.

"You can't wh...?" Her words were cut short as he turned, and not walked, but actually *ran* away from her.

Her mouth automatically dropped open in disbelief. After so many years of being shot down, you would think that she would be used to his constant rejections, but yet again she felt the familiar sting in her heart.

You'll never learn, her mind pressed.

CHAPTER 3

Avery eventually managed to gather what was left of her dignity. She released her breath in one quick exhale as she proceeded towards her car. She blinked away the oncoming tears as she started the engine.

She was beginning to realize that anything serious with Sebastian was completely out of the question. She loved him. More than she cared to admit. But when would enough be enough? At that exact moment, she decided that she needed someone to confide in, so she sent her best friend a text to meet her at a park nearby. Within seconds, Valerie replied that she was on her way.

~*~*~*~

Avery parked and trudged over to the picnic table where her best friend sat, swinging her legs over the edge like a little kid.

"Bad day?" Valerie asked.

"You could say that," Avery replied. She sat down next to her friend and stared off into space.

Valerie got straight to the point. "So, what's up?"

Avery groaned.

Valerie's legs stopped swinging. "That bad, huh?"

Avery nodded. "It's worse."

"Oh, do tell!" Valerie gushed. She was trying to keep from smiling with anticipation, but she was awful at hiding her emotions...good or bad.

Avery sighed as she mindlessly twirled the charm around her neck. "I'm thinking of ending everything with Bastian. I'm done trying. I don't know what else to do."

Valerie's facial expression shifted from shock to sadness and ended with confusion. "What happened?"

"Nothing. That's just it! Nothing has happened, and apparently, nothing is ever going to happen. I'm stuck in Friendsville, and it looks like I'm here for the long haul!"

Valerie frowned. "Aww sweetie, that sucks."

"Yeah, you're telling me!"

Valerie put her arm around Avery's shoulder. "So, what are you gonna do? Give him an ultimatum?"

Avery felt herself smile as she rolled her eyes. "Yes, Val, let me give him an ultimatum." She puffed out her chest and spoke with authority, "Either love me or leave me, but I'm not taking no for an answer!"

Her best friend clapped cheerfully. "There ya go! That's my girl, take charge!"

Avery laughed. "Did you not hear the sarcasm?"

Valerie gave her a playful shove. "Well, you do whatever you gotta do. I know how much you care about that boy, but he's not worth a broken heart. Especially if he can't see what he's got right in front of him!"

"Thanks, Val."

She smiled. "What are besties for?"

"Well, I should probably get home," Avery announced. "It'll be getting dark soon."

"Yeah, Lord knows we don't need to be on the cover of any newspapers tomorrow," Valerie replied jokingly.

Hurt covered Avery's face. "That's not funny!"

Valerie flinched. "I'm sorry. I didn't mean it like *that*."

"It's fine," Avery stated.

Though Valerie knew it wasn't fine at all.

~*~*~*~

Avery's mind was a jumbled mess the entire drive back to her house. She decided to take the long way home, giving herself some extra time to clear her head. But that seemingly wonderful plan was quickly squashed the moment she pulled into her driveway.

There, she found Sebastian sitting at the bottom of her stairs, waiting solemnly.

She parked and approached him as casually as possible...failing of course. "Hey," she said quietly. It was the only word she could think of, and of course, it came out shaky and way too high-pitched.

"Hey," he replied, keeping his face out of view.

Avery sighed and took a seat next to him. "I've been thinking..." she swallowed nervously before continuing, "...and as much as it kills me to say this, I think it might be time that we..."

Sebastian suddenly shifted his whole body in her direction, which caused her to stop mid-sentence. The look on his face was pure misery.

She debated whether or not she should continue with what she had planned to say.

The seconds ticked by and he never said a word. He just kept staring at her. She knew he was trying to figure out what was going on in her head. He always seemed to know what she was thinking or feeling, without her ever needing to say a word.

"Bastian, I..."

"I'm sorry I'm constantly being so difficult," he blurted out.

"It's not that you're difficult." She paused, and half smiled. "Well, you *are*, but that's not the point right now."

He smiled then, making her second guess everything she was about to reveal. Her heart stuttered at the sight of his perfectly shaped mouth. His soft pink lips curved just enough to form tiny dimples at the corners.

"You're staring again," he said softly.

She let out a nervous laugh. "You act like that's something new."

His grin widened. "I'll never understand the female mind, nor the attraction you have for me."

Her frustration and anger seemed to dissipate almost instantly as she leaned forward and used her fingertips to examine the features of his face. He shot her a playful glare as he gently pushed her away. Her smile faded as she awkwardly withdrew her hand.

"I don't do it to hurt you," he said quietly. He held her gaze this time.

There was that troubled expression on her face again as her eyes narrowed. "Do what?"

"Detach myself from you."

She sighed. "Then why do you do it? Especially when you know it hurts me."

He sighed too. "The reason goes hand in hand with my past."

"So, in other words, you won't tell me," she stated bluntly.

He noted the defeat in her voice. "Can't tell you," he corrected her. "Emphasis on *can't*."

She sighed again, deeper this time. Then she stood and looked down at him. "Can't. Won't. It's all the same to me, Bastian." She turned to leave.

Suddenly, he grabbed her wrist. "Avery, wait..."

This move completely caught her off guard. It wasn't aggressive by any means, more like a gentle grasp so she wouldn't walk away. And it was the first time since he had rescued her, six years ago to the day, that *he* had reached out and touched *her*.

She watched his facial expression change as their fingers slowly intertwined. Avery didn't want to move. She didn't want to breathe. She didn't want anything to ruin this moment.

Sebastian closed his eyes and gently rubbed the back of her hand with his thumb. *I said never again, yet here I am…again.* When he opened his eyes, he seemed even more conflicted.

"Are you okay?" she asked, her voice barely a whisper.

"No...I'm not," he replied softly. "I know you don't understand when I say that I can't give you answers." He looked up then, locking his intense grey eyes with hers. "I want to tell you everything, Av. I really do. I want to share all my secrets with you. I want to share all of myself with you. To let you know what makes me who I am and makes me...what I am, but it's just not possible right now."

Avery gripped his hand tighter. "But why? Why isn't it possible?"

He sighed and averted his gaze once more. "Because that's my curse."

She let out a sigh that sounded more like a small growl. "What does that even mean? Your curse? Are you some sort of werewolf or vampire or something?" She seemed a bit too excited about the likelihood that he could be either one of those things. "Because I could totally handle that!"

Sebastian laughed out loud. He hadn't meant to, it just sort of slipped out. "Those are just stories, Av. As in make believe."

"So, you're not a...?"

He shook his head, still clearly amused. "No, I'm not a werewolf...or a vampire."

"But you are something..."

Sebastian wasn't sure if she was asking him a question or making a statement. Either way, he chose not to respond.

Avery touched his chin and tilted his face to look at her again. "Nothing..." she paused, making sure she had his full attention, "...absolutely nothing you could say or do would ever change who you are to me or how I see you."

A faint smile graced his gorgeous face once more, which made her feel at ease for that brief moment. But smile or no smile, she was not prepared for what happened next.

He slipped his hand out of hers faster than humanly possible, then he stood and backed away quickly, looking down at the ground. "I...I...uh, I have to go!" he stammered. Then he ran away...again.

Avery stared after him with her mouth hanging slightly open. Then she threw her arms up in the air out of frustration.

"Ugh, FINE! Whatever! Go then!" she called out. She stomped up the stairs and slammed the door behind her. She wanted to cry. She wanted to scream. She wanted to fall on the floor and throw a full-blown tantrum.

"Why am I doing this to myself?" she said out loud. *More like why do I keep doing this to myself?!* She sighed for what seemed like the millionth time that day as she slid down to the floor and leaned her head against the door.

CHAPTER 4

Oh, how he hated having to keep secrets from her. As if things weren't complicated enough, he had just made them worse by running away like a coward twice in one day. Sebastian groaned inwardly. She was the girl who held his heart in the palm of her hand, but he couldn't let her know that...at least not yet. He couldn't allow himself to get any closer. Not without exposing everything he had been fighting so hard to keep hidden.

Then why do I keep giving her hope? Why do I keep leading her on? Why can't I just end it and walk away without looking back? He sighed, but what came out sounded more like a whimper. He knew exactly why he did all those things.

Sebastian closed his eyes and sat in silence for a while, reliving the intimate moment the two of them had just shared. He could still hear the sound of Avery's heartbeat increase when he didn't instantly pull away. He recalled the brief flash of excitement on her face and the warmth of her skin against his. Then he cringed. It was stupid to allow himself a moment to pretend he was normal. It was just a small slip up, but it was one that he couldn't afford to repeat.

He knew the risks. He could have easily lost control. In

fact, he almost had, which is why he fled. The Pure Ones were sure to find him if he continued down this careless path, but he just could not seem to help it. Avery was like a drug, and he was the addict coming back for more.

As fear and regret slowly rose within him, he swore under his breath and slammed his fist against the wall. The entire structure shook beneath his powerful strike. He took a step back and let out an irritated sigh as he stared at the huge hole in the wall of his living room. It reminded him of the hollow feeling he felt growing inside his own heart. He had been warned of the consequences. Being who he was...being what he was...getting too close to someone only meant that someday he would have to say goodbye.

He had never really worried about that sort of thing until the day he met Avery. He had lovers in the past, but nothing like this. His thoughts were always filled with her beautiful face, her soft touch, and her intoxicating laugh. She supplied his life with more joy than he could have ever imagined.

Though knowing how things would work out, he should have avoided her like the plague. But the more time he spent with her, the more his heart ached at the thought of watching her walk out of his life. He knew without a doubt that was going to happen. It was just a question of when.

Eventually, the torment would overtake him, and he would have no other choice than to confess it all. Though he was hell bent on holding out for as long as physically possible. Over the last six years, the pain had never grown above a dull ache when she was with him, and he was determined to keep it that way.

He leaned against the crumbling wall and let his body slide to the floor as his vision began to blur. He closed his eyes again, and for the first time in at least a hundred years, he let the tears fall. Soon he would lose her. He was sure of that fact. Still, her sweet words lingered in his ears.

You're wrong!

He gripped his chest and smiled through the pain. "If only..."

CHAPTER 5

Most of Sebastian's memories of his former life had long been forgotten. Not because he wanted to forget, but because he was forced to. He had no recollection of his mother or father, nor did he know if he had any siblings or living ancestors.

Sometimes he would have dreams about the same faces over and over. He believed that was his mind's way of giving him some sort of connection with those who he once knew and loved. It was a sad and lonely existence that he was doomed to endure for the rest of eternity. Everything started...and ended...because of a young girl named Adeline.

The year was 1817. Sebastian was seventeen-years-old and very much in love. Adeline Mary Andrews was beautiful and kind. She was fair skinned with long blonde hair and stunning blue eyes. To say she looked angelic would be an understatement. Their life together was perfect, up until one warm summer evening when the first incident occurred that would change Sebastian's life forever.

A fire tragically claimed Adeline's life. An accident that Adeline's mother, Moira, blamed him for. It was one of the few memories of his previous life that he was allowed to keep.

~*~*~*~

"You!" Moira cried out. "This is all your fault!"

Sebastian could not hear anything over the breaking of his heart as he stared at the charred remains of his beloved. Her empty, blackened eye sockets stared back at him, begging him to turn back time and save her.

"You let her die!" Moira hissed.

"NO!" he shouted. "I love her...loved her!"

Moira clamped her hand around his throat as he gasped for air.

"Please!" he whimpered.

Her grasp tightened as she lifted him off the ground with ease. Sebastian was stunned at the inhuman strength she seemed to possess. Moira closed her eyes, and her lips began to move. Sebastian fought to breathe, but no air was entering his lungs. Her hands clamped tighter. Surely she would crush his windpipe if things continued. Sebastian felt his life slipping away as everything around him began to dim. Just before he lost consciousness, he heard her utter the words, "You'll pay...forever!"

~*~*~*~

Sebastian wasn't sure what had been done to him when he woke up alone in the smoldering pile of ashes beside Adeline's corpse. His entire body began to feel as though it were on fire, burning from the inside out. He let out an agonizing scream as he tried to crawl away, attempting to stand as he began ripping off his clothes. Tears ran down his cheeks as his body crumpled back onto the ground. He called out for Moira, but only the echo of his own voice returned.

She had gone. Leaving nothing behind, except for him.

In the midst of the unbearable pain, his eyes began to glow.

What is happening to me? Sebastian thought frantically.

He opened and closed his eyes repeatedly, rubbing them in an effort to make the bright red light disappear. But then tiny sparks erupted from his fingertips. It felt as if his skin were being peeled away bit by bit. He let out a bellowing scream as his entire body suddenly burst into flames. He dropped to the ground again, rolling around in a desperate attempt to extinguish himself, but the flames only grew stronger. Hotter. Uncontrollable. He clawed at his face, struggling to end his burning torture as he screamed and cried out, begging for someone to help him. When he screamed again, flames shot out of his mouth like a volcano spitting out lava.

Moments later, as if an answer to his prayer, a small group of men appeared out of nowhere. Sebastian tried to ask them for help, but by that point, his mind was far too consumed with the endless, searing pain. The men picked him up and carried him through the forest, up a steep mountain slope. The entire journey took them a total of three days. All the while, Sebastian was in and out of consciousness.

Through his constant shouts and cries, he heard Moira's voice drift through his mind.

A lover's grasp shall be your fate.
Your dying heart they'll never take.
For once you utter love's three words
The darkened form will be returned.
Deny the curse and defy the night.
The tainted blood will destroy the light.

~*~*~*~

To this day, her final words continued to repeat in Sebastian's head as a deafening reminder of his misfortune. He used to perceive himself as lucky to be alive after the curse was bestowed upon him, but countless decades of constant sorrow and heartache later, he began to rethink his logic.

He learned that the three men who carried him out of the woods were called Pure Ones, gods or what have you. Their eyes glowed with an intense purple hue, though nowhere near as menacing as Sebastian's vibrant red. They became his mentors, his protectors, and his family. They informed him about Watchers; specific generations of humans who had been bestowed with magical gifts which were used to protect the Pure Ones' secrets. Watchers had been given the task of 'watching over' any Cursed Ones that were lost and in need of help. That is what Sebastian was now…a Cursed One. Though the Watchers weren't as strong or as fast, they were essential to the survival and concealment of his new-found family.

The Pure Ones taught him how to fight…and eventually how to kill. Sebastian also learned how to hide in plain sight, altering his appearance into any age he wanted to take. What he did not learn, however, was how to break the curse altogether. He was told it was impossible.

The Pure Ones taught him how to control his emotions to make the transition somewhat less painful, but never pain-free. The first time he purposely shifted into his Cursed Form, he was not prepared for the sight of his new 'body'. When the transformation was complete, he stared at his terrifying reflection. Like a ghostly apparition, he hovered above the ground. His glowing red eyes were menacing and creepy as they pulsed with his new extraordinary energy. His entire anatomy was see-through, like a wispy cloud of dark smoke. It was bizarre to feel entirely whole and yet look so incomplete.

After that day, Sebastian never looked upon his Cursed Form again. It was much too disturbing.

He initially thought the painful transition was the only aspect of the curse that he had to endure for the rest of his immortal life, which was not ideal, but he could learn to live with it. However, he soon found out there was much more to it. His new form craved blood. It thrived on it. And not just a drop or two, but a whole body full. So, he was taught to control his urges, only preying on humans who were already dying or recently dead. Fully draining them to consume their essence, or life force, to keep himself humming with power. If that weren't bad enough, there was one final aspect of the curse that he did not expect. The Pure Ones told him the story of how the Cursed Ones came into existence, only then did Moira's words make sense.

A lover's grasp shall be your fate.

Love. That was the trigger. If and when he fell in love, he would eventually be forced to reveal his Cursed Form.

Sebastian had stopped counting how many times he had gotten close to his lovers, only to lose them once his secret was out. He tried to run away once, to spare his young love such a heavy burden, but the distance meant nothing. The physical torment soon became too much for him to bear and he was sent crawling back to her, only to have her flee in terror once he transitioned. This would be his curse for eternity. Driven mad with internal agony until he confessed what he was. Only then would the pain stop.

Moira got exactly what she wanted. He would never find true love again because no one would want to stay with a monster.

So, for a long time, Sebastian had given up. He left the comfort of the place he had grown to call home…the sacred place he shared with the Pure Ones, as well as others who were in the same predicament he was. He disconnected himself with any shred of humanity left inside and let pure instinct take over. That was his life for the last hundred years. A lonely Cursed One without anyone to call his own…until he met Avery.

Now the pain was starting again. A pain that would only grow worse as time went on. A pain that would only end once she saw the darkness hiding beneath the surface.

He was going to lose her just as he had lost everyone else. This time, though, the torture he would feel *after* losing her may actually be worse than the physical pain that came with never telling her the truth.

CHAPTER 6

Avery watched the sun setting off in the distance. Soon the streets would be filled with pirates, ghosts, and princesses. Her stomach was already in knots, and her palms were starting to sweat. Tonight would be the fifth year in a row that she locked herself away from the world until All Hallows Eve was over.

Sebastian had texted her only mere moments ago, asking if she still wanted him to come over. It had become a tradition since the first day they met. She replied with a simple "No," though she secretly wished he would defy the odds and show up to her rescue once more.

Avery knew her parents had an office party to go to tonight, and they were still under the assumption that Sebastian would be coming over. She didn't want to ruin their night with her ongoing issues with this particular holiday, so she had kept the change of plans to herself. But who was she kidding? She knew she didn't want to be all alone tonight of all nights.

I should text him back and tell him that I've changed my mind. Her inner dialogue went back and forth repeatedly. *No, don't be a baby. You can get through one night by yourself!*

She turned off every light in the house, making sure to stay away from any windows without curtains. She didn't want any trick-or-treaters to know that she was home. A single candle flickered on the coffee table in the living room, giving just enough light to keep her from being in complete darkness. She paced back and forth across the room, nervously playing with her hands.

Her mind replayed bits and pieces of that horrible night. It was just enough to make her feel ill. *Sitting alone in a dimly lit room when I'm clearly terrified of the dark. Especially tonight. Real smart move, genius!*

She heard playful howls and excited chatter coming up the street. Her mind raced as more flashbacks toyed with her imagination.

Glowing red eyes.

Razor sharp teeth dripping with blood.

Screaming and screeching echoing from behind her.

She could feel her heart rate rising as she wiped the perspiration from her brow. This was going to be the longest night of the year for her...and she hated every long lasting second of it.

~*~*~*~

At least three times in the last hour there were knocks on her door. Each and every time she nearly jumped out of her skin.

"TRICK OR TREAT!" the children called out happily.

Avery covered her ears and whimpered to herself. *Just go away. Please just leave me alone.* For a while, after that, there were no more disturbances. Avery listened to the laughter and excitement of all the children passing by. She recalled feeling that way once, but that seemed like a lifetime ago. She glanced at the digital clock hanging on the wall. It was only 8:45pm. A groan escaped her lips. Time seemed to be moving like a snail stuck in glue.

~*~*~*~

Meanwhile, Sebastian had been pacing back and forth in his living room with his phone in his hand for the past forty-five minutes. He had already called Valerie and asked her to stop by to check on Avery for him, but that still hadn't satisfied the urge for him to rush straight over there himself. His stomach was twisting, and his mind was reeling. He sighed heavily as he sat down on his couch. A minute or so later he jumped to his feet, picked up his keys, gathered up a few items, and headed out the door. *I can't just sit here and do nothing.*

He cut off his headlights as he parked in Avery's neighbor's empty driveway. She didn't need to know he had disobeyed her orders to stay home…though she would find out soon enough.

As he strolled up the long walkway, a few kids were knocking on her door shouting "Trick or Treat". He cringed internally as he heard Avery's heartbeat thudding rapidly within her chest. He noted that all the lights had been turned off and most of the curtains were drawn. He wanted to go inside. He wanted to yell at all the children to run along. He wanted to tell them to skip this house and just move on to the next. He wanted to protect her. He wanted to comfort her. But tonight, she didn't want him there. Not that he blamed her; it was his fault after all. If only he hadn't run away. He let out a small sigh as he wrote a short note and then taped it to the large bowl he had brought with him. As he disappeared back down the driveway, a little fairy and a green ninja strolled past. He glanced back over his shoulder and smiled as their little faces lit up.

Happy Halloween, Avery…

~*~*~*~

Avery heard footsteps approaching her door yet again. Children giggled and squealed and then trotted happily away. A little while later, there was a knock on her door.

"Av, it's me. Open up!"

Avery let out a huge sigh of relief and welcomed Valerie inside.

"I know this is usually your tradition with Sebastian, but since you foolishly told him to stay home tonight, I thought I'd fill in."

"How did you…?"

Valerie smiled timidly.

"Ah. He called you, didn't he?"

Valerie nodded.

Avery sighed with relief. "Thanks, chick. I'll be honest, this year is harder than all the others for some reason."

"Because he's not here?" Valerie asked, already knowing the answer.

Avery shrugged. "Partially." *More like completely.*

"Well, at least you're changing things up this year." Valerie smiled again. "That's a good start."

Avery raised an eyebrow. "Changing things up?"

Valerie motioned outside. "The little set up on the steps. It's cute."

Slightly confused, Avery peeked outside. Four little kids dressed up as 'The Ninja Turtles' approached her steps. They dug through a large bowl of candy, picked out a few items, and then ran back down the driveway.

Avery opened her door and stepped outside. There was a perfectly carved jack-o-lantern with a candle inside sitting next to a large bowl of candy with a piece of paper taped to the front. She picked up the paper and recognized his handwriting right away.

Happy Halloween, trick-or-treaters.

Please don't knock on the door. Instead, help yourself to some candy.

Have a safe and fun night.

Bastian. She smiled to herself. Avery placed the paper back on the bowl and joined her best friend back inside.

Valerie grinned. "Let me guess…"

Avery tried to hide her ever growing elation.

"Even when he's in the doghouse, that boy still manages to pull out all the stops, eh?"

Avery smiled momentarily. "It's majorly complicated."

~*~*~*~

Throughout the rest of the night, footsteps and giggles came and went outside while Avery and Valerie enjoyed playing hide-and-seek and Marco-Polo in the dark. They gorged on handfuls of candy that they had stolen from the bowl out front, until finally, the clock read 11:59pm. Midnight was the cut off for trick-or-treating in their neighborhood. A mandatory curfew that was put in effect six years ago after the terrifying encounter had happened to Avery.

Valerie blew out the candle on the coffee table while Avery flipped the light switch for the front porch.

"There's still some candy left over!" Avery announced cheerfully. "Wanna veg out with me for a bit longer?"

Valerie was already picking up her purse and keys. "Sorry chickadee, I can't. I told Chase we'd hang out tonight after the curfew."

"You and Chase, huh?"

Valerie shot her a playful glare. "It's not like that. Not yet anyway."

Avery chuckled. "Well, considering how late it is, I probably won't hear from you till late afternoon."

Valerie shrugged with a complacent smile forming.

"That look says it all," Avery stated with a giggle.

Valerie held up her pointer finger as her smile widened. "Not another word, woman!"

Avery zipped her smiling lips.

After a quick kiss on the cheek and a bear hug, her best friend was gone. Avery plopped down on the couch and let out a contented sigh. Halloween was over, and she had survived it once again. She was just settling in for the evening when her phone chimed on the coffee table.

Bastian: Just wanted 2 check on u and make sure u were ok.

Avery: I'm fine…just glad the night is over.

Bastian: I wish I could have been there with u.

She smiled while playing with her necklace as she stared at his words.

Avery: I'd be lying if I said things wouldn't have been easier if u had been.

Sebastian's heart instantly felt lighter.

Bastian: Did the trick-or-treaters leave u alone?

Avery: Yes. Thank u 4 that.
Bastian: Of course. Well, g'night then.
Avery: G'night.

Avery didn't want that to be the end of the conversation. She wanted him to show up at her door, take her in his arms, and tell her how much he missed her. *Maybe one day.*

She changed into her PJs, grabbed a few pieces of candy, and slipped under her covers. She chuckled to herself as she popped a piece of chocolate in her mouth. *I hope I don't find ants in my bed tomorrow. Sweet dreams.*

CHAPTER 7

After texting with Avery, Sebastian sat at the edge of his bed staring out an open window. The streets were quiet now as all the trick-or-treaters had finally gone home. A gentle breeze caressed his face as he closed his eyes and thought back to this very night six years ago. Those images always haunted his mind each and every Halloween, so he wasn't surprised when they found their way to the forefront of his thoughts.

He remembered the look of horror on Avery's face as he chased her down the street. He could still hear her terrified screams echoing in his ears. But most of all, he remembered the hunger growing inside of him; the one part of his existence that he had never been able to control. The hunger that almost cost him the love of his life.

A rush of relief flooded his body as he envisioned himself holding onto her in the azalea bushes. Somehow his humanity had flipped back on. It was an unexpected occurrence that he chalked up to being a random glitch…a glitch that he would forever be thankful for.

Sebastian opened his eyes and reached underneath his bed. His hands instantly landed on the cold metal box he knew would be there. He wiped the dust off the lid as he slowly unhooked the latch. Inside were pictures and keepsakes from when his new life began, along with two old crinkled newspaper clippings. The first one had Avery's picture on the front from when she was interviewed after the attack. The other one read: **THE RED SLICER STRIKES AGAIN**.

The Red Slicer. That is what he was dubbed after three more bodies were found with their throats slashed. Sebastian slammed the box shut as a feeling of disgust overwhelmed him. He hated what he used to be…what he feared he could easily become again.

In that moment, he recalled meeting Isabelle and Elliot Smart for the first time. They had seen Avery's interview on the news and immediately knew it wasn't just some sadistic person playing a sick joke. They knew a Cursed One was to blame, and they needed to find him before anyone else did…or before he claimed another victim.

Sebastian remembered feeling uneasy and suspicious when the Smarts first approached him. However, once he saw the markings covering their arms, he instantly knew they were the Watchers that the Pure Ones had told him about. It took a little bit of coaxing, but eventually, they gained his trust, and he allowed them to take him home. That is when he met their sons, Jonah and Chase. They too had markings that only he could see. A brilliant blue hue that was rhythmically pulsating through the symbols beneath their skin, which started at the base of their shoulders and ran all the way down to the top of their wrists.

Isabelle and Elliot tried to teach Sebastian other ways to control his hunger, but for a while he struggled to live by their rules. They were trying to stop any other mishaps from occurring. Mishaps like the bodies he had left all over town. After living for so many decades without his humanity, change was proving to be hard for him. But after the fourth body had been found, Elliot knew they had to do something drastic, or Sebastian would have to be turned back over to the Pure Ones. He was becoming much too dangerous, and soon they would not be able to hide him any longer. There was only one way the Pure Ones would have dealt with him after all his reckless behavior: Death.

With that threat lingering over his head, Sebastian was willing to try harder to fit into the human world. The Smarts set up a volunteer program at the hospital for all the teens in their area. It was an easy cover. Sebastian could volunteer during the day and then slip into the morgue at night to take the life forces of those who had recently passed on. It was slightly morbid, but it was a better alternative to murder. The life forces of humans were the only reason Sebastian had survived as long as he had. It was absorbed into his tainted body, giving him unlimited strength and power. Not that he needed it while living amongst humans, but someone like him could never be too careful.

Today it had been over four years since he had visited the morgue. He knew one day his hunger could come back full force, but he was determined to survive without stealing any more essences…even those from the dead. He would always be a monster, but being able to control some aspect of his curse made him feel less powerless.

CHAPTER 8

Avery's stomach was filled to the brim with butterflies as she waited anxiously on the front steps of Sebastian's house. When his car came into view, she suddenly felt as if she may throw up. *Just breathe. Just calm down and talk to him. You can do this.* She stood on shaky legs as she wiped off the back of her pants and gave him a little wave. She couldn't see through the dark tinted windows if he waved back, but she just assumed that he had.

Sebastian was pleasantly surprised to see her when he pulled in his driveway. As he got out and started walking towards her, he heard her heart begin to race faster. *She's either very happy to see me, or she's still upset with me from yesterday. I guess I'm about to find out which one.* "Well hi there," he said sweetly.

Avery swallowed down the lump growing in her throat and said, "Hi." It was all she could get out.

"Is everything alright?" he asked. "Or did you just drop by to say hello?"

She shuffled her feet anxiously as he unlocked his front door. "I...uh...I kinda need to talk to you."

"Okay," he replied as he gestured for her to come inside. A million things ran through his mind as he began to wonder what she needed to say.

She hovered in the foyer as he tossed his jacket on the back of the couch and placed his keys on the coffee table.

"Do you wanna sit down or...?"

Avery hesitated. She glanced at the door behind her and then back into the living room. *You can do this*, she told herself again.

By this point, Sebastian was growing increasingly curious as to what had her acting so jittery.

Avery forced her wobbly legs to cooperate as she made her way to where Sebastian was waiting. She didn't have enough courage to sit next to him, so she plopped down on the loveseat across from the couch.

He cleared his throat in an attempt to get her to look at him. "So, what's going on?"

She bit her lip, looking everywhere except into his eyes. "Well, I um..." She shifted nervously in her seat. "I need to ask you something."

He leaned back comfortably and propped his feet up on the coffee table between them in the hopes that if he seemed more relaxed, she would relax too. A few moments of silence later, it seemed to be working.

She took in a deep breath and let it out slowly. When she finally spoke, her words completely caught him off guard. "Are we really friends or do you just stick around because you feel like you have to...because of our past?"

Sebastian's forehead wrinkled in confusion as he sat up and propped his elbows on his knees. This time, it took *him* a few seconds to gather himself before he was able to give her an answer. He cleared his throat. "Of course we're friends, Av!" *I honestly wish we were more.* "There are no obligations whatsoever. I'm here because I want to be here. Why...why would you even think like that?"

Avery sighed, mostly with relief from hearing his words, but partially because she was still unsure. "That's just how it feels sometimes, especially when you act like you did yesterday. It's been driving me insane for a while now."

He exhaled a short burst of air. "Well, I'm sorry if I've made you feel unwanted or uncomfortable. I didn't realize."

"It's not just a few random times, Bastian," she stated. "You do it all the time! You always have."

He wasn't sure what to say or how to respond, so he just stared at her.

Avery took his silence as a clue that she should probably elaborate. "Remember when we were thirteen and Chase triple-dog-dared-you to simply hold my hand? I knew you didn't like me in 'that way', but I never expected you to react the way you did."

"I honestly don't recall how I reacted," Sebastian replied. "Though I do remember Chase wanting to play that game all the damn time."

She chuckled. "Well, basically you outright refused and said you weren't in the mood for playing games."

Sebastian sighed. "Well, in my defense I was only thirteen. I was probably embarrassed. Who knows?"

Avery nervously fiddled with her fingers. "Okay then…what about when we were fifteen? We got paired up during drama class to do a slow dance for a mini play. Do you remember that?"

He nodded. "Vaguely."

"You went behind my back and told Mrs. Ellis that you needed to be switched with another partner. The next thing I knew, Jonah was taking your place. Then when we were sixteen at Paige's birthday party, we played spin the bottle. When my spin landed on you, you got up and left. And I don't mean that you just left the game. You left the entire party!" She paused and sighed. "You're constantly going back and forth when you're around me. One minute you're okay being close to me, and then the next minute you're freaking out and literally running away."

Sebastian was speechless. He hadn't realized how obvious he had been about needing to keep an emotional distance from her. He made a mental note to work on his avoidance skills. "Av, I had no idea that my actions were affecting you so deeply."

At that very moment, he made a decision. A decision that went against everything he had originally planned. A decision that he probably should not spend any amount of time even considering. He stood then and walked around the coffee table.

Avery's heart began to thud loudly in her ears when he sat down next to her.

"I think it's time that I shared some things with you." He sighed heavily. "Maybe it will help you to understand why I do the things I do...and why I can't do certain things as well."

CHAPTER 9

After Avery had gone back home, reality began to set in. Sebastian started wondering what the hell he was thinking! *Promising to show her things about myself that she'd never seen before? What in the world was that about?* Sebastian never made a promise unless he planned on keeping it, so he was quite annoyed at himself.

He spent the entire afternoon, as well as the majority of the evening, cursing at himself and trying to figure out what he could reveal. If he disclosed too little, she would wonder why he made such a big deal about his past. If it were too much, she would call him a freak and then run for the hills. So where was the middle ground? *Is there actually a middle ground to who I am? If there is, I'd better find it fast!*

As the hours ticked by, Sebastian laid on his bed staring at the ceiling. As if he didn't have enough to dwell on, his mind began to replay every single time that he had shown his Cursed Form to the women in his past. He cringed and wrapped his arms around himself as he recalled the horror in each of their eyes as he transitioned right in front of them. He could still hear the echoes of their bloodcurdling screams as they fled. He remembered feeling broken and helpless; frustrated and lonely. Now those feelings were resurfacing, causing him to doubt all the hope he originally had about making things work with Avery.

In the early morning hours, he finally succumbed to sleep, though it was anything but pleasant. The inner torture had begun, and there was no way to shut it off.

CHAPTER 10

The very next morning, Avery texted Sebastian and told him that she was ready to hear whatever he had to say whenever he was ready to talk…hoping he would get the hint.

An hour went by, and he never replied. She did, however, hear from Valerie. Apparently, Chase had kissed her last night, which left her wondering where they stood. Valerie was driving herself crazy wondering if they were still just friends. Were they boyfriend and girlfriend? Did he regret kissing her? Did he want to do it again?

Avery tried to reassure her best friend that everything would be perfectly fine, until Chase called and Valerie had to go. The juicy new details would be given later, which Avery could not wait to hear about.

She tossed her phone on her bed and willed it to ring. *C'mon, Bastian. Where are you?* She thought about sending another text, but she didn't want to come across as needy. *He said he was ready to tell me something from his past. I just need to be patient. I can do that. Right?*

She let out an irritated sigh. "Ugh, just call me dammit!" As if right on cue, her phone went off, alerting her to a new text message…but it was only Jonah. Avery sighed again.

Jonah: Hey, Av.

Avery: Hey. What's up?

Jonah: R ur parents home?

Avery: No…

Jonah: So ur alone?

Avery: Yeah…why?

Jonah: Just wondering.

Avery: Ok. Why?

Avery: Hello?

Avery: Jonah!?

And that was it. Avery stared at her phone, growing more and more annoyed by the minute. She let out a frustrated growl. *What is with these damn boys? It must be 'piss off Avery day' or something!* She slammed her phone down on her dresser and left the room. Thirty minutes passed without any other texts or calls. Then there was a knock on her front door.

"Who is it?" she grumbled.

"It's me," his deep voice replied.

Avery felt a rush of emotions come over her as she reached for the handle. She was happy and angry; sad and confused; hurt and delighted. Though the moment she opened the door and saw the look on his face, all the negative feelings faded instantly.

He smiled half-heartedly. "Hey there."

Helloooooo dimples! "Well hi," she returned with a smile. "Come on in."

"I'm sorry I didn't reply to your text. I was with Jonah discussing…stuff."

Avery closed the door. She wanted to ask what sort of 'stuff' he was referring to, but she knew better than to think he would actually give her a real response. So, she just continued smiling and gestured for him to come sit with her.

~*~*~*~

Sebastian momentarily lost himself in his thoughts from earlier that day. He woke up to the sound of his cell chirping in his ear. He knew it would be from her, so he smiled as he reached for the phone.

Avery: G'morning, Bastian. Whenever ur rdy 2 talk, I'm rdy 2 listen.

Sebastian groaned. *Uh oh. The talk… That was supposedly happening today.*

He wanted to write her back; he really did, but he just wasn't sure what to say. All that time he had spent thinking last night, and he still hadn't come up with a solution. He was worried that if he hurried over there, he might make a mistake. *What if I disclose too much about myself…or what if I show her something that she's not ready for?* Immediately another idea popped into his head. *I guess I could just tell her I jumped the gun yesterday and that I'm not ready to talk yet. That could be my ticket out of this mess!* Then reality slapped him in the face. *But what if she decides to give up on me? What if she realizes that I'm not worth waiting for anymore if I'm going to keep dragging this out?*

Sebastian rubbed his throbbing temples. He had to get another opinion on what he should do. So, he got up, got dressed, and headed straight to the Smart's house. He parked at the end of their driveway and cut off the engine. He didn't want to chance waking everyone up with the rev of his loud-as-hell Dodge Charger. He grabbed the hide-a-key from underneath a mosaic covered flowerpot on the front porch and let himself in. The house was quiet as he made his way down the hallway toward Jonah's bedroom.

He cracked open the door and walked to the end of Jonah's bed. "Sorry to wake you so early," he murmured. "…but I need some advice."

Jonah rubbed his eyes and squinted up at Sebastian. His bed-head hair was sticking up everywhere. "Ask away," he said while yawning.

"Yesterday I told Avery that it was time I shared some of my secrets with her. Now she wants to talk."

Jonah patiently waited for an actual question.

Sebastian sighed and sat on the edge of his friend's bed. "What can I say to her? Every time something gets brought up about my past we end up going in circles. Which never ends well."

"It usually ends with you bolting," Jonah mumbled under his breath.

Sebastian rolled his eyes. "I don't appreciate the condescending tone, but you're right. And that's exactly what I want to avoid this time."

Jonah yawned again. "Well, then something's gotta give."

"Yeah, I know…but what can I give?" Sebastian rubbed his forehead and closed his eyes. "What exactly can I do to give her some sort of insight into who I really am without revealing it all too quickly…or freaking her out?"

Jonah pulled his blanket back over his head. "Just think of the least scary thing about yourself and show her that."

Sebastian let out a dissatisfied grunt and smacked Jonah's legs. "Thanks for the not-so-useful advice."

"Anytime," Jonah replied arrogantly. "Now if you don't mind, I'm going back to sleep."

Sebastian let himself out, returned the hide-a-key, and headed straight to Avery's.

~*~*~*~

"Earth to Sebastian!" Avery waved her hands in front of his face.

Sebastian blinked himself back to the present. "Uh, sorry. Lost in thought."

She gave him a faint shy smile. "I noticed."

"So…" Sebastian cleared his throat. "You wanted to have our talk?"

"Yeah. I think it's about time, don't you? Unless…you've changed your mind."

Sebastian felt his heart sink, but he managed to keep his composure. Avery was still waiting for him to sit with her at the kitchen table.

"No, I haven't changed my mind."

The moment his butt touched the seat cushion, it was as if he had pressed START for Avery to pour out everything she was thinking. She was talking incredibly fast, so he wasn't sure if he was supposed to respond to anything or just sit and listen.

Her heartbeat was steady and strong, telling him that she was confident in whatever it was that she was saying. Normally he hung on every word that came out of her beautiful mouth, but this time he felt as if he was listening to Charlie Brown's teacher. All he heard was, "Wahh wahh wahh. Wahh wahh wahh wahh."

Sebastian struggled within himself. *Do something! Just do what Jonah suggested. Show her the least scary thing you can think of.*

Avery continued, "Wahh wahh wahh. Wahh wahh wahh wahh."

All of a sudden, Sebastian reached across the table and took her hand. Avery's words trailed off, and her eyes widened momentarily.

Great. I haven't even done anything yet, and she's already freaking out. Sebastian watched the corners of her mouth slowly turn up. *Okay, now would be the time to do something,* he told himself. *Now dammit! Do something NOW!*

He entwined his fingers with hers, squeezing lightly. Warmth began to radiate from his skin, sending small pulses of heated energy through his hand into hers.

Her mouth slowly fell open as little vibrations surged through her palm. It felt as if a honeybee were buzzing against her skin. "Do you feel that?" she whispered. After the words had spilled out, she felt like a complete idiot. *Why do you blurt things out before thinking?* She scolded herself.

Sebastian instantly severed contact and swore under his breath. "I'm sorry. I didn't mean to..."

She stopped him before he could finish. "So, you felt it too? What was that?"

He didn't answer right away. "Does it frighten you?" he asked hesitantly.

She just continued to stare at him, still enjoying the fact that only moments ago he had been holding her hand.

His lips pressed together showing his annoyance with the lack of a response. "Does it frighten you?" he repeated a bit more sternly.

She ignored his irritation and shook her head. "No, it

doesn't."

His skeptical gaze seemed to be seeking for any sign of doubt, which she knew he wouldn't find.

"Wait!" She reached for his hand. "Are you saying...*you* were doing that?"

He looked away. "What if I said yes? Would you be afraid?"

She shook her head slowly. "To be honest, I'd be more fascinated than scared." Then she locked her eyes on his. "So, you were causing that funny sensation?"

"Yes." He swallowed nervously as he entwined their fingers once more. "You've wanted to see past my walls for some time now." He swallowed again and stared right at her. "I'm ready to remove a few bricks."

The metaphor he used could not have been more perfect. A ping of excitement upped the amount of butterflies already swirling in her stomach. *A few bricks here and there and eventually his wall will be gone!*

He paid close attention to her facial expression as he sent a stronger surge of energy into her hand. "Are you sure this isn't freaking you out? Even a little?"

She shook her head again as she felt another rush of butterflies combined with the warmth that he was radiating.

"Av, do you trust me?" he asked softly.

"With my life," she replied quickly.

Sebastian smiled. "Then don't let go, okay?"

Without hesitation, Avery nodded.

She watched curiously as he closed his eyes and inhaled deeply, then blew out his breath slowly. The warmth from his hand began intensifying with each intake of air. Avery's heart felt lighter as she realized that he was showing her a side of himself that she had not known existed; a side of him that, within the bounds of reality, should not even be possible. Her eyes wandered down to his now *glowing* hand. Then suddenly, hers began to glow too. The vibrations had subsided, but her palm was starting to feel extremely warm. She didn't mean to, but she started to panic.

The instant her heartbeat rose, Sebastian's eyes flew open, and his steady breathing quickly became erratic. He spoke through gritted teeth, "I can sense your anxiety, but I would never let anything bad happen to you!"

Avery struggled within herself for a few seconds before finally swallowing down her unwanted fears and forcing herself to relax.

As quickly as it came, the tightness in his jaw disappeared. A few more minutes passed before he spoke again. "You can look down now," he whispered.

Her gaze eventually wandered back down to their hands, and a small gasp escaped her lips. "Wow!" she uttered breathlessly. The red glow was nearly blinding. And every fiber of her being was telling her to pull away, but then she heard Sebastian's voice.

Trust me.

She looked up to see him staring directly at her. His intense grey eyes were mesmerizing as he locked his gaze with hers.

Trust me, he repeated. *I would never hurt you.*

Though she clearly heard his voice, his lips never moved. "How…how did you do that?" she asked, clearly spellbound.

"It's complicated," he replied out loud. He tried to pull his hand away, but she squeezed her fingers tight and held him in place.

She raised her eyebrows and tugged him closer. "Let me revel in this for a few more minutes."

He noticed the bemused expression on her face. "You're enjoying this a little more than I expected."

Avery looked down at their hands again. "This is amazing," she whispered. "Is it some sort of magic trick?"

"No, it's definitely not a trick." He smiled faintly and lessened his grip. This time, though, she didn't fight him.

As he slowly pulled his hand from hers, the brilliant glow began to fade. He let his fingertips linger next to hers, causing the faint light to pulsate. It seemed to match her heart with each steady beat until he finally pulled away, completely severing contact. Then the glow was gone.

After briefly studying her hand, Avery turned her attention back to Sebastian. His facial expression seemed torn between relief and fear.

"Please don't tell anyone about this," he whispered.

She reached out to touch his cheek, half expecting to feel the same intense sensation all over again, but only the smoothness of his soft skin graced her fingertips. "Not that anyone would believe me if I did...but what will it take for you to understand that I accept you for who you truly are? Secrets and all."

He turned away from her. "One day you may retract that statement."

Avery frowned. "I've said it countless times before, Bastian...you're wrong! I'm not going anywhere."

"And as I always say in return, I'm never wrong," he replied.

She raised an eyebrow and smirked. "Are you hinting that you're some sort of psychic too?"

"No." He stood and took a step away from her, causing the chair to scrape loudly against the floor.

She stared at his back. "So, what are you exactly? A superhero?"

"More like an abomination," he said quietly.

Avery opened her mouth to protest, but he beat her to it.

"I was worried about how things would go today."

She tilted her head to the side in an attempt to see his expression. "Were you having second thoughts about...all this?"

He sighed, making his shoulders rise and fall. "Second thoughts. Third thoughts. Fourth, fifth, sixth..."

She walked around to stand in front of him. "What changed your mind?"

"I was afraid that you would give up on what we have if I kept you in the dark any longer," he admitted dismally.

She could see the hopelessness on his face as she took a step closer, struggling to keep her hands to herself. "It makes me sad that you thought you'd lose me if you didn't open up when you weren't ready…but I'm also thankful that you finally did. It really means a lot. A lot more than you think."

The tone of her voice and the look on her face told him everything he needed to know. She wasn't giving up on him. If anything, she was going to push harder to learn more about him. That thought caused him to smile just enough for his dimples to show.

Avery smiled too. "Soooo…can you show me that glowing thing one more time?" she asked eagerly.

Sebastian laughed out loud.

It was the first time in a long time that Avery had seen him look genuinely happy. The brooding expression that usually graced his gorgeous face had momentarily disappeared.

He was still grinning as he held out his hand. "Alright, one more time."

CHAPTER 11

When Sebastian got home that night, he was feeling something that he had not felt in centuries. Elation. His mind would not stop replaying the very moment when he revealed 'the glow' to Avery. For such a long time, he had been terrified of revealing anything pertaining to his other side, but the look of acceptance on her face and the gleam of wonder in her eyes was so unexpected that it nearly sent him over the edge.

Needless to say, he was more than a little eager to tell his friends what had happened, so he called Jonah and Chase and invited them over.

The three of them discussed and re-discussed how Sebastian should handle the situation and what he should do next, though the lack of interest from Jonah was a little disheartening.

"You're the one who told me to show her the least scary thing about myself!" Sebastian reminded him. "I thought you'd be happy for me."

Jonah shrugged. "Yeah, I know…and I *am* happy it worked out for you. I just didn't think you'd actually go through with it."

Sebastian let out an irritated sigh. "So, you gave me advice hoping that I wouldn't follow it? Where is the logic in that?"

"I think you should just focus on the fact that by listening to me, your relationship with Avery can progress now. She passed the first test." Jonah smiled, hoping it would ease the tension that was growing between them.

"It wasn't a test," Sebastian stated firmly.

"It kinda was," Chase interjected.

"As long as she doesn't tell anyone, things will be fine," Jonah added.

"She wouldn't do that," Chase stated confidently.

Sebastian's good mood was starting to falter. *What if she does tell someone? I'm already tempting fate by being involved with a mortal again. If I keep up this charade, the Pure Ones are sure to find me. More importantly, they would find her!*

The more the boys talked, the more Sebastian began to feel uneasy. So, when Monday morning rolled around, he just could not bear to face Avery. Not when he was having so many doubts about everything. He decided it was best if he just stayed home from school. That way he would have a little extra time to get his head on straight. It was a last-minute decision that neither Jonah nor Chase were even aware of. However, when the sun rose on Tuesday, he wasn't feeling any more confident about what he had done. In fact, he was feeling quite pessimistic. He ended up staying home for the entire week. Apparently, he needed a lot more time than he originally thought. And now it was Friday. Five days had passed since the glowing-hand-holding-incident had transpired and Sebastian had been avoiding Avery at every turn.

She had called and texted him at least thirty-seven times and shown up at his house on four separate occasions. Sebastian ignored her texts, he forwarded her calls to his voicemail, and he pretended he wasn't home when she came by…though his car was clearly sitting in the driveway.

To say that he had been feeling apprehensive about revealing one of his secrets to her would be an understatement. And though it killed him to admit, a little piece of him began to regret it. It made him feel vulnerable, something he was not used to experiencing. The only positive thing that could come of this situation, was that if he continued to show the pieces of himself gradually over time instead of waiting until the last and final moment like he always had in the past, then maybe the pain would never become unbearable and there would be a small chance that he may not have to lose her after all. Though that fate rested in Avery's hands…and that scared the hell out of him.

Could she see past the monster within and love me anyway? He honestly wasn't sure. After all, a little bit of a glow and some heat was nothing compared to his Cursed Form. *She seems okay with things right now, but what if she starts to fear me?* He wasn't sure if he could bear for her to look at him with pure repulsion.

Both Smart brothers agreed on at least one major thing: He was not handling the situation properly by distancing himself from her all over again, especially after showing her 'the glow'. A fact they made sure to drill into his head each and every time they had spoken with him that week. Deep down Sebastian knew they were right. After all, Avery had waited six long years for this, and he was doing what he did best…ruining it. He picked up his phone and hovered his thumb over the reply button.

"Just get it over with," Jonah pressed.

Sebastian felt his steady hands begin to tremble. "This whole thing has my nerves shot to hell," he stated, mostly for himself.

"Waiting is only going to make it worse," Chase told him.

"Make it short and straight to the point. Like ripping off a Band-Aid," Jonah said.

Chase looked at his brother in a state of confusion. "That made no sense at all."

Jonah shrugged. "He knows what I'm trying to say! Right, B?"

Sebastian waved his hand in dismissal as he worked up the courage to send a reply.

~*~*~*~

Meanwhile, Avery couldn't tell Valerie the actual truth, so she fabricated a simpler more plausible scenario. She told her that they had held hands and that Sebastian had finally shown her a deeper glimpse into who he was. Fairly accurate, just without the glowing and heated details.

"If the boy finally decided to let you in and then he turns around and slams the door in your face…I'm pretty sure that means he changed his mind."

"I think there's more to it," Avery argued. "We connected. There's no way he's just gonna shut me out all over again."

Valerie pursed her lips and shook her head. "You held hands, Av. Not that big of a deal in my book."

"It was a big deal to *me*," she countered. "You know how long it has taken for us to get to this point."

Valerie sighed. "I know, sweetie…and I'm not trying to downplay your feelings or burst your happy little fantasy bubble, but as your best friend, I have to call it like I see it. I feel like he's just playing with your heart."

"He's not," Avery replied sternly.

Valerie picked up Avery's cell phone and dangled it in front of her face. "Have you looked at your phone lately? Fifteen calls and twenty-two texts that have gone unanswered. You're borderline stalker material!"

Avery grabbed her phone. "Maybe he's sick. He did miss school after all."

Valerie exhaled a quick puff of air. "Or maybe not. It's been five whole days with zero contact. That's a pretty big red flag if you ask me. And I bet you he's been in touch with Chase and Jonah. Those three are inseparable. So, there is no excuse for him not to get in touch with you."

Avery slumped back against the couch cushions. *Could Val be right? I mean, it has been a whole week since he's said a single word to me.* She shook her head. *No. After everything I learned that night, he wouldn't just push me away again. Right?* She sighed to herself.

Unaware of Avery's internal dialogue, Valerie was worried

that her best friend was upset with her. "Look, I'm on your side regardless of how things work out. And I'll be here to pick up the pieces if need be."

Avery forced a smile. "Thanks, Val. I appreciate it."

There was nothing she could say or do that would ever make Valerie understand. Not without breaking her vow of secrecy to Sebastian. And she would never do that. So, for now, her best friend would have to be kept out of the loop. Which was easier said than done, considering that they have always told each other everything.

Suddenly, her cell chimed in her hand.

Bastian: I'm sorry 4 the lack of communication. I'd like 2 see u. Is now a good time?

An unwanted sensation of doubt and confusion came over Avery as she stared at his text. "He wants to come over," she stated quietly.

Valerie didn't say another word. Instead, she shrugged and stood up. "Since I already know what you're going to tell him, I'm gonna go."

"Don't be mad at me," Avery grumbled, though her words sounded more like a whining child.

Valerie smiled then. "I'm not mad, just concerned." She kissed Avery's cheek. "Call me later, 'kay?"

"I will, I promise."

Valerie hesitated before linking her pinky finger with Avery's, leaning in closer. "Use your head, not your heart," she whispered. Then she darted out the front door.

Avery let out the breath she had been holding and sent Sebastian a reply.

Avery: Now is fine. I'll c u soon.

CHAPTER 12

When Sebastian arrived, his facial expression was tense, his posture was rigid, and his body language was uncomfortable at best. He seemed to be fidgeting with his hands and constantly shifting his legs.

"Are you okay?" Avery finally asked.

Sebastian let a nervous laugh slip out. *No, I'm not.* "Yeah, I'm fine."

"I'm pretty sure you're lying," Avery teased. She had never seen him like this before. He was completely coming unglued.

Nervous laugh number two escaped Sebastian's lips. *Pull yourself together! What the hell is wrong with you?* Then almost as if a switch had been flipped, his awkwardly adorable behavior turned into a cold and distant demeanor. "I'm, uh…suddenly not feeling well. Maybe it's best if I go home and we can talk later." *Stupidest. Line. Ever.*

The look on Avery's face said that she wasn't buying it, but he knew that she wouldn't confront him about it.

She raised an eyebrow. "Or…why don't you cut the crap and calm down and talk to me?"

Sebastian's eyes widened. Okay, so he was wrong. He could

not believe she had actually called him out. Apparently, exposing 'the glow' had ignited a hidden passion inside of Avery; and in turn, it had transformed him into a fumbling idiot.

She inched closer. "I know you're probably feeling strange about the other night…and I get it. This is crazy…"

You have no idea, he thought to himself.

"But I want you to stop feeling like you can't be yourself with me."

He stared at her blankly. "I'm always myself," he stated.

She gestured from his head to his toes. "You don't have to be Mr. Perfect all the time. Let your guard down and stop acting like the world is out to get you. Stop hiding from me."

He snorted in response.

"I'm serious," she stated. "Lose your composure for once. Act like a complete doofus and make a fool out of yourself. Have fun."

"I do have fun," he countered.

Avery laughed quietly and shook her head. Then she immediately got up and turned on the radio. She scanned the stations until a familiar tune flowed through the speakers. "I think it's time I discovered another one of your secrets."

He gave her a questioning glance. *Oh no.* "How exactly are you going to do that?"

She held out her hand as a comical grin spread across her face. "With your permission."

Sebastian felt himself smile too. She wasn't seeking to learn anything about his past. She just wanted to see him less serious…less uptight. He liked this new side of Avery. And at that moment, he wondered why he hadn't done this a long time ago.

"C'mon," she urged. "I can already see the wheels spinning in your mind. Don't overthink it. Just give me your friggin' hand."

The moment he stood, the song on the radio changed, and he froze. "I can't dance to this…it's Britney Spears."

Avery smirked. "I'm impressed that you even know who

that is." Then she laughed as she began singing along, bouncing around, and flailing her arms in the air.

Screw it, he thought to himself. *Time to be a doofus.* Sebastian suddenly launched into a full-blown spaz attack. He was shaking his butt, jumping up and down, and waving his arms like the Chicken Dance mixed with the Macarena. It was quite freeing to forget about everything and just let loose. He made a mental note to do it more often.

Avery had stopped singing and dancing to gawk at him, covering her mouth to stifle multiple giggles.

Sebastian was oblivious to the fact that he was currently the object of her entertainment. Though when 'Raise Your Glass' by Pink came on, Sebastian stopped for a moment. He locked eyes with Avery, who was currently beaming from ear to ear.

"I don't think I've ever seen you like this," she stated happily.

He smiled wide. "I don't think anyone has."

"Well, I like it." She hesitated for a second before grabbing hold of his wrists, pulling him towards her.

It was a new and exciting feeling to allow Avery a glimpse of who he truly was instead of his usual brooding self, but he had almost forgotten that it would come with a price. As the two of them moved with the music, Sebastian felt the ache in his chest begin to intensify.

A few more songs played before the radio announcer started talking. Their dance fest soon turned into a casual dialogue, which eventually shifted into 'goodbyes' and 'see you laters'.

~*~*~*~

That night, Sebastian didn't dream about the usual faces from his long-lost past. He dreamed of his dorky dancing with Avery while she laughed and giggled at his goofiness. The dull ache in his chest had gotten worse, but his blissful thoughts seemed to mask the pain for the time being.

Avery fell asleep with a permanent smile plastered across her face. She could not believe that Sebastian had finally let his guard down…and it was even more incredible than she ever imagined.

CHAPTER 13

The next morning, Sebastian woke to a gnawing pain shooting throughout his entire body. Suddenly, Moira's voice flashed through his mind. *A lover's grasp shall be your fate. Your dying heart they'll never take.* An anguished expression covered his face as he squeezed his eyes shut. He attempted to dull the pain by healing himself, but it was not working like it should.

Just push through until it passes, he grunted. This time, though, something was different. The pain should not have been spreading so fast.

Over the course of an hour, Sebastian fought through the spasms and soreness as he attempted to get himself up and moving. Getting dressed was a pain in the ass…literally. Shifting his body and lifting his arms and legs made him feel like he was being slammed into a stone wall repeatedly. His cell phone rang from the opposite end of the house, and he groaned as he shuffled his way down the hall.

Chase's name flashed across the screen.

"What's up, Chase?"

"Hey Bas, are you busy today?"

Sebastian let out a painful sigh. "Not really. Why?"

"Well…I kinda wanted to ask you for a favor."

"What do you need?"

Chase cleared his throat nervously. "Well, I asked Val on a date…to the movies…and I'm flipping out."

Sebastian smirked. "So where does the favor come in? You want me to take her instead?"

"No!" Chase exclaimed. "Not even close! I was thinking…maybe you and Avery could come along, like a double date type thing? That might make the transition easier."

Sebastian began to pace uncomfortably. "Transition, eh?"

Chase rolled his eyes. "Sorry bad wording…but yeah, transitioning from 'just friends' to hopefully something more serious. You know I kissed her right?"

"No, I didn't know that, but I guess I could ask Av if she wouldn't mind helping me babysit you two," Sebastian replied. "What are you and Val going to see?"

Chase chuckled. "I'm going to ignore your petty attempt at mocking me! But anyway, I honestly have no idea. I told her it was her choice."

"So probably a chick flick," they both said in unison.

Sebastian grunted and sighed again as he shifted his position. "Well, let me call Av and see if she'd like to go. I'll call you right back."

"Sounds good," Chase said cheerfully. "See ya."

Sebastian hung up and then dialed Avery's number. Going out in public probably was not the best idea given his current level of discomfort, but having something to keep his mind occupied may help with keeping the pain at bay…at least enough for him to function at a somewhat normal capacity.

"Well hello there," Avery chirped. "How's my favorite dance partner doing?"

Sebastian could not help but smile. "I'm a little sore," he replied. Even though it had nothing to do with dancing. "How are you?"

"I'm alright, just hanging out with my mom. We're watching TV and doing some laundry."

"Would you like to accompany me to the movies today?

Chase and Val are going on a date and asked if we'd like to tag along." That wasn't exactly how he wanted to phrase the question, but alas, there it was.

There was a slight pause before Avery replied. "Isn't that sorta like crashing their first date?"

Sebastian shrugged on his end of the line. "I guess...but Chase seemed adamant about wanting us to go. Personally, I think he's just nervous."

Secretly, Avery wished Sebastian would ask her on a date, though she knew that was not likely to happen. "Well okay. What time should I be ready?"

"Uh...shit! I didn't even ask."

Avery giggled. "To be safe, I'll just get dressed now. Pick me up whenever they're ready to go."

"Alright, see you soon."

Sebastian hung up and called Chase back. "So, we're both in. What time does the movie start?"

"Meet us there in an hour. That should be more than enough time to park, get snacks, and find our seats."

~*~*~*~

An hour and fifteen minutes later, Sebastian was sitting beside Avery in the darkened theater. *Perhaps this wasn't such a good idea*, he thought to himself. Sitting there waiting for the movie to begin was pure torture. His head was pounding, his stomach was queasy, his extremities felt like they were being pricked with pins and needles, and his entire body was blazing hot on the inside. Sweat beads gathered on his forehead and upper lip faster than he could wipe them away.

Halfway through the movie, Avery's focus was drifting away from the screen. Chase and Valerie were practically swallowing each other's faces...and her eyes kept wandering down to Sebastian's hands. He was wiping them against his jeans over and over as if he was anxious and his palms were sweaty. She stole a glance in his direction to find that his eyes were squinting, his lips were pursed, and his brow was furrowed in a pained expression.

She nudged his shoulder gently and leaned closer. "Are you

feeling okay?"

The moment Sebastian realized that she was staring at him, he removed any sign of discomfort from his face. Over the years, he had become a master at hiding his feelings and emotions. It served him well when facing an opponent.

He shot her a smile that made her heart skip a beat. "I'll be okay. Just…an upset stomach," he whispered.

A rush of courage swept over Avery as she placed her hand on his leg, which happened to land right on top of his fingers as well. "Are you sure? We can leave if you need to," she whispered back.

The moment she touched him, it was like putting ice on a fire. It was a split second of relief from the burning sensation that continued to plague him from the inside out. His jawline tensed. "I'm alright, but I appreciate your concern," he replied quietly.

Avery let her hand linger there for a few more seconds. Once she pulled away, she immediately wished she hadn't. He did too. The cooling sensation was gone. Part of her wondered how long he would have allowed her to touch him.

She tried to keep her attention on the romantic comedy that was playing, but all she could think about now was the feeling of his warm skin against hers.

Sebastian's inner turmoil was temporarily repressed as his focus shifted away from himself and onto the sound of Avery's heartbeat rising rapidly. He leaned towards her. "I guess it's my turn to ask if you're alright?"

She instantly blushed, thankful that he could not see her reddened cheeks in the darkness. "I'm good, just enjoying the movie." *And being so close to you.*

A little while later, laughter erupted throughout the crowded theater. Chase and Valerie finally pulled apart long enough to realize that the credits were about to roll.

"Great movie, huh?" Valerie gushed. She wiped her lips and straightened her shirt.

"How would you even know that?" Avery muttered under her breath. "You were too busy acting out your own make-out scene."

Chase laughed, and Sebastian smirked, but neither of them said a word. Avery and Valerie continued their playful banter back and forth as the four of them headed toward the parking lot. A twinge of jealousy suddenly rose within Avery as she watched Valerie effortlessly take Chase by the hand. Though the feeling only lasted a second, Sebastian took notice. He followed her envious gaze and then 'accidentally' brushed the back of his hand against hers.

Avery's breath caught in her throat as a small gasp escaped her lips. Sebastian found it amusing that she attempted to cover it up with a fake cough. So, he did it again. He took a sideways step and brushed against her hand once more. The pitter-patter of her now rapidly beating heart told him that he shouldn't push her much further, but he just couldn't resist. This time, though, he teasingly lingered his fingers right next to hers, knowing that she could sense their close proximity. Her posture suddenly stiffened as if she were trying to keep her hand in that perfect position.

They were a mere ten feet away from his car at this point. *It's now or never*, he told himself.

Sebastian grabbed hold of her hand and tugged her closer. Momentarily stunned, Avery stopped walking and glanced up at him. He smiled just enough for his dimples to show, which caused her to smile too as she resumed walking again.

Externally she was cool, calm, and collected. Inside, though, she was a squealing, giggly, frantic ball of nerves. If only she knew that her heartbeat always gave her away.

CHAPTER 14

Over the next two weeks, Sebastian and Avery's friendship was quickly becoming something more. They hadn't put a label on it, well Sebastian hadn't, but they were definitely passed the friend-zone. Sebastian picked her up each and every day for school. They held hands as they casually strolled down the hall to their classes. He had even asked her to be his date to the prom. Everything seemed to be falling into place perfectly, at least in Avery's eyes. She could not be happier. She was on cloud nine with no intention of ever coming down. Sebastian, on the other hand, was in more physical pain than he had ever been in the past. None of his other experiences were anywhere near this bad. With each passing day, it was becoming harder and harder for him to hide his discomfort. His curse was living up to its name, and he was beginning to wonder if this was an omen of what was to come.

One afternoon, in particular, Avery was nestled comfortably in the curve of his arm while they watched re-runs of 'The Walking Dead'. She loved the feeling of his strong muscular arms wrapped around her. He made her feel safe. He made her feel special. He made her feel loved. And it was at that moment that she realized she had completely, without any doubt, fallen head over heels in love with him.

Almost immediately, Sebastian noticed the abrupt change in her heartbeat. His instincts told him something big was definitely about to happen, but it wasn't until she looked up at him that he knew exactly what she was going to say.

Don't, Av. Please don't.

Avery stared at him for a moment and smiled, then turned her attention back to the TV. She sucked in a deep breath, taking in the delicious smell of his cologne as she snuggled closer against him. Sebastian wrapped his arms tighter around her and let out a temporary sigh of relief, but it was extremely short lived. Avery's voice came out loud and clear even though she said it in a whisper.

"I…I love you, Bastian."

Momentarily stunned by the words that had just left her mouth, she waited impatiently for him to reply.

He had always known that sooner or later he would run out of ways to avoid the inevitable, but he did not think today would be 'the day'.

No. I'm not ready yet! I need more time, he thought desperately.

"Avery, I…"

For a brief moment, Sebastian imagined what it would have been like if things were different…if he were just a simple man. A human without tainted blood running through his veins. He would have caressed her beautiful face and kissed her tenderly as he whispered over and over how much he loved her too. Instead, he sighed deeply as he looked down into her brilliant green eyes. "I can't."

His words were like an emotional slap in the face as Avery slowly slid out of his embrace. "Y-you…don't love me?"

He pulled her back into his arms as a feeling of hopelessness overtook him. "I'm so sorry." And he truly was.

She wasn't sure if she should laugh because he was holding her or cry because it felt as if he were letting her go. She pushed him back so that she could look at his face again. He tried to avoid her burning gaze, but eventually, he gave in. Her eyes were glistening with unshed tears, and her bottom lip was quivering.

"There's not even a small part of you that loves me?" she whimpered.

His mind was crying out… *Yes! My God, yes! I love you with every fiber of my being!* …but he knew he couldn't say those words out loud. It was too soon. She was just getting used to the idea that there was something possibly supernatural about him. If he transitioned into his Cursed Form right here and now, she would never recover. The occasional flashbacks from that night were already having a huge impact on her life, and he refused to push her over the edge. He would rather break her heart than break her spirit.

With that thought running through his mind, somehow he was able to retain his composure long enough to deliver the final blow. His lips brushed against her ear as he squeezed her tighter. "I can't say it back, Av. I'm sorry."

A small sob escaped her lips as she fought to get out of his grasp. Her entire body was shaking as she tore herself away from him. She wrapped her arms around herself and backed away. "I want you to leave," she ordered quietly. When he didn't move, she screamed at the top of her lungs. "I SAID LEAVE!"

CHAPTER 15

This was it. The moment Sebastian had been dreading for the past six years. He was losing her. Though this was not the way he had expected. *He* shouldn't be running away; *she* should be. He stumbled out the front door as Avery slammed it shut behind him.

"I do love you," he whispered, knowing that she could not hear him.

Almost immediately after the words left his mouth, a burning sensation began to pulse through the soles of his feet, making its way up his legs. *Oh no! No, no, no, no!*

He gripped the railing, swaying side to side, barely making it down another step when the burn reached his stomach. He instantly doubled over and let out a quiet grunt. *Hurry*, he told himself. *She can't see you like this!*

He could hear her broken heart beating steadily over the sound of her muffled cries. Sebastian struggled to place one foot in front of the other as he continued down the stairs. The burning soon engulfed his chest, filling his lungs with invisible flames. He gasped, sucking in the cool air surrounding him, but the scorching pain blazed on. His throat felt like it was about to swell shut and his eyes began to water. He was almost to the bottom step. *Just a few more feet,* he told himself. But time was quickly running out. His fingertips began to spark, sending tiny flecks of light bursting off his skin as if he were holding a sparkler in each hand. Any minute now he was going to transition...right in front of her house!

He let out a painful moan as his eyes began to glow. A deafening screech erupted from his mouth as his body began contorting. He started to panic. *NOOOOO!*

Before his rage took full control, he raced down Avery's driveway as fast as he could, all the while, screaming and cursing and fighting the losing battle within himself. He completed his transition a few moments later. His Cursed Form fled down the dimly lit street, racing away from the pain; but no matter how far or how fast he ran, the pain remained, attached deep into his soul.

CHAPTER 16

Severe.
Relentless.
Agonizing.

Those were just a few of the words Sebastian would use to describe the unbearable amount of pain he had endured over the last week and a half. Being in his Cursed Form should have numbed the burning completely, but the invisible lava-flow raged on as if it were coursing through his veins.

Sebastian ultimately returned to his human form, causing the pain to double and then triple, until it ultimately reached a number that he was not able to put into words. He cried out as he collapsed inside his foyer. He grunted and groaned as he struggled to dial Jonah's number. His hands trembled so much that he dropped his cell phone countless times. Each time becoming more and more frustrated and upset. He was on the verge of crushing the stupid phone into tiny little pieces when the line finally began to ring.

"Well, it's about damn time! Where the hell have you been? You missed Thanksgiving! Mom and dad have been looking for you for almost two weeks! We've all been really worried!"

Sebastian opened his mouth to speak, but an intense groan came out instead.

"B?"

Sebastian tried to talk again. This time he managed to get out a single word. "Come." Then the phone fell from his trembling hands, clattering to the floor.

Jonah didn't hesitate. He raced outside and got in his car as fast as he could, with Chase close behind. "We're on our way, B. Just sit tight. We're coming!" Jonah's sneaker was pressed down so hard on the gas pedal that he thought his foot might go through the floorboard.

"What's going on?" Chase asked his brother.

"No idea," Jonah replied. "But whatever it is, it's bad."

Houses passed by in a blur until the boys pulled into Sebastian's driveway.

Jonah and Chase raced up the walkway and flung the front door open without even attempting to knock. They found Sebastian slumped over only a few feet away.

He was curled up in a fetal position, his hands clutched tightly around his knees, with his eyes squeezed shut. The pain had finally become too much. Sebastian seemed to be gasping for air by the time Jonah and Chase got to his side.

Jonah dropped to his knees. "What's happening, B?"

"Can't…breathe," Sebastian gasped. His chest felt so tight that it mimicked the feeling of being suffocated. The air went in, and the air went out, but still, it felt like he was dying.

"What should we do?" Chase asked. The worry was evident in his voice.

Jonah touched Sebastian's shoulder and sighed. "We need to get him to the morgue. He can consume a few essences, and he'll be back to normal."

"NO!" Sebastian shouted. His body started shaking. *No!*

"You're not really in a position to argue," Jonah stated bluntly.

Sebastian attempted to pull himself to a sitting position, but his body would not cooperate as he dropped back to the floor. He still managed to glare at Jonah and whisper "No," again through gritted teeth.

As the minutes passed, he screamed out in agony over and over as tears welled in his burning eyes.

Chase dragged his brother to the other side of the room and lowered his voice. "We can't force him to do that."

Jonah's forehead wrinkled, and his eyebrows arched so high that they nearly disappeared into his hairline. "You got a better idea, bro? Because right now we don't have many options. Look at him! It's either the morgue or he stays like this until he confesses his love to Avery." Jonah lowered his voice to an aggravated whisper, "And I don't see the latter one happening just yet...do you?"

Chase shook his head. "Bas doesn't want to take the essences of mortals anymore! We both know how hard he's worked and how long it's taken him to get to this point. I refuse to have our best friend resent us because we were too stupid to come up with a better plan."

"This plan isn't stupid!" Jonah snapped. "The people are dead. D.E.A.D...dead! It's not like he's taking their souls or damning them to hell! He's not hurting anyone! It's logical. And it's an absolutely straightforward solution to ending his pain!"

"I've never...stolen a soul...or damned anyone...to hell," Sebastian panted.

"You know what I meant," Jonah stated flatly.

"Well...there is another option..." Chase said quietly.

Jonah sighed. "That's not a solution. It's a temporary fix of the underlying problem!"

Chase stood his ground. "A short-lived patch will buy Bas more time...and it won't cause him to lapse back into the monster that he hates. Win, win."

Jonah rolled his eyes and grumbled. "Alright fine." He trudged back over to Sebastian, speaking directly to his mind so that Chase wouldn't hear. *It's our job as Watchers to protect your secret, B...not to hinder the outcome of the curse. We can't make a habit of this.*

I know that, Sebastian replied angrily. *But don't act like this is something you've had to do before. I've never asked you to use your markings…and I won't hold it against you if you choose not to. It's your choice. I can deal with this on my own if I have to.*

Jonah sighed deeply. *You know damn well there isn't a choice here! I would never leave you to suffer like this.*

Sebastian wanted to smile to show his thanks, but his jaw was too tense to move.

Chase and Jonah knelt down on opposite sides of Sebastian's body.

"Are you ready?" Jonah asked his brother.

Chase nodded. "Are you?"

"Let's do this," Jonah replied assuredly.

The Smart brothers placed their hands on Sebastian's shoulders and began to chant together, both out loud and into their friend's mind. *"The curse runs deep. The curse runs true. A watchful eye will see it through."*

The markings on the boys' arms began to glow, pulsing waves of cooling energy into Sebastian's body. *"The pain we take. Replaced with peace. A Watcher's vow never recedes."*

Almost immediately, Sebastian felt like he was being doused with cold water. He sucked in the deepest breath he could manage, extinguishing the burning sensation that filled his lungs, but that was where the relief stopped. Jonah and Chase had done all they could. Now it was up to him to put an end to his torment once and for all.

CHAPTER 17

Chase and Jonah watched anxiously as Sebastian began to pace back and forth. The expression on his face gave away the fact that he was still in an extreme amount of physical agony.

Chase nudged his brother and silently mouthed, *Say something!*

Jonah turned his attention back to his friend. "You need to call Avery."

Sebastian grunted. "I know…"

"You need to talk to her while you still can…before the pain gets worse again."

"I know…" Sebastian replied, clearly annoyed.

"So, what are you waiting for?" Jonah paused, waiting for an answer. When he didn't get one, he added, "She's not gonna leave you, man! You already showed her 'the glow' and guess what? She's still here! In fact, she told you she loves you. Isn't that what you wanted?"

Sebastian froze and let out an irritated, painful sigh.

Jonah mimicked him and threw his arms in the air in an exasperated fashion. "You're gonna have to confess it all eventually! The pain isn't going to stop until she sees you in your Cursed Form, so you might as well get it all out there now!"

"I'll lose her!" Sebastian growled. *I'm not ready to lose her.*

"Wake up and look around, B! You've already lost her!"

Sebastian's shoulders rose and fell as he looked around his living room. Jonah was right. Avery hadn't stepped foot in his house in weeks…and he hadn't stepped foot in hers either. Not since the I-love-you incident. The lingering scent of her coconut shampoo was long gone.

"Just show her what you've been trying so damn hard to hide! That's all she wants!" Jonah pressed. "It's what she deserves!"

"That's asking a lot, don't you think?!" Sebastian countered.

Jonah let out another exasperated sigh. "I'm not saying to put it all out there at once like, BAM 'here's my super-creepy-monster-demon-side…do you still wanna be with me?!'"

Sebastian couldn't help but smile then. "So, what exactly are you pitching, J?"

Jonah shrugged nonchalantly. "Just a few little things here and there. You could start off with, 'Hey, not only do I glow and radiate heat, but I can heal…I can read your mind…I can teleport…'"

Sebastian held up his hand. "I cannot teleport!" he stated humorously.

"Teleport. Drift. Whatever man, same difference! Regardless, the more you tell her, the less pain you'll have. Things will get easier. You'll be happy, which means Avery will be super happy. Then the big finale…TADA! She's still there by your side!"

"Riiiiiiiiight," Sebastian replied sarcastically. "Let me get a pen so that I can jot all those amazing ideas down!"

Both Smart brothers shook their heads.

"What's the worst that could happen?" Chase asked.

Sebastian rolled his eyes. "What's the worst that could happen?" He put his finger on his lip as if he were in deep thought. "Hmm, let me think! Oh, I know…she'll run away screaming because I'm a FRICKIN' MONSTER!"

Jonah shrugged. "It's not like you're some vampire out to drink her blood."

"Or a werewolf trying to rip her apart," Chase added with a grin.

Sebastian smiled momentarily. *I should not have told them she said that. Now I'm never going to hear the end of it.* "Neither of you are helping."

"So, you'd rather have her think that you don't give a shit about her? That you're just some pigheaded jerk who broke her heart? That's much worse than the whole truth if you ask me!" Jonah stated.

"Well, I didn't ask you!" Sebastian snapped. He closed his eyes, blocking out everything going on around him, and thought of Avery. Instantly he could feel himself being pulled toward her. Both Jonah and Chase's voices now seemed miles away.

Like a ghostly haze, Sebastian drifted down the familiar street, following the sound of her heartbeat...through her front door...down the hallway...into her room. Then the fuzzy picture in front of him slowly became clear.

She was curled up on her bed with her face buried in her pillow. His wispy projection drew closer. He could see her entire body trembling as tears streamed down her cheeks, falling one after another.

A distressing twinge gripped his heart. *I caused this.*

He opened his eyes, causing the images to instantly disappear as his projected form was pulled back into his body. Chase and Jonah were staring at him.

"Did you see her?" Chase asked.

Sebastian sank to his knees.

"I guess he did," Jonah replied to his brother.

Sebastian shook his head. "I can't just show her who I am...what I am. Not yet. It's too soon."

Jonah threw his hands in the air. "What other option do you have? She loves you; she'll understand."

"Really? You think so?" Sebastian countered. Then suddenly, a deafening roar erupted throughout the room as a strong, violent wind began to whip around them. Sebastian transitioned to his Cursed Form in what seemed like a blink of an eye.

Chase and Jonah both blocked their faces.

"IF MY TWO BEST FRIENDS CAN'T EVEN LOOK AT MY CURSE, WHAT MAKES YOU THINK THAT AVERY WILL?" Sebastian shouted. His gruff voice sounded demonic as his desperation was rapidly turning to rage.

The shrilling roar grew louder and louder, piercing the boys' ears.

"Sebastian, stop!" they both called out. "You've made your point! Now stop!"

The wind slowly began to subside as the room became silent once again. Sebastian's human form gradually returned. His back was turned toward them as his shoulders slumped forward. "I need to be alone," he stated glumly.

Chase opened his mouth to object. "But..."

Sebastian clenched his jaw. "Just...go! Now! Both of you!"

Jonah grabbed Chase's arm and headed for the front door. "We'll talk later then."

Sebastian didn't say a word, only nodded once and waved them away.

"I hate when he shifts without any warning. After all these years, I still need to brace myself for his...other side," Chase whispered.

"He was just showing off," Jonah stated loudly with a smirk.

Sebastian smiled faintly. He knew his friends were trying to get a rise out of him...but he just wanted to be alone. "Close the door," Sebastian stated firmly.

When he heard the click of the door shutting, he leaned his head in his hands. His thoughts drifted back to Avery, immediately taking his projected form back to her room. He would have given anything to hold her right then and there. His gentle whispers of *I'm sorry* echoed over and over in his mind. Though he knew she couldn't feel or hear him, he stayed beside her until her sobs eased into mere sniffles.

Emotionally exhausted and heartbroken, Sebastian eventually opened his eyes to find himself still sitting on the floor in his living room. He leaned his head back against the wall. "I don't know what to do," he whispered to himself.

"Yes, you do," came a voice from across the room.

He looked up to see Chase standing there with his arms crossed casually across his chest. Sebastian sighed. "I thought you left."

"I did," Chase replied. "But I came right back."

"Of course, you did." Sebastian could tell by the look on his friend's face that he was debating on speaking his mind. "Whatever it is, just say it."

Chase swallowed down his doubt. "Jonah's right ya know. You can't let Avery believe that you would just give her up without a fight."

Sebastian groaned.

Chase took a step forward. "You love her; I know you do…and she truly loves you too. So, are you gonna let her continue to think that everything you two had meant nothing? That you decided she wasn't good enough to know all your dark secrets, so you just up and left?" He paused and waited for a response. When Sebastian sat there silently, Chase got angry. "What the hell is wrong with you?" The tone of his voice surprised both of them as he took a timid step back.

Sebastian could feel himself losing control again. "EVERYTHING!" he shouted. "Everything is wrong with me! I'm a complete freak of nature, Chase! I'm a monster! I've lost the only girl I've ever truly loved…and she doesn't even know how I really feel because I have to lie to keep her from seeing my Cursed Form! I've lost everything and everyone in my life, all because of this stupid curse! The pain is already unbearable, and it's only going to get worse!" *How can I possibly endure more?* The tears started to fall before he had a chance to stop them while he continued to scream and shout and lash out.

Sebastian grabbed the first thing he could get his hands on…a lamp…and threw it against the wall. He stared at the broken pieces littered on the floor by his feet. The shattered fragments reminded him of his broken heart. Of Avery's broken heart. This only fueled his rage.

"Bas, you need to calm down!" Chase repeated those words over and over, but to no avail.

Sebastian was now blinded by dire fury. Another lamp was thrown. Holes were punched in the walls. Books and magazines were ripped to shreds. Next was the coffee table, literally smashed to tiny splinters. He tore the area rug down to little pieces of stuffing. The love seat followed, and finally the L-shaped couch. By the time Sebastian was done, the living room had been completely demolished.

Out of things to break and out of breath, he collapsed to the floor next to Chase. "I'm sorry about that," he said breathlessly.

Both of them looked around at the mess.

Chase shrugged. "I didn't get turned into tiny particles of Chase-dust, so I'm alright."

They both chuckled.

A few silent moments passed before Chase spoke again. "Sooo...are you good now? Feeling any better?"

Sebastian didn't reply right away. He continued looking around until his labored breathing returned to normal. "I have to tell her," he stated aloud. "That's the only way either of us will have peace. And who knows, maybe she will be able to see past the final part of me." *God, I hope so.*

Chase forced a smile. "When?"

Sebastian stood and wiped the debris from his pants. "Right now."

"Right now?" Chase repeated timidly.

Sebastian headed for the door. "Yes now!" He could hear his friend's heartbeat rising.

"Um...there may be a...sliiiiiight problem with that," Chase stated hesitantly.

Sebastian's irritation level was starting to grow again. He turned around with a blank expression. "What did your brother do?"

"Weeeeell...right before you came out of your, um...dream

state…Jonah went to see Avery."

Sebastian began to see red. "He…WHAT?!"

"Well, he…" Chase cleared his throat. "I mean…*we,* thought it might help things along."

Sebastian held up his hand to hush his friend. "I need absolute silence!"

Chase nodded and made a zipping motion across his lips.

Sebastian closed his eyes and began to concentrate. *Jonah better not have done what I think he has!* Sebastian felt himself drifting yet again. He relived the scene of him tearing apart his living room, only in reverse. When his mind started seeing Jonah, he followed him as he got into his car and drove straight to Avery's house. Sebastian could feel himself filling with malice as he watched Jonah casually stroll up her driveway and knock on the door. When Avery answered, her eyes were swollen and puffy from crying. Sebastian wished that he could look away.

"What do you want, Jonah?" Avery sniffled.

"Do you have a minute? It's about B."

Her eyes lit up for a split second before a look of devastation covered her face. "Unless he's in the hospital or some other type of emergency, I don't want to hear it."

As she pushed the door closed, Jonah put his foot in the way. "He's not in any hospital, but this is urgent."

Sebastian was not sure if it was out of pure curiosity or perhaps the determined look on Jonah's face, but Avery finally let him inside. Jonah followed her into the kitchen.

She wrapped her arms around herself and stared him down. "Okay, so what's this about?"

"B is my best friend, and normally I'd never do anything to betray his trust, but I can't let things go any further without you knowing the truth. It will be better for both of you in the long run."

"The truth?" she repeated.

Jonah sighed and his gaze intensified. "About B's past. About why he distances himself from you. Basically, everything."

Avery's arms slowly slid to her sides. There was a part of her that craved to know all the secrets that Sebastian had been hiding all these years, but at the same time, she felt that it was far too deceptive to hear it from his best friend. "I don't know if that's such a good idea. If he wanted me to know, he would have told me himself."

Sebastian felt a rush of relief. He had pushed her past her breaking point, and yet there she was, still putting his needs first.

Jonah held up his hand. "I know you wanted to hear it all from him because that's important to you and blah blah blah, but you know as well as I do that B is just too damn stubborn, and he's not going to jump unless someone gives him a push first. Well, this is me giving him a huge shove."

"I don't know, Jonah. He's going to be so angry…" she whispered.

Jonah nodded. "I know, but you need to understand that he's not what you think he is."

Her eyebrows rose as her forehead creased.

"When he told you that he couldn't tell you about his past, he wasn't kidding. He's been trying to protect you."

Avery sighed and rolled her eyes. "You're making about as much sense as he did when he tried to explain it…without actually explaining it! Why would I need protection from his past? It's over and done with! The past is just that…the past!" Suddenly, she gasped as if the perfect explanation just popped into her head. "Unless…is he in the Witness Protection Program or something?" *Holy crap! That would make perfect sense!*

Jonah's expression instantly turned grim. "No. Nothing like that. B is…well, he's cursed."

Avery stared at him…really stared at him. "Cursed?" she repeated questionably. "Like hexed from a voodoo doctor or something?" She shook her head and looked away, pursing her lips. *Witness protection or magical voodoo? This is nuts.* She gestured toward the front door, glaring in Jonah's direction. "You can go home now."

Jonah rushed in front of her to block the doorway. "Just

listen to me, Av!" he begged. "I don't have a lot of time. B is going to be furious with me once he figures out what I'm doing...and then the shit is gonna hit the fan, so please just sit down and give me the benefit of the doubt!"

Sebastian felt his rage building again as he realized that Jonah was serious about telling his deepest darkest secrets without his permission.

Avery hesitated for a moment before she sat down. "Okay, I'm listening."

"Well, Sebastian isn't an ordinary guy," Jonah started. "He has...powers..."

Avery bit the inside of her cheek, clearly annoyed. "I know that. I saw 'the glow', remember?"

"Okay...but I bet this is something you didn't know. He may look like he's only eighteen, but he's much older. Like decades of years older..."

Avery started shaking her head doubtingly.

"And his eyes, they glow too...which I guess is similar to what you saw with his hands," Jonah continued, "but he wasn't always this way. He used to be an ordinary person...like you."

"Don't you mean like us?" she corrected.

An uneasy expression crossed Jonah's face. "I'm not exactly normal."

"So...you're like him then?"

Jonah shook his head. "Not even close. I'm still human...I just have a little something extra. I'm a Watcher."

Avery's eyebrow rose. *Did he just admit that Bastian isn't human? What the hell?*

Sebastian had seen and heard enough. He pulled his projected form back to his body. "Chase?" he called out angrily.

Footsteps raced back down the hall. "Yeah, I'm still here!"

"You might want to call your brother and give him a heads up that I'm going to kill him!"

Chase swallowed hard as a nervous laugh left his mouth. "Not literally though, right?" His tone was more than a little concerned.

Sebastian stepped outside and slammed the door, nearly separating it from the hinges, and Chase was left wondering if he actually meant what he said. The scariest part was that Sebastian himself wasn't even sure. He raced over to Avery's house on foot, using his unbelievable speed, and stood outside her kitchen window just in time to catch more of Jonah's one-sided conversation.

"The Pure Ones were made up of four brothers: Hale, Kade, Ivez, and Dray. No one knows exactly where they came from, though it was rumored that they existed long before the creation of time itself. So, for millions of years, they were revered as gods. The Pure Ones have supernatural powers that are incomparable to anything you've ever seen in superhero movies. They lived a luxurious life out in the open, taking care of the land and all its inhabitants. Under their watchful eyes, the world knew only peace and prosperity."

This sounds like an old-timey bedtime story. Okay, Jonah, I'll play along. Avery gestured for him to go on.

Jonah sighed. "Well, eventually Ivez fell in love with a human…which was forbidden. Humans and gods were never meant to procreate."

Avery nodded as if she understood. "But obviously they did, or Bastian wouldn't be here, right?"

Sebastian covered his mouth to stifle his shocked response, though he quickly composed himself. *She thinks I could be a god? I'm not sure if I should be flattered or appalled.*

"B isn't a god," Jonah snickered. "But as I already said, he is cursed."

Avery cocked her head sideways with an annoyed expression. *Ohhhh, okay. Right, that makes perfect sense.* She rolled her eyes. "Can you just skip ahead to the part that has to do with Bastian then, please?"

"This all has to do with him…and I promise it will all make sense once I'm done."

And now he's repeating himself. Avery leaned back in her chair and impatiently waited for Jonah to continue.

"Ivez was so blinded by his feelings for a mortal that he

gave a piece of his life force, or what we call his essence, to her. It was the only way for them to be together forever, making her immortal. But in his haste, he overlooked the fact that a human body isn't capable of holding on to such immense power."

"So, she died?" Avery interrupted. Her tone was less than interested.

Jonah shook his head. "No. She was consumed by the intensity of the energy flowing within her. As you can imagine, she started wanting more."

Avery shifted uncomfortably in her seat. "So, did he give her more of his power?"

"No. But he did try to teach her the Pure Ones' ways. He tried to show her how to use her newfound talent for the well-being of humankind, but she was too selfish. Unbeknownst to Ivez, she had turned to the darker side of their magic, which caused her to lose touch with every shred of her humanity. She was slowly becoming a monster, and he didn't seem to notice. Over the years, she began claiming other humans for herself. Cursing them to live a life of misery and taking away their chance to find love. Watching them wreak havoc all over the world. When Hale, Kade, and Dray found out what she was doing, they gave their brother only one option: To kill her. She was becoming too dangerous and uncontrollable."

Avery sighed as if she were bored. "So, he killed her…"

Jonah ignored her distinct disinterest. "Ivez couldn't do it. And that was the last mistake he'd ever make. Somehow, against all odds, she managed to take the rest of his essence for herself. No one knows if it was by force, or if he gave it to her willingly, but the outcome was still the same."

Avery's mouth was now hanging slightly open. *Jonah is really taking this made-up story all the way.*

"His brothers, the remaining three Pure Ones, found Ivez's lifeless body in his bed chamber. After that, they created Watchers like my family and me. Generations of humans that are endowed with exceptional gifts. We don't have glowing hands or superhuman strength, but we keep their secrets safe, and we protect them. We have these markings under our skin that only the Cursed Ones can see, and we may or may not have the ability to heal…but that's a story for another time."

Avery chuckled to herself. *Riiiiight.* "Um, okay…"

"Well, the first batch of Cursed Ones that Ivez's lover, Moira, created were made with small pieces of his essence, which accidently made them part god and part human like she was…a very dangerous combo as I already stated earlier. But over the years, Moira eventually learned how to claim humans without giving any of her remaining essence away. B was her last victim before she died. According to B himself, the Pure Ones discovered him in mid-transformation in the woods near Moira's house that had been burned down. So, they took him to their sanctuary for his own safety. Shortly thereafter, the peace brought to the world by their hands ended. They no longer ruled with compassion and mercy. Instead, they turned to fear and hostility. If anyone defied their rules or betrayed their kind, they were tortured and usually killed. A select few were chosen to become Warriors. B was one of them. But after many years of carrying out their horrible requests, he didn't want to live that life anymore. He's been in hiding because he fled from their sanctuary. He wants to be free. If they were to find out his whereabouts, they wouldn't hesitate to take back what is rightfully theirs. His essence. That's why we've fought so hard to keep his secrets hidden, and why he's had to distance himself from you. He was protecting himself by keeping you in the dark. And protecting you from being caught in the crossfire." Jonah stopped talking when he noticed the look on Avery's face.

She leaned forward, clasping her hands together, then she licked her lips and cleared her throat. "So, let me see if I understand this correctly, Jonah…you're saying that Bastian is some superhuman mutant with incredible supernatural abilities, and he's being hunted by some other mutants with a god complex…and his only hope of survival is you and your undercover Watcher-spies who just happen to have invisible magic markings that only Bastian and his cursed friends can see? Does that just about cover it?"

Sebastian instantly felt himself relax. *She doesn't believe him! That's good. That means I have more time.*

But then Jonah had to go and open his big mouth again. His facial expression was serious, and his voice was stern. "I get it, Av. You don't believe me, and that's fine. But…what if I said that I could prove it?"

Avery raised her eyebrow as a skeptical expression covered her face. "And how are you going to do that?"

"Do you remember the night you met B?"

Sebastian's eyes widened. *He wouldn't dare…*

Avery's body posture went rigid. "Of course, I do! What kind of question is that?"

Jonah cleared his throat as a nervous twisting feeling filled his stomach. "Well, then this should make things crystal clear. The creature you saw…the one with the glowing red eyes? You're gonna think this is beyond crazy, but…"

Suddenly, Sebastian's entire body began to waver as he balled up his fists and let out an ear-splitting roar.

Both Jonah and Avery jumped.

"What was that?" she whispered as she reflexively grabbed Jonah's arm.

"I'm not sure," he lied.

Sebastian could feel himself losing control. His friend had betrayed him in the worst possible way, and there was no going back now. Sebastian's rage grew hotter beneath his skin.

Avery peeked through the curtains. The clear blue sky overhead was becoming darker and darker as the wind began to blow and howl. The trees were shaking wildly, sending their leaves twisting and swirling to the ground. What was left of the setting sun was rapidly disappearing as more and more menacing storm clouds moved in. Lightning flashed, and moments later, thunder rumbled off in the distance, and the skies opened up. Rain and hail poured down so hard that she could barely see anything past the glass. A few tiny pieces of hail pitter-pattered against the window, causing Avery to gasp as she backed away. Another loud crash startled her again. This time, though, it was at the front door.

"Could be a large piece of hail," Jonah offered. "Or a tree branch."

But the banging continued over and over, getting louder each time. Then all of a sudden, it sounded as if a bomb had been detonated right outside. The huge bay window in the kitchen where Avery had just been standing imploded, flinging shards of glass and chunks of wood in every direction. Avery and Jonah's arms went up over their faces as they tried to shield themselves from the flying debris. They were both thrown backward as rain began pouring inside, soaking the hardwood floors. It was then that they both heard Sebastian's voice calling out Avery's name. She managed to get to her feet, taking a step toward the gaping hole in the wall.

Jonah jumped up and grabbed her arm, pulling her back. "DON'T!" he shouted. "It's too dangerous!"

She had no idea that he wasn't talking about the weather. "Sebastian's out there," Avery argued, "I can't just leave him stranded in this crazy monsoon!"

She pulled free of Jonah's grip and raced to the front door. The instant she turned the handle, the wind ripped the door right out of her hand, flinging it open violently.

"BASTIAN, WHERE ARE YOU?" she called out. The rain was coming down so hard that it practically drowned out her voice.

Avery held onto both sides of the door jambs and slowly poked her head out. Instantly she was soaked from head to toe, but she didn't care. She narrowed her eyes and tried to scan her front porch, but the thick sheet of rain was nearly impenetrable.

"BASTIAN!" she shouted as loud as she could. "BASTIAN, WHERE ARE YOU?"

She could barely make out Jonah's voice screaming at her to close the door, not that it mattered now. The kitchen was a lost cause.

Avery wasn't even aware of his feeble attempts to pull her back inside. Her concern was elsewhere. That is, until two glowing red eyes came into view. They cut through the dense rain like lasers burning through paper. Flashbacks of those same eyes sent Avery into panic mode. Her anxiety level was just about to reach maximum capacity when Sebastian rushed inside with incredible speed and secured the door behind him. The instant the door clicked shut, the storm completely dissipated.

The three of them were all breathing heavily, scattered around what was left of the soaking wet kitchen. Sebastian studied Avery's face. Her wet hair was matted to her forehead, and there was a small gash on her cheek as well as one across her chin. Droplets of blood and water dripped down her face. His heightened sense of hearing could make out every little plop as they landed on the flooded floor.

"Is everyone okay?" Sebastian asked as he pulled Avery to her feet.

"Yeah, I think so," she replied breathlessly.

"I don't know," Jonah stated. "Are we?"

Sebastian knew that question had a double meaning. Jonah wanted to make sure that he wasn't in the line of fire, which Sebastian was still unsure of.

He ran his finger over the cuts on Avery's face, hoping to heal them before she even realized that she was hurt. It had been so long since he had seen her in person. He had to fight the urge to take her into his arms.

"Are you alright?" she asked quietly.

"I'm fine," Sebastian replied. He didn't mean to, but he looked directly at her when he answered.

Oh, my God! Avery's eyes grew wide as she quickly backed away, slipping and sliding in the water and nearly losing her balance.

Sebastian caught her arm just before she fell over.

"Your eyes," she whispered.

He shot Jonah a displeasing glare. He could feel his rage building again, but then he felt Avery's hands touch his cheeks. She slowly brought his face back down to hers. He swallowed nervously as she stared at him. He wanted to turn around and flee. It was unnerving to have her see this particular side of him, mostly because it linked him to the most terrifying night of her life.

"So, it was all true then?" she asked, baffled. "What Jonah told me about Ivez and Moira…and the Pure Ones? It's all…real?"

Sebastian blinked a few times, clearing his glowing vision and returning his eyes to their natural color. Then he stood up straighter, pulling away from her and turning towards Jonah. He was suddenly furious all over again.

Avery glanced back and forth between both men.

Jonah stepped closer. "Don't be mad at her," he stated. "This is all on me."

Sebastian trudged towards him, splashing water with each step. "Oh, I know this is all on you!" He grabbed hold of the collar on Jonah's shirt and pulled him up off the floor so that they were nose to nose. "You're supposed to be my Watcher and my best friend! Yet you go behind my back and divulge some of the most intimate parts of my life? What the hell were you thinking?"

Jonah gulped. He had never been on the receiving end when Sebastian was angry. Though he knew his friend had every right to be pissed-off after what he had done.

"Bastian let him go," Avery coaxed gently. She placed her hand delicately on his shoulder.

Sebastian's nose was flaring like a bull preparing to charge.

Jonah was too embarrassed and afraid to hold Sebastian's furious gaze any longer, so he turned his head away. *I'm sorry, B. I was only trying to help.*

"Let him go," Avery repeated. This time, she gave Sebastian's shoulder a slight tug.

His rigid body began to turn, so Avery tugged a little harder.

In one swift motion, Sebastian had released his hold on Jonah's shirt and was now fully facing in her direction, still clearly seething.

"It's just you and me now," she said as she reached out for

his hands. The instant their skin touched, Avery felt his warmth radiating.

All the anger and frenzied madness he was feeling only seconds ago seemed to melt away. He sighed and reached out to her mind. *Oh, Av. How do you always do that to me?*

She replied with her own question out loud, only because she didn't know how to respond telepathically. "Do what exactly?"

He didn't answer. He thought it best not to.

"You can leave now, Jonah," Sebastian said, without taking his eyes off of Avery.

"I'm going," Jonah stated. "Can we talk…later…about all this?"

Avery watched Sebastian's eyes narrow again as his jaw clenched.

"Goodbye, Jonah," she stated firmly. She hoped that he would get the hint and leave before Sebastian got pissed-off again.

To get to the front door, Jonah would have had to walk past them, but he was still too rattled to do that. So, he opted for the only other option. He jumped out of the broken window.

Avery chuckled, and Sebastian fully smiled then, causing small crevices to appear on his cheeks. Avery wanted to touch his adorable dimples, but as she reached out, he blocked his mouth with his hand.

She grinned. "How did you know what I was about to do?"

"You were staring right at them," he stated, seemingly amused.

"You're waaaaay too perceptive," Avery replied with a smirk. "Is that another one of your…gifts?"

He shot her a playful glare. "No. It's just one of the reasons I hate to smile. They drive me crazy."

They drive me crazy too, she thought.

He looked away for just a moment as his smile widened. She had no idea she had just sent that statement directly to him. One day he would teach her how to control the transfer of her thoughts, but that all depended on if she accepted him in the end.

Avery shuffled her feet, causing ripples in the shallow water that pooled around them. "So...your eyes glow too, huh?"

Sebastian ran his hand anxiously through his hair. "Yeah..." *The bigger question is, has she finally put two and two together?*

Avery stood still for a moment, shaking her head. "Why didn't you just tell me this stuff a long time ago?"

Okay, so I guess she hasn't. He sighed. "I wasn't sure if you were ready to deal with the consequences of knowing certain things about me."

She nodded as if she understood what he meant. "Why do I get the feeling that there's a lot more?"

He could hear the apprehension in her voice. "Because there is." Disappointment covered his face.

She looked at him in a way that made him feel like he could tell her anything and she would never judge him or push him away, but that didn't erase all the what-ifs running through his troubled mind.

He cleared his throat. "Well, I should probably get started on cleaning up the destruction that I caused."

There was at least three inches of standing water in her kitchen, and it was slowly seeping into the carpet in the living room which was connected through a small hallway. Sebastian knelt down and placed his hand on the soaking wet floor. He began radiating an extreme amount of heat at a very rapid pace. The water promptly began to bubble and hiss as it quickly turned into steam, evaporating faster than Avery expected. Within minutes, they were in a hot sauna. She could barely see him walking by only a foot or so away. When the fog-like vapors disappeared, the floor was entirely dry without any visible damage at all. The huge hole in the wall, however, now that was a different story.

Avery glanced at the remnants of the window and then at Sebastian. "So, that whole bizarre weather, all the rain and hail, and thunder...that was...you?"

He saw no need to beat around the bush at this point, though his heart rate had definitely raised a few extra beats per minute. He simply nodded, keeping his eyes glued to hers.

Avery seemed to be in deep thought for a moment. "Hmm, so you're a weatherman?"

Sebastian continued studying her. "You could say that."

"This is completely crazy and pretty much impossible…"

Sebastian gulped without her noticing.

"…but I'm pretty sure I can handle it all," she replied confidently.

He wanted to believe her. Really, he did, but decades of consistency in this particular area of his life had taught him to remain guarded.

She noted the skepticism covering his face. "You don't believe me." The tone of her voice wasn't upset at all. She just seemed to be stating an observation.

Sebastian wasn't sure how to reply. *I want to.*

Sensing that his lack of communication was an indication that the conversation wasn't going to progress any further, Avery changed the subject. "So, what should we do about the window? I honestly don't have the money to fix it, and if my parents come home from my dad's company retreat to this…" She glanced around and sighed. "I don't think we would be able to explain it to the insurance company."

Sebastian smiled. "I'm the one that broke your house, so I'll be the one to take care of it."

With that, she was ushered out the front door and into the passenger seat of her own car. They drove to the nearest building supply store where he bought a bunch of plastic drop cloths and some duct tape. Avery wasn't sure how those particular items were going to help, but she didn't say a word. They arrived back to her house in record time, and Sebastian began the simple task of framing the window with the plastic on the exterior of the house. Avery helped by holding a ladder steady while he securely taped down every corner. He repeated the same process on the interior.

"It's just a temporary fix for the time being…mostly to

keep out bugs and any other critters that might try to get inside until I can fix it. I promise to have it taken care of by tomorrow afternoon at the latest. But you may want to sleep somewhere else tonight." *I'd offer to let you stay at my place, but that would be a terrible idea.*

"Alright. Thank you." Avery wasn't sure if he was going to repair the window himself with some mystical carpenter power, or if he would hire someone to do it. Either way, she was grateful. "Soooo, why don't I get us something to eat, and we can hang out and talk for a little while?"

Sebastian knew exactly what she wanted to talk about: Him. His past. And everything Jonah had told her.

A few minutes passed, and he had yet to give her an answer.

Noticing his reluctance, Avery spoke again. "Look, you don't have to talk about anything you don't want to." She certainly had things she didn't want to discuss. Like the fact that she had foolishly professed her undying love for him and he hadn't said it back. As the memory replayed, her heart throbbed a little.

Sensing the sudden change in her heart rate, Sebastian ultimately agreed.

Avery prepared a ham and cheese sandwich with a side of potato chips and a glass of orange soda for each of them. Sebastian offered to help, to which she politely declined. They ate on the living room floor in awkward silence, both avoiding direct eye contact.

She took a swig of her drink and sat the glass down on the coffee table with a loud clank. "Why does this feel so uncomfortable all of a sudden?" she asked bluntly.

Sebastian shrugged as he took another bite of his sandwich. *Because I've never willingly opened myself up to anyone before.* That is what he wanted to say, but he just couldn't bring himself to.

"Be honest with me." Avery paused, and Sebastian waited. "Were you ever going to tell me these things about yourself?"

He swallowed the bite he was chewing and then lost his appetite. He cleared his throat before speaking. "Eventually, yes."

"Are you still angry with Jonah?"

Sebastian clenched his jaw and nodded once. "Yes."

"Do you wish I'd stop asking you random questions?"

He smiled then. "Yes."

His consistent short answers were more proof that this was extremely difficult for him, but at least she could tell that he was trying. Avery propped her elbow up on the coffee table, leaning her chin on her open palm. "Okay, I'll make you a deal. If you answer three more questions for me, I'll never bring up any of this again…until you're ready."

Sebastian's head shot up. His forehead and his nose were crinkled in confusion. "Just three questions?"

Avery nodded. "Any three I choose, but you can't give me one-word answers." She held out her hand. "Deal?"

He pondered for a moment, wondering which questions she would ask and how he would answer. Avery's mind was racing, and Sebastian's stomach was slowly churning within itself.

He stared at her hand hovering in the air in front of him. "Alright, deal."

They shook hands.

Now came the hard part. Sebastian was on the edge of his seat, almost on the verge of feeling sick.

"Okay, I've got my first question. Are you ready?"

He nodded yes, but inside he was saying *no*.

She cleared her throat softly before she spoke. "Are you really eighteen like I am?"

His face suddenly looked distressed. "No, I'm not," he whispered.

"Then how old are you?" she pressed.

He rubbed his temples and swallowed hard. "Does that count as your second question?"

She shook her head. "It goes along with the first since you aren't giving me much to go on."

He sighed and shifted a few inches away from her. "I've been eighteen more times than I can count."

Avery's breath caught in her throat as she waited for him to actually answer her question.

This game was harder than Sebastian had imagined it would be…and this was just the first question. A simple one. How was he going to feel if she asked something with more depth? He collected himself and released his clenched fists. "I grew up in the 1800s," he finally said.

Avery's mouth hung open, but only for a second. "So, that would make you like…"

He did the math for her. "Two-hundred-fourteen."

Avery was speechless for quite some time after that. In fact, she wouldn't even look at him. Revealing things that were normal for him, yet strange to her, definitely was not going to be as easy as he had hoped. Sebastian knew this was much more than she bargained for, but in his defense, he did warn her.

Avery finally looked his way again. "How old were you when you were…cursed?"

"Seventeen."

She eyed him suspiciously. "Like really seventeen or…?"

One corner of his mouth twitched. "Yes, the one that comes after sixteen."

"How are you not aging?"

He opened his mouth to answer, but she quickly asked another question.

"Are you going to stay looking eighteen forever?"

He arched his eyebrows. "Are those the last two questions?"

Avery shook her head. "No, they still pertain to question number one."

Sebastian felt himself getting flustered. "Av, the deal was three questions. We're technically past that."

At that moment, she wished she hadn't ever made the stupid deal. She wished she could take it back so she could gather as much information about him as possible. "Okay, I'm sorry."

"So, do you want me to answer those or do you have

something else you'd like to ask?"

"I want to know how you're not aging."

He let out an uneasy sigh. "The simplest way I can explain it is that I can be any age that I want to be at any time, but I'll always look like me. I can't shape-shift to look like you or Chase or Jonah or anyone else."

She stared at him, dumbfounded. "Uhh…"

I think I just confused her even more. He ran his fingers through his wavy brown hair as he thought of how to explain things clearly. "Let me try to put it another way. Okay…" He shifted his body so that he was facing in her direction. "So, let's say that I wanted to be an older version of myself tomorrow, like fifty-years-old. Then I'd look fifty. The next day I could choose to be eighteen again, so I'd look like the eighteen-year-old version of myself. Does that make sense?"

Avery tried to wrap her mind around this bizarre new information, but she just could not imagine how that could work. "Can you…show me?"

Sebastian was a little taken aback. "Like right now? I don't know if that's such a good idea, Av."

She crossed her arms. "Are you afraid that I won't think you're good looking anymore if I see you as an old man?"

Sebastian erupted with laughter. "Not exactly."

She grinned. "Then show me. I won't ask you for anything else. This will be it."

Sebastian's lighthearted mood was short lived. "I don't know…"

Avery instinctively clasped her hands on top of his. "Please?"

Should I do this? "This type of thing isn't for the fainthearted."

She shot him a smug look. "My heart is just fine."

He smiled briefly, but it was definitely forced. "You might want to prepare yourself then," he stated.

"I'm prepared," she said quickly, though she wasn't really sure how she could prepare for something like this.

Here goes nothing… Sebastian hesitated before he finally

closed his eyes and took in a slow deep breath. When he let it out, his hair suddenly began to lighten. The dark brown began to fade away as silver and white came through. His skin started to age and wrinkle. More pronounced smile lines appeared at the edges of his eyes. His full pouty lips began to thin out.

Avery felt like she was watching an age progression video in slow motion. It was unbelievable…and crazy…and extraordinary.

It only took a few minutes for Sebastian to complete his aging metamorphosis. When he opened his eyes, Avery was staring back at him completely stunned.

"It must be so weird to look in a mirror and see yourself like that," she said quietly.

"You get used to it," he replied matter-of-factly. Though for over eighty years before he met Avery, Sebastian didn't even feel his physical body, let alone see it. He had stayed in his Cursed Form, running from his past and living with his own inner darkness.

She continued staring at him, studying him. He thought for sure that she was going to ask to touch his skin to make sure it wasn't a mask or a trick of some sort, but she never did. She kept her distance, just observing curiously.

Eventually, he couldn't take her gawking stares, so he shook his head quickly. The aging seemed to flake away and fall off as if he had painted it all on. Moments later, he was his eighteen-year-old self again.

After that, Avery kept her word and didn't mention anything else pertaining to his past, though he could tell she really wanted to.

CHAPTER 18

That night, Avery stayed at a friend's house just as Sebastian had requested. She listened to Valerie giggle and swoon on the phone with Chase while she engrossed herself in a 'Supernatural' marathon. Quite fitting considering what she had just found out a few hours earlier. As she watched the show, she began to wonder what other abilities Sebastian was capable of.

Can he turn invisible? Can he stop time? Can he fly? Does he have super strength? She had so many questions that would have to go unanswered…for now.

Later that night, she listened to a mini argument of "You hang up first. No, you. No, you hang up". Avery was pretty sure that Valerie eventually fell asleep with Chase still on the other end of the line, because a soft muffled snore was now coming from her room.

Avery was in the guest bedroom wide awake, staring at the ceiling fan as it spun around and around, just like the thoughts in her head; thoughts of everything Sebastian.

He can alter his age, his eyes glow, his hands glow, he can radiate heat, he can speak telepathically, and he can basically control the weather… What are you, Bastian?

Avery woke up way too early, thankful that there was no school so she could recuperate after such a restless night. Her ever growing thoughts had kept her up most of the evening, and they were still nagging in the back of her mind.

She left Valerie a note saying that she had headed home early. The sun was barely peeking over the horizon when she pulled into her driveway. She expected to see the huge hole in the side of her house still covered with plastic. Instead, the siding appeared brand new, and the window was entirely intact. She parked and then walked over to inspect it closer, running her hands along the recently finished outer wall. She wasn't sure how Sebastian could have gotten such a massive amount of work done in such a short amount of time, let alone matching the color of this particular spot so perfectly with the rest of the house…unless he repainted the entire exterior.

But he couldn't have done that. Could he? Maybe it's the lack of lighting. I'll check again after the sun has a chance to rise a little more.

When Avery went inside, the kitchen was in perfect working order. The table and all its settings appeared untouched. No broken glass, no splinters, no water damage, nothing out of order. She was beginning to wonder if she had imagined the whole situation that had taken place yesterday. That made more sense than the likelihood of an explosion tearing apart her home and Sebastian aging right in front of her eyes.

~*~*~*~

By 10:15am, Avery had checked, rechecked, even quadruple checked the exterior of her house. The siding was seamless. There were no visible signs to show any remodeling had ever taken place. She stood with her hands on her hips, staring and pondering. *Have I gone completely crazy?* Suddenly, her phone chimed in her pocket.

Bastian: G'morning. How was ur night?

She decided to keep quiet about the possibly fictitious hole in the wall on the off chance of sounding like a fool.

Avery: It was restless 2 say the least.

After hitting SEND, she headed back inside.

Bastian: 2 much on ur mind?

Avery: Yeah.

Sebastian groaned as he stared at his phone. *Did I reveal too much?*

Bastian: I'm sorry. Maybe we should keep my…um, reveals 2 a minimum 4 a while then?

Avery's eyes lit up, and she sighed happily. "I'm not crazy. That's good news."

Bastian: How does the wall look?

Avery: Perfect…like nothing happened. How did u do that?

Bastian: I'm just that good.

Avery smiled. She was imagining the cocky expression that must have been gracing his gorgeous face when he sent that text.

Avery: haha…well, I appreciate it!

Her mind was repeating the same question over and over. *How did he really fix the hole? Maybe he'll tell me next time that we're face to face.* Which would be sooner than she thought.

Bastian: Knock knock.

The exact moment she read the text, she heard a knock at her front door. Avery grinned as she opened the door to see his smiling face.

He held up a bag of Dunkin' Donuts. "Time to celebrate!"

Avery smiled wider. "And what exactly are we celebrating?"

Sebastian stepped inside, placing the bag on the kitchen table. "Hmm, breakfast?"

Avery regarded him suspiciously as her smile reached maximum capacity. "No, seriously…what are we celebrating?"

"Progress," he replied with a smirk. "Lots of progress."

Ahh! Those dimples! Avery thought her face might crack.

CHAPTER 19

Sebastian and Avery sat down next to each other, playfully bumping elbows as they enjoyed their tasty treats.

"So, are you all packed for the Everglades trip on Monday?" he asked as he reached for another chocolate glazed donut.

Avery wiped away some stray sprinkles lingering on her lips before she replied. "With all the scheduling issues this trip has had over the last few months, I've packed and repacked so many times that I've lost count. August 12th, when the trip was originally planned for, I was all packed and ready. When it was rescheduled for September 9th, I packed all over again. Though I'm sorta glad that those dates got changed because warmer weather in the Everglades would have meant being eaten alive by mosquitos! Then I packed once more for October 20th, only to be told it was postponed yet again. Now we're not supposed to go until December 8th? At this point, I won't believe we're actually leaving until we get there!"

Sebastian chuckled. "I haven't packed a single thing…on any of those dates. I probably won't until Sunday night."

"That's because you're a guy. You all tend to be

procrastinators and last minute-ers." Avery flicked a piece of glazed donut in his direction. She snorted and then burst out laughing when it unexpectedly stuck to the side of his face.

His dimples began to show as he casually took the gooey dough from his cheek and glanced in her direction. She saw a hint of mischief in his eyes as he grabbed a cream filled donut in each hand.

"I'm sorry," he stated with a sly smirk.

Avery gasped as her mouth fell open. "You wouldn't!"

She could not have been more wrong. Before she had any time to react, Sebastian had squeezed and mashed both donuts right into her hair. Avery squealed and giggled as she attempted to get away, but there was nowhere she could go that Sebastian couldn't get to faster.

Super speed...check!

They chased and dodged each other around the kitchen and down the hallway into the living room. Her high-pitched shrieking only stopped when Sebastian respectfully conceded. Although by this point, Avery's long brown hair was covered in frothy whipped cream and sticky donut particles. After a few more minutes of playful banter, Sebastian helped to rinse out her hair in the kitchen sink. A shower would have been much easier...and faster, but Avery was enjoying being in such close proximity to him. Plus, she was reveling in the fact that his body was pressed up against hers as his hands gently massaged her scalp.

In the midst of the hair-washing chaos, Avery's mom walked through the front door. Water spatter and donut remnants welcomed her home. She stared at the crumbs all over the floor and then gave her daughter a questioning stare. "Do I even want to know what went on in here?"

Sebastian pointed to Avery, whose head was still under the faucet. "She started it."

Avery giggled.

Her mom just shook her head and smiled before walking away. "I just came home for a minute to grab a few things that your father forgot to pack. That man always becomes so scatterbrained when we have to go on these company trips. He's lucky this one was only a short drive away. I'll leave you two to finish…whatever it is you're doing."

Sebastian turned off the water and handed Avery a towel. He chuckled to himself as he realized just how much of a mess the two of them had made. "I'm beginning to see a pattern here," he stated quietly.

Avery raised an eyebrow as she twisted her hair up in the towel. "What are you talking about?"

Sebastian smiled wider. "Your kitchen and I don't seem to get along. Whenever we cross paths, destruction follows."

Avery's mouth slowly turned up as she too noticed the donut covered floor, table, and walls. Then she laughed so hard that she snorted like a little pig.

Sebastian nudged her shoulder gently as he leaned in closer. "Just remember that this time the mess is your fault," he whispered.

She fully smiled then. "Yeah, yeah! I take complete responsibility. Just help me clean it all up!"

"And if I don't?"

Avery turned around to hide her amused expression. "Then you'll find yourself covered with the rest of the donuts in this bag!" She could practically feel Sebastian's gaze burning a hole in the back of her head, so she turned around, grinning from ear to ear.

Much to her surprise, he was holding a glazed donut in his hand as if ready for another sugary battle. He smirked as his lips curled up. "You were saying?"

The confident, pompous look on his face nearly sent her over the edge with laughter yet again. So, she held up her hands as a sign of defeat. "Okay, okay…I surrender!"

Sebastian kept his eyes glued to hers as he slowly lowered his glazed weapon, placing it back on the table. Moments later he was sweeping the floor, sending the crumbs flying out the front door and down the steps. Avery was trailing after him with a Swiffer mop to clean up the sticky residue left behind. Then they wiped down the walls.

She looked around. "Phew! Alright now that that's taken care of, I'm going to change my shirt since *someone* got it dirty…but I'm not going to name any names! Then we can listen to some music for a bit."

Sebastian grinned. "*Someone* might be up for another dance session if the music is right."

Avery chuckled. "Well, you can dig through my pile of CDs and pick out whatever *someone* may want to listen to."

As she walked away, Sebastian began searching through her rather large CD collection. The first few were burned CDs that she had made herself. *Av's mix 2011. Av's dance mix 2012. Av's top songs of 2013.* Sebastian smiled as he picked up the last one. *Av and Bastian 2014.* He opened the case and slipped it into the player just as Avery came back into the living room.

"Did you find something good?" she asked.

"I think so," he replied nonchalantly. Then he pressed PLAY.

A beautiful piano riff filtered through the speakers and Avery's eyes widened as she made a quick dash for the stereo. She hit STOP before the words started. Sebastian could hear her heartbeat rising higher and higher. When she turned around to meet his gaze, her cheeks were flushed.

She let out a nervous laugh. "You saw the title?"

He nodded. "Yes, I did. Which is why I wanted to hear what was on it."

Avery cringed and turned away again. "Well, this is embarrassing."

"I thought it was lovely," he stated. "From the few seconds I got to hear anyway."

Avery sighed to herself as her heart began to race faster. *I can't believe I left that damn CD out in the open like that! I shouldn't have taken it out of my room. Ugh!*

Sebastian interrupted her inner dialogue by pressing PLAY once more. This time, though, he blocked her path so she couldn't cut it off. She struggled against him as the piano riff filled his ears again.

"Bastian, please!"

He wrapped his arms around her as the lyrics finally began to come through. Chantal Kreviazuk's lovely voice singing 'Feels Like Home' filtered through the speakers.

> Something in your eyes makes me wanna lose myself...makes me wanna lose myself in your arms.
> There's something in your voice...it makes my heart beat fast...hope this feeling lasts for the rest of my life.
> If you knew how lonely my life has been and how long I've been so alone.
> If you knew how I wanted someone to come along and change my life the way you've done.
> It feels like home to me.

If only she knew how much the words resonated with him as well, maybe she wouldn't have felt so uncomfortable. "So, this song...and all the others on this CD...they remind you of me?"

Avery sighed and slumped her shoulders while still in his embrace. "Are you really gonna make me answer that?"

Sebastian smiled and glanced down at her, though she avoided his stare. "May I borrow it?" he asked, sounding hopeful.

She instantly looked up then. Her forehead and nose were wrinkled. He wasn't sure if it was out of confusion or displeasure. "Bastian...no."

The tone of her voice was definitely full of the latter. "But why?"

Avery lingered in his arms even though she desperately wanted to pull away. "These songs have meaning for me. They are basically my feelings put perfectly into music. I tried telling you how I felt once...remember? It didn't exactly go my way."

Sebastian felt a twinge of guilt as he recalled the exact moment when she confessed her love for him. A moment that he will both cherish and detest for the rest of his life. "Of course, I remember..." He sighed as he cupped her face in his hands.

This unexpected move caused Avery's heart to stutter and her breath to catch in her throat. *Oh, my God, is he going to kiss me!?*

Their eyes were locked as Sebastian leaned in closer. He smiled faintly as his thumbs caressed her cheeks. Then his mouth parted as he leaned down to kiss her...on the forehead.

Disappointment covered Avery's face. *Or not...*

Sebastian's lips curled up to form his perfect dimpled smile as he leaned down once more. Avery could feel the warmth of his breath against her skin as he hovered dangerously close to her mouth. She swallowed nervously as her heart continued to flutter out of control. Sebastian slowly slipped his left hand around the nape of her neck, pulling her even closer. His right hand found the center of her back, holding her in place. He didn't think about the searing pain that would engulf him if he were to take this next step. He didn't worry about the consequences that would unfold. In fact, the only thought running through his mind was how amazing it would feel to press his lips gently against hers. So, that is exactly what he did.

The instant their mouths touched, he was flooded with all the emotions that he hadn't allowed himself to feel. This time, though, he didn't push them aside. He didn't fight them at all. For the first time in over a hundred years, he gave in. He felt the full weight of the wonder and love and desire that he felt for her. He felt an immense sensation of euphoria swelling from within, from the soles of his feet to the top of his head.

When he finally pulled away, he realized that he had been holding his breath the entire time.

"Wow..." Avery whispered breathlessly.

"Yeah..." Sebastian whispered back.

Avery smiled and closed her eyes as she wrapped her arms around his waist and leaned her head against his chest. As the melody continued to play, she began to sing along quietly. "Well if you knew...how much this moment means to me...and how long...I've waited for your touch. And if you knew...how happy you are making me...I never thought that I'd love anyone so much..."

Sebastian tightened his grasp around her in the hopes that she would understand the non-verbal cue showing her that he was feeling the same way…that he did, in fact, love her too. It was then that the oxygen seemed to leave his body. A moment later, he collapsed on the floor. Everything after that seemed to happen in slow motion. He could see Avery's panic-ridden face shouting at him and shaking him. Through his fuzzy vision, he watched her run down the hall to get her mother, who immediately dialed 911. Then everything went black.

CHAPTER 20

When Sebastian awoke, he was in an all too familiar place. Jonah and Chase were hovering nearby. He sat up, clutching his chest where the burning pain was supposed to be.

"What happened?" he asked. His voice came out hoarse at best, so he cleared his throat and asked again.

"We were going to ask you the same question," Chase stated solemnly.

Neither he nor Jonah would look at him.

Sebastian sighed and rubbed his forehead. "The last thing I remember, I was just dancing with Avery."

Jonah sighed too, but his sounded more like an irritated grunt. "Just dancing with Avery? Seriously, B? There's no such thing as *just* anything when it comes to you two. You need to be more careful, man!"

"I am careful!"

"Obviously not!" Jonah countered. "And we're all paying the price for your slip up!" His eyes finally made contact, blazing with anger.

Worry began twisting knots in Sebastian's stomach. "What? What are you talking ab…?" He stopped in his tracks when he noticed the dark red blotches running down Jonah's arms. Then he saw the same thing on Chase. He instantly got up and touched their skin. "What is this?!"

Jonah jerked his arm away.

"Our markings started to glow, so we knew you were in trouble," Chase stated. "But then…"

Jonah interrupted his brother. "Then all of our markings started to glow. Me, Chase, mom, dad…it eventually became so bright that it burned right through our skin, leaving these painful scars behind." He gently ran his fingers down his arm.

Sebastian took a few unsteady steps backward and fell onto the couch. He was feeling disoriented as he glanced around the Smart's living room. *How can this be happening?*

Jonah sat down next to him. "Mom and dad were listed as your emergency contacts, not that we needed to wait. We were all out the door before we even got the call."

"From what we were told, you were getting pretty violent before we arrived," Chase said. "Dad had to use a tranquilizer on you."

"Did I shift?!" Sebastian asked frantically. "Did I hurt anyone?!"

"No, no. Nothing like that," Jonah replied in a calmer tone.

Sebastian breathed a temporary sigh of relief.

"But you were in pretty bad shape," Jonah continued. "It took all of us…and a few others…over an hour to get you to stop having violent spasms."

Sebastian's forehead creased. "Others?"

"Yeah. Up until about fifteen minutes ago, our house was filled with Watchers trying to help you." Jonah looked away. He was becoming highly agitated again. "But you should know that each and every one of them left with the same scars…and they were all much weaker than when they arrived." Jonah's jaw clenched and his fists balled up. "Your choices are affecting everyone around you! But you're far too self-absorbed and obsessed with Avery to notice!"

Chase stepped in between them. "Cool it, bro! Bas didn't know this was going to happen," he stated firmly. "And besides, everyone is fine."

"That's just it, Chase! B never knows when something is gonna happen!" Jonah turned his attention back to Sebastian. "There are far too many things that could trigger your curse…and because you've decided to take things into your own hands, now we have no idea what we're dealing with! You're getting careless, and we're all going to suffer for it! Tonight could have ended in an entirely different way if we hadn't had help."

Sebastian's mind was a jumbled mess. "What…what are you saying?!"

Jonah swallowed hard as his glaring gaze focused solely on Sebastian. "I'm saying that if you don't stop what you're doing with Avery, you're going to change…into something dark."

Sebastian stared at his friends, blinking absentmindedly.

"You've altered your curse," Chase said softly. "That's the only way I know how to say it."

Sebastian's eyes widened. "WHAT?! What are you guys talking about? That's impossible!"

Jonah slammed his fist against the coffee table. "NO! What's impossible is the fact that it took thirty-two Watchers over an hour just to get you back to normal…well, normal for you! This whole genius plan you have to slowly show parts of yourself to Avery so you can have a chance of her accepting you in the end? It's not going to work! You're delaying the inevitable and destroying yourself at the same time!"

Sebastian stared blankly at Jonah. "No…that can't be what's happening! Avery has accepted everything I've shown her…everything I've told her! This plan will work. I just need a little more time!"

"You're out of time!" Jonah seethed.

"That's enough…both of you!"

All three boys looked up to see Isabelle standing in the hallway.

Sebastian leapt to his feet and rushed toward her, wrapping his arms around her neck as he began to weep onto her shoulder. "I'm so sorry! I didn't know…"

"Shhhh," she whispered as she gently caressed his back. "It's not your fault."

Jonah stood and threw his hands in the air. "Like hell, this isn't his fault!"

"I said that's enough!" Isabelle repeated sternly. "I'm sure Sebastian feels bad enough already…there's no need to make him feel worse!"

Jonah shook his head in disagreement with his mother, but out of respect, he kept his mouth shut and stormed off to his room. As he passed them by, he sent a thought directly to Sebastian. *Your carelessness is going to get us all killed…by your hands or the Pure Ones! Make a choice while you still can.*

Sebastian flinched when he heard Jonah slam his door. Though, regardless of how angry Jonah was, his words rang true. Maybe Sebastian was getting careless. He was more in touch with his humanity than he had ever been before…and it felt good. However, he also needed to be aware of all the changes he had been feeling. He wasn't human anymore, so he shouldn't pretend to be.

Isabelle released her hold on him and smiled sweetly, though there was a shimmer of doubt in her eyes. "We know you didn't mean for any of this to happen."

Elliot came up behind his wife. The same dark red blotches that covered Jonah, Chase, and Isabelle also ran down his arms.

Sebastian could not bear to look at them anymore. He was too ashamed. "I'm so sorry," he whimpered.

Elliot reached out and embraced Sebastian as if he were his son. "You have nothing to be sorry for," he said quietly. "You were trying to make a real life for yourself. You didn't know this would be the outcome. None of us did."

Sebastian broke down yet again.

Isabelle touched his shoulder. "We think it's best if you stay here with us…at least until we can figure out what we're dealing with."

Sebastian wiped his face with the back of his hand and nodded. *What were they dealing with? 'You've altered your curse.'* Those *were Chase's exact words. What exactly did that entail?*

"You can stay in the guest bedroom," Elliot told him. "You'll be safe here. We've already brought over some of your belongings."

"Thank you," Sebastian replied, though he kept his gaze angled down at the ground. As he walked toward his new room, he noticed the distinct outline of a magical wall.

"The room has been spelled for your protection...and ours," Isabelle stated.

"I understand," Sebastian said weakly.

"We would never hold you against your will," she said softly.

He offered her a faint smile. "I know that."

"But we're trusting you to do the right thing," Elliot added.

Sebastian's shoulders rose and fell slowly, defeated. "You're talking about Avery, aren't you?"

Isabelle took a step closer to the doorway. "It's not safe for her to be around you...at least not right now."

He nodded as tears filled his eyes once more. "I'll take care of it." Then without any hesitation, he crossed through the one-way barrier into his invisible cage.

CHAPTER 21

Saturday morning, Sebastian headed over to see Avery. Within seconds of him knocking on her door, she grabbed his arm and pulled him inside.

"Oh, my gosh, I'm so glad you're okay!" She wrapped her arms around his neck and squeezed. "I've been calling and texting you for the past few days! I was so worried!" She dragged him to the couch as she began to happily babble on and on about how glad she was that he was okay and how incredibly thankful she was that he had finally let her in.

Sebastian tried to interrupt. "Av, can you stop talking for a second? I need to…"

She continued to discuss how excited she was to get to learn more about him, and how much she was looking forward to whatever the future held for them.

"AVERY JUST STOP!" he shouted.

Her eyes widened as she backed up involuntarily.

Sebastian blew out his breath in a long slow exhale. "I'm sorry I yelled at you like that…but I think I might have made a mistake."

Instantly her smile faded. *This crap again?* "Don't do that,

Bastian. Don't you dare push me away again. Not now!"

"I don't know what else to do," he admitted honestly. His voice was quiet, full of desperation.

"Talk to me," she urged. "Tell me what's going on in that confusing mind of yours!" She tapped his forehead.

He looked away. He found it easier to speak to her when he couldn't see the expression on her face. "I thought I was ready," he said softly, "...for all the repercussions that came along with letting you in and showing you all these different aspects of myself, but I was wrong."

"Not ready?" *Is he kidding?* Avery could not believe what she was hearing. "It's been six years, Bastian! We're closer than we've ever been! If not now, when?"

He could feel her staring at him and hear her heartbeat rising, but he didn't dare meet her gaze. "You may never be ready for everything that comes with my past, Av."

She scoffed. "So, we're back to that? How many times do I have to tell you that I'm not going anywhere?! How many times have I already proven that? I mean, just the other day, we were lying here cuddled up on my couch. Now you're saying you want to give up...again?"

He turned back around with an angry scowl. "Don't you get it? It always comes back to my past...it always will!"

His ill-natured tone caught her off guard, but Sebastian was feeling rather exasperated at this point. Avery was as stubborn and hard headed as they come. It was actually one of the many things he loved about her, but right now he wished she would just drop it so he could do what he came there to do...though at that moment, he wasn't exactly sure what that was.

Her mouth was still moving. Words were still pouring out. She was still objecting.

He sighed and rubbed his temples. He wasn't making any headway in this situation at all, and he knew she would not stop asking questions until she got more answers...which was something he could not afford to let happen right now. Not with the new information that he had learned about himself. He should not have shown her his other side at all. This situation right here and now proved that she wasn't ready...or maybe it proved that he wasn't. *Ugh!*

If only he could ask her to stay away for a little while so he could figure out what was happening to him, but he knew she wouldn't do that. At this point, her curiosity could get her killed. There was only one way for him to protect her now.

Sebastian had never used his mind-altering powers on Avery before. Part of him was scared to. Scared that the effects may be permanent, but regardless of that possibility, and as much as it tore him apart inside, he had to make her see him differently. He had no other choice. She gave him no choice now. He had to make her despise him...hate him. His heart completely disagreed, but it was the only way to keep her safe from the new seemingly-uncontrollable monster inside himself.

His face slowly shifted into a serious expression. At first, he played it cool. Just a few smart-ass remarks to get a rise out of her. Then he rose the stakes by provoking an argument. A few moments of petty bickering and small accusations, then their voices were raised just below yelling level.

Avery begged him one last time to explain himself...to trust her...to finally let her see past his walls. When he refused, that was the last straw. When she spoke, he could tell that it was hard for her to say.

"This friendship of ours...or whatever messed up relationship that we have going on between us..."

He braced himself for the hurtful words he knew were coming.

She bit her lip to hold back her tears. "We should just call it a ship because it's starting to sink and I just...I just can't do it anymore!"

She waited impatiently for him to say something. To say anything really, but he just swallowed hard and looked away.

"So, that's it?" Avery asked unbelievably. Her voice was breaking, along with her heart. She was now holding his hand as tight as she could.

Sebastian could feel the tenderness and love pulsating from her skin directly onto his. He absorbed as much of those feelings as he possibly could. He wanted to be able to remember how passionately she felt about him, but after only a few moments, he closed his eyes and drifted gently into her head. Her mind was flooded with emotions. She was happy and relieved that he was allowing her to touch him again. She was also fascinated, irritated, and confused all at the same time.

I wish there was another way. I'm so sorry, Av. One by one, he began to take away her pleasant thoughts, popping them like iridescent bubbles floating in the air.

She seemed disoriented for only a second, but it was enough for Sebastian to know that his 'procedure' was working. Avery shook off the odd sensation she was feeling and tried again to focus on the fact that Sebastian was still holding her hand.

Disengage, he told himself. *You have to detach yourself from her, or this won't ever work!* He released his grasp and discarded her hand in a manner that made it seem like he was disgusted that he had ever touched her at all.

She stared at him in disbelief. "What the hell, Bastian?"

His eyes narrowed, and his jaw clenched. "Does that change how you see me?"

Her mouth hung open. He was openly mocking her, and she knew it.

Sebastian felt horrible, though he never showed it. He made sure to keep his facial expression blank.

"You're just trying to antagonize me," Avery stated firmly. "But I won't let you! You're not going to push me away anymore. You cared enough to show me pieces of who you are, so why are you doing this now?" When he didn't respond, she took a step closer and tried to wrap her arms around his waist. "I'm not giving up on you!"

Sebastian stood as still as a statue with his arms limp by his sides, refusing to return her embrace. He pushed deeper into her mind, twisting all the wonderful moments they had shared into uncomfortable and insignificant recollections of the past. One by one, he was slowly erasing any and all positive aspects of himself from her thoughts. He could see her struggling internally. Hell, he was too. This was the last thing he ever wanted to do to the one person who meant the world to him.

Avery knew something wasn't right. Then as if a light bulb turned on in her mind, a disheartened expression covered her face as she gaped in his direction. "Bastian, whatever you're doing…however you're doing it…stop! Please stop!"

He felt a rush of guilt and sadness come over him. *TURN IT OFF*, he yelled to himself. *Turn it off before you ruin everything!* So, he did. He turned off his emotions and let pure instinct take over. The shift in his demeanor was almost instant as he physically pushed her away…hard. Something that he would have never, ever done.

She stumbled slightly, catching herself just before she would have fallen over. The disheartened look on her face would have sent him into an urgent spiel of apologies, possibly even tears, but the new unemotional version of himself didn't care whatsoever.

Sebastian spoke his next words slowly, carefully, and full of resentment. "I've told you time and time again, Avery…everything you see and believe about me…is a lie!" His voice was low, and void of any feelings whatsoever.

Avery's mind was racing. The way he said her name…the malice behind it…broke her heart even further. *Why does he want so badly to prove me wrong?*

Sebastian could hear her heart rate quicken, and her breath sounds increase. The tension between them was starting to rise, and emotions were already running high. The inevitable was sure to ensue. He just had to push a little further.

Flashbacks of their past were slowly altered or completely deleted faster than she could recall them. Within seconds, he found just the right spot and tempers immediately flared.

"It's your fault that I'm alone!" she suddenly exclaimed. For an instant, she was thrown off by the words that had just come out of her mouth.

Sebastian's callous shell glared at her as he continued to alter more and more memories.

Avery scowled back at him. "Don't give me that look! For

the past six years, I've been so wrapped up in you that I didn't give any other guy a chance! Everyone thought I was bat-shit-crazy after I told the police what I saw the night that we met! And you didn't even back me up! You made me look like a fool!"

"That's your own fault!" Sebastian countered. The animosity in his voice was like a dagger through her heart. "I didn't ask you to sit here waiting for me like a dog waiting for her master! I didn't ask you to give up your life for me! You did that all on your own! And I don't owe you anything when it comes to that night. *I* saved *you*, remember? So, if anything, you are indebted to me!"

Avery's eyes widened. *Did he just compare me to a dog?!* She balled up her fists at her sides and screamed out of frustration as she stomped towards him. "You're the most difficult person I know!"

He pushed further into her mind. *You're finished with me. You don't care about me anymore.*

She pointed her finger directly at his face. "No more, Bastian! I just can't take it. I'm done!"

He leaned closer until they were nearly nose to nose. "You're right," he replied through gritted teeth. "This. Is. Done!"

She watched him walk out the door without another word, flinching as he slammed it shut behind him.

Avery's eyes were filling with angry tears as she gripped the necklace he had given her for her sixteenth birthday. Then, before she knew what she was doing, she had followed him outside. She ripped the chain from her neck and threw it at him. The vial shattered at his feet just as she turned to walk away. "I hate you," she whispered under her breath.

As her final three words echoed in his ears, Sebastian's emotions turned back on without his permission. He was almost halfway down the driveway when his heart began to break apart in his chest. But then he heard her voice once more.

"Don't you dare walk away from me!" she cried out.

Sebastian stopped short and reluctantly turned around. He could hear her footsteps approaching, hard and fast.

Her tear-stained cheeks and blurry eyes greeted him as they were now face to face again.

Sebastian was fighting back tears of his own as he struggled to turn his emotions back off, but he just couldn't bring himself to do it.

Avery's face was full of confusion and panic. "Something's wrong," she whispered. The hysteria was evident in her voice. "Something's wrong!" she repeated louder. Her breathing quickly became erratic as a rush of fear engulfed her. She looked him right in the eyes. "Bastian, what's happening to me? I'm remembering things, but they…they're all wrong and twisted! It's like a distorted version of my life!"

Sebastian stared blankly at her. After all, what could he say? *Oh, it's nothing to freak out about. I just reached inside your brain and jumbled a few of your memories so I can keep you safe from whatever is happening to me with my curse.*

When he didn't answer, Avery began to pace directly in front of him. She closed her eyes and started mumbling indistinctly while hitting herself on the forehead and saying "Why can't I remember?" and "I'm not crazy!" over and over.

Sebastian could not understand what was happening. *Why isn't it working? I altered and removed her thoughts perfectly. By my calculations, she should be running in the other direction by now!*

Suddenly, Avery began gasping for air. She stumbled backward a few steps before collapsing to the ground. Sebastian, with his lightning-fast reflexes, caught her head just before she would have hit the concrete.

"What have I done?!" he asked out loud.

He listened carefully to every aspect of her body. She was breathing regularly now. Her heartbeat had gone back to its normal rhythm. All of her organs seemed to be functioning properly. He checked her mind last, mostly because he was scared of what he would find.

A pile of mush? A shredded hunk of meat? A vacant hole-filled mass?

As he entered into her memories, his brow furrowed. Somehow her brain was healing itself. Every single memory that he had wiped away or altered was slowly reforming; recreating every little detail just as it had been. He was dumbfounded, yet so relieved. At least he knew now what had caused her to faint. It was her body's way of protecting itself while it fixed the problem. A problem that he had created.

With a deep, remorseful sigh, he scooped her up into his arms and carried her inside.

~*~*~*~

Avery awoke a few hours later with a throbbing headache, wondering if what she experienced had actually happened or if it was just a bad dream. She made her way into the kitchen for some Excedrin just as her parents walked through the front door.

"Hey, mom, dad…how was the trip?"

"Long," her dad replied.

Her mom chuckled. "It wasn't that bad, but we're glad to be back home. How was your freedom?"

"Fine," Avery replied. "Uneventful."

"And Sebastian? Is he okay?"

Avery hesitated before answering. "Um, yeah. He seems much better."

Her mom nodded. "That's good to hear. Did the doctors find out what was wrong?"

Avery shrugged. "I'm not sure."

"Hmm." Her mom sat down her suitcase. "So, what happened to your necklace?" she inquired.

Avery automatically reached for her neck.

Her mom motioned toward the front door. "There's glitter and little shards of glass in the driveway."

"Oh…I, uh, I guess I must have snagged it on something," Avery stammered. *So, it wasn't a dream after all.*

"Well, would you mind cleaning it up? I'd hate for someone to hurt themselves or for any stray animals to cut their paws."

Avery nodded as she headed outside with a dustpan and small brush. While she swept up the tiny flecks of glitter and glass, she replayed the fight with Sebastian over and over…and over. She could still see his hardened face in her mind, along with his hurtful words. She cringed. Some of the details were a little fuzzy, but unbeknownst to her, that would not last long. She sighed as she picked up the three grains of rice that had been inside the vial and rolled them around in her palm. Things with Sebastian seemed to be coming to an end. At least that was what she was afraid of.

CHAPTER 22

Avery went back inside and placed the three grains of rice in her jewelry box. She stared at them and sighed as she closed her tear-filled eyes, remembering the day he had given her such a unique gift on her sixteenth birthday.

~*~*~*~

Two years ago...

"Do you think he's gonna show up?" Avery asked sadly. She was sitting at one of the empty tables in the concession area while most of her friends were zooming around the skating rink.

Chase plopped down in the booth across from her, offering a sweet smile. "If Bas said he was coming, he'll be here."

"Cut the crap!" Jonah stated rudely. He slid in the booth next to his brother, shoving Chase all the way to the other end. "B isn't gonna show. He probably never even planned on coming. He just told you what you wanted to hear. That's just how he is."

Avery shook her head, trying to retain a somewhat happy composure. "No. He wouldn't outright lie to me. He swore that he was going to make it."

Jonah rolled his eyes and stood up, nearly falling over when his left skate caught a metal bar underneath the table. "Well, you might want to get used to broken promises. B isn't who you think he is." With that, Jonah rolled away.

Avery swallowed anxiously.

"Ignore my brother," Chase said kindly. "He's just taking his frustrations out on you because he and Bas got into an argument earlier today, so Jonah probably doesn't want to see him. If Bas told you he was coming, then trust him." Chase gave her shoulder a gentle squeeze and then went to join the rest of their friends on the skating rink. "Hokey-pokey time!"

Avery giggled. "I'll join the next round."

Every year, for as long as she could remember, her parents always threw her a party at the roller-skating rink. It had become somewhat of a tradition that Avery claimed she would never get too old for. She always felt so free while she sped around the rink on her rollerblades. She enjoyed the loud music. It allowed her to tune out everything and everyone around her and just live for the moment. No worries, no cares, no troubles, no fears. Nothing except the rumble of her blades racing across the slick wooden floor. This year, however, her feet were planted firmly on the carpet.

As she was lost in her thoughts, watching her friends putting their left foot in and their left foot out, someone popped a balloon right next to her ear.

What the hell? She jumped and let out a squeaky little yelp before turning around to find two familiar boys she went to school with. Both of them were doubled over, laughing hysterically.

One boy with dark hair mimicked her scream as he started jumping around, acting like a scared little kid. The other one openly mocked her by pretending to cry.

"Poor baby, were you scared?"

Avery wasn't sure how to react to such idiotic immaturity. When she attempted to skate away from them, they blocked her path.

"Come on! We're just teasing, Avery. Don't be such a party

pooper," the blonde one told her.

"Don't you mean party popper?" the other boy chimed in. "Get it? POP-er. Like a balloon popping?"

She rolled her eyes. "Real mature guys."

They continued to taunt and tease her for a few more seconds. Then suddenly, both of their childish smiles disappeared, and their faces went pale.

"Is there a problem here?" Sebastian's deep voice came from behind her.

Avery crossed her arms awkwardly across her chest without turning around.

"Nah man, we were just messing around," the blonde boy replied.

Sebastian stepped between them and Avery. There was only about an inch difference in their heights, but Sebastian and his tenacious demeanor seemed to tower over them both. "It might be time to take your messing around elsewhere." He stared them down like a lion stalking its prey.

Without another word, both boys turned and quickly walked away.

Sebastian eventually turned back around and smiled down at Avery. "Sorry, I'm late."

She laughed nervously and uncrossed her arms. "It's totally okay."

He raised an eyebrow. "You didn't think I was coming?"

She bit her bottom lip and looked at the ground, which clearly gave her away.

He smirked, causing one of his dimples to show. "I wouldn't miss your birthday, Av. Not for anything. Besides, I got you something." He handed her a small black box with a little silver bow on top.

A tiny box. Could this be jewelry? Butterflies filled Avery's stomach as she carefully lifted the lid. Inside was a silver chain with a small glass vial filled with tiny flecks of glitter and sand. At first, she wasn't sure what to make of it.

Sensing what he perceived as disappointment, Sebastian whispered in her ear. "Look closely."

Upon closer inspection, Avery noticed three small grains of rice amongst the sparkling glitter. She turned the vial on its side and twirled it slowly until she saw there was something written on each grain. The very first one she found said 'Avery'. She swirled the vial again. The second grain read 'Sebastian'. She began to smile now. One last twirl revealed the last grain to say 'Oct. 31st, 2008', the day they met.

"This is beautiful," she said softly as she continued to rotate the vial. *This is probably the most unique and thoughtful…and dare I say it, romantic gift that I've ever received.* She read the grains over and over again.

"It pleases me that it pleases you," he replied graciously.

She tried to hide her growing grin. "I absolutely love it!"

~*~*~*~

Avery came back to the present, holding the spot on her neck where her necklace used to be. Her mind replayed the hurtful expression on Sebastian's face when he stared at the broken vial at his feet. *Way to go conscience, as if I didn't feel guilty enough already!* She took in a slow, deep breath and blew it out. The moment Sebastian gave her that necklace still ranked pretty high on her 'amazing meter'. The only thing that could ever top it would be if he were to confess his undying love for her. She scoffed at herself. Right now, that seemed rather unlikely, if not completely implausible.

CHAPTER 23

Avery woke up bright and early Monday morning before the sun had risen. She needed to be at school by 5:00am so she wouldn't miss the bus for her senior class trip. She stared out the window of her mom's SUV for the short drive to the school, allowing herself to get lost in her thoughts…mostly about Sebastian. They had not spoken at all since their fight two days ago. She wasn't even sure if he was going to show up today, but part of her hoped he would.

When her mom pulled into the parking lot, there were signs set up to show where the drop off point was. So, they drove around to the back of the school.

"Thanks, mom. I'll see you in a few days," Avery said groggily as she got out and hefted her overly-stuffed duffle bag over her shoulder.

Her mom gave her a tight hug and a kiss. "Have fun and be safe, honey! I love you."

"Thanks, mom. Love you, too," Avery replied as she headed for the back entrance to the gym.

Inside she found a handful of her classmates waiting quietly on the old wooden bleachers. Her sneakers squeaked on the recently polished floor, echoing throughout the large room before she found a seat on the bottom row.

About fifteen minutes later, the majority of the seniors had arrived. The gymnasium was now filled with muffled chatter, countless yawns, and even a few snores.

Jonah and Chase were hovering near the door as Valerie and her cousin, Paige made their way inside. Then Kyle Cross, a trombone player in the school band, who happened to have a long-time crush on Avery, walked in with his best friend, Rhett. His eyes locked onto Avery's and he immediately jogged over and plopped down beside her.

"Mornin', Av," he said cheerfully.

Avery smiled. "Morning, Kyle."

"Ready to see some gators?"

As always, his deep southern drawl made her smile. "As ready as I'll ever be."

The principal, Mrs. Drennon, walked to the middle of the basketball court with a microphone in her hand. "Alright everyone, calm down and have a seat." She waited a few minutes for everyone to sit down and hush. "I know all of you are super excited and ready to get out of here, but I need your attention for just a few minutes. The buses will be arriving shortly, so I'd like to go over a few rules beforehand."

A few students moaned and groaned, but Mrs. Drennon ignored them and continued on. "There will be no reckless behavior on the buses. You will remain seated and talk amongst each other quietly. When we reach our destination, you will be polite and listen to the chaperones, no wandering off. That is not the place you want to find yourself lost and alone. And finally, once we get to the hotel tonight, there will be no fraternizing. No girls will be allowed in the boys' rooms, and no boys will be allowed in the girls' rooms. Is that understood?"

Every single senior replied with "Yes, Mrs. Drennon" completely out of sync.

She smiled. "Okay then, please gather your belongings and follow me."

The entire senior class shuffled around in a disorganized manner, tripping over each other and shouting, as they made their way off the bleachers and toward the back door. One by one their bags were loaded into the storage compartment underneath the bus. When it was finally Avery's turn to board, she noticed Jonah and Chase sitting directly behind the bus driver. An empty space was behind them, and then Valerie and Paige occupied the third seat.

Valerie motioned for Avery to join her, so she scooted over, practically smushing her cousin against the window.

"Really, Val?" Paige squeaked.

Avery sat down, but half of her butt was hanging off the seat. "I don't think this is going to work," she said with a giggle.

"Two to a seat, ladies," Mrs. Drennon announced as she stepped onto the bus. "One of you will need to move." Her attention was then directed to the back. "Alaric put Daren down! This isn't a wrestling match!"

Avery began to pout as she slid into the vacant seat in-between her four friends. *I guess I'm the odd woman out today.*

As she was sitting there, listening to the consistent babble of her classmates, she started to feel a bit lonely.

Valerie gently bonked her on the head. "I miss you," she whined as a fake pout formed on her crimson lips.

Avery peeked over the seat and grinned, though Valerie couldn't see her mouth. "I miss you, too! I hate being so far apart!"

Valerie hugged herself dramatically. "This distance is just too much!" Then she abruptly turned to Paige, "Switch seats with Av!"

Paige glared at her. "Very funny, har har har!"

As they continued their playful banter, Avery felt someone bump into her elbow. She turned around, and lo and behold, Sebastian's earnest gaze met hers as he sat down next to her.

Her smile instantly faded.

"Hi," he said softly.

She stared at him for a few uncomfortable seconds before

she replied. "Um, hi."

He leaned over and whispered in her ear so that only she could hear him. "I'm sorry about my behavior the other day. I feel horrible about it."

Avery broke eye contact with him and glanced at her feet. *Good. He should feel horrible.* "Yeah, that was messed up," she whispered back. "And the thing you did with my mind…" She snuck a peek in his direction.

He sighed and looked away, frowning. "I can't apologize enough for that. I'm utterly ashamed of my actions."

Avery sat there for a few seconds before she asked, "Why would you do something like that?"

He sighed again, but he looked at her this time. "I thought I was doing the right thing. It may sound farfetched, but I honestly thought I was protecting you."

"Protecting me by modifying my thoughts?" Her tone was skeptical at best. "How am I supposed to trust you after that?"

"You know me, Av. You know I'd never purposely do anything to hurt you."

"Oh, now you're saying I know you?!" Her voice raised slightly, "What about all the times you've repeatedly told me that I don't really know you, hmm? You can't have it both ways, Bastian. All this back and forth bullshit is starting to give me whiplash."

Sebastian was feeling disgusted with himself by this point. "You're right. I have said that to you far too many times, but that's only because of the parts of me that I haven't shown you."

Avery let out an exasperated sigh. "So, show me already! I'm dying over here!"

"This isn't the time…or the place to discuss certain things," he replied quietly.

He looked as if he were about to say something else, but the remainder of the seniors had made their way onto the bus, stopping directly beside their seat, which caused Sebastian to have to scoot closer in Avery's direction. She couldn't help the butterflies that instantly filled her stomach when the smell of his cologne reached her nose.

She decided to use this moment to try to push her thoughts into his mind, though she was not entirely sure how. She squinted her eyes and furrowed her brow, concentrating as hard as she could. *What about like this?*

Sebastian's mouth twitched.

Avery smiled faintly. *So, you can hear me?* She stared at him, patiently waiting to see if she was getting through.

He smiled then. *Yes, I can hear you.* The aisle had cleared, so Sebastian sat up normally again.

So… Avery cleared her throat. *Can we discuss what really happened to you the night you lost consciousness at my house…or is that off limits like everything else?*

Sebastian shifted awkwardly. He could easily hear the annoyance and apprehension in her voice. He swallowed the lump that was forming in his throat. *I'm not sure how to explain that.*

Avery sighed heavily. *Of course not. I expected nothing less.* She crossed her arms and shifted toward the window. *Never mind, Sebastian. Just forget I asked.*

He flinched at the harsh tone when she said his full name.

The doors to the bus closed with a loud thunk as the driver started the engine and pulled out of the school parking lot.

Sebastian placed his hand on Avery's knee. *I'm not meaning to sound cryptic. I'm honestly trying to find the words to explain things to you.*

She stared at his hand. Then at his face. His soft grey eyes were pleading for her to believe him…to give him a chance to make things up to her.

It was hard for Sebastian to keep up with what Avery already knew about him and what she didn't. He was always worried about disclosing something that he wasn't supposed to, or revealing something she wasn't prepared for. This situation wasn't any different. He racked his brain for all the parts of himself that he had already revealed as he attempted to get his wording right. *You can't screw this up,* he told himself. *She's already on the verge of losing all the faith she had in you! Show her you're still worthy of her trust!*

A second or so later, Avery's gentle voice came into his mind. *I'm pretty sure you didn't mean for me to hear that.*

Sebastian felt his face redden. *Shit. No, I didn't.* He sighed heavily. *I'm all out of whack these days. I can't seem to focus on anything, so that may happen more often. I apologize ahead of time for any other crazy thoughts that may be sent your way.*

The stressful look on his face caused her heart to ache. *I still believe you're worth trusting, Bastian. I never actually doubted you. I was just afraid of what you did to me…of what you could do to me…and I'd be none the wiser.*

The two of them locked eyes then.

He gave her knee a gentle squeeze. *I swear on my life that I will never meddle with your thoughts or use any of my abilities on you without your permission ever again. You have my word.*

Seeming temporarily satisfied with that statement, Avery gestured in front of them. *And what about things between you and Jonah?*

Sebastian groaned out loud.

"What's got you two looking all sappy?" Jonah suddenly blurted out.

Both Sebastian and Avery glanced up. The faint light from the passing street lamps illuminated the interior of the bus just enough for them to see him staring at them over the seat with a what-the-hell expression on his face.

Then Jonah smiled as he pointed at the two of them. "Ohhh, you guys must be…"

"THAT'S ENOUGH!" Sebastian roared.

Avery jumped, and Jonah's eyes widened as a slow sheepish grin spread across his face before he slid back down into his seat.

All eyes were now gawking in their direction.

Jonah's voice drifted into Sebastian's mind. *Just so we're clear, I wasn't going to say anything that would have exposed you.*

Sebastian groaned and offered up a short apology to the entire bus load of his peers; then he turned back to Avery. She was staring at him with a hopeful expression.

He forced a smile. *Sorry about that. Like I said, I'm a little on edge these days.*

She nodded. *I guess that answers my question, though, huh?*

Sebastian leaned his head back. *Things are slowly working themselves out, but I fear it may take a while to get back to where we were.*

Avery glanced his way. *What happened between you two? As long as I've known you both, you've been inseparable…aside from the issues you guys had when my kitchen exploded.*

He tried to suppress a smirk. *I'm not going to live that down, am I?*

Probably not. Avery grinned. *Now, back to you and Jonah…*

Sebastian blew out his breath in one long, slow exhale. *His whole family, as well as a few other Watchers…all got burned because of me.*

Avery looked surprised. *Burned? As in you set them on fire?*

No! Well…not on purpose! There weren't any flames, at least not that I know of. But their injuries happened because they were trying to help me. Sebastian stared at her with such intensity. *You can't see what I see…the burn marks covering their arms.* He swallowed and blinked away the images creeping back up into his thoughts. *It's just a constant reminder that it's not safe to be around me.*

Avery kept her eyes locked onto his. *It's ironic that you'd say something like that because I feel completely safe when I'm around you. I always have. When you're not altering my thoughts, that is.*

He sighed again and then he took her by the hand. *That's exactly how I want you to feel. Safe and secure. Minus the mind-altering part.*

Their telepathic conversation dwindled down to nothing after that as the two of them sat in actual silence for a while. A short time later, Sebastian shifted his legs so he could access his front pocket. He pulled out his iPod Classic and then he took out a pair of earbuds. It was at that moment, Avery realized she had left hers in her duffle bag that was currently under the bus.

She grumbled to herself, which came out much louder than she anticipated.

Without any warning, Sebastian's fingers moved her hair out of the way. Then he placed one of his earbuds in her ear. 'Without You' by My Darkest Days began to play.

Avery smiled to convey an unspoken thank you. And as she listened to the words, she began to wonder if he had purposely picked this song just for her. Wishful thinking, but she just could not help herself.

If only she could hear the thoughts running through his head saying that it *was* for her.

Once the song ended, she casually gestured toward his iPod.

Sebastian glanced at the title at the top. *A-List*. He hesitated momentarily, speculating if she would figure out that the *A* actually stood for her name and not the generalization of being a 'top list'. As he placed the iPod in her hand, he anticipated a questioning glance, but she just scrolled through all the songs, completely oblivious. His heart stuttered as he thought about how easy it would be to confess that each and every one of them were for her. Instead, he looked away as 'Closer To You' by Adelitas Way began to play.

Being in such a confined space with her, listening to love songs, and not having any way to escape was becoming rather arduous...more so than he expected. Needless to say, a rush of relief instantly fell over him when Mrs. Drennon announced that they would be pulling into a rest station momentarily.

The bus pulled over and parked...and not a moment too soon. Sebastian hit STOP just as 'Riot' by Rascal Flatts started. The yearning to reach out and touch her had finally reached its limit. The instant the doors of the bus opened, Sebastian rushed off so fast that he was practically a blur. Avery was slightly stunned by his hasty exit.

"Guess he really had to go," Chase offered jokingly. Then he shot his brother a serious look.

~*~*~*~

After spending fifteen to twenty minutes eating snacks and stretching their legs, it was time for all the seniors and chaperones to re-board. Valerie asked Jonah to switch seats with her so she could sit with Chase. Jonah obliged. Paige wasn't too thrilled to be sharing a seat with him, mostly because he was always such a smart-ass, but she kept her opinions to herself and focused out the window. Sebastian was the last person to step foot back on board. As the doors closed behind him, he took a deep breath and found his seat next to Avery.

Just as the bus pulled back onto the highway, Avery reached out to him telepathically. *Are you okay?*

He offered her a faint smile. *I'm better now.*

She sighed softly. *What made you rush off like that?*

Sebastian anxiously rubbed his palms against his jeans. *You want the truth?*

She rolled her eyes. *No, I want you to lie to me.*

Sebastian noted the sarcasm and chuckled halfheartedly.

She raised her eyebrows. *So?*

He sighed. *It's getting more difficult.*

She sighed too. *That's pretty vague, Bastian. I need a little more than that.*

He shifted uncomfortably in his seat. *Hiding myself from you…it's getting harder.*

But that's a good thing, though, she stated. *Isn't it?*

The distressed look on her face gave him no other choice than to lie. So, he forced another smile. *Of course, it is.* Then to ease the tension, he slipped his hand into hers.

Avery hesitated, but shortly thereafter, she relaxed and leaned her head against his shoulder. With that, everything went back to the way it had been. Perfectly imperfect.

The rest of the bus ride was spent just like that. Hand in hand, side by side, song after song, heartbeat matching heartbeat. Before they knew it, they had reached their destination: An Everglades airboat park.

CHAPTER 24

The entire senior class was divided up into three groups to go on three separate airboat rides. As their names were randomly called out, Sebastian was placed in Group-one. Valerie, Paige, and Chase were in Group-two. Jonah, Kyle, and Avery ended up in Group-three.

When Sebastian refused to board the first boat, he could see Mrs. Drennon staring in his direction from the corner of her eye.

"Mr. Taylor, you need to go with the rest of your group," she instructed him.

Sebastian straightened his posture. "May I speak with you a moment?" he asked her confidently.

Mrs. Drennon looked somewhat annoyed, but nodded and waved him over.

Sebastian glanced over at Avery as he casually strolled toward their principal. His mere presence commanded respect. It was how he walked, how he carried himself, how he talked. Seconds later, he had whispered something into Mrs. Drennon's ear.

Her expression was slightly puzzled as she stood there

staring at him. Then she sighed dramatically. "Mr. Smart, will you please switch groups with Mr. Taylor?"

Both Chase and Jonah started walking toward the first boat.

Mrs. Drennon cracked a smile. "Sorry, I was referring to Jonah."

Chase stepped back into his group as Jonah made his way down the short dock. He and Sebastian barely acknowledged one another as they passed by each other.

When Sebastian took his place in line next to Avery, she smiled in his direction and then shyly looked away.

Jonah plopped down cheerfully in-between two female classmates.

One by one, the loud airboats pulled away from the dock. Sebastian and Avery were the last two seniors in their group to climb on board. The dock shifted and swayed with the movement of the water, causing the airboat to drift back and forth a few inches. The driver offered Avery his hand and pulled her on board.

There were three rows of short benches in the center for everyone to sit. The last two were already filled, leaving a few spots open at the front. Sebastian sat with his elbows propped up behind him on the furthest edge of the bench. Avery squeezed into the small space between him and Kyle. As everyone else slid down to make more room for themselves, Avery stayed put. She was enjoying being scrunched so close to Sebastian.

He noticed the fact that she hadn't moved over, so he casually draped his arm across the back of the bench. His fingers lightly grazed her shoulder as he tapped them carelessly on the metal frame. She closed her eyes as his touch sent a tingle down her spine. She was pretty sure he had done it on purpose, so she glanced up in his direction. His mischievous grin told her that she was right. He gently wrapped his arm around her, clasping his hand on her shoulder. Avery was so distracted by his touch that she was barely aware of the safety instructions the airboat driver was telling everyone.

"Alright guys and gals," the man stated in a southern

accent. "My name is Mr. Mitch, and I'm gonna be your airboat guide for the next couple hours! I need ya'll to put your headphones on for safety purposes, and we'll be on our way!"

Avery came back to reality just as it was revealed that the driver was Kyle's uncle. She could definitely see the family resemblance. Short auburn hair. Noses turned up slightly at the end. Chins with a small indentation in the center.

Kyle stood up, hugged his uncle, and proudly introduced him to some of his close friends who happened to be in the group. As if sensing her eyes on him, he turned and gave Avery a wink. Then he leaned over and whispered something into his uncle's ear.

Mr. Mitch smiled in her direction and then addressed the entire group. "Okay ya'll, please keep your head, hands, feet...and any other relevant body parts inside the boat. There are wild animals out here, and I don't wanna return anyone half off."

Muffled laughter and giggles broke out.

"Let's be safe and have a great time!" Mr. Mitch finished. Then he started the engine.

Everyone cheered as the boat slowly left the dock. The thunderous noise from the motor didn't allow for much conversation unless you wanted to shout to the person sitting nearby. The headsets they were given didn't do much for blocking out the loud roar either. The wind whipped through Avery's hair as she watched the tall grass blowing and swaying gently in the breeze. The sky was a perfect shade of pale blue with random puffy clouds floating by. The water was calm and dark; the only movement being the large ripples breaking the surface as they raced on. A few birds flew away as the engine roared closer and numerous turtle heads peeked from beneath the murky water.

Avery took her camera out of her pocket and snapped a few shots of the landscape. Then she angled it so that she could sneak a picture of her and Sebastian together, though the flash instantly blew her cover. *Crap*.

"May I?" he asked, gesturing towards her camera.

She bit the inside of her cheek as she handed it over. Much to her surprise, Sebastian held it out in front of them both.

Her heart seemed to skip a few beats as he leaned his head against hers and took the photo.

If you wanted a picture with me, all you had to do was ask. He smiled as he placed the camera back in her hands, just in time for Mr. Mitch to whip the boat around in a circle, causing little waves to swell and splash up over the front.

Mr. Mitch faked stalling out a few times, causing the entire boatload of students to freak out and then laugh it off. A few minutes later, they had turned down a very narrow passageway with huge cypress trees on both sides. The branches and leaves formed a thick canopy overhead, providing temporary shade from the sun's burning rays. Small patches of tall grass lined the middle as they continued on.

A giant alligator drifted close to the boat as Mr. Mitch slowed to a stop. He went into a spiel about their eating habits and their habitat, etcetera. When the alligator bumped its enormous body against the left side of the boat, a few girls sitting on that side squealed and screamed, then attempted to climb over other students to get away.

Mr. Mitch immediately calmed everyone down and then revved the engine, causing the alligator to swim away as the boat raced further down the narrow waterway. "We don't need any sharp-toothed hitchhikers!" he called out jokingly.

Laughter erupted yet again.

This guy is hilarious, Avery thought to herself.

Yes, he is, Sebastian replied.

Avery kept her eyes angled at her feet as she smiled. *That wasn't meant for you. How do I turn this off?*

Close your mind to me.

She pursed her lips and shot him a playful glare. *If I knew how to do that, I would have already.*

He smiled then. *Close your eyes.*

She instantly did as he instructed.

Now picture an open door in your mind. Then imagine that I'm standing on the other side.

She nodded involuntarily.

Now close the door.

Shortly after that, Avery opened her eyes, and their telepathic connection was severed.

"See, it's that simple," Sebastian said out loud.

Avery immediately closed her eyes again. She opened and shut the imaginary door repeatedly, checking to see if it worked.

"Are you enjoying slamming the door in my face?"

Avery's eyes flew open as she began to laugh uncontrollably. Sebastian couldn't help but to chuckle right along with her. No one else seemed to be paying them any mind since the boisterous sound of the motor practically drowned them out.

Mr. Mitch slowed the boat down again. "Alright guys and gals, this is where we're supposed to turn around and head back to the docks."

A few moans and groans escaped the lips of every single senior on board.

"But by request from my nephew," Mr. Mitch continued, "we're gonna go on a little detour that he and I used to take after hours when he was a kid."

Hoots and whoops echoed all around.

Avery noticed Sebastian's posture instantly went rigid. There was also an apprehensive expression on his face that she just could not ignore.

"Is something wrong?" she asked quietly.

Sebastian shot her a faint smile and told her that he was fine, but his mind was saying *this is a bad idea.*

After speeding down the open waterway for at least another thirty to forty-five minutes, Mr. Mitch finally announced that they had made it to the secret destination: Another short, narrow passageway through more tightly knit cypress trees. This time, though, it was much more cramped. Sebastian wasn't sure the boat was going to fit, but Mr. Mitch didn't even bat an eye as he slowed to a crawl and pushed forward.

"Watch out for fallin' snakes!" Mr. Mitch exclaimed.

Everyone giggled at his comment, but alas, he wasn't kidding. As the large boat was forced into the small, confined space, the sides scraped and bumped against the roots of the trees that were sticking out of the water, shaking them slightly. Shrieks and obscenities were repeatedly shouted as snakes of all colors and sizes were dropped in and around the boat.

Sebastian jerked Avery closer and shielded her from the falling reptiles. With his quick inhuman-like reflexes, he caught multiple snakes before they landed on her.

The majority of the slithering serpents were harmless tree snakes, but a few pythons and water moccasins happened to be amongst them. Everyone began running around the limited space in a feeble attempt to get away, tripping over one another and knocking each other out of the way. Sebastian could feel his rage growing as he glared at Mr. Mitch, who sat idly by, smiling and continuing to trudge forward.

"Are you going to do something about this?" Sebastian called out. "Some of these snakes are venomous!"

At the mere mention of the word 'venomous', the atmosphere on board shifted into total hysteria.

"It's a little more overgrown than I remember, but we're almost through!" Mr. Mitch called back. Then he gunned the engine, causing everyone to topple backward.

Sebastian clutched Avery against his body just seconds before they hit the metal flooring. Most of the seniors landed on top of one another...and on top of some snakes as well. Kyle and Rhett nearly fell overboard, but they grabbed hold of the metal benches, saving themselves. Moments later, Mr. Mitch had finally gotten past the slithering invasion and made it into a large clearing. Sebastian and a few other male students were throwing the last remaining snakes overboard. A few of the girls were still screaming. Others were crying.

Mr. Mitch offered up an apology for scaring everyone, stating that he had the situation under control. Sebastian could tell he was being sincere, but that didn't take away the fact that the only way out of this secluded place was to go back the way they had just come.

"What now?" someone asked.

The airboat was floating in the middle of a circular swamp, completely surrounded by enormous cypress trees.

Mr. Mitch grinned and gestured all around them. "Now we explore!"

"You want us to get off the boat?" Avery asked in disbelief. "No way!"

Many others agreed with her. Poor Kyle hung his head in embarrassment and slumped onto the closest bench.

"Alright, alright. Calm down, ya'll. I'll turn us around, and we'll head back." As Mr. Mitch drifted the boat toward the tree line, the engine stuttered and choked and eventually cut off completely. He casually started it up again and attempted to turn the boat around in a wide circle. Once more the engine puttered and spluttered to a stop. He tried a few more times to restart it, but it never roared back to life. He didn't seem rattled at all as he told everyone to remain calm, not to worry, and to enjoy the sights and sounds of nature while he figured out what was wrong. He swore that he would have the airboat up and running in no time.

It wasn't until a couple of hours had passed that the panic began to set in all over again, and Mr. Mitch finally picked up his radio to call for help.

"Dockside, it's the Mitchster. I'm havin' a bit of engine trouble. Can you send out another boat to pick up my group? We're in the Hideaway Enclosure."

As luck would have it, the only reply was the sound of distorted, crackling static. Mr. Mitch tried again; the same result. They had gone too far out, and his receiver wasn't working. Go figure. A few seniors offered him their cell phones, but there was no reception.

The white, cotton clouds overhead were quickly turning a dark grey, and thunder boomed in the distance. A cool breeze sent a chill through Avery's entire body, causing goose-bumps to cover her arms. It was getting late, and soon the warm sun would start to set. They could only hope that the airboat would be fixed before it got dark.

Avery nudged Sebastian gently. *Are you doing this? The weather?*

He shook his head. *No, it's not me.*

Her wide eyes stared at him. *Can you stop it?*

I can't alter the natural order of Mother Nature. I can only manipulate things on a small scale. Sebastian could sense Avery's anxiety growing, so he wrapped his arm around her shoulder and pulled her closer. Then he leaned toward her ear and whispered, "Everything is going to be okay."

Almost instantly she felt better. They could have been stranded in the middle of a desert with no water and no signs of life, but if Sebastian told her they were going to be fine, she would have believed him…or at the very least, felt safe again.

For the next thirty minutes, everyone chatted amongst themselves as Mr. Mitch was attempting to remove any debris that could be causing an issue with the engine or the fan blades. He had one foot on the metal cage where the blades were, and one foot firmly planted on some roots of nearby trees. He slipped a few times, nearly losing his balance, but he hadn't fallen into the water.

Kyle, Rhett, and a few others were trying to help keep the boat steady while gusts of wind kept drifting it away from the tree line. Suddenly, there was a loud bang on the underside of the boat, which caused the entire floating piece of metal to shift sideways.

Mr. Mitch had two choices at this point. One, stay in his current position and hope that the students were able to get the boat back to its original location before he did a complete split…or two, let go and take his chances in the murky water. Either way, the water was most likely where he was going to end up. He only had a few seconds to make a decision, so he opted for the least painful. He released his hold on the fan's cage and dropped into the water.

The soft splash alerted the rest of the seniors that someone had fallen overboard. Mr. Mitch struggled to swim through the dense moss, grass, and branches hiding under the surface as he made his way to the side of the boat. Just as Kyle and Rhett reached for his hands, Mr. Mitch felt a hard tug on his left ankle. He disappeared for only an instant, but the frenzied look on his face as he re-surfaced caused Sebastian to rush over immediately. Kyle was clinging to his uncle's hand as another more violent tug took him back underwater. This time, though, there were a lot of tiny bubbles.

When the alligator emerged, the entire lot of students were in shock. The length of it was longer than the whole airboat! The third-time Mr. Mitch disappeared under the dark water, he didn't resurface. As the seconds ticked by, everyone began to fear the worst. Then suddenly, they all heard another splash.

Avery only caught a glimpse of Sebastian's backside as he dove into the darkened water. She let out a frantic scream as she rushed over to where he had just been. "BASTIAN!"

All the other seniors hovered close by, holding their breath as the water became still. Kyle moved next to Avery, taking her trembling hand into his, clutching it tightly.

Avery's heart was in her throat as she scanned the entire area, hoping and praying that Sebastian's face would appear. *Please be okay, please be okay, please be okay!*

Literally a second or so later, a few feet away, Sebastian, Mr. Mitch, and the enormous alligator all broke the surface together. Mr. Mitch was gasping for air and screaming for help with the alligator still clamped onto his lower body. Sebastian was struggling to keep them both afloat as he headed back toward the boat. He was bobbing up and down while spitting and coughing out mouthfuls of water as he stared at the seventeen pairs of eyes watching helplessly.

"I'll need...all the help...I can get...once we get...closer," he told them.

Everyone scrambled about, positioning themselves with their arms outstretched.

"We're ready," Kyle called to him, "but what about the gator? How are we gonna get it to let my uncle go?"

Sebastian could hear the hysteria in Kyle's voice as he inched his way closer. "One problem...at a time. I just want...to keep him...above the water."

All the while, Mr. Mitch was thrashing and splashing and screaming. Sebastian wasn't sure how he was going to detach the sharp-toothed hitchhiker. He was currently focused on making sure Mr. Mitch wouldn't drown. Then without any warning, the alligator started spinning its body into a violent death roll before it dove back under, dragging a terrified Mr. Mitch down with it. Sebastian, slightly startled, sucked in a deep breath and disappeared again.

Moments later, there was a brilliant flash beneath the depths of murky water. It lit up the entire swamp as if someone had turned on a flood light. Everyone on board the airboat was stunned and wondering what in the world was going on, but Avery knew exactly what was happening. Sebastian had used 'the glow'. A few bubbles drifted up from the darkness before the water became unusually calm. Time seemed to stand still as they all continued to search for any sign of their friends.

Bastian? Avery frantically called out to his mind. *Bastian, are you alright? Can you hear me?* She was on the verge of tears waiting for a reply.

A second or so later, his sweet voice drifted into her mind. *Concentrating. Above water soon.*

She blew out a huge sigh of relief before kneeling at the edge of the boat to wait for him.

When Sebastian finally dragged Mr. Mitch to the surface once again, he was limp and unresponsive, but the alligator was gone. As a handful of senior boys hoisted them both back on board, the seriousness of the situation became utterly clear. Mr. Mitch's left foot had been completely torn away. What was left of his muscles, tendons, and skin looked like they had gone through a meat grinder. His left arm and torso also had deep lacerations and missing chunks of flesh. Blood quickly pooled into the boat, circling his body with a large red puddle.

"Oh, my God!" Kyle cried out. "Uncle Mitch! Please tell me he's not dead!"

"He's still alive," Sebastian reassured him. *For now.* "He's just unconscious."

Kyle dropped to his knees beside his uncle as tears streamed down his cheeks.

Sebastian looked over at Avery; wet tendrils of hair were falling over his face. *I've got to cauterize these wounds, or he's going to bleed to death...but I can't do that with everyone watching me!*

She stared back at him. *What can I do?*

"Does anyone have a lighter?" Sebastian asked while putting pressure on Mr. Mitch's leg in an attempt to slow the bleeding.

Multiple lighters were gathered up and brought over to him.

For once I'm thankful to be surrounded by smokers! "I'm going to need help holding him down so I can use the flames to cauterize his wounds," Sebastian stated.

Kyle and Rhett were the first to volunteer, followed by Alaric and Daren.

"I need two of you on each side to hold down his shoulders. This is going to be extremely painful if he wakes up." Then Sebastian turned to Avery. "I need you to hold up a jacket or a shirt to block what I'm doing. If he comes to, he doesn't need to see this."

Avery immediately got the hint. She nodded as one of the football players offered her his jacket.

Sebastian blew out his breath. "Is everyone ready?"

Avery, Kyle, Rhett, Alaric, and Daren all nodded nervously.

"Alright, then...here we go." Sebastian flicked one of the lighters, hovering the flame over Mr. Mitch's ankle. He waited until Avery had the jacket high enough to block his hands and then he radiated as much heat as he possibly could, pressing his palm against Mr. Mitch's butchered appendage. The instant he made contact, Mr. Mitch came to and began screaming and thrashing his entire body. The four boys were clearly having a hard time holding him down, so two more seniors rushed over to help. Avery was nearly knocked out of the way, causing her to temporarily lose her grip on the jacket, but she quickly re-positioned herself back in front of Sebastian's glowing hands.

With all eyes now focused on Mr. Mitch, Sebastian was able to make his move. He threw the lighter down as he began touching each and every injury as fast as he could. Some needed more heat than others, but he finally managed to stop the blood from flowing. Mr. Mitch eventually passed out again.

"We have to get him to a hospital," Kyle said while choking on tears. "He can't die out here!"

The skies had gotten darker, and more storm clouds had moved in, blocking out the sun.

"Do you know the way back?" Sebastian asked Kyle.

He nodded. "Yeah, but that won't matter much if we can't get the engine workin'. We're miles from the dock."

Sebastian brushed his wet hair away from his eyes. "One task at a time," he stated confidently. "We need to get out of this secluded area. If we can get back out in the open, another airboat will be able to find us. We were due back hours ago, so surely they've sent someone out looking for us."

After a bit of maneuvering, and lots of cussing, the airboat was finally back at the entrance to the narrow passageway. All the seniors divided up equally on either side of the boat, pulling and pushing against the roots of the trees. Though backtracking turned out to be easier said than done; the boat kept scraping against the trees, getting stuck repeatedly. Sebastian was becoming increasingly frustrated while trying to keep over a dozen hungry and tired teenagers focused and cooperating. That was worse than wrestling an alligator...and he would know. The good news, though, if it even qualified as good news, was that no snakes had fallen on them this time. It was a slow and tiring process; one only made harder by the fact that it started raining.

Stranded in the middle of the Everglades with a dying man on board of a nonworking airboat was bad enough, but add being in the midst of a monsoon, surrounded by ginormous alligators, and having the chilling wind whipping through their soaking wet clothes. That would definitely qualify as a horrible field trip experience.

Sebastian wasn't quite sure how much time had passed since they started their journey, mostly because he didn't want to think about it, but when the boat finally reached the covering that led back out into the open swamp area, night had fallen.

Avery huddled closer to Sebastian, pressing herself against his chest in an attempt to escape the cold sting of the rain. When she started to shiver, he began pulsing a small amount of heat into her body.

She glanced up in his direction, though she couldn't really see his face in the darkness. *Thank you.*

You're welcome.

"I think I found a flare gun!" Kyle suddenly called out.

All eyes instantly turned in his direction.

"Will it work in the rain?" someone asked.

Avery could barely see Kyle shrug through the torrential downpour.

"I dunno."

"Use it," Sebastian called to him. "It might be our only chance."

Kyle's hands were shaking as he pointed the flare gun straight up in the air. He counted down from three…two…one…and squeezed the trigger. A bright ball of light shot up into the air, illuminating the entire area for a mere second before fizzling out.

What seemed like an eternity later, a strobe light appeared as a speck in the distance, and the sound of a gentle hum grew louder. Everyone on board began screaming and shouting while waving their arms in the air. "OVER HERE! WE'RE OVER HERE! WE NEED HELP!"

Two airboats approached, immediately taking Mr. Mitch off first. Kyle went with his uncle, as did Rhett. The second airboat eventually carried the rest of the seniors back to the docks where they were informed that Mr. Mitch had been airlifted to the nearest hospital.

That is when the questions started…

How did this happen?

Why would he take the boat out so far?

How were his wounds cauterized?

Then everyone began to tell the story of what Sebastian had

done; though thankfully 'the glow' in the water seemed to have slipped their minds.

The instant Sebastian's feet touched dry land he was surrounded by the staff of the Everglades Tour. They thanked him repeatedly, all revering him as a hero after word spread about how he had risked his life to help Mr. Mitch. Sebastian forced a smile and shook countless hands before being ushered onto the remaining bus. He was in no mood to be the center of attention. He just wanted this horrible day to be over with.

CHAPTER 25

The ride back to the hotel was relatively quiet aside from the gentle hum of the bus engine and the occasional snore from one of their classmates. The minimal chatter eventually ceased into complete silence. It was then that Sebastian became overwhelmed with an excessive amount of rage. His eyes began to glow, and his head began to pound. He felt sick to his stomach, like something was trying to tear him apart inside.

Avery was oblivious to what was happening beside her. She was exhausted and hungry and cold, and her eyes felt extra heavy. All she could think about was the cozy bed she knew would be waiting for her back in the hotel room. When she leaned her head against Sebastian's shoulder, the strange feelings he was experiencing disappeared as if they hadn't been there at all.

He pushed his delirious thoughts aside, chalking them up to being a side effect of the day's hectic events. He wrapped his arm around her, radiating a small amount of heat once again. So little in fact, that she didn't even notice. She thought it was just his natural body heat keeping her warm.

When the bus finally pulled into the hotel parking lot, the

students slowly made their way inside. Most of them went up to their rooms to shower and change; others headed straight to the dining area to get something to eat. Sebastian's growling stomach overshadowed the fact that he was uncomfortable in his wet clothes, so he sat down at one of the tables and ate whatever food was placed in front of him. He wasn't sure if he was even tasting what was going into his mouth. All he knew was that his belly was getting full and his hunger pains were dwindling away.

Avery sat across from him, casually sipping ice water through a straw. In the time it had taken her to eat her meal, Sebastian had devoured at least three full plates. A contented sigh left his lips as he finally glanced in Avery's direction. Her amused expression made him wonder how long she had been watching him.

"Are you full now?" she asked quietly. There was a small grin on her face.

Sebastian smiled and rubbed his extended tummy. "I'm pretty sure I've still got room for dessert."

Avery laughed out loud.

"I'm kidding," he stated.

He stood and held out his hand, helping her out of the booth. They were the last two to leave the dining room, and the hotel lobby was practically empty as they made their way over to the elevators. Sebastian insisted on making sure she got to her room safely, so as the doors opened smoothly on the fifth floor, he politely escorted her to her door.

Avery pulled out the keycard she had been given and slipped it into the lock.

Sebastian gave her a hug and a quick kiss on the forehead. "I'm in room 608 if you need me for anything."

~*~*~*~

A little over a half hour later, Avery still had not been able to fall asleep, through no fault of her own. So, she snuck out of her room and headed straight for the elevator. She pressed the number six and waited patiently for the short ride to end. She peeked her head around the corner once the doors slid open.

With the coast clear, she half walked, half jogged to Sebastian's door. Her hand hovered in the air for a few seconds before she finally knocked.

Sebastian had just gotten out of the shower when her familiar heartbeat filled his ears. He threw on his pajama pants just as he heard a quiet knock-knock-knock. When he opened the door, Avery's eyes widened, and her mouth dropped slightly.

She was not prepared for the image in front of her. *Whoa.*

He stood there shirtless with a towel draped over his shoulder, his damp hair partially covering his face. A few stray droplets of water were making their way down his muscular torso, disappearing into the small line of dark hair below his belly button.

Sebastian cleared his throat as he propped his arm up on the door jamb, cluing her into the fact that she was standing there with her mouth hanging open.

She recovered quickly, just not fast enough. *Oh God, how long have I been gawking at him?* She cleared her throat and blinked away the shock that had spread across her face. "Uh…can I come in?"

He smirked as he moved out of the way, gesturing for her to come inside without saying a word.

"I can't sleep," Avery grumbled. Her voice sounded completely drained. "My roommate was snoring so loud, I think the walls were shaking."

"I thought you were sharing a room with Valerie," Sebastian replied as he closed the door behind them.

Avery sighed and allowed herself to fall backward onto his bed. "Val got paired with Paige." She groaned and curled up in a fetal position. "I'm just so frickin' tired! All I wanna do is sleep." Her eyelids fluttered open and closed repeatedly; each time getting heavier and heavier. She sighed again as her eyes forced themselves to close for the last time. Before she could stop herself, she had fallen asleep in Sebastian's bed.

He shook his head smiling as he whispered, "Sure, go ahead and take my bed. I don't mind at all." Then he gently slid the covers out from underneath her and draped them up to her chin. *So much for the fraternization rule*, he thought humorously.

~*~*~*~

The following morning, it took Avery a few minutes to realize where she was. She stretched and rubbed her sleepy eyes before she sat up and looked around. A few blinks later, her vision had adjusted to the dimly lit room. The curtains were drawn, but a small stream of light shown through in the center, landing directly on Sebastian who was sleeping soundly in a chair nearby. He was still shirtless, looking incredibly sweet and innocent. He had a sweatshirt draped over his upper body like a blanket, and his legs were stretched out to their full length. His head was tilted slightly to the side, and his lips were parted. Avery's heart fluttered as she watched his chest slowly rising and falling.

Though the peaceful moment didn't last long. Images of Mr. Mitch's mangled body started playing on a loop in her mind that she was unable to stop. She began crying quietly as she pulled her knees to her chest and buried her face in her hands.

Sebastian woke up to the sound of Avery's frenzied thoughts shouting loudly into his mind, though he knew she hadn't meant to send them to him. In a flash, he was by her side. He closed his eyes and tried to connect his mind to hers as he wrapped his arms tightly around her.

I'm here. Everything is alright; you're safe now...let me take it all away.

Almost immediately, their mental connection stabilized. As his soothing voice entered her mind, Avery pressed herself against him as the horrific pictures continued to dash back and forth in her head.

He hesitated, waiting for permission to alter her thoughts as he had promised, but as the seconds ticked by, he realized she wasn't going to give it to him. She was far too immersed in the gruesome images floating around, threatening her sanity. Sebastian's moment of uncertainty faded away as Avery let out a muffled cry against his shoulder.

Then, as quickly as they came, each and every detail of the sights, the sounds, and the smells of that horrible memory began to disintegrate from her mind. The gory mash-up of pictures slowly drifted away as if they were ashes being carried by the wind.

It took a few minutes for her to regain her composure, but when she did, she looked up into Sebastian's soft grey eyes and gave his neck a squeeze. "I'm not sure how you are able to do that…but thank you."

Sebastian held her for a little while longer before helping her sneak back to her room. She showered and changed just in time for all the seniors to be called down to the main lobby of the hotel.

Mrs. Drennon was standing in the middle of the entrance hall as all the students gathered around her. She waited a few moments for the chatter to cease. Her facial features were soft, but her expression was stern. "First, I wanted to let everyone know that we heard from the hospital this morning. Mr. Mitch underwent emergency surgery in an attempt to save his leg. He may be in intensive care for quite some time, but the doctors are hopeful that he will be on the road to recovery very soon; thanks in large part to those involved in his rescue."

All eyes landed on Sebastian. Their heartfelt stares of admiration should have made him feel proud and appreciated. Instead, he felt uncomfortable and awkward.

"With that being said," Mrs. Drennon continued, "if any of you feel the need to make a quick phone call to your parents or speak with a counselor, please let me or one of the chaperones know and arrangements will be made immediately. Those of you who may be having a hard time dealing with what happened, you are more than welcome to return home, and you will receive a partial refund. The school staff, chaperones, and I have also decided on a change of venue for the remainder of the trip. The seniors who choose to stay will be going to the Megawaves Water Park." She paused as a muffled discussion broke out amongst the entire group. Her voice grew louder to be heard, "The buses will be leaving in two hours, so you have more than enough time to make your decision, pack, eat breakfast, and change into your swim attire. For now, everyone is dismissed! I'll see you all in two hours in the front foyer."

Sebastian gently nudged Avery's shoulder and reached out to her telepathically. *Are you going back home?*

She kept her eyes angled at the ground as she nervously played with her shoe laces. *I'm not sure. Maybe. What about you?*

Sebastian shrugged. *I am if you are.*

Avery looked up then. There was a faint smile on her beautiful face. *Thanks, Bastian.*

~*~*~*~

Two hours later, the majority of the seniors were standing out front, waiting to load their luggage onto the bus. Much to Mrs. Drennon's surprise, only three students opted to go home.

"Alright! All aboard the splish-splash express!" she said happily.

Avery chuckled as she followed Valerie onto the bus, with Sebastian close behind. When they arrived at the Megawaves Water Park, everyone was all hyped up and ready to go, but before anyone could leave, Mrs. Drennon had all the seniors line up along the side of the bus.

"Alright ladies and gents, let me have your attention for just a moment. Today is meant to be a day of fun and relaxation, but I also want everyone on their best behavior. I don't want to find out that any of you were mistreating the property, its inhabitants, or its guests. Because if I do, drastic measures will be taken! You're old enough to know when it's time to act like adults and when it's time to let loose and be wild and crazy." She stared directly at Alaric and Daren when she spoke. "Let me give you a hint, today is not a wild and crazy time, okay?"

The two boys looked stunned as if they weren't expecting to be called out in front of everyone.

Mrs. Drennon continued with a smile, "I want each of you to choose a partner. And no, I don't care how juvenile that sounds! He, or she, will be your buddy for the duration of our time here."

Sebastian looked at Avery from the corner of his eye. *Buddy?*

She grinned. *Buddy!*

"We will reconvene back at the entrance in four hours for lunch. Please mind your manners and above all else, be respectful!" Mrs. Drennon clasped her hands together excitedly. "Now go have fun and enjoy this lovely day!"

With that, the seniors divided up and took off in different directions.

Valerie shuffled her way over and tugged on Avery's hand. "Wanna buddy up?" she asked cheerfully.

Avery glanced at Sebastian as if that was the only answer her best friend needed.

"I see." Valerie crossed her arms and just stared at the two of them, sizing them up. Then a smile broke through her serious expression. "Can you at least tell me where Chase went then?"

Sebastian pointed to a small group of their peers nearby. Valerie gave Avery a brief hug before she walked away, purposely swinging her hips from side to side in quick thrusts.

"That's sure to get his attention," Avery called after her.

Valerie burst into a fit of giggles as she glanced over her shoulder. "That's the plan," she called back.

~*~*~*~

Sebastian shot out of a water slide and eagerly waited for Avery to come whooshing out behind him. Out of nowhere, his vision started changing from a blotchy red tint to a dark haze and back again. He dropped to his knees, clutching his chest as a spasm of pain shot through him. A few people passing by stopped to see if he was okay, to which he obviously lied. He happened to notice Jonah in the wading pool nearby, surrounded by a group of girls he didn't recognize.

Sebastian sent him an urgent telepathic message. *J, I need you!*

I'm a little busy, Jonah replied curtly.

I know you're still upset with me…but I need you to put that shit aside…because right now I've got a problem!

Jonah glared in Sebastian's direction. *WHAT…do you want?!* When their eyes met, Jonah gasped. *Oh, shit!* "I'll be right back, ladies!" he stated aloud in a playful tone. Then he casually strolled away from their close-knit group and rushed to Sebastian's side as soon as he was out of their view.

Chase was waiting for Valerie at the end of another slide a few feet away when he noticed the tension growing between his brother and Sebastian. "Please don't tell me you two are gonna have it out right here?"

"No, but we have a huge problem," Jonah replied.

That is when Chase saw the red glow of Sebastian's eyes. "Oh man! We have to get him out of here. Right now!"

Sebastian started to panic. He was in the middle of a crowded, public place, on the verge of completely losing control. *I don't know how much longer I can hold back!* A deep growl resounded in his throat. *Something's wrong!*

"Mom did warn you that going on this trip was a bad idea," Chase whispered.

I don't need any I-told-you-so's right now, Chase. Just get me the hell away from everyone!

The three boys trudged their way through the mass of people. All the while, Sebastian was grunting and groaning and grinding his teeth. Without so much as a second glance from the park staff, Jonah and Chase basically dragged Sebastian out the front gate and around to the back of the park near the tree line.

By this point, Sebastian was doubled over and panting heavily. His vision was now shifting from a fierce red to completely black. "You both…need to get…away from me!" he growled.

At that very moment, Avery came running around the corner. "What are you guys doing out here? Is Bastian okay?"

Sebastian let out a threatening roar. "GET HER THE HELL OUT OF HERE!"

Jonah began pulling Avery away, but of course, she fought

against him.

"What's happening? What's going on?" she asked frantically.

Sebastian didn't even think twice about what his face may have looked like when he turned his head. All he was worried about was getting his friends somewhere safe, Avery especially. He glanced in her direction, locking his glowing eyes with hers.

A terrified expression graced her lovely face as she finally stopped struggling against Jonah's grasp.

"RUN!" Sebastian shouted. "You all need to RUUUUUUN!" Then he took off, sprinting in long strides like a marathon runner.

At the exact same time, Jonah and Chase each grabbed one of Avery's wrists and raced away in the opposite direction, pulling her toward the park entrance.

Sebastian didn't look back. He forced his legs to move faster and faster. He needed to get as far away from them as possible before his transition completed. Then suddenly, it was lights out.

CHAPTER 26

Night had fallen by the time Sebastian came to. He found himself on the freshly cut lawn in front of the Smart's house.

What the…?

His entire body ached, and he couldn't remember a single thing that happened after he transitioned, which was very unusual. He groaned as he reached up to cradle his aching head in his hands. That is when he noticed the copper smell. His hands…his arms…his clothes…all stained red with blood. But who's blood? That was the most important question. *Think*, he told himself. *What's the last thing you can remember?!* Sebastian squeezed his eyes shut and racked his brain. *The water park. Jonah. Chase. Avery.* Then he gasped. *Oh, dear God, please don't let this be theirs!*

He hesitated before sucking in a deep breath, filling his nose with the sickly-sweet odor covering his body. He braced himself for the worst; then he let out a momentary sigh of relief. The scents were unfamiliar. *It's not theirs…but then that still begs the question…whose blood is it?*

Suddenly, headlights approached as a vehicle pulled into the driveway. Isabelle and Elliot got out of their car, making their way up the stone walkway. Sebastian tried to find his footing as he stumbled toward them, only to collapse on the ground at their feet.

"Sebastian?!" Isabelle exclaimed in disbelief.

"What happened, son?" Elliot asked him.

Sebastian was feeling so drained that he could not find the words to speak. He was in too much shock to even stand.

Isabelle and Elliot carried him into the house, but it wasn't until he was under the bright lights in their living room that the horrific picture became clear. He was drenched in blood from head to toe. The red liquid in his hair was still damp as it trickled down his face, dripping onto the beige carpet. They looked him over, checking to see if he was injured…he wasn't.

"Oh no!" Isabelle whispered frantically. "No, no, no! What have you done?!"

Sebastian could not stop trembling as he held his bloodstained hands out in front of himself. "I…I don't know," he stammered. "I don't remember! I can't remember anything after I…!"

Isabelle quickly turned toward her husband. "We have to bring the kids back home! We have to make sure they're all safe!"

Sebastian mindlessly sat down on the couch, not even thinking about the mess he would leave behind. "I didn't hurt them. I wouldn't…"

"You just said you don't know what you did!" Isabelle snapped.

She immediately apologized and sat down next to him, but he couldn't bear to look at her. He was ashamed and completely mortified.

"Why don't you go clean yourself up," Elliot told him as he dialed the emergency contact number on the field trip form. "Then we can talk about…whatever you may remember."

Sebastian nodded, still avoiding looking directly at either of them. He stood, and then noticed the rust colored stain he had left behind on their beautiful suede sofa.

"Don't worry about that right now," Isabelle said softly.

"Go take your shower." She turned to her husband again. "Let me know the second you find out if the kids and their chaperones are alright."

Elliot nodded. "The line is ringing."

Sebastian could hear the uncertainty in their voices, but he was too emotionally weak to say anything else. He headed down the hallway, all the while feeling their eyes on his back. He closed the bathroom door behind him and walked over to the mirrored cabinet that was hanging over the sink. A few drops of blood dripped into the bowl as he gripped the edges of the white porcelain. It took him a few minutes to gather enough courage to even look at himself. When he did, he wished he hadn't. He didn't even recognize the reflection staring back at him. *Holy hell.*

He let out a shaky sigh as he stared at his unfamiliar bloodshot eyes. He was about to look away when a brief flash of black crossed his vision. His brow furrowed slightly as he leaned closer toward the mirror. He studied his eyes for a second or two and then couldn't stand the sight of himself anymore. He tossed his ruined clothes into the trash before stepping into the shower. As the warm water washed away the gory mess covering his body, he pressed his forehead against the cool shower wall and began to weep quietly.

~*~*~*~

"I called the hotel and spoke with Mrs. Drennon," Elliot stated. "She informed me that everyone was doing well and enjoying their trip, but that Sebastian had been picked up by a family member because he was feeling sick…"

Isabelle exchanged a wary glance with her husband. "Should we be proud or concerned at the fact that our boys know how to lie so well?"

"For this current situation, I'm going to go with proud."

Not even a second later the phone rang. "Hello," Elliot answered. All the color seemed to drain from his face.

"What is it?" Isabelle asked anxiously.

Her husband didn't answer. Instead, he turned on the TV with the phone was still pressed against his ear. "Yeah, I'm seeing it," he said to the caller.

Isabelle's forced smile faltered as Sebastian came back into the living room. The bold italicized headline flashing across the screen immediately captured his attention.

THE RED SLICER: BRUTAL MASS MURDERER STRIKES AGAIN!

Sebastian instantly cried out as he dropped to the floor, landing on his knees. His eyes were glued to the TV, and suddenly, he couldn't breathe…he couldn't move. *This isn't happening! I didn't… I couldn't have done this!* When he finally found his voice again, his anguish-filled eyes looked up at Isabelle. He didn't want to ask, but he had to know. "How many…?"

She couldn't look at the screen any longer, so she met his horrified gaze. "Thirteen…so far," she replied quietly.

The news broadcaster's voice was now a distorted mash-up of noise in Sebastian's mind as the images of multiple body bags were being shown. The scene looked like something from a horror movie. Police cars were surrounding the area. Red and blue flashing like a constant strobe light. The building in the background was barely standing. Some type of bar from the looks of it. The front door was lying on the ground. Most of the windows had been broken, leaving behind jagged spikes that resembled the jaws of a great white.

A muffled cry escaped Sebastian's lips as bile rose up into his throat. The knot in his stomach got tighter and then his head began to throb. When his vision started to change, followed by a sudden rush of aggression, he gasped. *I'm on the verge of another shift*, he thought helplessly.

"ISABELLE!" he cried out. "ELLIOT! It's going to happen again…right now! I…can't…stop it!" Then he let out a deafening scream as his body began distorting.

"Spell the guest room!" Isabelle frantically told her husband.

Elliot was already on his way down the hallway before she had finished her sentence.

Sebastian wrapped his arms around himself.

"HUUUURRRRRYYYYY!" he growled in a deep, gruff voice.

"Hold on, Sebastian! I just need a few minutes!" Elliot called out.

"We may not have a few minutes!" Isabelle called back. She placed her hand on Sebastian's shoulder in an attempt to both comfort him and to let him know that he needed to hold on for just a little longer.

Sebastian was shouting and screaming and cursing as he struggled to keep a hold of his humanity. "I can't...! It's happening...NOW!"

Elliot raced back into the living room and grabbed hold of Sebastian's left arm. Isabelle grabbed his right. The two of them attempted to drag him down the hall, but much to their surprise, Sebastian fought against them. It took every ounce of strength they had within their Watcher abilities to force him to cross the newly spelled barrier. And it was definitely a close call. They barely got him over the threshold before he fully transitioned on the other side. The transformation seemed to happen in slow motion, as if having him pass through the barrier caused him to change from a handsome teenage boy into a gruesomely terrifying monster.

The Smarts were both staring in complete disbelief at Sebastian...or rather, not staring at Sebastian. The creature hovering in front of them radiated absolute malevolence. Its dark, deep-set eyes were empty and void of any emotion. In the midst of its smoky mist-like form was a 'face'. Its features were similar to that of a human skull, but its appearance was cracked and broken; missing huge chunks of bone as it wavered in and out of view. During a normal transition, there were still bits and pieces of Sebastian's features while he was in his Cursed Form. This time, though, there were no remnants whatsoever of the pure soul who once stood in its place.

Isabelle swallowed nervously. "What...is...that?" she whispered.

"I've never seen anything like this before," Elliot replied. "I don't think any Watcher has."

The dark creature tilted its head from side to side,

narrowing its dark eyes as if studying them. Then it lunged forward, barely moving an inch, but it was enough to make Isabelle jump back.

"It's testing us," Elliot told her. "We mustn't back down."

The dark creature's crooked jaw twisted into a smile as if it understood what they were discussing. Then it raised its gruesome hand and placed it against the barrier.

"Sebastian…I know you're in there," Elliot spoke aloud with authority. He was scared, but he never showed it. "You need to grasp hold of your humanity and come back to us."

The dark creature began to shake and twitch. It took the Smarts a moment to realize that it was laughing at them. The creature's sinister grin widened, showing its long, serrated teeth. A threatening growl resonated deep in its throat as it slammed both fists against the magical wall. The light from the hallway illuminated the ripples that were expanding across the invisible prison as the creature's fists hit again and again.

Isabelle took a step away from the doorway, closer to her husband. "Sebastian? Can you hear us?"

The dark creature didn't respond. Instead, it flung itself against the barrier repeatedly, each time more combative and determined than the last.

~*~*~*~

The Smarts took turns guarding the warded room throughout the night. The dark creature hovered near the doorway, occasionally ramming itself full force against the barrier. When Chase and Jonah arrived home the next morning, they were in for a rather large surprise. Their parents tried to explain the events that had transpired over the past twelve hours, and the boys explained what had taken place at the water park. Isabelle had called every Watcher they knew to try and figure out what they were dealing with, but so far none of them had ever heard of a Cursed One shifting to their Cursed Form and losing all sense of time or themselves…or turning into something entirely different altogether.

Jonah and Chase were not prepared for the sight of their friend when they finally wandered down the hall. Any and all attempts to reach Sebastian's inner humanity continuously failed. And just as they were beginning to lose all hope that he would ever return, the dark creature slowly began to pace. It slumped against the magical barrier, glaring menacingly at its captors. As it slid to the floor, human features slowly began to reform. After a short length of time, Sebastian's red eyes gradually broke through the darkness. He sucked in the deepest breath imaginable as he crawled on his hands and knees away from the door, panting and gasping heavily.

"Mom! Dad!" Chase called out. "Get in here. He's back!"

Isabelle and Elliot rushed forward. "Sebastian! Are you okay?" they both asked in unison.

Sebastian was disoriented and breathing laboriously. "What...what happened?" he asked, looking back toward the doorway.

Elliot stepped up to the invisible wall, making sure to stay on the outside of it. "What do you remember, son?"

Sebastian sighed and closed his eyes. "I remember seeing the bodies on TV...I was feeling scared...and then enraged...and then..." He was shaking his head with a perplexed expression on his face. "...then I felt emptiness, darkness...I felt...cold."

Elliot walked through the barrier.

Sebastian's bloodshot eyes stared back at him. "It was bad...wasn't it?" The tone of his voice was tense and sad.

Elliot sighed and offered his hand. "Yes, it was."

Sebastian instantly stood up. "Did I hurt anyone?! Are you all alright?" His eyes darted back and forth, studying each of them carefully.

"We're all fine," Elliot replied. "You didn't hurt anyone. Your...form was trapped in here."

Sebastian's eyebrow rose. "Why did you say it like that? What are you not telling me?"

Elliot looked back at his wife with a pained expression. "How do we explain this?"

Sebastian waited impatiently for someone to tell him what the hell was going on, while anticipation and panic were growing inside his gut.

Isabelle crossed the barrier and sat down on his bed. She sighed and forced a smile as she tapped the spot next to her. When he sat down beside her, she proceeded to tell him everything they had seen, heard, and experienced while he was in his strange new form. Sebastian sat with his head in his hands, unsure how to react to the information he had just learned.

~*~*~*~

The following days, he stayed locked up in his room behind the magical barrier. He refused to leave for any reason whatsoever. He didn't trust himself anymore.

With him safely tucked away from the world, rumors were starting to run rampant in the halls at school. With the amazingly impossible rescue of Mr. Mitch still fresh in the minds of his classmates, then his mysterious disappearance from the senior field trip, and now he was missing school…it wasn't hard for people to come up with their own interpretation of the strange series of events.

Though Jonah and Chase tried to do damage control, there was only so much that two eighteen-year-old boys could do with a high school full of peer pressured, drama seeking, self-centered, unapologetic teenagers.

CHAPTER 27

Avery was literally freaking out. It was now day three since Sebastian had disappeared from their senior trip. Three incredibly long days that she had spent in multiple states of panic; so much so, that she was barely able to function. Her life had been completely turned upside-down, and she still had no clue what had actually happened.

She replayed the moments of that day over and over. She could still see the strange distortion of Sebastian's face and the fear in his eyes. She knew without a doubt that whatever was going on with him had to do with his past, mostly because everything had to do with his past, but she just could not figure out how to put all the pieces together.

Chase eventually called to let her know that Sebastian was okay and that he was staying with his family, but that she was not allowed to see him…though that didn't stop her from trying. She showed up at the Smart's residence every day, sometimes multiple times per day. She had even spent a night in her car in front of their house in the hopes that she would at least catch a glimpse of him…no such luck.

His face never left her mind. Even her dreams were filled

with images of his perfect smile, his adorable dimples, and his gorgeous eyes. She had called and texted him repeatedly; she even opened the door of her mind and shouted his name, but silence was her only reply…and it was driving her crazy!

Of course, Sebastian had listened to each tear-filled message and read every heartbreaking text. It was tearing him apart inside to know that he was hurting her by staying away, but Isabelle and Elliot were firm with their rules…

One: No contact with anyone outside of the family. No texts, no calls, no visitations.

Two: No leaving the house without permission unless accompanied by a Watcher; which included any projected forms. No school.

Three: Report any changes in mental, physical, or emotional state right away.

The no contact rule was mostly referring to Avery. He needed to refrain from any and all communication with her until they knew what they were dealing with. It was safer for everyone…and as much as he hated it, he knew it was for the best.

For the past three nights, he had listened to Avery cry herself to sleep while she called out his name. He wasn't sure how much more of this emotional torture he would be able to endure. The pain he was causing her by sticking around was completely unfair…to both of them, especially when he knew the ending was just around the corner. *But how can I leave her?*

He had repeatedly tried over the past six years to walk away, long before he started to fall in love with her, but something within his tainted heart just would not let her go. And now here they were…two broken hearts with a vast trail of shattered hopes.

This time he didn't have a choice. It didn't matter how he felt about her. It didn't matter that his heart was breaking into a million pieces. It didn't matter how conflicted he was. This time it was truly a matter of life or death. He would have to give her up to keep her alive. *God, I don't want to give her up.* Sebastian's heart ached as he closed his notebook and put down his pen. He let out a deep, sorrow-filled sigh as he glanced out the window.

In the wee hours of the morning, before the sun had a chance to rise, he left the safety of his warded room…with permission from Isabelle…and headed over to Avery's house.

He sat in his car, staring toward her darkened window, smiling half-heartedly at the thought of her sleeping peacefully only a few feet away. Then he remembered what he was there to do. In his trembling hands, he held a letter. A letter he had spent the last few days writing and revising over and over. It had to be perfect…though he wasn't sure how any goodbye could be perfect.

Just as the sun began its ascent over the horizon, Sebastian gently pushed into Avery's mind. He wasn't sure how much time he had, and he wanted to make sure to be back in his room before any more strange transitions had the chance to overtake him.

Avery, he whispered into her mind. *Avery, wake up.*

She made a few incoherent noises as her eyes fluttered halfway open. "Bastian?" She glanced around her dimly lit bedroom.

I'm outside, he told her.

Avery shot up and peeked through her curtains. Her heart dropped, and a smile spread across her face involuntarily when she saw that his car was parked out front. *You're really here! I'll be out in a second.*

I'll be waiting.

She jumped out of bed, splashed some water on her face, and put her hair up in a messy ponytail.

The thought of seeing her again caused a tightness to grip Sebastian's chest, making it hard to breathe. He glanced down at the letter that he was practically strangling in his hand as his palms began to sweat. Suddenly, he felt the need to flee. *I can't do this!* He shifted out of neutral, hovering his foot above the clutch. In one swift movement, he could easily shift into first gear and just drive away. *No.* He shook the thought from his head. *Remember what Isabelle said. I'm not safe anymore.* Sebastian let out a painful sigh as he shoved the wrinkled piece of paper into his pocket.

A moment later, Avery appeared at the end of her driveway.

As he opened his car door and stepped onto the sidewalk, she couldn't hold back her emotions any longer.

She rushed forward, holding him as tight as she could, pushing into his mind. *Where have you been? Why haven't you been answering me?*

He welcomed her embrace. *There have been some unforeseen complications with…my curse.*

She squeezed him a little tighter. *Whatever it is, we'll get through it together. I'm just so glad to finally see you.*

He pulled back and smiled at her, hoping that she wouldn't notice the sadness lingering in his eyes. He was trying to retain a somewhat pleasant composure, at least while he was in her presence. The two of them stood there silently together in the pale light from the half-risen sun.

Sebastian was stalling. He didn't want this moment to end…but then thoughts of the brutal images he had seen on TV slipped back into his mind. So, he cleared his throat in the hopes that he wouldn't sound upset. "I have something I need to give you."

He fumbled around in his pockets as if he didn't know exactly where he had put the letter only moments ago. He finally pulled out the folded piece of paper, and his tattered heart sank a little further in his chest. He hesitated as he placed it in her hand. "Read this after I'm gone," he said quietly. Then he pulled her into his arms again.

A wave of regret slowly washed over him as he leaned his head against hers, breathing in the sweet smell of her coconut shampoo.

She wrapped her arms around his waist, completely oblivious to what was happening between them, and snuggled her face against his broad shoulder.

He listened closely to her heartbeat thudding rapidly in time with his. Another sigh left his mouth. This time, a small whimper escaped.

Avery pulled back so she could look up at his face, but Sebastian would not let her see him cry. He sniffled once, kissed her on the forehead, and rushed back to his car before she had the chance to see the tears welling up in his eyes. His back was facing her as he spoke. "Goodbye, Avery." Then he climbed into the driver seat, revved the engine, and sped away as fast as he could.

Avery was slightly puzzled as to why he didn't even give her a chance to reply with her own goodbye, but she would soon figure that out once she read the letter that she had almost forgotten was in her hand. She unfolded the paper and began reading his slightly messy handwriting.

Avery...

I've been writing and re-writing this letter for the past few days. I just couldn't seem to get out what I needed to say. I'm still not sure if I can, but if you're reading this, then I guess it means I've done the unthinkable. I've said goodbye. It pains me to even think about the fact that this letter is currently in your hands and you're reading these words.

I don't want you believing that I wanted this ending for us, or that I've stopped caring about you or our friendship because I haven't. I don't want this at all, but unfortunately, circumstances are now spiraling out of my control, and I have no other choice.

I can hear you crying. You're calling out my name right now as I'm struggling to put these words on this piece of paper. I want you to know that I'm desperate to reply, but it's not safe. I'm not safe.

I'm so sorry to have hurt you once again, but I promise

that it will be the last time. I'll think of you always, and you will forever be in my heart.
    Sebastian

Avery read the letter over and over until tears blurred her vision. She glanced down the road where Sebastian's car had gone. *He can't do this*, she thought to herself. Then she reached out to him mentally. *I won't let you do this! Do you hear me, Bastian? I REFUSE TO ACCEPT THIS!*

Sebastian heard her clearly, but just like before, he didn't respond. As he pulled into the Smart's driveway, he rushed inside. "Chase?"

"He's not home," Isabelle replied. "He's with Valerie."

Shit. Sebastian blew out his breath in one quick huff as he ran his fingers through his hair.

Then Jonah came around the corner. "Where were you?" he asked.

"With Avery," Sebastian replied sullenly. "I need you to do me a favor."

Jonah's eyebrows rose. "What were you doing over there?"

Sebastian ignored his question and replied with a statement of his own. "I need you to take my car and park it at my place. I can't have her knowing where I am."

Jonah eyed him skeptically. "What? Why?"

Sebastian tossed Jonah his keys. "Because…it's necessary given my current situation."

"What did you do?"

"What I had to," Sebastian stated sadly. "Now please take my car before she shows up looking for me." He turned and wandered down the hall toward his warded room.

Jonah slipped on his sneakers and did as Sebastian had asked him…and not a moment too soon. On the short walk back to his house he saw Avery's car pulling into his driveway. She was barefoot and still in her pajamas. The distressed look on her face told him that this meeting was not going to go well.

"Where is he?!" she demanded in a serious tone.

Jonah played dumb. "Chase is at Val's, but he'll be home

later tonight."

Avery glared at him. "You know damn well I'm not talking about your brother! Where is Bastian?"

Jonah shrugged as he kept walking. "I haven't seen him."

Avery held up the letter from Sebastian and practically shoved it into Jonah's face. "Well, did you know about this?"

He grabbed it out of her hand and quickly skimmed over it, then he sighed as he gave it back to her. "No, I didn't," he replied honestly, his face softening. "But I understand why B would write that."

"Well, how about you explain it to me then, because I feel like I'm always the last to know what the hell is going on with him!"

Jonah shook his head. "I can't do that, Av. Not this time."

For a half second, Jonah thought she was going to walk back to her car and just drive away. Instead, Avery paced back and forth a few times and then started to scream. And not just a small, little, frustrated scream. What came out of her mouth sounded like the wail of a pissed-off banshee.

Sebastian, who had been acutely aware of Avery's arrival, was listening to the entire conversation from the safety of his room, but when he heard her start to scream, he took a chance and peeked through the blinds. "Isabelle?" he called out.

She was already on her way down the hall. "Yes?"

"I need you to take down the barrier, please."

She appeared outside of his bedroom door with both hands on her hips. "You finally cut ties with Avery, huh?"

He nodded. "She said she refuses to accept it."

Isabelle couldn't help but smile then. "Take it from a woman who knows a thing or two about what it's like to be a teenage girl in love...you don't break up through a letter or a text or a phone call. You do it face to face."

"We didn't break up...we weren't even together..."

Isabelle's smile dwindled as she dispelled his room. "We both know she's more than just a friend to you."

Sebastian stepped through the doorway. Avery's screams were still echoing all over the neighborhood.

"You may want to hurry," Isabelle said as she gave him a gentle shove down the hall. "Most of the neighbors will be wondering what all the fuss is about."

Sebastian took a second to brace himself for the whirlwind that was about to blow his way when he opened the door. Then he turned the handle and stepped onto the front porch.

Isabelle was right. People all over the block were peeking out of windows; others were standing on their front steps or their lawns, gaping in Avery's direction.

Her grief-stricken eyes landed on him immediately as her screams finally stopped. "Why do you keep doing this?" she called out. She started walking towards him, her bare feet traipsing through the grass. When she got to the bottom of the stairs, she stopped. "After all the progress we've made. After all the hurdles we've overcome. Why do you keep trying to push me away or make me hate you? Is that really what you want? Seriously? Because if it is, I swear to God that I'll walk away right now and never look back! I'll never think about your stupid face ever again! So, tell me, IS THIS REALLY WHAT YOU FRICKIN' WANT?!" Tears were falling down her face now, though they weren't just tears of sadness anymore, they were from anger and frustration as well.

Shit… Sebastian gulped as he fixed his gaze on Avery. "No…it's not what I want at all." He said the words so quietly that he wasn't sure it was even audible. Sebastian could see Jonah out of the corner of his eye. He was staying as far away from them as possible.

Avery's shoulders were rising and falling quickly as her breath came in short powerful bursts. "Then why do you keep doing this shit to me, Bastian?! Why do you keep toying with my heart…and my mind?! Is this just some kind of sick game to you? Because I'm waaaay past my breaking point!"

Sebastian wanted to break down and tell her the entire truth so she would finally understand that his actions weren't malicious at all…that he wasn't being an asshole…that he wasn't playing games. But when he opened his mouth to speak, Jonah interjected.

"No one is playing games here, Av. I mean, look at the guy! Does he seem to be enjoying any of this?"

Avery glared at them both. *Of course, they are taking up for each other; that's what best friends do! They're both being...jerk-faces!* She shook her head, keeping her eyes narrowed, mostly in Sebastian's direction. Then she pointed directly at him. "You've been keeping me at a distance since the first day I met you! Part of me finally understood your reasoning once you decided to let down your walls and I got to see some of the..." She paused and looked around, lowering her voice so that none of the neighbors would hear, "...unique abilities you have, but if you're not going to let me all the way in, then why bother at all? You've pulled me closer only to push me away more times than I care to count! You've hurt my feelings and broken my heart on far too many occasions..."

Sebastian wanted to interrupt. He wanted to tell her how sorry he was for everything he had ever done to her, but the look on her face told him to keep his mouth shut.

Avery's bottom lip was quivering now. She was on the verge of a total meltdown, but somehow she held herself together. "If you're going to leave, you better make sure it's for good this time because I just can't..." Her voice broke, and she looked away. She sighed and quickly composed herself once more. When she turned back around, Sebastian felt like a dagger had just pierced his heart. She took a step toward him as she crumpled his note up into a ball and then tossed it on the ground at his feet. "When you're ready to say goodbye..." *And break my heart for the last time.* "...be a man and say it to my face, not through a stupid letter."

Ouch. Sebastian cringed at her final words, especially the ones she didn't speak out loud. He knew that she knew that he had heard her. With that, she turned and trudged back to her car and drove away.

Jonah glanced over at his best friend. "Well, that was...intense."

~*~*~*~

Avery pulled into her driveway and shut off the engine. She

167

leaned her head against the steering wheel as her emotions finally overflowed. In that moment, and in the few that followed, she hated that she loved him so much. She sat in her car and cried for over an hour before forcing herself to head inside. She climbed back into her bed and pulled the covers completely over her head. *Love sucks.*

<u>CHAPTER 28</u>

Day after day passed with zero contact between Avery and Sebastian. And those precious days were taking a toll on them both.

Avery couldn't eat. She couldn't sleep. She couldn't concentrate in school. Christmas had come and gone. It was her favorite holiday…with the bright twinkling lights, the red and white gift-wrapped presents, the delicious array of food, the merry laughter, the gathering of family and friends…and yet this year, it held no joy for her whatsoever. Her entire life had been turned upside down in a blink of an eye. She had known for years that Sebastian was hiding something crucial about his past, but when he was faced with the choice of either telling her everything or letting her go, she never thought he would actually choose the latter.

~*~*~*~

At the same time, Sebastian was dealing with his own inner turmoil. "I'm doing the right thing," he stated confidently. Then his certainty faltered. "Aren't I?"

Jonah shrugged and continued enjoying his lunch. He was getting a bit tired of the whole Sebastian/Avery drama.

Chase, on the other hand, was more than happy to share his opinion. "You definitely did the right thing. It's not like you had a choice, ya know?"

Sebastian sighed. "She hates me now," he mumbled.

Jonah scoffed. "Just shut up already! You had your chance to tell her everything, no strings attached. You gave it a shot. You bombed. She's gone. It's over."

Chase's mouth fell open…and Sebastian's would have too, had he not been leaning his chin on his fist for support.

Jonah took another bite of his sandwich. "She's not worth it," he stated matter-of-factly. "I mean sure, Avery is an awesome girl, and she's a good friend, but in the bigger scheme of things she's just some chick you feel obligated to because you almost killed her…but you 'saved her' instead." He sarcastically made little quotations with his fingers.

Rage began to simmer beneath Sebastian's semi-collected exterior. "Seriously, J? Are you really gonna go there? Now?"

Jonah shook his head nonchalantly with his mouth still full. "What are you gonna do, B? You gonna try to kill me too?"

Chase waved his napkin in the form of surrender as he elbowed his brother…hard. "Damn bro, tone it down a bit! Let's all just take a little breather here."

Jonah rubbed his side as he shot his brother a sideways glare. "Just get over yourself," he mumbled under his breath to Sebastian. "Everyone is sick of your constant woe-is-me bullshit!"

Sebastian whispered back through gritted teeth, "You really want to start shit…without your parents around to protect you?"

Chase gulped and lowered his voice. "You guys need to chill out before someone says something they're going to regret."

Jonah avoided Sebastian's burning gaze as he continued to eat his lunch as if nothing were out of the ordinary, but his cocky smirk was the last straw.

Everything that transpired after that seemed to happen in slow motion. Sebastian lunged across the table, flinging food and drinks everywhere as his massive body slid over the smooth surface with unforeseen ease; then he clamped his hand around Jonah's neck, lifting him straight into the air. Jonah's feet were dangling high above the floor as Sebastian's mouth slowly curled into a threatening snarl.

The explosive reaction made Chase jump up and instantly lock eyes with his brother. "This is bad," he stated out loud as he struggled to loosen Sebastian's grip. "This is really bad!"

The look on Jonah's face said that Chase needed to do something fast. Sebastian's grey eyes were beginning to fade to black, which meant at any moment he could be on the verge of a not-so-normal transformation.

GET A HOLD OF YOURSELF, Jonah shouted into Sebastian's mind. *B, pull it together man! I'm sorry I went off like that, but you need to calm the hell down!* Jonah kicked and thrashed and pulled at Sebastian's steel-like grasp to free himself, but nothing was working.

Sebastian began to shake as a response to the frenzied madness that was building within himself. Slowly he tightened his grip as his vision became dark and fuzzy. Then he raised his other arm, balling his hand up into a fist. The first punch was a warning of what was to come if someone didn't 'batten down the hatches' so to speak. Jonah's cheek screamed from the impact, but it was nothing compared to punch number two. The ringing in his ears was a clear sign that he was indeed in dire straits…that and the fact that he was currently having trouble breathing.

The markings on Jonah's arms were glowing vibrantly as Chase repeatedly tried to pull Sebastian back, but as the minutes passed, his markings were beginning to dim. Soon the damage would be irreversible. Jonah's face was slowly turning red, and his eyes were starting to bulge. The strangled retches and grunts coming from his throat were gradually fading away.

Just when all hope seemed lost for the Smart brothers, a familiar shout rang through the house.

"SEBASTIAN!" Isabelle cried out.

Jonah and Chase's mom had just walked through the front

door, arms full of groceries.

The sound of her voice stopped Sebastian right in his tracks. His fist was hanging in mid-air, lingering centimeters from Jonah's discolored face. The rage slowly began to disappear when he glanced up to see her terrified gaze staring back at him.

She dropped everything she was holding and rushed over, causing all the contents to spill onto the floor. "What...are you doing?" she asked, clearly baffled by his behavior. "Let him go!"

Sebastian glanced back at his best friend, who was now barely conscious, still dangling from his grasp. Alarm bells were going off in Sebastian's head. *What am I doing?!* He instantly released his grip, causing Jonah to drop to the floor with a loud thud.

Chase crouched down next to his brother, looking briefly at Sebastian. The sadness in his eyes was overshadowed with fear.

Sebastian knelt down beside them. "I'm...I'm so sorry!" He could see the damage he had done. His handprint was clearly outlined as a deep purple bruise on Jonah's throat; not to mention the blood and bruises covering his best friend's face. The sight instantly made Sebastian sick to his stomach.

Luckily, Jonah's Watcher abilities had kept him from experiencing the full extent of Sebastian's power. If he had been just some regular-average-joe, there would be no coming back from his injuries.

Sebastian's wide, shock-ridden eyes stared down at the aftermath of what he had done. *What is wrong with me? I could have just killed my best friend.* As quickly as inhumanly possibly, he stood and backed away.

Distance. What he needed right now was distance. And a hell of a lot of it.

Chase and Isabelle were both tending to Jonah and not paying Sebastian any mind as he rushed down the hall and flung himself through the barrier that surrounded his room. He couldn't...no, he wouldn't...allow himself to hurt anyone else that he cared about.

CHAPTER 29

Over the next three weeks, Sebastian had shifted into his Dark Form at least once per day…sometimes twice if he was unlucky enough. It was a horrible experience for everyone involved. The Smarts were all on edge. Sleep was a distant memory of the past. And on top of taking turns guarding the magical wall, Isabelle and Elliot still had to go to work and keep up appearances; Jonah and Chase still had to attend school and act like everything was normal. Life was an ever-changing, chaotic mess with a constant feeling of dread hanging in the air.

Then one fateful day, as if an answer to their prayers, a phone call from a fellow Watcher changed everything.

Through a-friend-of-a-friend-of-an-acquaintance-of-a-person-of-a-whoever-of-a-someone-of-a-blah-blah-blah, they had finally found a Cursed One who had gone through a similar experience; though not nearly as severe, but it was a start. And with everything going on in their lives, they desperately needed a starting point. Isabelle and Elliot immediately set up a meeting for the very next morning so they could finally get some answers.

Sebastian woke up to the sound of an engine revving to life out front. He shot up just in time to see Isabelle's car pulling out of the driveway. As he placed his palm on the cool glass of the window, he felt himself smile for the first time in almost a month. Today might be the day he could possibly be getting his life back; which meant that maybe, just maybe, he could restore whatever had been broken between himself and Avery.

~*~*~*~

Pacing.
Checking his phone.
Looking out the window.
Pacing some more.
Fidgeting.
More pacing.
Dashing back to the window.
Looking up and down the street.
Checking his phone.
Sighing.
Back to pacing.

That is what Sebastian's entire morning and most of the afternoon consisted of.

With an exasperated huff, he fell back onto his bed. His feet wanted to continue carving a groove into the carpet, but he just could not handle being upright anymore. His back was killing him…but that is what happens when you don't sit down for nearly ten hours straight.

~*~*~*~

It was close to five o'clock when Isabelle and Elliot finally pulled back into the driveway. The ache in Sebastian's back magically disappeared as he pressed himself against the window. All his instincts kicked in as he studied their facial expressions and their body language while they casually strolled up the walkway toward the front door. Neither of them appeared upset nor distressed. In fact, if he allowed himself to believe it, they looked rather content. *This could really be it!* He eagerly waited at the opened doorway of his room as he heard muffled voices at the front of the house.

"They're back!" Chase hollered.

"So...what's the news?" Sebastian called out. He physically could not wait anymore. Anxiety was eating him up inside.

Elliot was the first one to come strolling down the hall with a half-smile on his face, followed by Chase and Jonah.

"Well, we have some answers," Elliot stated. "Some were more helpful than others, but I think it's safe to say that we finally have a handle on what we're dealing with...and even a possible way to contain it."

Sebastian felt a rush of relief flood over him.

"The Cursed One we spoke with, Luca, had something similar happen to him about twenty years ago. Though he was quite reluctant to share his story."

The optimism Sebastian felt only a few seconds ago began to dwindle. "Is there a way to stop this or not?" he asked bluntly.

"Yes," Elliot replied matter-of-factly. "But, it's not without risks."

Sebastian placed his hand on the barrier. "The risk of doing nothing has to be worse than whatever the solution is!"

Elliot nodded once. "I agree, but in the end, the choice is solely yours."

Isabelle came down the hall to join her family. "Have you given him the news?"

"Partially," Elliot replied.

Sebastian was getting flustered by this point. "Guys...please! Tell me already! I'm dying over here!" *For all I know, I could be!*

Jonah and Chase looked back and forth between their parents just before Elliot disappeared back down the hall. When he returned a minute or so later, he was holding a long leather strap with intricate designs and symbols etched down both sides.

Chase gasped. His eyes were wide and full of fascination. "Is that what I think it is?"

Elliot nodded.

None of the Smarts had ever seen a Strap of Virtue before,

though they had read all about them in the old Watcher journals that were handed down from generation to generation. These rare straps were used by the Pure Ones throughout history to cure the sick and save the dying. Rumors spread that they were all destroyed once the Pure Ones' reign ended. And Sebastian had not seen one since his departure over eighty years earlier.

Jonah suddenly snatched the strap away. "Whoa! Dad, are you crazy?" He turned to face his mom. "You guys can't be serious?" Lastly, he stared at Sebastian. "You can't do this, man. They'll sense their magic and come straight for you! Not to mention the fact that we don't even know how this could affect your other form! For all we know, that Luca guy could be full of shit or lying! What if this makes it worse?"

Elliot took the Strap of Virtue back from his son. "Luca's Watcher is a very reliable man, known for his blunt and often too true nature. This isn't a lie. He witnessed everything first hand."

"Is he still with the girl?" Sebastian suddenly blurted out.

"What?" all four of the Smarts replied at once.

"Luca…is he still with the girl? The one he loved when all this started happening to him?"

Isabelle frowned. "No. He's not with her anymore."

"Why? What happened?" Sebastian asked.

"She left when she saw his Cursed Form," Isabelle replied quietly.

Sebastian took a step back as his stomach did an uneasy flip. "But…she loved him?"

Isabelle sighed and took a step closer to the doorway. "She claimed to…but I guess it wasn't real, undying, head over heels love."

Sebastian kept pushing for more answers. "What all did he reveal to her?"

Elliot spoke up. "That's not essential right now. We need to focus on…"

"NO!" Sebastian shouted. "This is important! If he went down the same path that I have, I want to know what happened to him…and the girl he loved!"

Elliot started to argue, but Isabelle cut him off. "Luca showed her everything. Everything leading up to his Cursed Form." Her sad eyes held Sebastian's defeated gaze.

Sebastian felt lightheaded and sick to his stomach. "She stuck around through it all? Only to…to leave him anyway? So, he did it all for nothing?"

Elliot sighed. "As I said, he was reluctant to talk about it."

Sebastian didn't say anything else. The story he just heard circled around in his head over and over. *She left him. Luca trusted someone enough to reveal it all…and she left him. He lost himself, and he lost his love. For nothing.*

Isabelle didn't need to be a mind reader to know what he was thinking. "She isn't Avery. And you're not Luca. Don't you dare try to compare the two because it's not the same! Deep down in your soul, you know that."

Sebastian didn't want to think about any of it anymore. He glanced down at the strap, fully aware of the fact that the moment he connected himself to the energy within it, that his days of a semi-normal life were over. The Pure Ones would sense their power being used and they would send a search party out for him, or they would come for him themselves. That thought made him shudder. He may have to give up everything to run. A sharp twinge gripped his heart when he thought about the possibility of never seeing Avery again.

"Please…" Chase pleaded. "There has to be another way." He clearly agreed with his brother on the matter.

Sebastian sighed. "There isn't any other way. If there were, I would have done it already."

Elliot reached through the magical barrier and placed the Strap of Virtue in Sebastian's hand. "It's up to you. Take some time to think about it before you make your final decision."

A split second later, Chase stepped through the barrier and grabbed Sebastian's shoulder. "Don't do this. Please. We'll figure something out."

"I can't live like this anymore, Chase," Sebastian said quietly. He glanced in Jonah's direction. "I can't risk hurting any of you ever again."

The bruise on Jonah's neck was long gone, but the memory was still fresh in all of their minds.

Chase's eyes began to fill with tears as he released his grasp on his friend's shoulder.

Sebastian sighed again. "We won't have long once we do this," he stated sternly.

"Nothing is happening tonight," Elliot told him. And his words were not a request; they were an order. "I can't have you rushing into something like this. You must be entirely sure. We have to weigh all the pros and cons."

"I'm already aware of everything I need to know," Sebastian replied. "I want to do this."

Elliot shot him a don't-argue-with-me stare. "It's not happening tonight. That's final!"

Sebastian turned away. "Tomorrow then."

"No," Elliot spoke with authority. "We have the strap. It's not going anywhere. You will take a moment to think about what this will mean for you. No matter what the outcome may be, your life will never be the same again. Don't let something…or someone…cloud your judgment."

The *someone* he was referring to was Avery. Sebastian knew it. Isabelle knew it. Jonah and Chase knew it.

"Promise me," Elliot finished.

Sebastian sighed heavily while staring at the leather strap in his hand. The designs were pulsing with a brilliant red hue in a perfect rhythm to his heartbeat. He closed his eyes, feeling the surge of immense power starting to swell from within. The magic called to him. It begged him to use it. And for a moment, he was reminded of the Warrior he once was…of the life he once lived…of all the blood he once shed. It took every bit of strength in him to break concentration long enough to toss the strap onto his bedside table. As he watched the red glow begin to fade away, he realized Elliot was right. He needed to take some time and think this through. "Alright, I promise."

CHAPTER 30

Two days later, the magical wall which had been spelled to keep Sebastian inside was constantly shifting. The Smarts determined that it was based on Sebastian's mood and state of mind. One moment it would be translucent, then the next it would be so hazy that they could not see past it.

Tuesday was one of the bad days. Sebastian had transitioned early that morning, and his Dark Form had torn apart his room. Since then, the wall had been shaking and vibrating so violently that it seemed to be on the verge of a total collapse.

Isabelle made multiple attempts to reach out to him, but neither her thought projected words nor her verbal ones could get through. He had completely blocked everyone out, including Jonah and Chase. Sebastian kept the leather strap next to his bed, staring at it occasionally, but never touching it.

After a brief discussion as a family, the Smarts came to a unanimous decision. Something had to change, or they would surely lose Sebastian altogether. So, in turn, their bold new plan would stop the problem in its tracks...or cause the situation to completely blow up in their faces...either way, they had to take action.

Avery was practically in tears when Chase showed up at her house and said that she needed to come over, and fast…that Sebastian needed her. She was both excited and nervous at the thought of seeing him, especially after their last encounter. Her stomach was filled with anxious butterflies as they pulled into the Smart's driveway.

Chase didn't waste any time dilly-dallying. He jerked the car door open and literally pulled Avery toward the front steps. His long strides were hard to keep up with as she tripped and skipped all the way inside.

"Mom! Dad! She's here!" Chase called out.

Avery anxiously lingered in the living room, waiting for whatever was about to take place.

Isabelle appeared at the end of the hall just outside of Sebastian's room. The expression on her face was somewhere between relief and apprehension as she gestured for Avery to come closer…but Avery didn't move right away. A growing pang of worry began to form a lump in her throat as she finally took a small step forward. The atmosphere was thick with tension, making the hallway seem endless. One more step. Then another. And another. Her heart was about to explode from her chest by the time she made it to the end of the hall. Then Isabelle's face softened.

"He's in a pretty bad place," Isabelle stated quietly. "I think you may be the only one who will be able to reach him."

Avery swallowed hard as she tried to wrap her head around the seriousness of whatever situation she had just found herself in. "I'm not sure if I can do anything," she replied sadly. "He hasn't talked to me in a long time. I don't think he wants me around anymore."

Isabelle sighed, her forehead creasing with worry as she glanced over her shoulder. "Sebastian is a good guy, Avery. He cares for you very deeply, but he's not your typical teenager." She turned back around, narrowing her eyes in Avery's direction. "I know he's told you bits and pieces about himself. And I'm sure he's mentioned our abilities as Watchers too, so this should be somewhat easy for you to grasp."

Avery held her breath, waiting for whatever else Isabelle was going to say.

"The room he's in has an invisible ward surrounding it, keeping him inside."

Avery's confused expression shifted into disapproval. "You're...you're holding him hostage?"

Chase stood next to his mother. "No, Av. He's not a prisoner."

"We're trying to keep him safe," Isabelle told her. "But right now, we can't give him what he needs."

"Why not?" Avery inquired.

"Because he needs...you," Chase spoke up.

Avery's heartbeat began to pound in her ears. *He needs me.* She closed her eyes and reveled in those few precious words. *He needs me.* Slowly she stepped around Isabelle and Chase, until she was standing just outside Sebastian's door. She could see him sitting on the bed with his back to her, staring out the window. "Bastian?" she said softly.

He didn't move.

"Bastian...can you hear me?" she said a little louder.

He remained eerily still.

Avery sighed out of frustration. "BASTIAN!" she shouted.

Suddenly, his head half-turned. His stare seemed hollow as he glanced at her from the corner of his eye.

Oh, Bastian. The pain you're in...why?! "Isabelle said I could see you," Avery said quietly.

Sebastian turned all the way around then. The sight of her beautiful face nearly sent him over the edge. "Avery?" he whispered in disbelief. His hair was sticking up everywhere, and dark bags were under his tired eyes as he fumbled and stumbled to get to his feet.

She smiled as her eyes filled with unwanted tears. "Yeah, it's me."

A hushed laugh escaped his lips as he began to cry. He rushed toward the open doorway and placed his hands on the magical wall. Almost immediately it began to distort and sway turbulently. Avery couldn't see it, but Isabelle and Chase could.

"I've missed you so much," Sebastian cried out.

Avery sighed. "I've missed you too…but…I didn't think you wanted to see me." As she raised her hand to place it on top of his, Isabelle pulled her back.

"What are you doing?" Avery asked, confused.

Isabelle lowered her voice. "We can't allow you to go inside. He's not stable."

"Please…" Sebastian begged. "I only want a moment with her! I *need* a moment with her!"

"I'm sorry, Sebastian. It's not safe; you know that."

The saddened expression that had graced his exhausted face mere moments ago quickly faded away. "Let her in."

Isabelle stood her ground. "The answer is no."

Instantly his gentle demeanor vanished. His lips curled back over his teeth as he growled with indignation. "Then. Let. Me. Out."

Isabelle just shook her head.

Wrong answer. He balled up his fist and punched the magical wall as hard as he could.

Avery jumped back, as did Isabelle and Chase.

When Sebastian slammed his fist again, the wall instantly started to vibrate even more violently than before. This time, though, the entire structure of the house began to rumble and shake. Another powerful strike of his fists caused a dark acidic substance to start oozing and dripping from the top of the barrier.

Avery frantically looked around. "What's happening?"

Elliot came racing down the hall. "What the hell is going on? Sebastian, stop this! You need to calm down!"

Sebastian was grunting and groaning on the other side of the barrier. His self-control weakening to the point of no return.

Avery had no idea what was happening, and she couldn't see the reason for all the panic. All she knew was that Sebastian was less than a foot away and there was something very, very wrong. He needed her…and little did everyone else know, she was about to close the small gap between them. She rushed past Isabelle, nearly knocking Chase over, as she entered Sebastian's room.

The instant she crossed the threshold of his doorway, it was as if someone had dropped a pebble into the middle of a pond. Tiny ripples in the outline of Avery's body expanded across the entire magical wall, causing the powerful spasms and distortions to cease almost instantly.

Sebastian latched onto Avery so fast; it was like they were magnets being drawn together. The clash of their bodies mimicked the sound of an avalanche rumbling down a mountainside. Her legs wrapped around his waist and her arms locked around his neck.

Overcome with emotion, he sank to his knees, keeping his arms wrapped tightly around her. She could feel his body trembling as he choked back muffled sobs. She caressed his back and ran her fingers through his tousled hair. She didn't even realize she was crying too, until her nose started running. She sniffled once, causing him to bawl even harder.

Isabelle cautiously ushered her family away from the door. "Let's give them some privacy." Then she sent a thought directly to Sebastian. *You let us know the instant something doesn't feel right and we'll get Avery out of there.*

He barely nodded in response.

As the Smart's footsteps disappeared down the hall, Sebastian reached out to Avery's mind. *I can't believe you're here. I thought I was dreaming when I saw you.*

Avery sniffled again. *I would have come sooner…but I thought the deafening silence between us had been your way of saying a final goodbye.*

Sebastian whimpered out loud. *I never want to say goodbye. Ever.*

Even in her mind, she could hear the tortured sadness in his voice. *I hope you mean that this time, Bastian, because I don't think I can handle another one.*

He pulled her tighter against him, holding her as close as physically possible without completely crushing her. *I swear on my life that I will never utter that word again.*

All he could think about was Luca and his beloved. Luca had revealed himself to the girl he cherished more than anything in this world, and she had given up on him and left him. Sebastian had to see if Avery still loved him; really, truly loved him. It took a while for him to calm down long enough to release his hold on her, though Avery didn't seem to mind at all. It had been so long since she had been this close to him, she was reveling in every single second. When his body finally stopped shaking, Sebastian pulled himself away from her. Not entirely, but just enough so he could see her face. He knew he must look awful, all puffy faced and snotty, but he needed to look into her eyes. When he met her gaze, it was as if time stood still.

It's there, he thought joyfully to himself. *The love is still there!*

Avery felt her heart skip a beat. She had never seen him look so desperate...so vulnerable...so exposed. A smile formed on her trembling lips as another tear made its way down her cheek. The seconds seemed to tick by ever so slowly while they studied each other closely.

As her fingers gently caressed his face, Sebastian closed his tear-filled eyes, delighting in the fact that she was once again touching him. How could he have been so blind...so stupid? How could he have ever thought that being without her was a good idea? He opened his eyes again. The startled expression that came across Avery's face told him that his eyes were probably glowing.

Oh, no! Are they red or black? He wasn't sure. A momentary jolt of panic shot through him as he pushed her away, scooting back as far as possible, covering his face with his hands. "Get away from me! Get out of the room, now!"

"What? Why? What's wrong?"

He could hear the confusion and worry in her voice, but there wasn't enough time to explain. "My eyes!" he cried out.

"Your glowing eyes don't scare me anymore." Her tone was much more relaxed now.

He still had his hands pressed against his face, blocking his hazy vision. "Av, please! Get out of the room! Cross the barrier! I don't want to hurt you!"

She wasn't leaving. Instead, her footsteps were getting closer.

"Avery! Stay back!"

She wasn't listening.

He felt her hands land softly on top of his. With a gentle tug, she pulled them away from his face.

Sebastian squeezed his eyes shut tighter. *Oh, God, please...not now...not with her in here!*

"Bastian," she said softly. "Bastian, look at me."

He shook his head. "No! No, I can't. You need to get away from me! ISABELLE!"

Avery was cupping his face in her hands now. "Look at me," she whispered.

Isabelle's fast paced footsteps came racing down the hall. "What's wrong? What's happened?"

"He's fine," Avery said. "We're fine."

Like hell we are, he thought to himself. *God, why didn't I just tell her about all this when things were still good between us? If I had, she wouldn't be questioning my regard for her safety!*

Isabelle instantly connected to his mind. *Sebastian...are you alright? Talk to me. Tell me what we're dealing with here...*

His instincts were telling him that everything was alright...that he was safe...that Avery was safe. And not once in his entire existence had he ever second-guessed his hunches, but this time he actually had doubts.

He sent a thought directly back to Isabelle. *My eyes started to glow...*

Isabelle instinctively stepped into the room. She was ready to fling herself...and Avery...out into the hall at a moment's notice. "Maybe you should come back into the hallway with me, Avery. Until we can be sure he's truly alright."

"No. He's not going to hurt me!" Avery cleared her throat and turned her attention back to Sebastian. "Look at me, Bastian," she repeated slightly louder. "Trust yourself and look at me."

What seemed like an eternity later, Sebastian's eyes slowly

fluttered open. A brilliant red hue illuminated the entire room, covering every inch of every surface with a crimson tint.

"See," Avery told him. "I'm not afraid."

But he was. He was terrified. What if the darkness broke through when she was this close to him? What if Isabelle couldn't get her out of his room before the shift took over his body and his mind? What if he woke up to find both of their lifeless bodies at his feet? All the 'what ifs' running through his mind were making him paranoid. He slowly backed up, causing Avery's hands to fall away.

She frowned at him. "What's going on in there?" She pointed to his forehead.

He was silent for a moment as he turned his face away from her. *Isabelle…please give us a few minutes alone.*

She nodded, trusting that Sebastian had things under control for the time being, and backed up into the hall.

Sebastian waited until her soft footsteps faded into the next room before he spoke again. "Av, do you remember when you asked me if I was a werewolf or a vampire?"

"Yes…" She eyed him suspiciously, half expecting him to finally admit to being one of those things, or possibly a hybrid of both. After all, it would make perfect sense given what she had learned about him so far.

He was having trouble holding her gaze while his eyes were glowing. "I was telling the truth when I said I'm neither of those things, but…from a fairytale standpoint I am more lethal than both of them combined."

Without skipping a beat, Avery replied with complete confidence, "Whatever you are, I trust that you'd never hurt me."

The edges of his mouth curved upward slightly. *Whatever I am.* It amused him that this sort of conversation had become somewhat routine for her. "No, I would never do anything to purposely harm you, but…"

"No buts about it." She scooted closer to him. "I know you."

And she did know him. She knew him better than anyone

in his life ever had. Yet she still didn't know all of him.

"I can tell this is hard for you," she continued. "But you don't need to hide things from me anymore. Whatever it is that you're struggling with, I already told you that I want to face it with you."

The unfailing faith she had in him caused his heart to ache. He wanted to let her all the way in. And in that moment, his mouth made the decision for him. "You know about my curse?"

She nodded. "I know as much as you've allowed me to."

How can I put this...? He rubbed his temples as if his head were hurting. "It's altered itself somehow."

Her eyebrows shot up. There was something about the way he worded that sentence. Like his curse could do things on its own. Like it was some living, breathing being. Like it was alive. "What...do you mean?"

Sebastian sighed as an uneasy feeling filled his stomach. *How much should I tell her? Would she really be able to handle this? She's done incredible so far with everything I've thrown her way, but what if this is the last straw? What if this turns out to be the one thing that pushes her over the edge to make her finally leave me like Luca's beloved left him?*

The sound of Avery's voice ended his thoughts. "You still think I'll walk away." It wasn't a question. It was a blunt statement.

For a split second, he wondered if she had actually heard his personal thoughts. He shook his head. No. They were his own. She just knew him too well. "A little," he replied timidly. "But I have my reasons to feel that way."

She nodded as if she understood. Then she spoke again. Her words made him feel like he had gotten hit in the gut with a baseball bat. "You do realize that *you* have been the one to constantly push *me* away, right? Not once have I walked away from you, but you have repeatedly walked away from me. I wish you'd get that through your thick skull. I haven't gone anywhere. Not when I saw 'the glow'. Not when I found out you could control the weather and change your appearance.

Not when I saw your eyes change…"

He held up his hands in surrender as a small smile formed on his lips. "Okay. Okay, I get it."

She crossed her arms across her chest with a faint triumphant smile on her face. "Then why continue with the secrecy?"

His smile instantly faded. So did the glow in his eyes. He sighed and rubbed his temples again. "I can't explain it."

"I should have seen that one coming," Avery said under her breath. She looked annoyed now.

Sebastian sighed again and reached out for her hand. "I don't fully understand what's happening. That's the truth."

"Try." Her voice was sweet, though her facial expression was anything but.

He thought about his Cursed Form. He thought about the night he almost killed her. He thought about how she would feel about him once she knew that he was the source of her nightmares. There was no way he could bring himself to mention that particular detail. Not in this moment. "My curse…it's…it's turning me into something that I don't want to be. Something dark. Something…evil."

Avery had no clue what he was talking about, but his words sent a chill down her spine.

"I have no control anymore," he continued. "I used to have somewhat of a hold on when I'd…shift." He paused, waiting to see how she would react.

A hint of curiosity shone in her eyes, but she didn't recoil in any way.

So far so good. He tried to calm his growing nerves as he went on. "Without control, I have no memory of what I do or where I go."

"Like you're possessed or something?"

He shrugged. "Yeah. I guess that's the best way to put it." *More like Dr. Jekyll and Mr. Hyde.*

The two of them sat in silence for a few minutes. Sebastian wasn't sure what else to say, and Avery seemed to be letting things sink in.

"Can't Isabelle and Elliot help with whatever change is going on with you and your...curse?"

He cast a sideways glance at her. "Yes. Well, sort of. They're trying to," he replied. "But there's a catch." He tried to gather his thoughts, pushing away the nagging urge to grab the leather strap and start the extraction process himself.

"What...sort...of...catch?" She said each word slowly as if she wasn't sure she wanted to know.

Sebastian had just opened his mouth to give her an answer when Elliot appeared in the hallway outside his door.

"I'm sorry to interrupt, but it's time for Avery to go home."

She and Sebastian exchanged disheartened glances.

Elliot pushed into Sebastian's mind. *We have some important things to discuss.* His eyes gestured to the leather strap sitting on the new bedside table.

Sebastian followed his gaze and nodded once. *Alright. Just let me say goodbye properly.*

Elliot nodded back and gave them a few more moments of privacy.

Sebastian stood, pulling Avery with him. "We'll finish this discussion later. I swear it."

She wrapped her arms around his neck and gave his cheek a little peck. "Looking forward to it."

Though he said he would see her soon, their goodbye was still bittersweet...and Avery was left with a feeling of dread that she just couldn't shake.

CHAPTER 31

Sebastian watched from his window as Avery made her way toward her car. All the while, he could feel Elliot's eyes on his back. "I've made my decision."

Elliot stepped through the barrier. "I figured that."

Sebastian had already picked up the leather strap and was staring at it questioningly.

Elliot would not be able to do this alone. His singular Watcher abilities would not be enough to channel the amount of power that would be unleashed. It was going to take all of them to pull this off…if they could. Elliot shook the doubt from his mind. *This is going to work*, he told himself. Shortly thereafter, he called for his wife and sons.

Isabelle, Jonah, and Chase all stepped into Sebastian's room. In that instant, the feeling in the air changed. Senses were heightened. Worries were abundant. But that was all on the Smart's side.

Sebastian eventually turned around to face his Watchers. There was a calmness surrounding him. A look of utter clarity that seemed to dilute all the reluctance and uncertainty of everyone else in the room.

He was ready.

Everyone was silent for a moment as they all realized what was about to take place.

Isabelle was the first to act. She wrapped the Strap of Virtue around her husband's wrist, securing it with the small metal links. The instant the bindings were fastened, one side of the etchings began to glow a pale blue…the same hue pulsating from Elliot's markings.

Sebastian stepped forward and held out his arm, palm up. He and Isabelle locked eyes and smiled at one another. She gave his hand a gentle squeeze before securing the bindings around his wrist and taking a step back. Sebastian's eyes began to glow, causing the other side of the etchings to blaze a fierce and fiery red.

The next step was to link them all together. Elliot took Isabelle's hand, causing the pale blue on the etchings to brighten in color. Jonah and Chase followed suit. Soon their side of the strap was glowing an intense neon cerulean, too bright to even look at.

With the five of them securely bound and connected, Sebastian had to partially transition to his Cursed Form. This was both highly dangerous and extremely hard to do. Keeping himself connected to his human form while being torn apart by his curse wasn't exactly pleasant. Plus, he wasn't even sure which one of his forms would show up, but that was just part of the risks.

I hope you know what you're doing, Chase said directly to Sebastian's mind. He didn't want his family to know that he was afraid.

Sebastian gave his friend the most sincere smile he could manage. *I've got this, buddy. Trust me.*

Chase returned the smile before he closed his eyes and began reciting along quietly with his family.

With their bond completely established with the strap and the sacred chanting commenced, Sebastian immediately felt the surge of energy building. His essence was growing stronger, filling up with an insatiable hunger that he had not felt in years.

He closed his eyes to concentrate on his breathing. *Now comes the hard part*, he told himself.

Steady breath in, slowly blowing it out.

Over and over, steady breath in, slowly blowing it out.

Steady breath in, slowly blow…

The surge of power hit him with a force equivalent to a nuclear blast. Sebastian let out an earsplitting scream as he began the agonizing process that would ultimately lead to an incomplete transition.

None of his Watchers even flinched as he screamed over and over again. They were deep in a trance, chanting, and keeping their focus.

The strap's glow intensified just seconds before Sebastian's entire body contorted backward, severing his spinal cord right in half. Typically, the pain would have been short lived once he fully completed the transition, but this time he had no choice other than to endure it all. His ribs imploded all at once, puncturing his lungs and piercing his heart. This excruciating turn of events limited the amount of time he had left. As he used up the last remaining amount of air in his deflated lungs, he soon realized he would not be able to sustain half way. He had no choice now. A full transformation had to happen, or he would surely suffocate.

Tiny sparks shot out of his fingertips. Eventually, those sparks converted into full blown flames, turning him into a human flamethrower. In a bright flash of red light, his human form disappeared. Sebastian's Cursed Form sucked in a deep breath, filling his newly formed lungs with the precious oxygen they so desperately needed. He hovered in the air above his Watchers in his mist-like form. Their eyes were still closed, and their lips were still moving. His 'wrist' was still connected to his end of the strap, though he wasn't sure how.

Suddenly, Elliot collapsed; followed by Isabelle, then Jonah, and finally Chase. All four of them were immobile, lying on the floor. The vibrant blue emanating from their end of the strap suddenly disappeared, and with it, the strap snapped in two.

In that moment, Sebastian could feel the darkness

threatening to overtake him. Now that he had a taste of its power anew, he wanted more. The overwhelming desire to feel invincible again was a euphoric high that he did not want to come down from. It would be so easy to give in; to relapse back into the savage Warrior that the Pure Ones had turned him into...but then he heard Chase's voice in the background of his thoughts.

Remember who you are. Remember who you've become. You're not a monster anymore.

Sebastian glanced down to see Chase staring up at him. The poor guy. His body was weak, and his head felt woozy, but he still managed to reach out and connect himself to Sebastian's mind.

Think about Avery.

Sebastian struggled to maintain some level of self-control, but his mind, heart, and essence were now at war. *Avery.* He loved her. He had to fight for her. The winner of this battle would determine who Sebastian came back as...the cursed monster that Moira had created...or the man he had worked so hard to become.

What was only a few minutes felt like endless hours for Sebastian. He was literally fighting his inner demons...and for a long while he was losing. The pull to succumb to the limitless power was nearly too much. It was like a tug-of-war for his soul raging beneath the surface.

Just when he was on the verge of losing his ever-loving mind, he let out a boisterous battle cry, and his human form slowly began to return. At the exact same time, Jonah moaned softly and sat up, followed by both of his parents. The Smarts all glanced around, disoriented and dazed. Elliot removed what was left of the leather strap from his wrist and crawled over to where Sebastian was lying motionless on the floor.

Sebastian was soaked from head to toe in sweat, but he was thankful to be himself again. At least, he hoped he was still himself. He kept his eyes closed, focusing on calming his rapid heart rate, and his breathing.

"How is he?" Isabelle asked breathlessly.

Elliot checked Sebastian's pulse. "He's alive."

"Did it work?" Sebastian asked. His voice was hoarse and came out weaker than he expected.

"I hope so," Elliot replied. "Because the strap was destroyed."

A trickle of worry forced its way into Sebastian's thoughts.

Isabelle was beside him now, her steady heartbeat filling his ears. "Can you remember what happened?" she asked hesitantly.

Sebastian slowly opened his eyes, repeatedly blinking to get used to the bright light overhead. A faint smile formed on his trembling lips. "I…yeah, I remember it all. It hurt like hell." He shifted his gaze between the four of them. "Are you all alright? I saw each of you collapse one after the other."

Jonah spoke up first. "I felt the surge after you fully transitioned."

"Me too," Chase chimed in.

Elliot and Isabelle nodded in agreement.

Sebastian draped his arm over his face, covering his eyes. The lights were just too damn bright. "I'm sorry. I hadn't planned on things going that way."

"We know," Isabelle spoke up. "What's important is that it seems to have worked."

"We hope," Elliot stated quickly.

"The outcome is the same regardless," Sebastian said quietly. "The Pure Ones will be coming for me. Tonight. I can't stay here and put you all in danger."

Elliot stood on wobbly legs, straightening his posture to make himself seem taller and more authoritative. "You're not facing them alone."

Sebastian blew out his breath as he pulled himself up off the floor. After everything they had been through together, he knew his Watchers were not going to back down. So, in turn, he came up with the only compromise that could possibly work in favor of all involved. "I'll try to negotiate with the Pure Ones, or whoever they may send. I'll attempt to appeal to their good-natured past. Reminding them of the bond we once shared. If that doesn't work, you all can be waiting nearby out of sight…as a backup plan."

Instead of an argument, which was what he had prepared himself for, the response he got was surprising.

"Alright," Elliot agreed.

CHAPTER 32

Later that evening, Sebastian waited impatiently for the Pure Ones to arrive. He was on edge, pacing back and forth in the foyer of his home. He was going over and over Plan A in his head. Everything had been prepared perfectly…well, as perfectly as possible given the short amount of time allotted. The time. The place. What he would say. What he would do. Yet his gut was screaming at him to abandon ship. His instincts were the only reason he had survived off their radar for all these years, so he was having a difficult time pushing them aside. He kept telling himself that this was the only way.

Suddenly, his phone rang, derailing his inner dialogue. It was Chase. "What is it?"

Chase was breathing heavily as if he was out of breath. The sound of his fast-paced footsteps echoed on the pavement through the speaker. "I'm sorry, Bas! I didn't mean to…"

Sebastian's grip tightened on the phone as his instincts shouted *I told you so* in the back of his mind. "What happened?"

"Avery. She…she came by wanting to talk to you. I accidently told her you had gone home. It just slipped out…"

Oh, God! "How long ago?"

Chase continued with his labored breathing into the phone. "Not even five minutes. I thought I could catch up with her…I'm so sor…"

Sebastian didn't say anything else. He hung up and threw his cell across the room. The phone flew in a near-straight-line before smacking into the far wall and shattering onto the floor. "Great…just great," he muttered to himself. *Maybe she'll call to make sure I'm home…or maybe she'll wait to come over later.* Not that that would help matters in the slightest, considering the fact that he had just broken his phone. *Dammit.*

While he was lost in his worrisome thoughts, a familiar heartbeat suddenly filled his ears. Just as he glanced down at his watch, there was a knock at his front door.

"Shit!" he whispered anxiously under his breath. *Shit…shit…SHIT!*

Sebastian already knew she would be on the other side once he opened the door, but to visually see her standing there, knowing what was about to transpire, caused his eyes to widen both in shock and in fear. His mind raced, and his heart pounded. "Avery…" He paused and looked around at the area behind her. "Can we hang out later? I'm sort of in the middle of something." He tried to sound tired and bored…failing at both.

A frown instantly formed on her beautiful face. "Well, hi to you too," she replied with a sullen tone.

He continued scanning the surrounding area. "Now really isn't a good time," he stated quickly. "You need to go back home. We'll talk tomorrow, I promise." *Please go…please just turn around and go!*

She sighed quietly. "It's never a good time, Bastian, but I really wanted to see you. And after our last visit, I thought you'd be happy to see me again."

Please don't let them come yet, he begged silently. "I am happy to see you, it's just…" In the middle of his sentence, a crushing weight settled into the middle of his chest, and he could sense three powerful essences close by.

The Pure Ones had arrived…and there was no time to get

Avery to safety.

Without any warning whatsoever, he grabbed her by the arm and jerked her inside. He hadn't meant to be so forceful, but he practically threw her across the room to get her through the door before slamming it shut behind them. He turned around to find her staring at him with a disapproving glare.

"What the hell, Ba..." Her facial expression changed from pissed-off to freaked-out in about a millisecond.

That is when he realized that his face had begun contorting on its own accord. Having the Pure Ones in such close proximity had his Cursed Form itching to break free.

Avery opened her mouth. Sebastian wasn't sure if she was going to scream or say something, but he wasn't taking any chances. He was by her side in the blink of an eye, covering her mouth and holding her firmly against his chest. She struggled, but only for a moment. Then thunder boomed outside. He frantically glanced from Avery to the door and then back to Avery. Her wide eyes were full of apprehension. She was obviously scared, and for a brief moment, he allowed her to see that he was too.

He swallowed hard. "Please don't scream," he whispered through his disfigured mouth.

Slowly he removed his hand.

Where can I hide her? He thought to himself. Then...*light bulb moment!* He reached into his back pocket and pulled out a necklace. It was nearly identical to the one she had thrown at him during their fight...the one he had given her for her sixteenth birthday. He had replaced the vial, but he hadn't gotten around to filling it again.

Avery relived that horrible moment, feeling the familiar twinge of guilt rising up in the pit of her stomach.

Sebastian hooked the necklace around her neck and placed his hand over her heart where the vial lay. He exhaled long and hard as his shoulders slumped momentarily. Another thunderous boom reminded him of the harsh reality that he was about to face. With Avery here, Plan A was gone. It was time to implement Plan B...whatever that may be.

"Close your eyes," he whispered. "This is going to be bright."

She didn't even hesitate to do as he asked, and he quickly followed suit. The sudden flash of light was so bright that even though her eyelids were closed, she still had to cover her face to avoid the brilliant blast.

"Please don't take the necklace off," Sebastian whispered. "Not until it's over."

Avery was so confused. "Until w-what's over?" she stammered.

"I don't have time to explain," he said quietly. With that, he picked her up and practically shoved her into the hallway closet. As he peered down at her puzzled expression, he said, "Whatever you hear, do not open this door! And don't make a sound...okay?"

She was hurt, angry, confused, and scared; yet despite all that, she still trusted him completely.

"Okay?!" he repeated, slightly louder this time.

She nodded quickly.

More thunder crackled, and his head shot towards the front of the house. "Just remember, don't move and don't make a sound. Please!"

She nodded again.

Without waiting for her to respond verbally, he closed the door. He barely had enough time to place a small mirage to keep her hidden before he sensed the three Pure Ones' essences at the front door.

~*~*~*~

Avery was in complete darkness now, except for a small line of light coming from underneath the door. She heard Sebastian's footsteps walking away, then another loud rumble of thunder, followed by the front door opening and closing. For a split second, she thought he had left her there, but then she heard muffled voices. Shifting her body as quietly as possible, she leaned forward until she was lying sideways on the floor. As she peered under the door, four sets of feet came into view. Sebastian was closest to her. She would recognize those orange Converse shoes anywhere.

There were three other sets of feet standing in front of him. At first, Avery felt no need for alarm. The indistinct conversation seemed rather casual. There were even a few laughs traded back and forth. She was in the process of readjusting her body back into a more comfortable position when all hell broke loose. Thuds, loud crashes, and the sound of glass shattering seemed to echo all around. Someone let out a shout, followed by screaming and moaning, then shrieking. She barely had time to process what was happening as something…or perhaps someone…slammed into the door, causing it to shake and rattle on its hinges. Avery yelped involuntarily, then covered her mouth to keep a louder one from escaping. Scooting back against the wall, she pressed herself as far into the corner as she could manage.

An explosive boom resonated throughout the small confined space, causing the shelving overhead to collapse. Avery covered her head as clothing and boxes toppled down on top of her. The walls began to shake, and the floors started to vibrate. As the chaos continued, more glass shattered and a loud crackling noise sounded from above. She glanced up to see a jagged fracture line starting near the molding around the top of the door. It was slowly extending the full length of the closet. Bits and pieces of the ceiling were already crumbling away, falling like a heavy snowfall of drywall and plaster. It sounded like a tornado was ripping apart the house piece by piece. BANG…BANG…BANG came against the door again. Avery heard Sebastian's voice cry out repeatedly, each time more tormented than the last. It was a sound that she never wanted to hear again.

Avery squeezed her eyes shut and covered her ears as another loud thud hit the door. Tears silently made their way down her cheeks as the riot-like pandemonium carried on. Thud after thud. Crash after crash. Bang after bang. Then as quickly as the turmoil began, it was suddenly silent. Eerily silent. Except for the sound of her rapid heartbeat hammering in her ears. She sat very still. Holding her breath while listening for any sign of movement. She was about to lie back down to peek underneath the door when she noticed something seeping into the closet. The small line of light illuminated the red liquid as it crept closer. *Blood...*

She gasped and tried to scoot away from the growing puddle. Tears continued to fall down her cheeks as she sat there trembling in fear. Something horrible had taken place on the other side of her little closet haven, and she didn't want to see the aftermath. But then she heard someone say her name. It was very faint, but she definitely heard it. She waited a few more minutes, straining her ears to listen harder.

Avery.

There it was again. This time she recognized his voice. Gathering what little bit of courage she had left, she turned the knob, then pushed on the door. It wouldn't budge. She tried again, this time bracing her back against the wall and pushing with her feet. Slowly the door cracked ajar. She pushed harder. The hinges let out a strained creak as the door fully opened, smearing blood everywhere. Avery glanced around cautiously, as the chandelier hanging in the hallway, which was now barely connected to the ceiling, swayed back and forth. Electricity sparked and popped overhead like mini fireworks flickering through the air. Broken furniture and huge chunks of plaster and concrete littered the floor. Most of the walls were torn down, and the entire ceiling was missing in the living room. Needless to say, the whole house was in shambles, but the coast appeared clear.

Avery managed to find her footing by holding onto the door jambs of the closet. Her wobbly legs held her up as she began weaving through the carnage, lit only by the light of the full moon overhead. She followed the gory red trail until a lifeless body came into view.

"Oh, my God! BASTIAN!" she shrieked.

This time there was no hesitation...though she was having trouble staying on her feet as she struggled to get to him, slipping and sliding in his blood and tripping over the jagged remnants of his house.

"I'm coming, Bastian! Just hold on. I'm coming!" Finally making it to his side, she skidded to a stop and dropped to her knees. "Oh, my God," she repeated.

His face was so swollen that he was completely unrecognizable. There were so many wounds and gaping holes covering his body that she wasn't sure what she could do to stop the bleeding.

Then the panic fully set in. "SOMEONE HELP ME!" she screamed. "HEEEEELLLLP!"

She lifted Sebastian's head gently into her lap. "You're gonna be alright, Bastian! Just stay with me okay?! Can you open your eyes? I need you to look at me!" *Airway! I need to check his airway.*

His breathing was labored, his skin was draining of color, and his lips were beginning to turn blue.

"Bastian…can you hear me? I'm right here. Just hold on!" *Oh, God, please don't die on me!*

During the struggle to keep his heart pumping, Sebastian was quickly losing focus. *I need to see that she's alright. I need to make sure they didn't hurt her!*

Finally, he managed to flutter one of his eyelids open. He blinked a few times to clear his cloudy vision long enough to gaze up at her beautiful face. The red glow slowly faded back to grey just as their eyes met. Then he smiled that half smile that she adored. When he tried to speak, he managed to say only her name. "Av…ery…"

She shushed him gently as tears streamed down her cheeks. "Shhh, I'm here. Everything is gonna be okay."

That was a total lie. Things were not okay. Time was quickly running out…and they both knew it.

She looked around again. *Someone had to have heard all the commotion. Surely someone has dialed 911 already!*

All of a sudden, Sebastian's body stiffened and jerked as he began gasping for air. He tried to speak again, which only resulted in him coughing and choking and spitting out more blood. With each desperate attempt he made to take a breath, Avery could hear gurgling and bubbling sounds coming from his chest. His lungs were filling up with fluid.

"SOMEONE HELP ME!" she screamed again.

Avery knew Sebastian had very little time left. So, she was forced to make the difficult choice to leave him to find help, or stay and hold him while his life faded away.

Doing nothing was not the logical option for her, but just as she shifted his head back onto the floor, he began convulsing. With each violent shake of his body, blood spurted out of every open orifice. His nose. His ears. His mouth. Even his eyes were bleeding.

Avery grabbed hold of his shoulder and turned him on his side in a last-ditch effort to keep him from choking on his own blood.

"PLEASE!" she cried out. "Please don't die on me!"

After two more shallow intakes of air, Sebastian's entire body went limp.

In complete shock, she shook him lightly. "Bastian?!" She turned him back over and put her head on his chest. No sound of a heartbeat.

His angelic grey eyes instantly glazed over.

"NO!" she screamed. "NO! NO! NO!" Avery began pounding on his chest and blowing air into his lungs. "One...two...three...four..." She paused for a second to blow into his mouth. "One...two...three...four...Bastian PLEASE! BREATHE!" she shouted through tears. "Please don't leave me!" Avery screamed and begged for someone to help her while she continued CPR. She screamed until her throat was raw.

Then as if the angels had finally heard her prayer, Chase came running through what was left of the front door. He stumbled around in the moonlit room, nearly falling over the surplus of debris. Then he laid eyes on Avery.

"Oh SHIT!" he yelled. "JONAH, get your ass in here NOW!"

Jonah raced in. "What's wro...?" He too stumbled inside, tripped over his brother, and landed hard on his knees in the rubble. "Son of a bi...!" The pain shooting through his legs was quickly forgotten once he saw Avery in full hysteria trying to revive his best friend. "No! B!"

From that point on, it was as if time stood still. Avery couldn't feel anything anymore. Her legs were numb…her hands were numb…her heart was numb. She vaguely felt Jonah's arms wrap around her as he forcefully pulled her away from Sebastian's body. She felt so empty without him in her arms, like she was dying right alongside him. *Dying. No, he wasn't dying…he was dead.* Tears blurred her vision as she watched Chase jump on top of Sebastian. Everything after that seemed to be moving in slow motion. Over and over Chase tried to resuscitate his best friend…with no luck.

Avery began crying inconsolably, struggling against Jonah's grasp in a feeble attempt to get back to Sebastian. "Let me go!" she shrieked! "He needs me…I need…I need to hold him! I need to help him!"

Jonah held her against his chest. "I got you, Av. Let Chase do his thing…"

Chase stopped CPR and shook his head. "This isn't working. I can't sense his essence inside him."

Avery slipped out of Jonah's arms and dropped to her knees. *This can't be real. He can't be gone.*

"Do you think the Pure Ones took it?" Chase asked frantically.

"No way. B is too smart for that shit. It has to be around here somewhere," Jonah stated. "Start looking!"

Chase stood up and motioned all around him. "Look where, Jonah?! The house is barely standing! Everything is destroyed!"

Jonah was equally flustered. "Well, we know it's here somewhere! If they had taken it, B wouldn't be a mutilated frickin' mess!"

The Smart brothers both turned their attention to Avery at the exact same time. She was still staring at Sebastian, shaking her head, making little gasping sounds and whimpering to herself. She went to cover her face with her trembling hands, then let out a scream as she realized her skin was coated in his blood.

Jonah reached out and shook her. "Hey...look at me!"

Avery began to cry harder, but she did as he asked. Her blank stare was a telltale sign that 'no one was home'. It was as if an empty shell was staring back at him.

Jonah took a breath to calm himself. "Did B give you anything before...all this happened?"

Avery just whimpered.

"She's in shock, bro!" Chase yelled from across the room.

"I don't care! This is literally life or death!" Jonah called back.

Chase began digging around through the rubble. "If it was left in the open, it's destroyed...or floating around aimlessly somewhere. It's too damn dark to see in all the nooks and crannies. It has to be with her."

Jonah turned his focus back to Avery.

She was still staring vacantly at Sebastian. "He can't be gone," she whispered. A single tear ran down her cheek and landed on her hand, which was now clutching her necklace.

Jonah's eyes widened. "Uhhhh, Chase? I think I may have found it!"

Avery blinked a few times and then looked down.

Chase let out a sigh of relief as he made his way over to them, staggering and wavering through the mess.

Jonah pointed at Avery's neck. "Did B give you that?"

She sniffled and nodded.

Without even the slightest warning, Jonah snatched the chain right off of her neck.

Avery gasped and lunged for him. "Give that back! It's all I have left of him!"

The two of them wrestled for a moment until Chase intervened. "Give me the damn necklace!" he said sternly. When neither of them moved, he added, "NOW!"

Both Avery and Jonah reluctantly let go.

Chase walked confidently toward Sebastian, maneuvering through the huge chunks of concrete and wooden beams.

Avery was watching his every move. "What are you doing?"

she asked.

"This is the necklace Bas gave you two years ago, right?"

Avery nodded as a rush of sadness overwhelmed her. "Sort of. He had to replace it."

Chase held up the vial. "Well, this now holds his essence."

Confusion covered her tear-streaked face. "Is this my fault?" Her voice broke as she began to cry again.

Jonah rolled his eyes. He didn't want to waste time explaining things; he just wanted to try to bring Sebastian back.

"No. This isn't your fault," Chase told her.

"What if it doesn't work?" Jonah asked sadly, redirecting the conversation.

"It has to," Chase stated. "Bas is always prepared. He wouldn't have allowed the Pure Ones near him without some sort of backup plan."

Both Smart brothers looked at Avery and smiled halfheartedly. Avery's jumbled mind, shattered heart, and broken spirit knew they were talking about her when they said 'backup plan', but she had no clue what they actually meant. Standing on shaky legs, she forced herself to go into the other room. She didn't want to see whatever they were going to do with Sebastian's body.

Meanwhile, Jonah and Chase were discussing the best course of action to deal with the essence. "If B gave himself to Avery, then she has to be the one to do this."

They both glanced in the other room. She was sitting on the floor with her back to them.

Chase sighed. "She's not going to believe a word we say."

"Look at our friend, Chase! He's dead! I don't care if Avery believes us or not. She's doing it!" Jonah trudged toward her…stomping over the piles of plaster, wood, concrete, and glass.

Chase opened his mouth to object, but changed his mind. His brother was right. This was the only chance they had to bring Sebastian back…if it worked.

Jonah stormed into what was left of the living room. "I need you to come with me," he demanded calmly.

Avery continued sobbing, ignoring his request.

Thankfully, Chase came up behind them. "You're not gonna get anywhere with her by acting like an ass."

Jonah pulled his brother aside. "If we don't do this quick, B's essence is going to die...which means his body will die too! Then...it'll really be too late."

"I know that!" Chase declared curtly.

Jonah threw his hands up in frustration. "WELL....?"

Chase sighed. "For her to agree to do this, we're gonna have to explain what's going on."

The Smart brothers both stared at Avery. This time, though, she was looking back.

Chase knelt beside her and placed the necklace back in her blood-covered hand, closing her trembling fist around it. "You can save him," he said softly. "You can bring him back."

Avery shook her head in disbelief. "That's impossible."

Chase stood and pulled her up with him. "His mere existence is impossible, yet there he is. All his unique abilities are impossible, but I know you've witnessed them with your own eyes. It's a long story, but I promise that Bas will explain everything to you himself...considering this works."

"I...I don't understand," Avery stammered.

"I know. But please," Chase begged. "Please just trust us."

Avery looked down at her necklace. The little charm contained some sort of wispy, glowing mist. She inhaled sharply. "What is that?"

Jonah shoved his hands in his pockets and kicked at a small hunk of rock. "Basically, that's B," he said quietly.

"It's essentially his soul," Chase added.

Avery was even more confused.

Jonah scoffed. "Guys! Time...running out...can you like, hurry up!"

"What do I have to do?" Avery asked. Her face was pink and puffy from crying, but she seemed completely in control for the moment.

Taking advantage of her sudden moment of clarity, Chase led her back to Sebastian's bloody, battered body. "You have to will his soul back to where it belongs."

"How…how do I do that?" she whispered.

Both Smart brothers knew she was scared and in shock…probably thinking they were crazy.

Jonah placed his hand gently on her shoulder. "Break the vial to release his essence."

She swallowed the growing lump in her throat. "Then what?"

Jonah and Chase both smiled.

"You'll know," Chase replied.

Avery took a deep breath and placed the necklace on the floor beside Sebastian. She didn't overthink. She didn't question anything. She trusted her instincts as she raised her foot and slammed it down, breaking the vial into tiny little fragments. The moment the glass shattered, the entire house shook simultaneously.

Jonah and Chase exchanged puzzled glances.

"Was that supposed to hap…?"

Chase gasped, cutting her off. "Avery…the essence!"

She turned back around and her breath caught in her throat. Hovering in front of her was a large, grey, wispy form, swirling and twisting and flowing within itself. The unshapely form grew bigger. Spreading outward like a thick cloud of smoke, taking on a more human-like appearance as it swayed slowly from side to side.

"I…I need you to come back to me now," she said softly. "I don't think I can live without you." She sniffled. *In fact, I know I can't.*

The wispy form began descending, hovering just above Sebastian's body.

Avery smiled as her eyes started to blur again. "I'm so scared, Bastian. Since the first day we met, I've been scared of losing you. I don't know what happened tonight, or what's happening right now for that matter, but I need you. I need you here…with me." She placed her hand over her heart. "Please, come back to me."

Suddenly, the wispy smoke surrounded Sebastian's body

like a transparent casing and lifted him up off the floor. The essence lifted him higher and higher until he was floating above their heads. A split second later, the entire room lit up like an explosion.

Avery, Jonah, and Chase were caught off guard as they were all flung backward…practically landing on top of one another in the rubble.

Then in the blink of an eye…wind, thunder, and lightning erupted out of nowhere; engulfing the room in a violent turbulence. The vortex of air lifted and tossed huge chunks of debris in different directions.

Jonah and Chase knew exactly what was taking place, but they couldn't do anything to stop it…and they couldn't save Avery from what she was about to witness. Sebastian's Cursed Form was about to make an appearance. Ready or not, here it comes…

Sebastian's eyes flew open, blazing hot like fire. He sucked in a deep breath just before a loud, booming bellow escaped his lips. As the screaming continued, he opened his mouth wider, elongating and stretching the skin until his jaw completely disconnected. The flesh at the corners of his mouth ripped apart in protest, changing his face into a mutilated image straight out of a horror movie. Shortly thereafter, his entire body began distorting. Twisting, turning, and bending in ways that no human should be able to. With each new arc of his battered frame, crunching and cracking sounds rebounded throughout the room as his bones started breaking and reforming. Sebastian screamed again and again while the roaring wind continued to hold him in mid-air. He was growling and screeching and screaming as his deformed body finally began to deteriorate.

"WHAT IS HAPPENING TO HIM?" Avery cried out in a panic. She was shielding her face with both hands as she leaned in closer to Jonah and Chase.

Neither of them responded. They both just stood there, watching and waiting.

"WE HAVE TO HELP HIM!" she exclaimed frantically,

though she wasn't sure what any of them could do.

The Smart brothers had seen Sebastian transition countless times before, but this time was different. It was more intense. Scarier. And from the looks of things, much more painful. They could only hope that the Strap of Virtue had done its job and that Sebastian's darker side wasn't about to show up.

A brilliant flash of light, followed by a clamorous boom, temporarily blinded them all. It took a few blinks to clear their vision, which revealed the fact that Sebastian had completed his transformation. His newly formed 'body' was surging and pulsing with an unbelievable amount of energy.

Chase gasped, and Jonah gulped. Avery screamed in terror and backed away. This was not a typical transition by any means. The creature hovering in front of them held no affinity to Sebastian's Cursed Form at all. In fact, it held no resemblance to the Dark Form either. This thing was enormous and vile looking.

The creature's entire body was covered with some sort of black sludge, moving and churning and dripping, but never falling away. Each and every one of its features were exaggerated. From the face that was so sunken in that it appeared to be nothing but an endless black hole, so dark that you could see your reflection within it; to the twisted spine with each individual vertebra protruding from its back like giant spikes on a Stegosaurus.

The creature lowered its colossal form to the floor, testing out its large limbs one by one. Bending and flexing each joint one at a time.

Jonah and Chase looked at each other, both having the same panic-ridden thought. *The strap hadn't worked!*

Long, pointed fingernails clicked and scraped against each other as the creature wiggled its fingers mockingly in their direction. Without warning, it began to circle them, growling viciously.

"DON'T!" Jonah yelled.

The creature paused and stared back blankly with its dark soulless features.

"We could really use a barrier right about now," Chase muttered under his breath.

"Yeah, no kidding," Jonah replied sarcastically.

The creature opened its mouth and let out the loudest, longest, high shrilling screech they had ever heard. All three of them were instantly brought to their knees covering their ears.

"SEBASTIAN, PLEASE!" Jonah shouted.

"IT'S US!" Chase added.

But nothing could be heard over the ear-splitting shrieking. Sebastian's altered form lunged at them again. It grabbed one of Avery's legs, dragging her across the floor; over all the hunks of glass, rock, metal, and wood.

Both Jonah and Chase tried to get a hold of her, but the creature was just too fast.

Avery was screaming as loud as she could, but only a faint squeak could be heard.

The creature wrapped its grotesque fingers around her throat and lifted her into the air.

She struggled against it. Clawing at its arms and face, but her hands went right through the sludge-like mist as if she were slashing at nothing but air.

The creature squeezed its grip tighter.

Avery tried to scream, she tried to cry, she tried to breathe, but none of those things happened; instead she could feel her throat slowly being crushed.

Jonah and Chase were both yelling at the top of their lungs for Sebastian to put her down…not to hurt her. They tried to remind him of how much she meant to him…how much he loved her. But then they heard a loud, gut-wrenching pop. Their eyes widened in complete disbelief as the evil creature tossed Avery's body across the room.

She looked like a ragdoll as she flew through the air and smashed into what was left of the back wall. She hit the ground hard with a loud thud; her body bent in a strange, unnatural looking position.

Chase's legs abruptly gave out.

Jonah picked up a large piece of debris and hurled it toward

Sebastian's new form. "SNAP OUT OF IT, YOU IDIOT! YOU JUST KILLED HER, DAMMIT! YOU. JUST. KILLED. AVERY!"

The creature seemed to hesitate for a moment. It studied Jonah briefly, then turned toward Avery's body. It stared at her for quite some time before it let out another screech. Its long serrated claws began to mangle and scratch and rip itself apart.

Jonah and Chase watched in horror as the creature's eyes flashed back and forth from black to red repeatedly as it continued to mutilate itself.

Black. Red. Black. Red. Black.

Eventually, the darkness in his eyes seemed to disappear, and a brilliant, glowing red broke through. The creature then appeared disoriented as it frantically flung itself around the room, howling and shrieking like it was in pain. As it got closer to Avery's body, the howling slowly began to sound more human. Howl after howl, the creature descended closer to the floor. Sebastian's human form gradually took shape again as he dropped to his knees in front of her, screaming and crying. He grabbed hold of her lifeless body and cradled her in his arms.

He killed her. He had actually killed her.

Jonah and Chase raced over.

"Is she...?" Chase didn't get to finish his sentence.

Sebastian's reaction answered his question.

"NOOOOOOOOOOO!"

"Oh, my God!" Jonah whispered, his eyes filling with tears.

Sebastian was crying inconsolably. "What happened?!" he growled.

"It wasn't you," Chase replied sadly.

Sebastian looked up at his two best friends as tears blurred his vision.

"It wasn't the Dark Form either," Chase continued. "But somehow you managed to fight it off."

"The strap must not have had enough time to take full effect," Jonah half-whispered.

The seconds ticked by ever so slowly while Sebastian sat there rocking back and forth with Avery's dead body held tightly in his arms. He was sobbing against her cheek, running his fingers gently through her tangled hair.

Chase started crying too. "What are we gonna do?"

Sebastian stroked her forehead tenderly as tears streamed down his cheeks and fell onto hers. "She risked it all for me," he said softly, sniffling. "I'm going to risk it all for her."

Jonah and Chase exchanged nervous glances.

"Bas, I know what you're thinking right now…but it's…it's unheard of," Chase stated, wiping his eyes.

"And even if you could," Jonah added sadly. "There's no way you're strong enough to…"

"I HAVE TO TRY!" Sebastian shouted, cutting them both off. He had never actually seen it done before, but he remembered the myths being whispered throughout the centuries. Stories about Cursed Ones resurrecting people by giving away a piece of themselves. Not enough to curse the human, but just enough to bring them back from an untimely death.

Sebastian carefully laid Avery's body on the floor and took her hand. He kissed each of her fingers before clasping her palm firmly against his. "I'm so sorry," he whispered. "I'll give you everything if you'll just come back to me." Over and over, he repeated those words as he closed his eyes and tightened his grip.

"It's not going to work," Chase told his brother quietly.

Suddenly, Jonah gasped. "I beg to differ."

Chase followed his brother's gaze, and his mouth fell open.

Sebastian's hand was starting to glow an intense reddish hue. He smiled as he felt the warmth surging from his hand into hers. Then almost instantly, he cringed. Unimaginable pain engulfed his entire body all at once. It was excruciating. Worse than the pain he endured from his curse, but he kept pushing. He let out a rumbling roar that shook what was left of his house. "DON'T LET ME BREAK THE BOND!" he shouted.

Jonah and Chase raced to his side and clutched their hands to his, holding him in place.

Not that they could have actually stopped him if he had wanted to pull away, but it seemed to give him the initiative to press forward.

Every fiber in Sebastian's body was telling him to release her…to end the pain and just let go. Instead, he pushed harder. It felt like his entire body was on fire; being engulfed by hot, stinging flames and burning alive, but at the same time, it was as if he were also drowning; being pulled down into the deepest depths of the coldest ocean, unable to breathe. He let out another blood-curdling scream, unintentionally loosening his grip on Avery's hand.

Jonah squeezed tighter. "Don't let her go, B! It's almost over…just a little longer!" Not that he knew how much longer this would have to go on.

Sebastian gritted his teeth and forced himself to keep going. He had collapsed on the floor and folded in on himself, screaming and crying out in pain, but he did not release his hold on Avery's hand again. He kept pushing his energy into her. Further and further he pushed…pressing on through the waves of pain. Focusing all of his strength…until finally…it split.

He let out a deep, blaring wail as part of his essence was literally torn from his soul. The physical torture was unbearable, but it was done. A tiny, almost undetectable piece of his essence was now floating right above their clasped hands. It was brighter than the flame from 'the glow', but it was smaller and wispy in form. He waited for the pain to subside, but so far it had not dulled at all. He screamed and cried out over and over as he writhed on the floor in agony.

"I will myself to you," Sebastian hissed through clenched teeth. He painfully pulled himself up to look at Avery's face. "Avery, live again…please!"

With that, he let go of his essence. He watched the glowing trail gradually fade from his hand and be absorbed into hers. Avery remained unmoving as the red hue made its way up her arm and then slowly coursed throughout her entire body, lighting up her veins like a neon pathway beneath her skin. The seconds passing seemed endless while Sebastian, Jonah, and Chase waited; and waited…and waited.

Finally, after what seemed like an eternity, Sebastian heard the most beautiful sound in the entire world.

Her heart began beating again.

When Avery gasped her first breath, Sebastian's emotional pain lightened immediately. He watched her chest begin to rise and fall. She was breathing! She was alive! For a mere moment, he allowed himself to be happy, then he dropped back to the floor writhing and groaning in pain.

Avery's eyes fluttered opened, and she found herself staring up at the moonlit sky with countless stars twinkling overhead…where the ceiling used to be. It took her a moment to realize where she was as she slowly pulled herself into a sitting position and rubbed her throbbing head. She moaned softly as she tried to get her bearings while a deafening ringing thrummed through her ears. A moment or so later, reality came slamming down on top of her.

Sebastian was dead…and then he wasn't…and then he was a monster…and then he… She gasped. *He killed me!*

Suddenly, Chase was at her side. He was frantically pointing and mouthing something. She could see his lips moving, but couldn't hear anything he was saying. Her disoriented gaze eventually landed on Sebastian. As the ringing sound finally began to subside, she could hear his tortured screams.

The white parts of his eyes were so bloodshot that they appeared to be bleeding and his face was warped and twisted, somewhere between his human form and his Cursed Form.

When Sebastian reached out for her, Avery let out a small yelp and instantly scooted away, backing up as quickly as possible.

Sebastian's misshapen face frowned at her, and he couldn't find the will to speak. Every time his mouth would open, a gut-wrenching scream would escape. Finally, he managed to cry out her name, but even then, his voice came out sounding like someone under demonic possession.

For a brief moment, Avery covered her ears and had to

look away. She didn't want to admit it, but she was afraid. Afraid of what had just taken place. Afraid of what she was feeling. Afraid of…him.

It was at that exact moment the realization finally hit her. And she was surprised it had taken her so long to figure it all out…maybe because she didn't want to believe it could be true. All the clues had been right there staring her in the face the whole time. *He* was her nightmare…the terrifying creature that haunted her dreams.

Sebastian watched helplessly as Avery continued backing away. Unable to form any verbal words, he reached out to her mentally. *I'm so sorry*, he cried. *Please forgive me. I never meant for any of this to happen.*

Tears were building in Avery's eyes as his tortured voice danced within her mind. He sounded so hopeless…so distraught…so lost. She stole a glance in his direction.

He was staring at her with his arm still outstretched toward her, crying and screaming with his strange facial features twisted in agony. His bloodshot eyes were begging her not to go. *She's leaving me! Oh, God no! She's seen my dark side, and now she's going to leave me! I'll end up just like Luca!*

Avery hid her face again as everything over the past six years began to make sense. Sebastian had been telling her the truth the whole time. The reason he consistently distanced himself from her. The bizarre phenomenon that always seemed to take place whenever he was around. The never-ending secrecy. The half-truths and whole lies.

It must have been such a daunting and relentless process, always having to hide himself from her…from everyone.

Sebastian could not stay focused on anything anymore. The agony he was experiencing kept him from being able to disconnect his mind from hers. Now Avery could hear everything he was thinking. She could hear the panic in his strange voice as his jumbled thoughts raced around and around in both of their minds.

The monster inside me has finally won… I deserve this suffering! I deserve to watch her walk away! I deserve to spend an eternity of misery after what I've done! I killed her… Oh, my God! I can't believe she died by my hands! I'll have to live with this for the rest of my immortal life…for eternity! I'm not worthy of her love…I never was! I'm sorry…I'm…so…sorry.

Avery opened her eyes and held his pitiful gaze. As they stared at each other, she heard his voice once more.

I'm so scared, Avery! I can't lose you…I'll die if I lose you! I don't deserve your forgiveness, but I'm begging for it anyway!

With that, his thoughts were entirely overtaken by his screams. Any and all awareness of his surroundings disappeared. There was nothing but pain…the feeling of compressing and squeezing his lungs, bending and snapping his bones, burning and shredding his flesh. His tormented cries quickly became too much for Avery to take. The shock of knowing that he was in fact, the-one-thing-that-terrified-her-the-most was still very fresh in her mind, but at the same time, he was also the man who owned her heart…whether he wanted it or not. She pushed her fear and doubt aside and scrambled back towards him.

Dropping to her knees, she grabbed his hand and stared into his bizarre, bloody eyes. She repeated the same thing she told him right before he died in her arms. "I'm here, Bastian. I'm right here!"

Suddenly, he stopped moving, and everything was silent.

Jonah was the first to speak. "What just happened? Did he…?"

Chase leaned down and placed his fingers on the side of Sebastian's neck. "He has a pulse."

Jonah crouched beside his brother. "Maybe he passed out."

"No," Sebastian said hoarsely. "The pain is…gone."

Avery took a step back to allow Chase to help Sebastian to sit up, but the second she released his hand, he dropped back to the floor.

"AVERY!" he shouted. "I NEED AVERY!"

Immediately she was back by his side, reaching out to grab his hand. The instant their skin touched, the pain stopped again.

Sebastian let out a sigh of relief with a partial smile, revealing one of his dimples. "Don't let go," he whispered breathlessly.

She squeezed his hand. "I won't."

In an attempt to relax, he closed his eyes and let out a shaky breath, willing his body to calm down. Now that he was able to think clearly, he knew what was happening.

Avery, Chase, and Jonah waited patiently for Sebastian's irregular breathing to slow so he could speak. A little while later, he sat up again, still clinging to Avery's hand. She could feel him trembling as he began to explain what was going on.

"When I gave a piece of my essence to Avery, in a sense I...lost a piece of myself..." Sebastian held her gaze. "A piece of my soul is part of you now," he told her quietly. "I can't ever be whole again, not unless you're with me."

If only she understood the full weight of that one sentence.

Avery blinked a few times to avoid completely breaking down. "So, you're saying that unless I'm physically here within arm's reach, you're going to be in pain like that for the rest of your life?!"

Sebastian swallowed hard. "Maybe not to this severity, but yes, it will hurt when you're not around."

Jonah and Chase stared back and forth between Avery and Sebastian.

"Sooooo...what the heck do we do now?" Chase asked.

The four of them looked at one another, then at the mess surrounding them.

Sebastian stood, taking Avery with him. "The mirage I placed over the house will last until I remove it," he stated. "So, no one will ever know what's happened here."

"That's not the only issue," Jonah pointed out. "Avery can't exactly glue herself to you forever."

"You can take her home. I'll be fine," Sebastian replied without missing a beat.

"NO!" Avery objected as she squeezed his hand tighter. "I can't leave you here knowing that you'll be suffering in my absence!"

"You have school tomorrow," he reminded her. "You can't miss class on account of me."

"We…" she corrected him. "We have school tomorrow! And I'm not leaving you. That's final." She stomped her foot for effect, which only made them all laugh.

Sebastian smirked in her direction. "If I prove to you that I'm alright, will you let them take you home?"

She bit her bottom lip as she stared him down. "Maybe."

He gently pulled his hand away from hers and took a step back.

Jonah, Chase, and Avery were on edge. None of them knew exactly what was going to happen. Would the screaming start up again? Would he collapse? Would he be completely incapacitated by the pain? Then…nothing happened. No screaming. No crying. No writhing in a fetal position on the floor.

"See?" Sebastian smiled, showing both of his dimples this time. "I'll be okay. The pain isn't that bad right now. You need to go home and rest. You've…had a long day." His smile faltered as he recalled the memory of him holding Avery's dead body.

Chase eyed him suspiciously. "Are you sure you're alright?"

"Yeah, I'm fine," Sebastian lied. "Make sure she gets home safe, and we'll talk tomorrow."

"Our phones will be on," Jonah announced as he headed for what used to be the front door.

Avery hesitated. "I'll come over first thing after school." She wrapped her arms around his neck and gave him a gentle squeeze.

He held her tighter and longer than she expected. Later, she would come to realize that was a huge red flag that he was lying about his pain level.

He kissed her forehead and released his hold on her waist, lingering his hand in hers. "I'll see you tomorrow."

The moment the door closed behind them, Sebastian sank to his knees.

CHAPTER 33

That night, Avery found it extremely hard to fall asleep. After sneaking in the back door so her parents wouldn't see her blood-soaked clothes, she took a shower and climbed right into bed. Since she was absolutely exhausted, she expected to pass out right away; instead, she found herself tossing and turning…and crying. Lots and lots of crying. Her heart broke over and over as her mind replayed the evening's dreadful events. Sebastian's hole-ridden body…then him turning into that hideous creature. She wrapped her arms around herself as she recalled the terrifying sensation of her own life slipping away.

Somehow, at some point, she must have passed out. The only reason she knew this was because her alarm was now blaring loudly in her ears, annoyingly telling her to get her booty out of bed. She groaned, turned over, slapped the clock repeatedly until it stopped beeping, and then pulled the covers back over her head. *Maybe I should call him*, she thought to herself. *He won't mind if I'm just checking up on him.* Her phone was already in her hand when she looked at the clock again. 6:07am. She sighed. *He's probably still asleep…and I wouldn't want to chance waking him*. So, after a few more minutes of wallowing in her comfortable bed, she dragged herself to the kitchen. She made some breakfast, quickly got dressed, and finally headed out the door.

Jonah and Chase met up with her in the school parking lot.

"Either of you talk to Bastian this morning?" she asked, hoping to sound upbeat and not desperate.

Both Smart brothers shook their heads.

"Me neither," she replied, her happy façade quickly fading.

"Cheer up, Av. You'll see him right after school," Jonah told her.

~*~*~*~

The school day went on as usual. Normal classes. Normal tests. Normal lunch. Normal conversations. Normal everything! All the ordinariness was driving Avery crazy.

Today can't be normal! It just can't! I mean, after all, Sebastian and I both died last night!

Lunch had ended, and she was sitting in sixth period waiting for the teaching to start when her heart began to race uncontrollably. At first, she thought she might be having a heart attack or maybe a panic attack, but then her thoughts shifted to Sebastian.

He needs me, she thought frantically. *It's crazy, but I just know he needs me! What are you doing?* She scolded herself. *Get your ass out of this chair, run out of this classroom, and get to Sebastian! NOW!*

Without another word, or thought, she jumped from her seat. She grabbed her backpack, threw the classroom door open, and ran down the hall. Her algebra teacher was hollering at her to come back, but she didn't stop or turn around. There was no time; she just kept running. Avery raced across the parking lot, making it to her car in record time. She revved the engine and took off down the road.

The usually short drive to Sebastian's house seemed to take forever. When she finally arrived, she parked and ran up the walkway as fast as her legs would allow. She reached for the doorknob, realizing a tad too late that the door wasn't actually there, and fell face first into the rubble on the other side. She grumbled as she picked herself up. Then she heard a God-awful noise.

"Oh no," she whispered out loud to herself. "I was right!"

Sebastian's tortured screams were echoing down the hallway, filling her ears with the horrible sound and breaking her heart into pieces. She tripped and stumbled through all the debris before shooting down the hall faster than a bullet leaving a gun. When she entered his bedroom, he was curled up in a fetal position, gripping and ripping apart his covers in a feeble attempt to escape the pain. She practically threw herself on top of his body, holding him as tight as she could.

"*I never should have left you*," she cried out both vocally and mentally. "*I'm so sorry, Bastian!*"

She could hear his soft sobs in her ear as his entire body shook uncontrollably. Avery lifted herself up just enough so she could see his face.

He grabbed hold of her, keeping her in place. "Please. Don't. Move," he pleaded, completely out of breath.

She gently moved a few strands of hair from his sweaty brow and caressed his cheek. "I'm not going anywhere," she assured him.

He let out a shallow breath and closed his eyes. Tears continued to fall silently down his face and onto his pillow as the tremors continued to rage on.

Has he been in this much pain since I left? That question burned in the back of her mind; and she was going to ask...just not right now. Avery shifted herself next to him, making sure to keep physical contact.

He cradled her head in the curve of his arm as she listened to his heartbeat. For a while, the beats were fast and irregular, but gradually they slowed to a normal rhythm.

Avery sighed and cleared her throat. "So, um. I don't want to ask this, but...I have to know," she said quietly. "Have you been like this since...?"

He took a deep breath and let it out slowly before she even finished her sentence. "Yes," he admitted.

Avery frowned. "Why didn't you call me? I would have

come right back over!" Part of her was a little pissed-off at him for being so stubborn. And for what? What was the point of suffering all alone for an entire night and almost a full day, when her mere presence could have soothed him?

"You've given up enough of your life for me," he replied faintly.

Ah. So, there it is. She sat up in a quick fluid-like movement and looked down at him. "So, that's what this is about? Punishing yourself?"

As usual, he avoided her gaze.

"You can't walk away from me this time, so you might as well look at me," she stated confidently.

One corner of his mouth turned up.

"Oh, look at that. I see a dimple!" she added teasingly.

He fully smiled then.

She gently grabbed his face and turned him back towards her. His mind flashed back to the first time he had allowed her to touch him so intimately. She too recalled the same memory, only in her version it wasn't the sweet caress of her hands on his rugged face…it was the image of him running away from her. He saw the hurt on her face just before she looked away.

"I'm sorry," Sebastian said quietly.

Avery attempted a shrug. "It's okay. I'm used to it." Immediately she regretted those words coming out of her mouth.

Sebastian frowned and looked away again, feeling utterly ashamed.

"Thaaaaaat came out totally wrong!" she stated earnestly. "I didn't mean it like that."

"Doesn't make it any less true," he replied sadly.

She cleared her throat in an attempt to change the subject before she caused any further damage. "Are you feeling well enough to get in the shower? Then we can get rid of these ripped up, sweaty sheets."

Neither of them were sure of how showering was going to work, especially given their 'special circumstances', but neither of them disputed it.

Avery held Sebastian's hand as they made their way to the bathroom.

Sebastian took off his shirt and tossed it on the floor. Then they stared at each other for a brief moment. To say tension was in the air at this point would be an understatement. When he began unbuttoning his pants, Avery blushed and turned her face away.

"I, uh…" He cleared his throat. "I think I can handle a few minutes of pain to take a shower."

She felt her face redden deeper, hoping that he wouldn't notice. "Yeah. Um, okay. I'll be right outside the door if you need me."

Both of them hesitated before disconnecting their hold on each other. A moment later, Avery heard the water running, then the shower curtain scraping the top bar. Which meant, in theory, that he was able to shower pain-free. Though, no sooner had she pulled the door shut behind her, Sebastian grunted loudly and called out her name. She rushed back in and threw the curtain out of the way. He was doubled over with his hands resting on his knees, breathing heavily.

He looked up at her over his shoulder and let out a nervous laugh. "It would seem that being away from you is becoming more and more difficult."

Avery smiled involuntarily. "Had you said that a year ago, under different circumstances, I may have fainted."

They both chuckled.

"Let's try this again, shall we?" Sebastian said optimistically.

This time, Avery kept her hand on his back while he washed off, then when he turned around, she kept her hand on his chest, and her eyes squeezed shut.

Was it awkward? Pretty much. But did she *really* mind? Nope.

When the water turned off, and he was snuggly wrapped in a towel, she opened her eyes again. "So, how is this going to work exactly?" she asked.

Sebastian arched his eyebrow as he ran another towel over his face and upper body. "How will what work?"

She sneered at him playfully. "Um...the whole I-can't-leave-you-alone-because-you'll-be-in-excruciating-pain thing?"

"Ahh, that," he replied as he casually put on a clean shirt.

"Yes, that," she echoed.

"Well..." He cleared his throat. "I guess we just leave things as they are. It's not like we have much of a choice."

Her eyes widened. "Are you frickin' kidding me? There's no way in hell that I could leave you again knowing what I know now!"

A comical grin spread across his face as he reached for his boxers. "Well, unless you're planning on moving in with me and dropping everything else going on in your life so you can be here 24/7..." He paused, waiting to see her response.

Avery stared at him in stunned silence, but that didn't last long. She jerked his boxers from his hand and tossed them back onto the bathroom counter. "How can you be so relaxed about everything that's taken place over the last day and a half?" She frowned. "This may be normal in your crazy, messed up world, but this is not okay with me! You died in my arms, Bastian! I held you while you took your last breath. Do you even know what that did to me? And if that wasn't already horrific enough, I watched you transform into a demon straight out of hell...and you killed me! Yet you're joking around, smiling, and acting like nothing is out of the ordinary!" Her voice cracked. "Nothing feels right anymore, and I don't know what to do!"

He sighed as his cocky smile faded away. *Great, she thinks I'm a demonic creature from hell.* He took her hand off his chest and intertwined their fingers together as he sighed again. "Do you want to know the reason why I'm able to smile and act like everything is okay...even after all that?"

Avery nodded as she blew out her breath.

Sebastian cupped her face in his hands, tilting her head up so he could look directly into her beautiful green eyes. "You see me, Av. You truly see me. Not just who I am, but *what* I am...and you're still here!" He let out a hushed laugh as his eyes began to glisten. "You have no idea how long I've waited for this. So regardless of how we got here, I can't help feeling happy."

"So, the reason you refused to get closer to me after all these years…the reason you were so distant…it was because of that thing you turned into? That was the secret?" She acted as if it was no big deal.

"Yes."

For the next few minutes, time seemed to stand still. Neither of them said a word. They just stood there together.

Eventually, Sebastian pulled her closer and wrapped his arms around her shoulders. "I do have one question, though."

"Okay, what is it?"

"What made you stay?" he asked. "Why didn't you run away once you realized I was…a monster?"

Avery smiled as she leaned against his chest. "You're not a monster, Bastian."

"What made you stay?" he repeated, quieter this time.

The story Elliot and Isabelle told him about Luca kept circling in his mind. He didn't just want to know the answer; he had to know. He recalled seeing the fear in Avery's eyes as she backed away from him. At that moment, he knew she was going to run. He had braced himself for it. He had prepared his heart for the unbearable break it was going to feel…but when she turned around and was suddenly back by his side, he was completely baffled.

"You already know the reason," she replied timidly.

"Tell me." Oh, how he yearned for her to say those three precious words again, even if it was just once more.

Avery felt a rush of emotions overtake her. The last time she offered her heart to him, he had smashed it to pieces. She wasn't sure if she was ready to take that chance again, even if it seemed that he was currently feeling the same way.

Sebastian's heart was beating steadily in time with hers. The overwhelming moment they were sharing would soon be over. And the question still remained… Would she say it again?

Then all at once, reality slammed into him like an out of control truck on the highway. He hadn't actually confessed his love to her. She still didn't know how much he cared for her. *Oh, no!* If he were to say it out loud, would his Cursed Form come back? Would he still be in control of himself or would the evil creature return? Or worse... What if he killed her again? There was no way he would be able to split his essence a second time, so she would be gone forever.

Sebastian quickly decided to change the subject. "I'm starving. Would you mind accompanying me to the kitchen after I get dressed so we can get something to eat? Then I promise to have a more serious talk about our um...situation."

She nodded. "Okay."

~*~*~*~

Hand in hand yet again, they searched the kitchen for something that looked appealing to them both. While Sebastian was in the process of making sandwiches, Avery was staring at what used to be his living room. She replayed the grisly events that lead to its annihilation over and over in her mind. In a daze, she let her hand slip right off his shoulder.

Sebastian promptly gripped the granite countertop, nearly snapping it in half. "Avery..." he groaned.

But she didn't respond, nor did she touch him again.

His breathing increased without his consent as he flailed blindly in her direction. "Av...ery," he grunted louder. *Where is she? She wasn't even a foot away a second ago. I should have connected with her already.* Sebastian forced his eyes open. He repeatedly blinked to clear his cloudy, double vision, but it never went away. There was no sign of Avery in the kitchen or what was left of the living room. *Where did she go?* he thought helplessly. As he staggered down the hall, he had to lean on the wall for support to remain upright, all while groaning and calling out her name. He tripped and nearly fell a few times, but he had finally made it to his bedroom.

She wasn't there.

Sebastian called out for her again, louder this time. His steps faltered, and his body slammed into the floor before he could catch himself. This time he screamed. He screamed her name at the top of his lungs.

"AAAAAVVVVEEEEERRRRRRYYYYY!"

Still no sign of her anywhere.

He was dragging himself back into the hallway when a familiar voice resounded in his ears.

"She's not here," the female said in a sing-song voice.

Sebastian immediately felt his tainted blood run cold. He forced his tormented body to kneel, bracing his hands on the cool marble floor. When his head lifted upward, he found himself face to face with his past. "Adeline?" *I must be dreaming…or hallucinating.*

She started walking towards him, her movements fluid and graceful. She knelt down beside him, gently caressing his face. When she finally responded, her sweet voice sounded exactly as he remembered. "I can assure you that you're not. I am real."

Sebastian squinted up at her through the pain.

Long blonde hair framed her elegant face, and her blue eyes still sparkled when she smiled.

"But how? How…is this possible? You're…dead."

"Yes, I was," she said sadly. "But my mother sacrificed herself and willed her powerful essence into my body."

"Moira?" Sebastian continued to stare at his first love as unsettling thoughts raced through his mind. *Moira was the reason for the downfall and destruction of the Pure Ones' rein after what she did to their brother Ivez. Her betrayal caused them to lose their purity and become susceptible to darkness. If Adeline is back from the dead…with Moira's essence…*

Adeline's voice purred in his ear. "That's right, my dear. Put all the puzzle pieces together. You're almost there."

Sebastian nearly fell over as a wave of nausea overtook him. "Stay…out of…my head."

Adeline reached out and brushed his hair away from his face. "You look like you're in a lot of pain, my love. I could fix that for you." She smiled again, but this time there was a villainous look about her.

Sebastian doubled over, dropping back down to the floor. His situation was growing more urgent by the moment.

"How…can you…help me?"

"It's quite simple really," she said as she studied her long, manicured fingernails. "I'll just take back the piece of your essence that was given to that little wench and make you whole again."

Instantly rage overtook him. "WHAT…HAVE YOU…DONE WITH HER…ADELINE?" He shouted each word at the top of his burning lungs, pausing only to take in short bursts of air.

Adeline twirled her long blonde locks around her fingers seductively. "Aww, my dear sweet Sebastian, I've missed you so."

He attempted to stand, but he just wasn't strong enough. He lost his balance and slid back down, clutching his chest and groaning in agony. "Don't…hurt her," he pleaded. "Please."

Adeline's face hovered above him as his vision went hazy. Her devious smile was the last image he saw before he passed out.

CHAPTER 34

"Bas?"
"B, wake up!"
"Can you hear us?"
"WAKE UP!"
"C'mon man, open your eyes!"

Sebastian could hear Jonah and Chase's voices, but his body would not move. His insides felt as if they were made of lead and his eyes felt heavy...not just tired heavy, more like glued shut heavy. He made an attempt to speak, but only a moan escaped his lips.

"Bas, we're here!" Chase assured him. "What happened?"

Avery! Sebastian remembered being in the kitchen with Avery, then out of nowhere she just disappeared. And then Adeline was there... He began to panic. Flailing whatever limbs would cooperate.

Jonah tried to catch one of Sebastian's arms before it clocked him in the face. "Calm down, B! It's gonna be okay!"

Sebastian concentrated on the physical contact. It was the only thing keeping him from spiraling completely out of control. He needed to find Avery before Adeline did something horrible to her. *Calm down and focus.* Suddenly, his eyes popped open, but the rest of him remained immobile. His fuzzy vision landed on Jonah as he willed the rest of his body to move. *Come on, dammit! Move. MOVE!* As if it had been waiting for him to make the demand, his body finally obeyed. He sucked in a deep breath and shot straight up to a sitting position. "Where's Adeline?" he panted.

Jonah and Chase exchanged confused glances.

"Don't you mean...Avery?" Jonah corrected him.

Sebastian jumped to his feet. "No, I mean Adeline!" he replied crossly.

"Hold up!" Chase waved his arms in the air. "Are you talking about *the* Adeline? As in your dead first love?"

"Undead first love," Sebastian corrected. "Adeline isn't so dead after all."

Chase's forehead wrinkled. "Wait...are you saying she's like...a zombie?"

Jonah laughed unintentionally, then immediately cleared his throat. "Uh, sorry," he said sheepishly.

Sebastian would have gotten a good laugh about a zombified Adeline too, if he wasn't currently losing his ever-loving mind. "What time is it?" he asked. He needed to know how much time had gone by since he had passed out.

"Uh, it's five-ish," Jonah replied. Then he cocked his head sideways and looked at his best friend. "So, what does this have to do with Adeline exactly?"

Shit! Sebastian was pacing around the kitchen now. Looking for a clue or a possible scent that may have been left behind. "She took Avery over two hours ago. I have to find them!"

Jonah and Chase simultaneously looked at each other again. And it was at that moment, that Chase realized something that Sebastian and his brother had overlooked.

"Uh, Bas?"

Sebastian didn't pay him any mind as he continued his unproductive search.

Chase tried again to get his attention. "Bas?" When his second try went unnoticed, Chase upped his game. "BAS!

STOP! JUST FRICKIN' STOP FOR A SECOND AND LISTEN TO ME!"

Sebastian slammed one of the cabinet doors, causing it to embed itself into the wall. "WHAT?!" he growled back.

"Your pain..." Chase stated, as if waiting for something to click in his friend's head.

Sebastian took a moment to reconnect with himself. "Oh, no..." he whispered.

"What?" Both Jonah and Chase said together.

"My essence…" Sebastian uttered apprehensively. "…it's…whole."

"But how can that be?" Jonah asked.

"Maybe you healed yourself?" Chase offered.

Sebastian shook his head and placed his hand over his heart. "No. I can feel the piece of myself that I willed to Avery. It's irregular. Like it was ripped away by force."

Then he recalled what Adeline had said. *I'll just take back the piece of your essence that was given to that little wench and make you whole again.*

He began to imagine what Avery must have gone through for Adeline to take his essence away from her. He pictured Avery lying on the floor with Adeline's monstrous hands all over her body, tearing her apart internally, while reveling in every horrible moment. Avery must have been utterly terrified to be in such an unbelievable amount of pain. Sebastian slammed his fist down on the counter, breaking the granite right in half.

Chase hung his head. "You don't think Avery is...?"

"Don't even think like that!" Sebastian snapped. "I'll find her. I have to!" Without another word, he walked outside with his Watchers following close behind.

"So, you're not taking any supplies?" Chase blurted out. "Just the clothes on your back and the hope that you'll make it out alive? C'mon man, that's suicide!"

Sebastian sighed. "If I showed up at the Pure Ones' sanctuary with an arsenal of weapons, they'd kill me on the spot! There are probably hundreds of Cursed Ones residing there now, if not more. There is only one of me. I figure I have a better chance of getting Avery back if I show up and let them see that I'm not a threat. Maybe they'll make a trade. Avery…for my essence."

"You're an idiot!" Jonah exclaimed. "You think they're just going to let you waltz right in and take Avery home? There won't be any trading. They killed you once already. I'm sure they won't hesitate to do it again. It's clearly a trap! The second you show up, Adeline will rip your essence apart without batting an eye. Then just for kicks, she'll kill you. And I hate to be the one to say it, but Avery is probably already dead!"

Sebastian turned around and punched Jonah…right in the face.

Jonah stumbled backward a few feet and landed on his butt. "Are you frickin' kidding me?!" he groaned. "What the hell, B?! I'm on your side, dumbass!"

"She's NOT dead!" Sebastian yelled. "Don't EVER say that to me again!"

Jonah's nose was dripping blood all down his shirt. He was pretty sure it was broken.

Sebastian rubbed his throbbing temples and sighed. "I'm sorry…come here," he told him.

Jonah shook his head. "I'm fine. I'll deal with it. You go find Avery."

Sebastian walked over and cupped his hand over Jonah's nose. A bright red flash temporarily blinded both Smart brothers. Once the light faded away, Jonah's nose was fully healed, but Sebastian was gone.

Chase stated the obvious. "He went without us!"

"How noble," Jonah said sarcastically.

CHAPTER 35

Avery eventually came to and opened her eyes to find a vast wall of darkness. She blinked a few times in an attempt to clear her vision, but nothing changed. Wherever she was, it was pitch black and smelled like a mixture of mildew and sewage. The floor was hard, cold, wet, and somewhat sticky. *Eww.*

When she reached up to rub her temples, she felt something strange around her wrists. *What the hell?!* She adjusted herself to a sitting position and began tugging and pulling at the rusted metal. A rattling, clanking sound echoed throughout the room. Chains. Someone had literally chained her to a wall. A groan escaped her lips as she began to rack her brain for answers. She remembered being with Sebastian in his kitchen. Then suddenly, a woman had appeared. After that, there was a lot of pain. But that was it. Everything else was a total blank.

Considering the dire circumstances she found herself in, Avery was surprised at how calm she felt…though that was probably because the reality of her situation had not sunk in yet. The darkness helped with that. Had she been able to see her surroundings, panic probably would have been immediate.

Her head was pounding, and her entire body felt like a huge bruise. Her mouth and throat were dry, and her lips were chapped. She tried to swallow, but it felt like she had swallowed a handful of tiny needles. *How long have I been here? And where exactly is here?*

She sat silently in the darkness, listening to the sound of water dripping onto the floor. Then something ran across her bare feet. She yelped and instantly brought her knees up to her chin, wrapping her arms around her legs. Muffled shuffling sounds came from somewhere close by. That is when the rush of hysteria finally hit her.

Avery whimpered as she swallowed another batch of tiny needles. She tried to speak, but her voice box wasn't cooperating. In an effort to clear her throat, she coughed quietly. "Is someone there?" she asked. Her voice was hoarse, but at least she could talk.

More shuffling sounds and a few soft moans were the only replies.

Someone is in here with me! Avery wasn't sure if she should be relieved or frightened of that new revelation. "Where are we? Can you move?"

Still no response.

Straining her eyes against the darkness, she still couldn't see anything. Suddenly, there was a loud clanging sound as a door cracked open. Avery was partially blinded by a bright light as someone stepped inside and closed the door.

A man dressed entirely in black, most of his face hidden with some sort of mask, was standing just a few feet away holding a dimly lit lantern. His eyes were radiating a vibrant shade of red, similar to Sebastian's. As the masked man stepped closer, the little amount of light now allowed Avery to see an older woman chained to the wall directly across from her. They made eye contact briefly. Terror and sadness covered the woman's face.

"Get up!" the man ordered to Avery. His voice was so deep that it sounded inhuman.

"Leave her alone," the woman said quietly. "Please, just

leave her be."

He slapped the woman across the face. "SILENCE!"

She let out a small moan and began weeping quietly.

The masked man then turned his attention back to Avery. "I said get up!" His tone was angrier this time.

Avery's heart was racing, and her entire body was shaking, rattling her restraints. She wanted to do as he said, but she just could not move. She was literally frozen in fear.

The masked man sat his lantern on the floor and took an outraged step toward her. He grabbed hold of her upper arm and jerked her up to a standing position. The rusted metal that was binding her wrists cut deep into her skin.

Avery cried out. "Please, stop! You're hurting me!"

"Stop what?" he asked maliciously. "This?" The masked man lifted her higher.

The jagged edges of the chains sliced open both of Avery's wrists. She screamed out in pain as a warm trail of blood began running down her arms. "Please…" she begged. "Please, stop! I'll do whatever you say!"

The masked man loosened his grip but kept his hold on her as he leaned in closer. She could feel his hot, foul-smelling breath on her cheek as he whispered into her ear. "Yes, you will do exactly as I say! Now come with me!"

Avery was unshackled from the wall and led down a long, narrow corridor. She nearly lost her footing countless times, tripping and slipping on the slimy rocks underneath her bare feet. The masked man didn't stop moving; he just continued to drag her behind him. Soon they came to a large opening that led to an enormous cavern. Now that she could see more of her surroundings, Avery realized that she had to be somewhere underground. The nasty sewage smell was gone, replaced by a fragrant, earthy scent.

"Put her there," a female voice ordered.

Avery glanced up to see a beautiful blonde woman standing nearby.

The masked man directed Avery to a small cage in the far back corner.

She shook her head. "NO! No, please don't put me in there!" Avery struggled and fought and begged with all her might, but it just wasn't enough.

The masked man shoved her head first into the cage before he began chaining her ankles together with thick metal cuffs. She kicked and screamed and punched as hard as she could, but nothing seemed to deter this horrible man from his mission. Once he secured the chains on her feet, he grabbed hold of her lacerated wrists and slammed them down against the solid stone floor. Two loud cracking sounds seemed to echo in Avery's ears as she suddenly lost the will to speak...to move...to breathe. Feeling lightheaded and nauseated, she tried to scream, but what came out was just a hoarse whimper.

The masked man wrapped the cold, rusted metal around both of her now broken wrists.

Avery shuddered and cried out again and again as she writhed in pain on the floor.

Adeline casually walked over to the small cage and knelt down.

Avery's wide, tear-filled eyes locked onto hers. *Oh, my God! She was in Bastian's house right before I woke up here!*

Adeline's mouth curved up into a sinister smile. "Now connect the rest of the dots, and you'll realize *why* you're here."

Avery cried out again and again. "Please...help...me..."

~*~*~*~

Seconds passed...minutes...hours...and the throbbing never let up. Poor Avery had screamed so much that her throat felt like it was on fire.

"Oh, for the love of all that is holy...SHUT HER UP!" Adeline shouted. "I've heard enough of her whining for one day!"

The masked man bowed. "Right away, Lady Adeline." The latch on the cage door was unlocked. When he jerked it open and ducked inside, Avery tried to scoot away.

"Please don't! Oh, God, PLEASE!" she pleaded. "I'm sorry! I'll be quiet! I swear I'll..."

As the masked man reached out for her, she screamed once

more. Her tiny voice echoed throughout the entire cavern. Then he slapped her so hard that she blacked out.

The cavern became silent as Adeline walked away with a satisfied grin spreading across her face.

CHAPTER 36

Two days later, Sebastian had finally managed to make it to the Pure Ones' sanctuary…which was nearly twenty-thousand-feet up on the side of a mountain in the-middle-of-nowhere Alaska. His mind was a jumbled mess of emotions as he stood in front of the hidden entryway on the rock face. The last time he had been here, his life was incomparable to what it is now. He had a different outlook, different dreams, different friends…and a different hunger. He placed his trembling hand on the faded markings that covered the huge boulder in front of him. The instant he sent a heated pulse, the entire slab illuminated with his red hue. His throat suddenly went dry as the mirage lifted and a rock-shaped door slowly rolled away, rumbling the snow-covered ground beneath his feet. As he stepped inside, he could feel the air around him change drastically. *Be ready for anything*, he warned himself. Not even a second later, the heavy boulder slammed down behind him with a loud crash.

Sebastian now stood alone in the darkness. His eyes began to glow, allowing him to see his surroundings. In front of him was a long, narrow passageway that descended deep into the earth. Slowly and carefully, watching his footing and keeping an eye out above him for any traps, he made his way down. He found it somewhat comforting that after so many decades, he still remembered all the twists and turns and dead ends of this place.

He finally managed to make his way to the bottom where the slender passage opened up into a massive cavern deep within the mountain. Right away his eyes were drawn to a cage in the corner furthest from him. Horrible images flooded his thoughts as he recalled the abhorrent things he had been a part of down here after the Pure Ones lost their purity. Sebastian could hear Avery's faint heartbeat pulsating in his ears. He rushed across the room in stealth mode where he found her chained to a granite wall. She was unconscious and hanging limply by bloody wrists.

He cried out into her mind. *Avery?! Avery, can you hear me?!*

Her eyes fluttered open. "Bas…tian?" she whimpered weakly.

I'm here, sweetheart! Hold on! I'll get you out of there! He grabbed hold of the bars and attempted to pull them apart.

Suddenly, Avery let out a blood-curdling scream that was so loud it made the hair on the back of his neck stand up. She struggled against the chains in a feeble attempt to free herself. Then the painful reminder that her wrists were broken stopped her from moving altogether. She froze as tears rolled down her cheeks.

"Hold on, Avery! I'm coming!" Sebastian pulled harder, causing one of the bars to bend a little.

Avery screamed again. "STOP! PLEASE STOP! IT HURTS!"

Maniacal laughter echoed throughout the entire chamber. Sebastian let go of the bars as he scanned the seemingly empty room. The laughter continued. He focused hard, reaching out with his mind to pinpoint the source.

"There's no need to be sneaky," Adeline stated. "I'm right here."

As she stepped out from the shadows, Sebastian tried once more to free Avery. But the instant he tugged at the metal, she started screaming again.

"Go ahead," Adeline taunted. "The bars are infused with her blood. If you tear *them* apart, you'll tear *her* apart."

An evil smile spread across Adeline's face, making Sebastian want to rip her throat out.

He took his hands off the bars, hesitating for only a moment before stepping back. "Release her! You have what you want, Adeline. You got me back here. Avery has nothing to do with this!"

Adeline's delightful expression disappeared. Now she was glaring in Sebastian's direction. "That girl has everything to do with this!" she hissed. "You gave up your life with me to be with her!"

"You were dead...and I was cursed! I had no choice other than to move on. And besides, that was centuries ago. If you wanted to be with me so badly, why hide your resurrection? Why not come for me?"

Her face distorted for a split second. "I did come for you, but you had already left the sanctuary. You had chosen a different path." She frowned. "You moved on so easily, my love. Forgetting about me as if I were nothing...leaving me to rot! Yet you risked your very life to bring this girl back from the dead!"

Sebastian wasn't going to continue playing this game. "Let Avery go!" he stated adamantly.

The corners of Adeline's mouth twitched. "And if I say no?" She didn't wait for him to answer. Instead, she vanished down a darkened corridor directly behind her.

Sebastian immediately followed. At the end of the tunnel, he found a small room to the left that was unfamiliar to him. *It must have been built long after I left.*

As he entered, a lantern sat on a table, illuminating the small space. Luxurious bolts of silk and satin in multiple shades of purples and blues draped the ceiling and the walls. A large four poster bed overloaded with pillows of all shapes and sizes sat in the center of the room. Adeline was standing beside it, twirling her hair seductively like she always had.

She stared at him, smiling wickedly. "Hello again, my dear Sebastian."

The sweet tone of her voice sent a chill down his spine. He could feel her presence within his mind, searching his thoughts. Her grin widened as she began toying with his memories. Forcing him to recall distinct moments from their past.

He tried to push her out, but she was stronger than he anticipated. Against his will, Sebastian was forced to relive old memories the two of them had shared. He watched as he caressed her soft smooth body and kissed her plump pink lips. He heard himself whisper *I love you* in her ear as he pulled her closer. He told her how much he cherished her. How much he wanted her.

"Stop this!" he said bitterly.

Adeline stepped forward and touched his face. "But there's so much more…"

Sebastian growled menacingly, but Adeline just giggled.

She reached out again with her other hand to stroke his cheek. "You don't scare me, my love. You were mine once…or have you forgotten?"

He backed away, leaving her hands hovering in mid-air. "I haven't forgotten. Though I wish I could."

The instant he severed physical contact, her demeanor quickly shifted. "Tsk tsk, Sebastian. Falling in love always comes with a price…or haven't you learned that by now?"

Sebastian moved slowly and carefully across the room, keeping his eyes glued to hers. "Love? What happened to the girl I fell in love with? Where is the Addie I knew, who was so full of life? So full of compassion and kindness. You hold no resemblance to her whatsoever."

Adeline frowned momentarily. "Death changes a person. You of all…people…should understand that."

"Is that really it?" he countered. "Or did your mother's essence being harbored inside of you turn you into the cold-hearted bitch that she was?"

Adeline slapped him with every ounce of power she

retained, dislocating his jaw in the process. "Don't ever speak ill of my mother!"

He dropped to his knees, cradling his chin in his hands. It would be harder to speak now. Not that he needed his mouth to convey his words.

"Nothing more to say?" she mocked.

I've got plenty to say.

Her mouth twitched up into a smile once more. "Pity that I don't have time to listen."

You won't tune me out. Apparently, you've been searching for me for far too long to just toss me aside now.

She calmly strolled over to him, grabbed hold of his chin and lifted him up off the floor with ease. She pulled him closer, centimeters away from her angelic face, and then squeezed.

Sebastian flinched and accidently let a groan escape as the bones of his jaw crackled and crunched.

"Believe what you want," she hissed, "but you don't know me anymore...or what I'm capable of. You said it yourself. I hold no resemblance to the girl I once was." With that, she shoved him backward and turned away.

This was his chance. Probably the only one he was going to get. Sebastian let out a menacing growl and lunged at her, transforming to his Cursed Form in mid-leap. His wispy hands clamped around her neck, digging his razor-sharp claws into her soft, pale flesh. A single drop of blood ran down her collarbone, seeping into the white fabric covering her breasts.

Adeline stared into his glowing red eyes. There was a fierceness behind them that would have terrified her in the past, but this time, she knew something he didn't. When Sebastian's creature-like form gripped her harder, a villainous grin spread across her face.

"Go ahead and kill me if you like. Either way, you won't be leaving this room alive."

He snarled at her.

Adeline laughed. "I'm not scared of you, my love."

He shook his head and growled again, this time only an inch from her face. *I haven't been your love for centuries!*

Suddenly, Adeline's face went stone cold. "Release me right this minute…or I'll slaughter your precious Avery…" She snapped her fingers.

Within seconds, Sebastian heard Avery screaming.

STOP! He shouted into Adeline's mind. *Don't hurt her!*

"Release me…or she's dead."

The tone of Adeline's voice and the feral look in her eyes sent Sebastian's instincts into overload. He quickly returned to his human form and took a step back.

"That's a good boy," Adeline taunted. Then she snapped her fingers again. Immediately, Avery's horrible screams ceased. "I should probably go check to see if she's okay," Adeline whispered as she casually stepped through the archway leading back into the tunnel.

The savage-like expression on her face caused bile to rise into Sebastian's throat. He ran after her, slamming into a magical wall that now divided them. Her devious grin was the last thing he saw as she disappeared down the corridor.

Sebastian pummeled the invisible wall, but it held firm. Just like the barrier in the Smart's house, it was unbreakable. He was in the process of healing himself when he heard Avery start to scream again.

He called out to her distressed mind. *Hold on, Av. I'll figure out a way to get you safely out of here!* Sebastian looked up. There were no bars on the ceiling or floor, just solid rock. So, he slammed his fists on the ground, causing the entire cavern to rumble in protest. Punch after punch, he pummeled the floor.

Adeline reappeared in the doorway. "STOP!" she shouted. "You'll bury us all!"

Sebastian ignored her and continued to slam his mighty fists against the granite floor.

"Stop him!" Adeline ordered.

Instantaneously, three men dressed entirely in white stepped inside the veiled room. They were gigantic, the size of mammoths. There was no way Sebastian could take them all on. Not without some serious luck…which did not seem to be in the cards for him as of late. He was racking his brain to come up with a plan, when all at once they removed their cowls, revealing their glowing eyes; each set a deep, amethyst purple. Sebastian's morale promptly faltered. The three burly men standing before him were the three remaining Pure Ones. The strength possessed by just one of them outweighed his by an incalculable amount.

Sebastian reached out to his mentors' minds. *Dray? Hale? Kade?*

None of the Pure Ones looked him in the eye. It was as if he were a meaningless stranger to them all.

"Without purity, they are tainted," Adeline whispered. "They belong to me now."

Sebastian tried to push into their minds again, but the doors were locked, blocking him out. He surrendered without a fight as Dray grabbed hold of his shoulders and shoved him forward.

"Well, that was rather disappointing," Adeline declared unhappily. She stepped into the room with her hands on her slender hips. "I expected more from you."

Sebastian glared at her as he was ushered past. He may have been outnumbered, overpowered, and totally helpless, but he still held his head high. If he was going to die down here, then he would perish with his dignity intact. He just hoped that he would be able to get Avery out safely first.

"Bring the girl as well," Adeline ordered. "I want her to bear witness to this!"

"NO!" Sebastian shouted. His jaw still ached, but it was healing quicker than he expected. "Please, Adeline…spare her. I'll do anything you ask. Just please don't hurt her further!"

Adeline stared into his soft grey eyes that were full of desperation. She sighed as she tucked a few wavy strands of hair behind his ear. For that brief moment, Sebastian thought he had reached her softer side, but he could not have been more wrong.

She grabbed hold of his shirt and pulled him down towards her. He could feel her warm breath as her lips brushed against his cheek. "Begging is beneath you!" She spit out each word with so much hatred.

And with that, Sebastian was taken away…still begging Adeline to spare Avery's life. He was dragged down into one of the oldest dungeons deep within the mountain. He knew exactly what this particular room was for. After all, he had brought his share of 'traitors' down here back in the day. Many Cursed Ones, who had been accused of betraying the Pure Ones after they had lost their humanity, were brought here to die. The dank, dark room still smelled of death.

Soft footsteps approached as Adeline stepped inside. Beside her was the Dark-Warrior who broke Avery's wrists. He had her unconscious body draped over his shoulder. Her face was covered in dirt and smeared with blood; her hair was knotted and matted to her forehead.

A threatening growl rose up from Sebastian's throat as the Dark-Warrior opened the cell closest to him and tossed Avery inside. When she landed, her head slammed against the solid rock floor. She groaned slightly as she struggled to lift herself up, but her broken wrists refused to hold her weight as her hands flopped sideways.

Against his better judgment, Sebastian made a break for the open cell door. The Pure Ones didn't even blink as he rushed past. Hale grabbed Sebastian's forearm and twisted so hard that it snapped.

Sebastian screamed so loud that it came out as a mighty roar. "PLEASE!" he shouted. "Heal her! Don't leave her there to suffer like that!"

Adeline rolled her beautiful blue eyes as she stepped inside the cell with Avery. "Ugh, you're so pathetic!"

Sebastian held his breath, unsure of what Adeline was about to do.

She grabbed a handful of Avery's hair, pulling her up off the ground.

"Adeline stop!" Sebastian hollered. He wrestled against Hale's hold, even though his broken arm was burning in disapproval.

Adeline ignored him. "Would you like that, Avery? Would

you like me to take your pain away?" The tone of her voice was pretentious at best.

Avery whimpered. Her nose was running down her dirty face as tears poured from her puffy, swollen eyes.

"I. Can't. Hear. You," Adeline sneered.

"Y-Y-Yes," Avery stammered.

Adeline faked a frown. "Aww. Say please!"

"ADELINE!" Sebastian shouted her name with strict authority.

"Relax, my love. I'll heal her..." Adeline reassured him warmly. "When I'm done playing with her."

Sebastian fought with every ounce of strength he had within himself to escape his captors, but it was futile. The Pure Ones soon bound his hands behind his back and gagged him so he couldn't speak. In any other situation, in any other place, Sebastian would have been able to rip through the chains and heal himself, then reach Avery before anyone knew what hit them. But here in this sanctuary...every weapon, every door, and every form of restraint had been bound with the Pure Ones' magic. He was completely powerless.

Hale and Dray tightened their grasp on Sebastian's biceps as the Dark-Warrior wheeled over a tray full of medieval weapons.

Sebastian screamed and cried and struggled to free himself unsuccessfully. *Adeline, stop! Please, I'm begging you! Don't do this!*

She sighed and looked directly at him. "You have to understand that everything has consequences."

With that, the Dark-Warrior handed Adeline a 'morning star'. She tested the weight of the wooden handle as she pricked her finger on each of the sharp spikes covering the small, steel ball. "This one is perfect."

NO! Adeline NOOOOO! Sebastian turned his face back to Dray. *Please! Dray, help her! Avery is an innocent! We never harm innocents! She doesn't deserve this!*

Dray's face remained unchanged as he continued to stare straight ahead.

Sebastian watched helplessly as Adeline raised the spiked

weapon above her head and then slammed it down with so much force that the 'morning star' went straight through the middle section of Avery's right foot, obliterating the bones on impact, before embedding into the stone floor.

The earsplitting shriek that followed was unlike anything Sebastian had ever heard before…and never wanted to hear again.

A split second later, when Adeline forcefully dislodged the weapon, Avery screamed again. Her entire body began to tremble from shock.

Sebastian immediately reached out to her mind. *Oh, God Av…I'm so sorry I brought this upon you. Just stay focused on me, okay? Look at me, sweetheart!*

Avery began choking on her own sobs as she reached down, trying to cup what was left of her foot in her trembling hands. Three of her toes had been completely severed off. The other two were barely hanging on as blood squirted and poured from her mutilated appendage. She wanted to reach out to Sebastian's mind. She wanted to ask him why all this was happening…to beg him to help her…but she was unable to form even the simplest word or thought. Pain was all she knew now. Indescribable, incessant pain.

Tears spilled from Sebastian's eyes. *Look at me, Av. Stay with me…*

Avery began seeing double as she forced her blurry eyes to connect with his. Her breathing was rapid and shallow, and her entire body was shaking so hard that it looked like she was having a seizure. They both knew their situation was beyond critical at this point. One, or both, of them may not make it out of here alive.

"Next!" Adeline ordered wickedly.

The Dark-Warrior placed a large wooden cudgel in Adeline's awaiting hand.

She studied the thick club carefully, running her fingers over the heavy splintered wood. "Simple yet satisfying."

Avery screamed again while writhing in agony on the floor. She pushed herself backward with her left foot in an attempt to get further away, but there was nowhere to go. Blood pooled all around her, filling in the multitude of cracks on the stone floor.

Sebastian was screaming at the top of his lungs, but the gag muffled them to minuscule grunts. He struggled against the Pure Ones' iron grasp, knowing he wouldn't be able to slip out of their grip, but he was still going to try. His throat was on fire, and his eyes were overflowing with tears, but Adeline blocked him out. She didn't want to hear his pleas anymore.

Her face partially contorted to her Cursed Form as a malevolent grin reached her eyes. She raised the cudgel high above her head, letting it hover there for a few intense seconds to instill more emotional misery into Avery, who was already clearly terrified.

Sebastian reached out to Avery once more. *Keep your eyes on me, Av. Don't look at her! Don't focus on what she's doing! Just keep your eyes on me!*

Avery was crying so hard that she was barely able to breathe, but somehow she tore her terror-filled gaze away from Adeline and stared helplessly at Sebastian.

That's good, sweetheart. Just look at me. It's just you and me now. You're going to be okay.

Avery knew that was a lie.

Tears streamed down Sebastian's cheeks as he reassured her over and over that she was going to be okay. That everything would be fine.

Then Adeline struck the weapon down exactly three times. Each hit was so fast that Avery never had a chance to react. First, the cudgel crushed Avery's left knee with a loud crack…then her right knee. Lastly, Adeline swung it as hard as she could straight at Avery's face.

The slow-motion impact caused Sebastian to swallow down his own vomit as he heard every bone in her beautiful face shatter at the exact same time.

Avery's eyes widened with fear and unimaginable pain as she fell backward against the stone wall. She wanted to die. She tried to open her mouth to plead for her own death, but her fragmented jaw wouldn't move.

Adeline tossed the bloodied weapon down. It clattered to the ground with a reverberating clang just before she climbed on top of Avery's body and stared down at her prize.

Avery braced herself for another blow. This time, though, Adeline used her fists.

Sebastian wriggled and battled against Hale and Dray's hold…willing to do just about anything to get free. *ADELINE, STOP! YOU'RE KILLING HER!*

The final beating was so brutal that Avery's small human frame would not be able to take much more. Sebastian could hear her heart straining to keep her blood pumping. With each beat, more and more red liquid flowed out of her broken and battered body. The entire floor of the cell was now drenched in a shallow red pool.

Avery, don't you dare give up! You have to keep breathing! Stay alive! Please…

Adeline started screaming at the top of her lungs. "A LOVER'S GRASP SHALL BE YOUR FATE! YOUR DYING HEART THEY'LL NEVER TAKE! FOR ONCE YOU UTTER LOVE'S THREE WORDS! THE DARKENED FORM WILL BE RETURNED! DENY THE CURSE AND DEFY THE NIGHT! THE TAINTED BLOOD WILL DESTROY THE LIGHT!"

Suddenly, she stopped. She flipped her long, bloodstained hair behind her and let out a breathless, contented sigh. "Jealous rage really doesn't suit me, but I feel much better now."

HEAL HER! Sebastian ordered to Adeline's mind. *YOU SWORE!*

"Let me relax a moment to catch my breath…then I'll heal her!" Adeline smiled. Her sterling white teeth were spattered with red speckles and smudges.

A single moment turned into many as Adeline still refused to heal Avery, who lay dying only a few feet away, her heart barely beating now.

PLEASE, Adeline! Sebastian pleaded again. *I'll do anything!*

Just don't let her die!

Adeline strolled over to him and ripped off the gag. "You'll do...anything?" she asked mischievously.

He nodded quickly as he glanced back at Avery. "Anything."

Adeline licked her lips and walked back into the blood-soaked cell. She placed her hands gently on Avery's chest and closed her eyes. "This is for you, Sebastian."

A brilliant flash of purple light lit up the entire room. When the brightness faded away, Avery's wounds had all been closed, and her bones had been reset. Sebastian listened intensely. The seconds seemed endless while he waited...and waited...and waited...until finally, Avery's heart began to beat faster. A few minutes later, it regained a normal rhythm.

Sebastian was so overcome with joy that he began to weep. "Thank you!" he cried out.

Adeline shut the cell door and locked it behind her. "Now...I've kept up my end of the deal. It's your turn to give me my *anything*."

"What is it that you want?" His tear-filled eyes were darting back and forth between Avery and Adeline. He didn't care what was about to be asked of him. Avery was alive! That fact alone had him on such an emotional high that he was willing to comply with whatever the hell the crazy bitch wanted.

"Just a kiss," Adeline replied nonchalantly.

His brow furrowed as his gaze zeroed in on hers. "Just one kiss?"

"A real kiss," she rectified. "I want you to kiss me like you did when you loved me. I want to feel your true passion again."

One insignificant kiss was nothing when it came to keeping Avery safe, so Sebastian agreed.

Adeline immediately pressed her body against his, running her bloodied hands up and down his chest. "Oh, how I've missed this," she moaned. Standing on her tip-toes, she grabbed handfuls of his hair and pulled his face closer. She nibbled his lower lip before pressing her mouth firmly against his.

Sebastian could taste Avery's blood as Adeline slipped her tongue past his lips. At first, he fought it, barely engaging with her, keeping his body rigid and reserved…but then her voice echoed in his mind.

You're holding back, my love. Kiss me like you did when you loved me…or I'll keep your precious mortal here…torturing her every single day for the rest of her pathetic life.

The thought of Avery being kept here, having Adeline and her Warriors doing God-only-knows-what to her for hours…days…years, made his stomach twist. For he knew Adeline meant what she said. So, he did what he had to do. He slipped his tongue into her mouth and swirled it with hers.

Adeline continued to run her fingers through his hair, caressing his neck and shoulders, pulling his body hard against hers as if the closeness wasn't close enough. *Your bindings are going to be removed; then you're going to touch me like you used to.*

Abruptly Sebastian pulled away, staring at her as if she were out of her mind. *That wasn't part of the deal.*

She stroked his cheek with her fingertips. *That was before we had a captive audience.*

Sebastian could now see Avery from the corner of his eye. She had regained consciousness and was currently staring in their direction.

"Bastian…what…what are you doing?" she asked, clearly confused.

Adeline put a finger on Sebastian's lips to keep him from answering. Then she turned her focus to the Pure Ones. "Release him."

They didn't question her. They didn't hesitate. They simply removed the bindings and tossed them on the ground.

Sebastian's arms fell limp at his sides; his left one angled awkwardly due to the break.

Adeline gently touched his forearm, instantly mending the bone with just a glimmer of purple light. "There. Now that that's taken care of…" She linked her hands around Sebastian's neck dotingly. "Where were we?"

He didn't comply. Instead, he glanced back at Avery.

Her green eyes were shimmering with unshed tears. "Bastian?" she squeaked.

Adeline was growing increasingly agitated. *I suggest you play your part, my love, before I tire of your uncooperative behavior!*

Sebastian's eyes stayed locked on Avery's. "Forgive me..." he whispered.

Without any indication of hesitation, he wrapped his arms around Adeline's waist pulling her flush against his body, grinding his hips against hers as if they were making love in a vertical position. He brushed his lips against her mouth, lightly kissing down her chin and jawline, down to her neck. Adeline giggled gleefully as Sebastian shoved her against the cold stone wall. He started kissing her so vigorously that for a single moment, he forgot he was only acting.

Avery averted her eyes as she blinked away more oncoming tears.

Then as quickly as it started, Sebastian pulled away. He and Adeline were both breathing heavily, their faces flushed from exertion.

He scowled at her despondently. *Debt paid.*

Adeline moaned softly and touched her face with her hands. "I had forgotten how amazing you are. Thank you for that sweet reminder. I may want another taste later..."

Sebastian looked at the ground, utterly ashamed of what Avery must think of him now.

"It's time for me to freshen up," Adeline stated merrily. "I'll leave you two alone to get reacquainted."

When she snapped her fingers, the Dark-Warrior re-shackled Sebastian's wrists behind his back and forced him into the cell next to Avery's. Then he and the three burly Pure Ones followed Adeline into the outer corridor.

"See you both soon," she said sweetly.

The solid alloy door was slammed shut, leaving Avery and Sebastian alone in absolute darkness. As the heavy footsteps faded away, Sebastian reached out to Avery's mind. He was too humiliated to speak to her out loud.

Are you okay?

No reply.

He tried again. *Av, can you hear me? Are you okay?*

Avery could hear him just fine, but she couldn't bring herself to give him an answer. She cringed when she thought about Sebastian's hands touching every inch of Adeline's perfect body. A body that just happened to be covered with her very own blood. The disgusting images she had just witnessed toyed with her mind, repeating on a loop over and over…and over again. Her heart felt like it had literally been ripped right out of her chest. She was angry and cold and scared. She had just been tortured to the brink of death, still sitting in a puddle of her own blood, and yet, seeing Sebastian kiss and touch that horrible woman was the only thing on her mind.

Sebastian was crumbling internally as he listened to Avery crying quietly to herself. He tried again to reach out to her mind. *Avery…please talk to me. I need to know that you're alright.*

She couldn't bear to hear his voice anymore, so she slammed the door shut in her mind, locked it, and then threw away the imaginary key.

Sebastian flinched as he was forcefully blocked from her thoughts. Simultaneously, his heart constricted in his chest. His head was reeling as tears threatened to fall.

It was silent for a few more moments until Avery's voice broke through. Her words were barely a whisper, but they cut through his heart like a razor blade ripping through flesh.

"You still love her, don't you? That's why you never wanted to be with me."

An anguished expression covered his face as he gaped in her direction through the darkness. "NO!" he shouted. "No! Av, please wipe that thought from your mind!" He shifted his body so he was able to get onto his knees, then he shuffled his way closer to the bars that separated them. "Avery, I don't love her. I haven't loved her for well over a century." *It's you that owns my heart.* For half a second, he toyed with the idea of actually saying those words out loud.

Avery sniffled and then let out a distressed whimper. "Then

why, Bastian? Why would you…touch her…kiss her?" Her voice was a tiny squeak by the time she finished.

Sebastian leaned his forehead against the cool, metal bars and sighed. "I told her that I'd do anything to save you." He paused and sighed again as tears stung his eyes. "She was killing you, Av... I was listening to your heartbeat fading away. I had to do something…anything to make her heal you." He paused again as his voice cracked. "I would have never done anything like that on my own accord. I swear on my life that I didn't want to... You must believe me. Please…"

A heavy sob escaped Avery's trembling lips as her entire body began to shake.

"I'm so sorry," he whimpered. "I just wanted to save you."

He closed his eyes, pushing his projected form into the next cell. He could see perfectly now as if he had on night vision goggles. Avery was in the far corner, curled in on herself, hugging her legs to her chest. Her face was buried in her knees while she was crying. Sebastian felt his heart physically split in two. He knelt beside her, placing his hand on her shoulder.

She gasped and sat up, wiping her shoulder again and again. "Someone is in here with me!" she whispered.

He could hear the sheer panic in her voice, so he opened his eyes, causing his wispy projection to rush back into his body at lightning speed. "Avery, calm down!"

"No," she argued. Her terrified voice was getting higher, "I think there's someone in here with me!" She flailed her arms in the darkness. "Get away!" she whispered frantically. "Get away from me!"

"Avery, there isn't anyone else in here. It's just us."

"But someone touched me!"

At that very moment, Sebastian realized that somehow, against all odds, she must have actually felt his projected presence as if his physical body had been in the room. Maybe it was the immense power emanating from the Pure Ones' magic in this place, he wasn't exactly sure, but this fascinating fact temporarily took his mind off what was happening to them. He could hear Avery shuffling around in her cell, probably punching at the air while crying hysterically.

He tried again to calm her down. "Avery, I need you to listen to me." His voice was gentle but stern. "I need you to calm down. Can you do that?" He thought he heard an *uh huh* through her whimpers, which was close enough. "I want you to close your eyes and imagine me next to you." As he was telling her what to do, he closed his eyes as well. He felt himself drifting across the darkened room once more. When he found her again, she was curled up in a ball in the middle of the cell.

"I'm scared, Bastian," she squeaked, "...and I'm so cold." Her eyes were squeezed shut, and her entire body was trembling.

"I'm here with you now. I'm going to hold you, okay?"

"Okay," she whimpered.

He laid down beside her and wrapped his arms around her, pulling her close.

She gasped and began to panic all over again.

"It's just me," he said quickly. He shushed her a few times. "It's only me! I'll prove it to you, okay? I'm going to touch your cheek." He gently brushed his projected fingers across her cheek bone.

Her body began to relax. "How did you get through the bars?"

"I didn't."

"But I can feel you," she whispered. "How is that possible?"

"I'm not sure."

"Please don't leave me," she begged.

Sebastian nuzzled her closer. "I won't, I promise."

CHAPTER 37

Sebastian awoke on his side of the pitch-black dungeon. He could hear Avery's gentle breathing in her cell as two separate sets of footsteps were rapidly approaching.

"Avery!" Sebastian whispered. "Psst...Avery, wake up!"

She groaned softly.

The heavy latch on the thick alloy door scraped open.

Avery sat straight up and quickly crawled over to the bars that separated her from Sebastian. She reached out to hold his hand, then realized he was still bound behind his back. Her concerned eyes found his as a line of light poured in from under the door. "You were able to sleep like that?"

"Not comfortably, but being able to hold you...even in my projected form, made it bearable."

She smiled momentarily as more tears filled her eyes. "I don't want to die like this, Bastian. I want so much more out of my life. I just..."

Sebastian's facial expression wavered. "You're not going to die here, Av. You'll have everything you've ever wanted. I swear it." He swallowed hard as the thick metal door fully opened. There was so much more that he wanted to say, but he had run out of time.

Both of their hearts began to race as Adeline and her Dark-Warrior stepped inside.

"Sleep well?" Adeline asked. "I did. On my comfortable mattress with lots of fluffy pillows…and then I had breakfast in bed…"

"Drop the pleasantries, Adeline," Sebastian snarled. He grunted and groaned as he struggled to stand up. "Let's get this over with!"

"No!" Avery cried out. "Bastian don't!" She barely grazed her fingers against his arm before he was out of reach.

"He doesn't have a choice!" Adeline snapped. "At least he's smart enough to know that!"

Sebastian flashed Avery his dazzling smile, dimples and all. The door to her mind was open again, so he spoke directly to her. *I'll be alright*, he assured her. *I've been through worse.*

The Dark-Warrior unlocked the cell door and pulled Sebastian out with so much momentum that he lost his footing and stumbled right into Adeline's awaiting arms.

She smiled a twisted smile. "Remove his shackles and hold him down."

Two out of the three mammoth-sized Pure Ones suddenly appeared. Hale and Kade.

Avery shouted obscenities at the top of her lungs as the Dark-Warrior began removing Sebastian's metal bindings carelessly, ripping and tearing his skin in the process.

Sebastian's forearms and hands were now covered with deep scratches and small punctures, though not once did he cry out.

"Now…bind him with these," Adeline ordered ruthlessly. She placed a strange pair of handcuffs in the Dark-Warrior's hand. Inside each shackle was a sharp spike that ran straight through the center.

Sebastian's eyes widened as he recognized the device. *Cuffs of the Crux.* "Adeline, no!" His gallant exterior dissolved into a cowardly demeanor in an instant.

Adeline chastised him. "So, you can dish it out, but you

can't take it?"

"I'm not the sick, sadistic monster that I was back then!" he replied curtly.

The corners of Adeline's mouth turned up. "Aren't you, though?" She snapped her long, bony fingers again.

The bigger of the two Pure Ones, Kade, slammed Sebastian down on the granite floor, holding him by his throat with one hand as the Dark-Warrior prepared to attach his new restraints.

Sebastian refused to give in so easily this time. He fought with every ounce of strength that he had left. As he allowed the rage to empower him, he could feel his Cursed Form beginning to take hold, but Adeline was already one step ahead. She grabbed his forehead, digging her fingernails into his skull, pushing her essence deep into his mind. His head started twitching from side to side as if he were having a seizure. Suddenly, his body went rigid, and his eyes began to bleed a dark purple liquid.

"What are you doing to him?!" Avery shrieked frantically. "Stop it! Stop it, please! You're hurting him!"

Adeline's gleaming purple light began to fade as she retracted her nails. "You haven't seen me hurt him…yet!"

The Dark-Warrior didn't waste any time. He opened the first shackle and grabbed Sebastian's left wrist. Avery screamed in horror as she watched the three-inch spike penetrate straight through Sebastian's wrist, then it was latched to the other side of the cuff. But Sebastian didn't scream. He didn't flinch. He didn't move. Whatever Adeline had done seemed to have completely immobilized him.

Maybe that means he isn't feeling any pain, Avery thought optimistically.

Then she noticed a single tear falling down Sebastian's cheek; followed by another, then another.

He was, in fact, screaming and roaring and howling inside of his own mind, but he could not physically react. It was like being trapped inside his own personal hell with no chance of relief or escape.

Sebastian felt his right wrist being lifted up. He felt the

sharp stick as the point touched his flesh. Then he braced himself for the second spike to pierce all the way through. When the pain came, it was worse than the first time. He could feel his muscles and tendons being split apart…his nerves and veins being sliced in half. The bones were the worst part of it all. He felt the breaks immediately. The earsplitting pop echoed in his ears as the radius was fractured and the ulna snapped clean in two. Sebastian's terrified eyes were locked onto Avery's. She began crying hysterically as she struggled to reach out to him through the bars of her cage. Tears were streaming down his face as his wide eyes stared at everything and nothing at the same time. His vision came and went as he drifted in and out of consciousness over the next few minutes. Shortly thereafter, Avery dropped to the floor as her stomach turned inside out.

The Dark-Warrior pulled Sebastian's arms up with a quick jolt, sending another wave of mind-numbing pain shooting throughout his entire body. The throbbing sensation made him feel dizzy and nauseous. Then the Cuffs of the Crux were attached to a large hook swinging from a bulky chain overhead. The chain ran across the entire length of the room, ending at a large lever on the wall near the door.

"Raise him up," Adeline ordered.

The Dark-Warrior obeyed. As the chain was pulled tighter, Sebastian's arms were lifted into the air. He moaned and cried out internally as Avery begged the Dark-Warrior to let him go.

While hanging there, Sebastian's feet were still planted firmly on the ground, sparing his arms from bearing the full weight of his body. When Adeline noticed a flash of relief cross his face, she ordered for him to be raised higher. The Dark-Warrior turned the lever once more, causing the chain to rattle and clink as it was pulled tighter. Sebastian was barely on his tip-toes now as the paralysis finally began to wear off. He let out a strained howl as the metal spikes shifted inside his flesh.

Sebastian reached out to her mind. *Adeline…it doesn't have to be like this.*

She ignored him, tapping her fingernails carelessly against her chin as she began to circle him, letting her gaze drift up and down his outstretched body as she prepared her next move.

Sebastian's breathing was coming and going in short, fast bursts as dark red trails of blood continued to trickle down his arms, saturating his t-shirt and causing the dampening fabric to cling to his skin. His hair was sticking to his face, blocking most of his vision as his head lulled to one side. Feeling disoriented from the constant spasms of pain, he was having trouble keeping balance on the tips of his toes.

Avery was shouting something in the background, though Sebastian couldn't quite focus on what she was saying, but Adeline seemed to be enjoying the heightened sense of fear that was quickly filling the room.

"Hand me the urn," Adeline told the Dark-Warrior, who instantly obeyed. Her lips turned up into a wicked smile as she reached inside. When she removed her hand, an orange gooey substance was dripping from her perfectly manicured nails. "I'm sure you'll remember this," she stated pleasingly.

Sebastian swallowed hard and leaned his head back in an attempt to get away, but Adeline placed her hand around his neck, pulling him forward. She lingered there for a few agonizing seconds before slowly sliding her sharp nails down his chest, cutting his bloody shirt in half; then she ripped it away completely. Sebastian closed his eyes and cringed as she ran her fingers tenderly down his bloodstained torso.

She leaned her head against his chest, listening to his rapid heartbeat. "You're frightened," she stated humorously. "How interesting."

Her smile faded as she began circling him again, studying every curve and crevice of his perfectly contoured body. When she was standing directly behind him out of his field of vision, she tapped her tainted nails against the base of his spine.

Sebastian knew what was coming then.

Adeline slowly pressed her nails into his skin, twisting her pointer finger just enough to make a small slit in his flesh. "I'm sorry, my love," she said sadly. The distress in her voice sounded real this time. "…but you know what I must do."

Sebastian's jaw clenched as he growled and grunted through gritted teeth.

"What are you doing to him?!" Avery demanded.

Adeline didn't waste time answering such a trivial question from a stupid, annoying mortal. She sliced open a larger section of skin on Sebastian's lower back and then her hand began to tremble. Adeline quickly realized that she would not be able to go through with her plan unless she eradicated her love for him. *He doesn't love you anymore,* she told herself. *He doesn't care about you. You're nothing to him now.* She continued her personal inner spiel for quite some time while her fingers hovered over the small of Sebastian's back. *He hates you,* she told herself. *He loves…Avery.*

At the mere mention of Avery's name in her mind, Adeline regained her merciless composure. Without so much as a second thought, she plunged her tainted nails deep inside his body. There was a small clicking sound when she reached his spine; followed by a wail from Sebastian's mouth, which was so loud that the entire cavern shook, causing small pieces of granite to fall from the ceiling.

Avery shrieked and averted her eyes, thinking that Sebastian's spine was about to be ripped out of his body like a scene from one of those gory slasher films.

Instead, Adeline quickly grazed his spinal cord. Scraping it just enough to allow the poison to enter. Not even a moment later, she retracted her hand and sealed the wound with her purple glow. Then she wiped her bloody poison-covered hand on her long, elegant, white dress. "This is for reassurance that you won't be able to heal during your…session."

Sebastian sighed helplessly as he felt the neurotoxin starting to take effect. He had been taught this sick ritual in the past. He remembered feeling an extreme amount of guilt whenever he had to torture or kill his fellow Cursed Ones. He had to turn his humanity off each and every time in order to get the job done. Looking back, he could see how foolish he had been, but at the time he believed he was doing what was best for the Pure Ones' legacy. Little did he know that their morals had died with Ivez when their purity was ripped away.

Sebastian gritted his teeth and waited for the new waves of pain that he knew were coming. A millisecond later, his legs gave out, putting the full strain of his one-hundred-eighty-pound frame on the spikes inside his wrists. He screamed and shouted and pleaded for mercy as he struggled to grab hold of the chains above, but his fingers kept losing their grip.

"Mercy comes from love," Adeline purred. "You rejected my affections. Any leniency for you is unlikely." With that, she turned to the Dark-Warrior. "Finish the job."

She and the two Pure Ones left swiftly, leaving Avery and Sebastian alone with her ruthless minion.

The Dark-Warrior's eyes began to glow as he eased his partially disfigured face closer to Avery's cage, scowling and growling only inches away from the bars.

She took a couple of steps backward, returning his scowl, but not looking away.

The Dark-Warrior was suddenly intrigued. His lips turned up slightly. "You're not frightened of me?"

She didn't answer. She just continued to stare.

He abruptly turned around without another word and stood in the open doorway. "Lady Adeline," he called out. He must have explained himself directly to her mind because when she returned, she had a disapproving expression on her face.

"Sebastian, you've been a very naughty boy! Revealing yourself to this mortal girl, yet somehow she still has a fondness for you…that must mean you finally managed to find a loophole to my mother's curse."

Sebastian refused to acknowledge her words or her presence, which outraged Adeline to her core.

She let out a monstrous roar as she transitioned to her Cursed Form right there and then.

Avery staggered backward. "What in God's name…?!"

Adeline's Cursed Form held no resemblance whatsoever to Sebastian's demonic mist-like creature. She looked more like an abnormally deformed gargoyle. Indented and misshapen. Bent and disproportioned. Twisted and mangled. Adeline snarled in Avery's direction as her claws clickity-clacked on the cold stone floor. She paced back and forth, pressing her crooked, bulbous nose through the bars.

Avery pressed her body against the far wall and let out a terrified squeak.

Adeline's gargoylic-form laughed in response with a deep frenzied cackle.

"Leave her alone!" Sebastian commanded firmly. He was in no position to be barking out orders, but he had to get the negative attention away from Avery.

Adeline spun around. Her long canine fangs were dripping with saliva. She leaned closer, snorting and growling dangerously close to Sebastian's throat. He didn't move. Instead, he spit directly into her face, knowing he would pay for that childish act…probably with his life…but for that moment it was totally worth it.

Adeline's oversized paw gripped Sebastian's shoulder, digging her inch-long talons deep into his flesh. He grunted loudly, holding back a scream. A vicious grin spread across her hideous face as she began to drag her talons over his shoulder and down his chest. Sebastian let out a high-pitched shout as his defenseless body was slowly mutilated. Avery cried out repeatedly in the background, continuously losing her stomach contents as blood poured from Sebastian's gaping wounds. Just before Adeline's nails reached his ribs, she started to transition back to her human form. The claw marks got smaller and smaller as she continued to move her hand lower and lower on his torso. Just before she reached his belt, she withdrew her nails one by one, his face flinching with each retraction.

"Now comes the fun part," Adeline purred excitedly.

Avery and Sebastian both gulped at the same time.

The Dark-Warrior stepped forward, wielding an eighteenth-century dagger with intricate markings carved into the hilt, exactly like those etched on the Strap of Virtue. As his hand began to glow, so did the markings.

Avery watched Sebastian's face instantly drain of color.

The Dark-Warrior's thick boots thumped noisily against the stone floor. Each thud bringing him closer and closer to Sebastian's weakened and vulnerable body. The Dark-Warrior glared at his victim, wanting his glowing red eyes to be the last image Sebastian would see before his death.

"You don't...have to do this," Sebastian said weakly. Blood continued to drip onto the floor beneath him.

The Dark-Warrior looked toward Adeline, then Avery, and finally back at Sebastian. He repeated Adeline's words. "All choices have consequences. This...is yours." Without any hesitation, the dagger was brought up to Sebastian's throat, the sharp end of the blade pressing against his larynx.

Avery screamed.

"Do it...slowly!" Adeline commanded wickedly. "I want him to feel each and every centimeter of his flesh being sliced away as his essence is absorbed into the blade." She smirked and then added, "...while his little wench watches."

The Dark-Warrior nodded and pushed the blade just enough to pierce through the top layer of Sebastian's skin. A trickle of blood ran down his neck, filling the tiny indentation in the center of his clavicle.

"STOP!" Avery shouted through tear-filled eyes. "Please just stop!" She was gripping the rusted bars so tight that her fingers were turning white. "Please...I beg you. Don't take him away from me!"

Temporarily stunned by the despair in her voice, the Dark-Warrior unintentionally lowered the dagger.

Adeline's vicious gaze was now focused in Avery's direction. "Why do you care so much about this worthless disgrace of a man?"

"Why do you hate him so much?" Avery countered. "What could he have done to deserve all this? He's a wonderful and caring person! How can you do such horrible things to him?!"

Adeline sneered in her direction. "Wonderful and caring? That monster," she raised her voice as she pointed her bony finger in Sebastian's face, "...is a murderous leech who caused my death! He deserves every bit of torture that I plan to bestow upon him…which may include watching you die if you're not careful how you speak to me, mortal!"

"YOU WON'T TOUCH HER!" Sebastian roared.

Adeline suddenly reached through the bars and grabbed hold of Avery's hair.

Avery cried out in response as she struggled against the iron-like grip.

A sly grin spread across Adeline's angelically evil face. "And how do you plan on stopping me?" she taunted. Then she jerked Avery forward, slamming her face against the bars, shattering her nasal cavity.

Sebastian let out a long, deep, frustrated scream. He stared helplessly as Avery lay unmoving on the floor. Her hair was covering her face, but he could smell the blood that was now flowing from her nose.

Though Avery was unconscious, Adeline continued to speak as if she were still listening. "My death was the result of his mere existence!" She turned to face Sebastian. "I was working on a spell that would have saved you from the curse my mother was going to place on you…"

"I never…knew that," he replied softly.

"Of course, you didn't!" she seethed. "I burned alive before I got the chance to tell you!"

Sebastian's memory flashed back to that heartbreaking day. For a short while, he was able to tune out the current predicament he was in. He momentarily overlooked the horrible person Adeline had become and thought back to the time when she was a beautiful, kindhearted woman. A woman whom he once loved. "I can't take it back…and I can't alter the past…but I can try to…make it right…with the time we have now. Please, Addie…"

As the tragic memories faded away, Sebastian stared into Adeline's grief-stricken eyes. He was tied up, broken, and bleeding, yet he was more concerned with how he could help her move past her internal distress.

After a long moment, she finally spoke. "I appreciate the

apology, my dear Sebastian…but in all honesty, my heart has been hardened for far too long. The Addie you knew is long gone. I'm afraid it's too late now."

Sebastian opened his mouth to protest. "Adeline, please…"

She put her finger over his lips. "It's too late."

With a snap of her fingers, the Dark-Warrior was instantly by her side. And at that exact moment, Avery came to, groaning quietly as she gently touched her bloody, broken nose.

Sebastian's eyes darted in her direction just as a flash of silver plunged into his right side. He cried out in anguish.

The Dark-Warrior removed the blade in one swift motion, spilling blood all over the floor like a broken water valve that had burst open.

Satisfied that Sebastian's fate had been sealed, Adeline walked away, shutting the massive steel door behind her.

Shortly thereafter, the Dark-Warrior stabbed Sebastian seven more times. Twice in the back between his shoulder blades. Three times in the lower stomach. And twice in his left side. But the torture still wasn't over. Sebastian's arms and legs were brutally slashed, again and again, weakening his essence to the point of no return. The pain was so overwhelming, and each blow came so fast, that Sebastian couldn't even cry out. His face would contort into a scream…his mouth hanging open and his eyes bulged…but no sound followed.

All the years of training he had been given to hide his feelings and emotions from his enemies were completely worthless in these moments.

The Dark-Warrior finally positioned himself behind his victim as he brought the blade up to the center of Sebastian's throat. "The end has come for you, Warrior."

Sebastian held back a sob. "Avery…I need you…to look away now."

"I can't!" she squeaked. Her bloody, tear-stained cheeks glistened in the dim light from the lantern.

"Please," Sebastian begged. "I don't…want you…to see this." His voice seemed to be getting weaker by the minute.

"No!" Avery shook her head. "This can't be the last image I have of you!"

The Dark-Warrior closed his eyes, preparing his final assault.

"NO! PLEASE!" Avery shouted. "PLEASE DON'T!" She could feel the bile rising in her throat again.

"Wait!" Sebastian cried out hopelessly. "I don't...want her...to witness this!"

Surprisingly, the Dark-Warrior slowly lowered the blade. The red in his eyes gradually faded back to a pale blue as he turned his head away. "Make it quick," he stated in a harsh voice.

Sebastian made an effort to shift his body in Avery's direction. His tip-toes barely brushed the slippery, bloody floor as he painfully pulled himself up on the chains to turn slightly to the left. He grunted and whimpered as the metal spikes tore deeper into his wrists.

"I can't lose you..." Avery cried out despairingly. "Not like this! This can't be the end! Not when we never even had a chance to begin!"

He wanted to feel her loving arms around him, even if only for a second. "My last request..." he said weakly.

The Dark-Warrior waited.

"I need...to hold her...one last time."

Avery could not stop crying. "I don't want it to be the last time! Please just let us go...please! Oh, God...please..." She was in full-panic-hyperventilation-mode now. Her heart was beating so fast, and her breathing was coming in such quick bursts, Sebastian feared she might faint.

The Dark-Warrior's stance seemed to soften as he placed the bloody dagger on the table. He unlocked the cell door and swung it open. Avery yelped and backed away, but the Dark Warrior stepped aside and headed straight for the lever on the wall. With one quick spin, Sebastian crumpled to the floor with a loud thud.

"Go to him," the Dark-Warrior ordered.

Avery hesitated, looking back and forth between them.

Then Sebastian whispered her name. "Avery... Come to me...please."

She immediately rushed past the Dark-Warrior and raced to Sebastian's side. She knelt down beside him, lifting his head into her lap. She stroked his sweaty, blood-soaked brow and brushed his hair away from his face. Images from the first time he died in her arms slowly crept into her mind. She just could not stop crying.

The Dark-Warrior turned his back respectfully.

"Bastian...I'm so sorry!" Avery leaned her forehead against his as tears ran down her face, dropping onto his cheeks.

He sucked in a labored breath. "I don't have...much longer. I need you...to unhook...my restraints."

Avery shook her head. "No! I'm scared to even touch you! I don't want to make your pain worse."

Sebastian forced a smile just for her. "The pain of...removing them...will be less than...leaving them in." He raised his unsteady arms up as high as he could manage, which wasn't very high at all; and he was trembling so hard that the chains were rattling.

Avery briefly glanced at the Dark-Warrior, who was standing only a few feet behind her.

"He knows...I can't heal," Sebastian stated sadly. "...so, he...won't stop you."

Avery finally got her hands to stop shaking long enough to unhook the first shackle. She closed her eyes as she quickly pulled the huge spike out of Sebastian's wrist. He roared and shook violently in her lap as blood poured out of the wound. She dropped the cuff on the ground and wrapped her arms around his neck.

"I can't do this!" She was becoming hysterical again. "I can't be the one hurting you!"

Sebastian reached out to her mentally since he had momentarily lost the will to speak. The pain was just too much. *I know this is difficult for you, but I can't do it on my own. I need you, Av. I always have...and I always will.*

Avery's heart broke into a million pieces. "Please don't

make me do that again…please!"

Just one more time. He held up his other arm. Blood was seeping out, dripping onto the floor, and forming a small red pool in her lap.

Avery clicked the latch open. "I'll count to three," she told him. "One…two…three…" She slipped the last spike out, flinging it across the room.

Sebastian's screams seemed to last forever that time. And there was so much blood. Avery was surprised he was still conscious, let alone alive. As she gently pulled and tugged him closer, he wrapped his mangled arms around her, hugging her as tight as he could…which wasn't very tight at all. She could literally feel his life fading away…again.

Avery turned toward the Dark-Warrior, who still had his back toward them. "Please heal him!" she choked out. "I'll do anything. I'll give you anything!"

The Dark-Warrior stared at her over his shoulder, his eyes showing a fleeting glint of confliction. "I can't. I'm sorry. Lady Adeline's orders."

"Please!" Avery begged again. "Take me instead."

"NO!" Sebastian tried to yell. "Don't you…dare!" He used what little strength he had left to keep a hold of Avery's hand, but she easily slipped out of his delicate grasp.

"Take me instead," she repeated.

Sebastian rolled onto his stomach, trying to crawl toward her. *Av, don't! Avery, please…come back to me!*

The Dark-Warrior met her serious gaze. "My orders are to dispose of him…not you."

"Make an exception," she pressed. "Please!"

"DON'T…HURT HER…I BEG OF YOU!" Sebastian shouted as loud as he could before he collapsed back to the floor.

Avery sprinted back to his side, cradling him in her arms again.

"You've seen his Cursed Form?" the Dark-Warrior suddenly asked.

She nodded while staring at Sebastian, though that memory

seemed lifetimes ago.

"Why didn't you run?"

She tore her eyes away for a split second to stare at the Dark-Warrior, confused.

"When you saw his Cursed Form," he repeated, "why didn't you run?"

Avery laughed. Partly out of nervousness and partly out of irony. "I couldn't. He killed me first."

Sebastian tried to smile. "Not one...of my...finer moments."

The Dark-Warrior seemed overly interested to hear more. "How did you bring her back?"

Sebastian let out a shallow breath. "With a...piece of...my essence."

A single tear ran down Avery's cheek, landing on Sebastian's hand that was now barely clutching hers.

"Was it painful?" the Dark-Warrior pressed.

Sebastian sighed as he began to feel hazy. "Not as...painful as...the thought of...losing her...forever." Suddenly, he started gasping for air.

"No!" Avery cried out. "NO! No, no, no!"

Sebastian knew he didn't have long now. He was literally on death's door with his foot in the entryway. He wouldn't have the time nor the strength to tell her everything, so he pushed into her mind. He gave her the only thing he could. *Avery, I want to show you how I imagined our life together...*

As she heard his sweet voice in her mind, bittersweet images began to play in her thoughts like short little movies. **Sebastian was down on bended knee, his trembling hands holding onto hers for dear life, asking her to marry him. In an instant, it switched to their wedding day, surrounded by all their friends and family. She heard him say "I do" as he pressed his lips tenderly against hers. The picture shifted again. They were buying their first house with a huge fenced in backyard. She saw herself pregnant, sitting on the front** *porch swing. Sebastian was kissing and talking sweetly to her belly, rubbing the baby-bump tenderly with his palm. Next, she watched a little boy with Sebastian's adorable dimpled grin and a little girl with his beautiful grey eyes, playing in their back yard. Both were chasing a small, black dog while smiling and laughing and giggling.*

Avery was in utter shock, wishing she reach into her head and make those precious thoughts a reality.

Sebastian reached up and used what little energy he had left to heal her broken nose. *No matter what happens after I'm gone, please don't lose hope. Never forget…how much…I…*

Suddenly, Sebastian's entire body jerked with a violent spasm before going completely limp. It took a few intense seconds for Avery to realize that he had just died in her arms…again.

She screamed and cried and squeezed his bloody, battered body closer. "This isn't how it was supposed to end! You're supposed to be here with me! You promised to keep me safe! You promised you'd get us both out of here! You lied to me, Bastian! YOU LIED TO ME!" She turned her puffy, tear-stained face toward the Dark-Warrior. "Bring him back! Right now! Please, *oh-my-God*, please bring him back!"

"Why do you love him?" the Dark-Warrior asked. His face was stoic…as if this were just a normal everyday conversation…as if he didn't just torture and kill someone.

Avery's shock-ridden body wasn't sure how to respond. She was crying so hard that she couldn't see anymore, and her sobs kept getting caught in her throat, choking her. She wanted to punch the Dark-Warrior right in the face and then tear him apart. She glanced at the bloody dagger on the table nearby…and for a second, she toyed with the idea of stabbing him with it. She wanted to make him feel every bit of suffering that Sebastian had endured. It was the least he deserved after killing the love of her life. "What kind of question is that?!"

The Dark-Warrior narrowed his eyes and repeated the question. "Why…do you love him?"

She sniffled and attempted to compose herself. "Because he

saved me," she said sadly as she stroked Sebastian's cheek. "In so many ways he saved me. He made my life worth living. He is my everything!" She choked back a sob. "He...was my everything."

"Would you really do anything to bring him back?"

Such a stupid question. Avery nodded without taking her eyes off Sebastian. She just continued stroking his cheek.

"Then I may have a way."

Avery eyed the Dark-Warrior suspiciously. She wasn't sure if he was being truthful or just mocking her pain. "Why would you help us now? You just killed him...by order of that horrible bitch!"

The Dark-Warrior briefly looked away. "For decades I was forced to believe that all hope was lost for people like us." He gestured between himself and Sebastian. "But now I see that not all curses are meant to last forever. You helped to break his curse. I now have hope that I too may find love one day."

Another tear slid down her cheek, and Avery felt herself smile involuntarily as she thought about how much she loved Sebastian. "What would I have to do to save him?"

"You have to forget."

Avery's forehead wrinkled. "Forget what exactly? Everything that happened today? Done! Let's go, right now!"

The Dark-Warrior sighed heavily and shook his head. "You'll have to forget...him. Completely. It's the only way Lady Adeline may agree to do this."

Avery's mouth fell slightly open as she glanced back at Sebastian's lifeless body. "So, I won't remember a single thing about him? How we met...how much he means to me...or what we went through over the past few days? Nothing at all?"

The Dark-Warrior nodded once. "It will be as if he never existed. Your memories of him will be completely eradicated and replaced with someone else of significance in your life."

She blew out her breath and swallowed hard. Sebastian had tried to erase himself from her mind once before. That painful memory gripped her broken heart. She briefly wondered if she were to agree to this, would he leave her alone so the two of them could live out their lives separately? Or would he still come for her and try to make things right again?

Though she took her time to give the Dark-Warrior an answer, the decision had already been made. "If he'll live…I'll forget," she finally said.

CHAPTER 38

Sebastian woke up feeling rather disoriented. He forced his tired eyes open as he looked around, slightly puzzled. He was lying on a luxurious couch in an unfamiliar room. He blinked a few times in an attempt to clear his blurry vision as he stretched out his aching joints. *Where am I?* He glanced up at the painted stone ceiling. An oversized replication of Vincent van Gogh's 'Starry Night' covered the entire length of the dome-shaped roof. He was still clearly in the Pure Ones' sanctuary, but the last thing he recalled, was dying in Avery's arms for the second time in his life.

Then a familiar voice broke his concentration. "Ah, good...you're awake! The groggy sensation you're currently experiencing will wear off soon enough, and then you'll be good as new."

Sebastian immediately leapt to his feet. The hasty movement caused him to become light-headed, and he quickly lost his balance and fell backward over the couch. When he managed to find his footing, he swiftly moved as far away from Adeline as possible. "Where is she?!" he demanded. "What have you done with Avery?!"

Adeline sighed deeply. "You're healing at an exceptional rate, my dear Sebastian. Your most recent memories should not have returned so quickly. I had hoped you and I could have gotten to spend a little more time together before reality slapped you in the face."

Sebastian fully regained his clarity as he trudged towards her. "I swear to the gods if you've done anything …"

"Save it!" Adeline said condescendingly as she raised her hand to cut him off. "First of all, I don't answer to you. Secondly, I haven't done anything to your sweet, pathetic Avery. She's fine."

Sebastian was mere moments away from becoming unhinged. "I don't believe you! Where is she?!"

"Bring me the girl!" Adeline demanded aloud.

As if waiting for his cue, the Dark-Warrior dragged Avery in. She was limp and lethargic, barely able to stand.

A warning growl reverberated in Sebastian's throat as he readied his stance for a fight.

Adeline held up her pointer finger and smiled wickedly in his direction. "Just give me one moment, my love, and I promise everything will become perfectly clear." Then she grabbed hold of Avery's arm and jerked her closer. "Do you know this man?" Adeline asked as she gestured toward Sebastian.

Avery could barely move, let alone shake her head as she stared him right in the face. She seemed to study him for only a second. "No…I don't know him," she answered softly.

Sebastian felt his entire body tense up all at once as he recoiled in utter shock. "*What?*" He immediately reached out to touch her, caressing her cheek tenderly. "Avery…tell me what happened. What did they do to you?"

Adeline sidestepped, putting herself directly in-between them and pushed him back.

"What have you done to her?" Sebastian growled.

Adeline paid him no mind. Instead, she turned back toward Avery and faked a frown. "My dear girl, this man found you wandering around in the woods at the base of the mountain.

You would have died from hypothermia if it hadn't been for his bravery. You should thank him before you say goodbye."

"LIAR!" Sebastian shouted. He took a step closer to Avery. "You know me! You have to remember who I am! Just look at me...look at my face. You must remember something, anything!" Anguish filled his heart and soul as he stared at her vacant expression. "You're so much stronger than they could ever imagine...so I know you can undo whatever damage that's been done to your mind! Think, Av! Push through the mental block!"

Avery seemed confused as her brow furrowed, but a second or so later, her face went blank again. "Thank you for saving me," she whispered.

Adeline pat her on the head. "That's a good girl." Then she snapped her fingers once again.

Two more Warriors dressed entirely in black entered the room, their eyes glowing red. More Cursed Ones.

Adeline instructed them to take Avery back to her hometown. "Make sure she gets home safely. I'm sure the police were notified after her disappearance, so alter however many minds you need to, but leave no signs that you were ever there."

They both nodded as they half dragged, half carried Avery away.

Sebastian felt completely helpless. "No, wait! Av...you need to listen to me..."

But Avery didn't turn around.

Sebastian rushed forward, slamming face first into that damn magical wall again. He cussed under his breath. He couldn't protect Avery. He couldn't save her. All he could do now was stand idly by, watching and listening. But at least she was leaving this horrible place. That was the one good thing he could hold onto.

Adeline let out a contented sigh. "See, my love, I'm not so cruel and heartless after all. It would seem that I still have some compassion left in me."

Sebastian let out a low growl and staggered towards her.

The Dark-Warrior caught his arm and reached out to him mentally. *Don't! It's exactly what she wants you to do.*

Let. Me. Go! Sebastian snarled.

The Dark-Warrior's eyes narrowed. *I know you have no reason to trust me, but I need you to try.*

Why would I ever trust you? Sebastian countered back into his mind. *You tortured me for hours! You murdered me! You tampered with the mind of the woman I love! You're just as evil as Adeline!*

Sensing that violence was sure to ensue, Adeline excused herself, leaving the two Cursed men alone to continue with their private dispute.

The Dark-Warrior suddenly removed his cowl, revealing his entire face for the first time. His angry features seemed to soften, though his eyes still glowed brightly.

Sebastian stared at him for a moment, backing up slightly. *I know you…*

The Dark-Warrior's mouth relaxed. *Yes.*

A memory tugged at the back of Sebastian's mind. It was right there, but he couldn't access it. *How?*

The Dark-Warrior began unbuttoning his shirt, revealing a multitude of scars covering his entire torso.

Sebastian looked away in disgust. *I tortured you?*

I'm not offended that you don't remember me. You were a busy Warrior back then.

Sebastian cringed. *My how the tables have turned*, he thought to himself. Then he looked the Dark-Warrior in the eye. *I'm sorry.*

The Dark-Warrior rebuttoned his shirt and straightened his posture. *I suppose you could say that we're even now.* There was a hint of sarcasm in his voice.

Sebastian wasn't sure how to reply to that, so he just looked away.

The Dark-Warrior's voice entered his thoughts once more. *So, you truly care for that mortal girl, don't you?*

Just the thought of Avery filled Sebastian with another bout of despair as he stared down the narrow passageway where her heartbeat was slowly getting further and further away.

The Dark-Warrior took a step closer. *She begged me to save you. That girl of yours is quite relentless to get what she wants.*

Sebastian couldn't help but smile at that statement, but a second or so later his smile faltered. She wasn't 'his girl' anymore. She didn't even know him now.

~*~*~*~

The rest of Sebastian's day went by in a blur…and he spent most of it sulking by himself or sleeping. When night fell, Adeline removed the magical wall and brought him into the main cavern. He was surprised by the multitude of bodies wandering about. Most eyes were glowing red, only three sets were purple.

"Have you changed more humans?"

Adeline's twisted smile gave him the answer, though she verbally replied anyway. "A few here and there."

A few? he thought to himself. *More like a few thousand!*

"I was bored with the limited amount of company," she told him. As if that was supposed to make it alright.

As they made their way across the crowded cavern, he noticed the three Pure Ones standing against the back wall, away from all the Cursed Ones. Their vibrant purple eyes were solely fixed on him.

He was intrigued enough to ask the only question burning in his mind at that very moment. "How did your mother gain control of the Pure Ones…and pass the ability on to you?"

Adeline stopped short and turned around, a nefarious grin spreading across her face. "Would you like to see for yourself?"

Seriously? How could he say no?

Sebastian nodded eagerly as Adeline led him down a long, dark corridor tucked in the back corner of the cavern. He had to duck his head to keep from hitting the stalactites hanging from the cave ceiling as they made their way down. The temperature had dropped at least twenty degrees since they had begun their descent.

"Where are we going?" he asked, his voice echoing all around them.

"You'll see. We're almost there." Her voice bounced off the walls, entering his ears over and over. Then suddenly, she stopped. In front of them was a dead end, or at least it looked like one. Adeline placed her palm on the stone wall. A light purple glow pulsed, lighting up a small array of carvings that Sebastian hadn't noticed. The rock shook and wavered and then completely disappeared. Another magical veil.

Sebastian's eyes narrowed, searching the expanding darkness in front of them. His eyes began to glow, illuminating the cavern as he stepped inside. The room was small. Maybe ten feet long and five feet wide. Huge stalagmites grew up from the ground, making it impossible to walk very far. What captured his attention, though, was a large wooden coffin in the center of the room covered in dust and grime. He glanced back at Adeline as if asking permission to look inside.

She smiled as she gestured forward and then crossed her arms, casually leaning against the cave wall outside the doorway.

Sebastian stood at the foot of the coffin. He gripped the corners and gave a little tug, expecting some resistance. Instead, the old rusted nails broke in half, and the decrepit wood splintered, opening easily. He slid the lid to the floor, coughing quietly from all the dust before leaning forward. He expected to see the bones of some forgotten soul or maybe even some hidden treasure, but when the dust cleared, his wide eyes landed on the body of a man. No decaying flesh. No rotting smell. In fact, he seemed perfectly alive aside from the fact that his chest wasn't moving and he was as still as a statue. Sebastian's eyes glowed brighter as he took a closer look…then his breath caught in his throat.

Ivez?

"Amazing, isn't it?" Adeline's voice echoed loudly in the small room. "The long lost Pure One."

Sebastian could not take his eyes off of the body in front of him. *The missing Pure One? This isn't possible. This can't be real.*

Ivez had died long before Sebastian had become cursed. And his body was stolen shortly after his death, causing his existence to become a myth rarely spoken of. Nothing but a mere memory. Yet there he was. Alive-ish.

"How?" Sebastian asked. It was the only word he could find in his extensive vocabulary.

Adeline stepped beside him, placing her arm around his waist. "He was a gift."

Sebastian cast her a sideways glance.

"From my mother. She left some of her memories hidden within her essence. So, I found the unmarked grave, dug up the body, and brought him here."

That still doesn't explain how she took control of the other Pure Ones, he thought to himself.

As if she were reading his mind, she continued, "I can play the part of a damsel in distress quite well." She twirled her hair innocently around her fingers. "They took me in and welcomed me with open arms. Within a few days, I made my move."

Sebastian's eyebrows rose. "And what sort of move might that be?"

Adeline was clearly enjoying the attention he was giving her. "I thought for sure Ivez would have been drained dry and withering away, but to my surprise, he was still full of his life-giving blood."

Sebastian's chest felt tight. "You…you tricked his brothers into drinking his blood?" He couldn't believe what he was hearing.

Adeline seemed slightly annoyed now. "They didn't realize I was Moira's daughter. Their purity made them far too trusting. I simply put a drop of Ivez's blood in each of their goblets. Within a few days, all three of them belonged to me. Funny how something so insignificant could overtake three of the most seemingly powerful supernatural beings in existence."

Adeline's words struck down to the core of Sebastian's soul. "So…you're saying that you were here…in the sanctuary…before I left? But I never saw you…I would have sensed you! And you said…"

She cut him off. "I had to finish what my mother started. And you didn't sense me because I didn't want you to. My essence is far more powerful than yours, remember? Though, by the time I returned to claim what was rightfully mine, you were gone."

In that one moment, everything that had always been so complicated and unsettling about his past finally started to make sense. All the sudden changes in his mentors that had caused him to flee. All the violent and destructive behavior that seemed to go against everything they should have stood for and claimed to believe in.

Oh. My. God. Sebastian felt sick as he glanced back at Ivez. The horror of the lost Pure One's situation was finally sinking in.

Ivez was alive. Lying there in a dreamlike state...or coma, for the lack of a better word. Fully aware of his surroundings. All his senses still working. Conscious, yet stuck inside his own mind and body.

Sebastian took a step closer, angling himself so that he could look into the Pure One's eyes. They were distant and glassy, staring at the ceiling. But Sebastian knew Ivez could still hear, see, and feel, though he was unable to move or speak. What a terrible way to spend eternity. He wanted to speak into Ivez's mind, hoping he would be able to hear him, possibly even respond. The door to the Pure One's mind was ajar, so Sebastian gently pushed it open.

Ivez, can you hear me?

Nothing.

Ivez? My name is Sebastian. I'm a Cursed One. I was a Warrior for your brothers long ago.

Ivez's eyes glistened, but he remained perfectly still.

You can hear me, can't you? Sebastian felt a rush of excitement, though he had to keep it hidden from Adeline.

She was still rambling on about her terrible deeds over the last century, probably hoping it would impress him. Occasionally he would nod in response as if he were listening, but he kept most of his attention focused on Ivez's frozen face.

I will find a way to get you out of here.

All at once, an overpowering ache spread throughout his

head. Sebastian clutched at his temples, trying to will the sudden rush of pain away. Then he heard a loud, booming voice enter his mind.

DO NOT TRUST HER!

Sebastian accidently let a gasp escape, shifting Adeline's concerned gaze in his direction.

"Are you alright?" she asked. Her hand still lingered around his waist, tugging him closer.

"I'm not feeling well," he lied. "I think I need to lie down." He glanced at her, then back at Ivez.

I don't trust her. And I will find a way to free you.

There was no reply this time, but Sebastian hoped that Ivez had heard him. He watched in quiet misery as Adeline slid the coffin's lid back into place. He felt horrible knowing how dark and lonely it must be in that cold, splintered box.

Adeline ushered him out of the miniature mausoleum, using her purple glow to replace the stone wall, before heading back up the long passageway.

Sebastian grimaced as he passed by Dray, Kade, and Hale still standing against the back wall. Their vacant, expressionless eyes stared back at him.

I'll save them, he thought to himself. *I'll release them from Adeline's hold and restore their purity. Somehow. Then their true order will return.*

CHAPTER 39

Avery woke up in her bedroom, face down on her bed. She pushed herself up and wiped the drool from her chin. Her arms ached, and her head was spinning. Really, there wasn't any part of her body that didn't feel sore. *What in the world did I do to myself?*

She dragged herself into the bathroom and turned on the shower. As she began to undress, a scream erupted from her mouth. She stumbled backward so she could see herself in the full-length mirror hanging on the back of the bathroom door. Her long, dark hair was knotted and filthy, sticking out in every direction. Her eyes were puffy and bloodshot, looking like she had been crying for days. Her clothes were torn and splattered with various dark brown stains. She wracked her brain for an answer, but nothing came. *Memory loss, unexplained rips in my clothes, stains of an unknown substance covering my body. Was I drugged? Could these stains be blood?* She checked herself over. No cuts. No scrapes. No bruises.

Avery pushed aside her frenzied thoughts and tossed her ruined clothes on the floor. After her shower, she made her way into the kitchen where both of her parents sat at the dining table, chatting and eating breakfast as usual. They smiled as she joined them.

"Well, good morning sleepyhead!" her mom said cheerfully.

"Sleep well?" her dad asked.

She stared at them both. "Did I...go out last night?"

Her question seemed to have caught them off guard.

"Go out?" her mom repeated. She glanced at Avery's dad and shook her head. "No, you were in bed by eight o'clock. You seemed really tired."

Hmm. Avery's head was reeling. "Did I seem...okay? Like, was I upset or anything?"

Again, her parents exchanged glances.

"You seemed just fine," her dad replied. "Why do you ask?"

"The clothes I slept in were...dirty," she stated, deciding to leave out the rips and possible blood stains.

Her dad smiled at her. "Ah. Well, you did help your mom work in the garden for a bit. Maybe that's where the dirt came from."

"Oh?" *Since when did mom have time to be pulling weeds? The woman barely gets any down time between work and sleep.*

"I'm sure that's all it was," her mom agreed. "Nothing to worry about."

But Avery was worried. Something strange was going on. She heard her phone ringing in her bedroom, so she excused herself. Valerie's name flashed across the screen.

"Hey, chickadee!" Avery answered happily.

"Where. The. Hell. Have. You. Been?" Valerie was clearly pissed-off.

Avery dropped down onto her bed. "What do you mean?"

"What do you mean, what do I mean? You've been MIA for days!"

Days? That can't be right.

"The only way I'm going to let this go is if you tell me you were off somewhere romantic with Sebastian."

"Who?"

Her best friend suddenly gasped and then giggled. "So, you

were off with him? I knew it! What did you do? Where did you go?"

"I…I don't know who you're talking about," Avery replied honestly.

Valerie scoffed. "Whatever. Play dumb, but I want details later! I'm just glad you're back home safe."

"Yeah, okay," Avery tried to pretend like she knew what her best friend was talking about. "So anyway, what are you up to today? Wanna hang out?"

"Sorry my lovely, can't today. I've got a date with Chase tonight!"

Avery rolled her eyes and smiled. "Of course, you do."

"Well, you'd know all about that if you had touched base with me before you disappeared, but whatever! We definitely need to catch up later. I wanna hear all about your um, adventure…or whatever you were off doing. And I've got some equally juicy details for you too!"

"Yeah…okay. I'm sure you do…"

"Well," Valerie cleared her throat. "I'm off to get beautified! Again, I'm glad you're back home! Love you!"

"Love you, too! Have fun."

Cue the giggling. "Oh, trust me, I will! Buh-byes."

~*~*~*~

An hour had gone by since hanging up with Valerie and Avery had yet to leave her room. She sat on the edge of her bed holding her favorite book in her hand: 'The Fault in Our Stars' by John Green. She had read it a million times but never got tired of it. A smile crept across her face as she leaned back against her fluffy pillows and turned to the first page. *One million and one.*

Somewhere between chapter three and chapter four, her phone went off again. She checked the caller and answered on the third ring. "Hey, Jonah."

"Oh, thank God, you're okay! Where is Sebastian?"

There was that name again.

"How did you escape? Did they hurt you?" Jonah continued.

So many strange questions. "Ummm…" She drew out the word, unsure of how to answer his plethora of off-the-wall inquiries.

"Hello? Av?"

Avery cleared her throat. "I'm still here."

"Screw this phone bullshit. I'm almost to your house. I hope you don't mind the company because we need to talk! We've been so damn worried about you two!"

"Okay…um, see you soon then." Avery placed her cell phone down beside her book on the nightstand. *Why is everyone acting so weird? Talking about things that never happened. Asking about people I don't know. Has the entire world gone mad…or is it just my friends and family?* She heard a car door slam outside. "That must be Jonah," she stated to herself as she got to her feet.

Jonah waltzed into her house after only knocking one time. He flew past her parents, barely acknowledging them, and then slammed her bedroom door shut behind him, locking it.

Avery's eyes widened. Alarm bells started going off in her head as he lumbered toward her. The frenzied look on his face was rather unsettling.

"What…in the world are you doing?" She backed away as she spoke.

Jonah grabbed her by the shoulders, looking at her for a few seconds and then pulled her into his arms for a tight embrace. "I wasn't sure if I'd ever see you again," he whispered. He backed up then. "So, tell me how you escaped…and where is B? My parents are going out of their minds trying to find him."

Avery blinked a few times before pushing him away. "I honestly have no idea what you're talking about."

A puzzled expression came over his entire face. "You don't…" His brow furrowed deeper. "You don't know what I'm…?" He was positively confused. "This isn't funny!" he finally said.

"I'm not trying to be funny," she replied.

Jonah grabbed her upper arms and squeezed, leaning his face closer to hers. When he spoke, it was through gritted teeth. "Where. Is. He?!"

She winced. "Let go of me! That hurts!"

Jonah lowered his voice. "I will… When you tell me where B is!"

Avery wiggled and squirmed in an attempt to get out of his firm grip. "I don't know who the hell you're talking about! Now let me go!"

Jonah's face suddenly went pale as he released his hold on her arms. "You…you really don't remember him?" His voice was just above a whisper.

Avery rubbed her arms. "No, I don't!"

"SHIT!" Jonah shouted. "Shit, shit, shit!" He punched her closet door.

"What the hell is wrong with you? Have you lost your frickin' marbles?"

Jonah ignored her as he took out his cell phone and started dialing someone's number. "Chase? Yeah, I don't care if you're almost to Val's…listen, Avery's back. No, she doesn't know where he is. No, she doesn't. I don't know!" Jonah paused and sighed heavily. "She doesn't remember him, bro! Yeah, you heard me right. Exactly! Okay, meet me at home in twenty."

Avery was glaring at Jonah while still rubbing her arms.

"I'm sorry," he told her. "I'm really, really sorry." Then he walked out of her room.

A few minutes later, she heard him drive away. *What. The. Hell!*

CHAPTER 40

Jonah parked in his driveway, raced up the walkway and flung the front door wide open, yelling at the top of his lungs for his parents to get their asses into the living room. Not the best of manners, but this was an emergency! He didn't even wait to catch his breath before telling them all about Avery's memory loss and the fact that Sebastian was still nowhere to be found.

Over the next half hour, Elliot and Isabelle were on the phone with every Watcher they had ever come into contact with, trying to find the secret location of the Pure Ones' sanctuary. Jonah and Chase continued to reach out to Sebastian mentally. They had been trying for the past few days with no luck, but with Avery's return, a renewed sense of hope filled them both.

"Why doesn't he answer?" Chase asked. The pressure of mental telepathy was giving him a headache, so he leaned back against the couch and took a break.

Jonah sighed. "Maybe he can't because he's too far away."

They were both thinking the same thing, but neither of them dared to say it out loud.

Chase closed his eyes and fought against the oncoming

tears.

Jonah leaned back next to his brother. "B isn't…" His words came out in a weak whisper. "We'd know if he were gone."

That last sentence seemed to cheer Chase up a bit. "Yeah. As his Watchers, we'd know."

Jonah smiled half-heartedly.

Suddenly, Chase jumped to his feet. "Holy shit, dude! We are so frickin' stupid!"

Jonah leaned forward. "What? What are you talking about, bro?"

Chase looked at his brother as if an idea were about to burst through his skull at any moment. "Some of the old Watcher journals. Didn't they have maps in them?"

Jonah stood too and slapped himself on the forehead. "Why didn't mom and dad think of that?"

Chase shrugged.

"We have," their dad replied, unexpectedly appearing behind them.

"The sanctuary is clearly marked in at least three of them," their mom added. Her voice was soft and quiet, almost as if she had hoped they wouldn't hear her.

Jonah and Chase stared at their parents, both of their mouths hanging slightly open. "And we're still sitting here on our asses and making pointless phone calls because…?"

Elliot and Isabelle exchanged wary glances.

Chase and Jonah did the same.

"What are you not telling us?" Jonah finally asked.

"If Sebastian truly is at the Pure Ones' sanctuary, there's…nothing we can do for him. We can't fight an army of Cursed Ones on our own, let alone the Pure Ones."

Jonah was seething. "Like hell, we can't!" *How can they just give up like this? Why in God's name didn't they tell us? Why did they allow us to continue believing we were going to try and rescue him?* He glanced over at his brother.

Chase was already looking back, shaking his head. His breathing was uneven, and his fists were balled up at his sides.

"This is bullshit!"

"This is exactly why we didn't say anything," Isabelle said softly. "We didn't want to upset either of you."

"This is utter bullshit!" Chase said again. Then he stormed out the front door.

Jonah followed his brother, not bothering to waste his breath speaking to his parents.

Chase was leaning against the porch railing with his back to his brother. "You realize we're going to have to do this without them, right?"

Jonah nodded. "The thought had crossed my mind."

"We can't waste any more time. Who knows what's happened to Bas already! We have to go tonight!"

"We can't just take off unprepared, bro. That's exactly what we scolded B for!"

Chase turned around with a confident expression. "Oh, we'll be prepared!"

~*~*~*~

In the wee hours of the morning, Jonah and Chase snuck out of bed; fully dressed and ready to start their quest. They tiptoed down the hall, pausing just outside their parents' room. Gentle snores were coming from the other side of the door, so Jonah motioned for Chase to keep moving. The boys quietly rustled through the bookcases in their dad's office a few doors down.

"I got one," Chase whispered.

"Me too," Jonah replied.

They flipped on their flashlights and turned to the last few pages in each journal. Inside they found two large maps and one page of handwritten scribbles with precise directions…at least they hoped the directions were accurate. They nodded toward each other, turning off their lights at the same time. Next stop was the kitchen to fill their backpacks with crackers, bread, bottles of water, and a few canned goods.

"Don't forget the can opener," Chase whispered. "Or we'll be prying those cans open with our teeth."

Jonah chuckled to himself as he carefully dug through the

utensil drawer. "Got it," he whispered back.

The boys quickly made their way toward the front door. As it clicked shut behind them, they both blew out a sigh of relief.

Chase grabbed his brother's shoulder. "We need weapons."

"B's place?"

Chase nodded.

They couldn't risk starting up either of their vehicles on the off chance that they might wake up their parents, so the boys headed toward Sebastian's house on foot.

A short jog later, both Jonah and Chase made it to their destination. As they approached the front porch, they slowed their pace. Making sure the coast was clear, they took turns stepping through the mirage and into the chaos that used to be the living room. A hidden cache was behind a panel in Sebastian's closet. The boys raided his weapon supply and then borrowed his spare set of car keys.

'Operation Rescue' was officially under way.

CHAPTER 41

"The Watcher who wrote this was a moron!" Jonah exclaimed.

Chase grumbled in agreement.

The maps were totally confusing, and the directions were completely and utterly useless. It had taken them five days, two falsified passports, a crap-load of hiking equipment, nearly their entire savings, and most of their sanity to find the stupid sanctuary. Then there was the problem of how to open the solid stone door hidden behind a magical veil, but their markings proved to know a lot more than they did. A simple touch of the wall and the boulder lit up with their brilliant blue hue.

Jonah and Chase were terrified out of their minds as they descended into the unknown. The long, narrow passageways were dark and cold. Each one seeming to go on forever.

Countless times they found themselves at a dead end. With a spewing of swear words, they would make their way back to the main path and try again. And unfortunately for them, their markings were doing very little to help them light their way, the cave was much too dark.

"Flashlights," Chase grumbled. "Why didn't we pack the

flashlights?"

Jonah shrugged in the darkness. A flashlight was the last thing on his distressed and distracted mind. The main thought that was circling around in his head was the fact that if they were to get lost in this endless maze, they would probably never make it out alive.

At least three hours had passed since the Smart brothers first found the entrance to the Pure Ones' sanctuary…and they still hadn't found the right path.

~*~*~*~

Sebastian had been locked away behind Adeline's magical wall for the last five days. She still didn't trust him to be wandering around on his own, which was actually smart on her part, because he definitely would have caused some trouble while trying to escape.

He was sitting alone, dwelling on unpleasant thoughts, when two familiar heartbeats filled his ears. They were super faint, but he knew exactly who they belonged to. *Jonah? Chase?*

A jumbled mess of words and shouts and cries came through all at once. Of course, they were both talking at the same time.

Sebastian's level of desperation had completely vanished. *One at a time! Where are you? How did you find me? Is Avery safe?*

Again, both boys were trying to reply at the same time.

ONE AT A TIME! Sebastian shouted. Then it was silent. He could only assume that they were discussing among themselves who should talk first.

Jonah's voice was the one that came through. *Holy shit, B, you're alive! We've been so worried about you! And yes, Avery is safe, but you should know…*

He finished Jonah's sentence. *…she doesn't remember me. Yeah. I'm sorry, man.*

It was quiet for a moment or so before Sebastian spoke again. *So, where are you? How many Watchers have you brought with you?*

Well, we're in the main tunnel. Not lost, but not exactly on track either. A nervous laugh came through. *It's just Chase and me.*

You're joking, right? Just you and Chase? Sebastian was flabbergasted.

Yeah, it's just us.

Sebastian's head started to ache. *Are you kidding me? Turn your idiotic asses around right this instant! If I can sense you two morons, and I mean that with all the love in the world, then soon every blasted Cursed One in this place will know you're here! Including Adeline!*

Jonah stopped walking. He hadn't thought about that.

"What's wrong?" Chase whispered.

"They're going to sense us."

As if a light bulb went off in Chase's mind, he swore under his breath. "We suck at rescue missions."

Sebastian's voice came through again in a rush. *It's too late! The Cursed Ones are being gathered in the main cavern. I can hear Adeline ordering them to find you! Get out of here now!*

We can't, B! Not without you!

J, this is no time to argue! I can handle myself. You two need to get back to the surface!

Jonah and Chase stood there silently, contemplating their options.

"Maybe we should go back," Chase whispered. "Now that we know where this place is we can bring back-up. Plus, if they already know we're here then the element of surprise is gone."

Jonah sighed as he glanced behind him at the small dot of light flickering in the distance. "We were so damn close."

The boys heaved their backpacks over their shoulders and turned to leave. In the same moment, they heard footsteps coming up the tunnel. Loud, heavy, fast footsteps. And lots of them.

It's too late, Jonah told Sebastian. *They're here.*

Seven pairs of red eyes shone through the darkness. They were trapped.

~*~*~*~

Shortly thereafter, Jonah and Chase found themselves in the middle of an enormous cavern surrounded by Cursed Ones. Adeline stood at the very front, staring at the boys with a wicked smile.

She raised her arms in a triumphant stance. "Ah, the guardians have finally come to save their dear friend." She was openly patronizing them. "You think two little mortal boys with limited Watcher abilities can stand a chance against me and my army of Cursed Ones?" She paused, no doubt hoping to make more of a dramatic effect. "Not to mention the Pure Ones who just happen to be under my control."

Jonah and Chase gulped and huddled closer together.

Sebastian's voice filtered into their minds. *Your parents are here! They must have followed you…and they're not alone! Stand your ground and buy them some time to get down here!*

Jonah's frustrated and fear-filled voice came through. *How in the world are we supposed to do that?*

Chase withdrew a dagger from his backpack and held it out in front of himself.

Adeline nearly fell over with laughter.

Sebastian pushed back into Jonah's mind. *What's happening? Chase is pointing a dagger…at Adeline.*

Sebastian snorted. *I said stall, not antagonize my psychotic ex!*

Jonah reached out for Chase's hand and started lowering the weapon. "We don't want a fight. We just want Sebastian back."

Adeline bit her bottom lip as a small smile graced her face. "Oh, is that all?"

Someone this beautiful and majestic should not be evil. It goes against nature.

Sebastian grunted to show his annoyance. *Thank you for that little bit of scientific information, J. Now can you concentrate on the task at hand? That majestic looking creature, as you just put it, will rip your throat out without batting one of her pretty eyelashes. FOCUS!*

Jonah cleared his throat. "Yes, that's all we want."

Adeline took a step closer, as did the Cursed Ones. The circle was starting to close in, getting smaller and smaller.

"STAY BACK!" Jonah shouted. He grabbed the dagger from Chase's hand and waved it around. "BACK UP, YOU FREAKS!"

Sebastian's voice came through again. *Your parents are almost at the end of the tunnel. Don't let your confidence falter!*

Adeline was standing an inch away from the tip of Jonah's dagger. He thought about charging forward and stabbing her directly through the heart, but he knew her reflexes were much faster than his. He would be the one with the dagger protruding from his body instead.

Just when all hope seemed lost, Adeline's eyes shot up. She looked toward the tunnel just as Isabelle and Elliot stepped into the cavern. "Aww, the cavalry has arrived just in time to save the day," she paused again. "NOT!"

Jonah and Chase's parents began to chant quietly.

"Your meaningless words have no power here!" Adeline stated confidently.

Suddenly, two more Watchers stepped from the entrance corridor, then two more, so on and so forth; bringing their total number to fifty-eight. Their chanting became louder and louder as their voices mingled together.

The Cursed Ones disbanded their circle around Jonah and Chase and turned their focus toward the horde of Watchers behind them. Then all at once, the ground beneath their feet began to rumble and shake.

Adeline gasped. "That's impossible!"

Jonah and Chase could hear Sebastian calling out to them. *What the hell is going on out there?*

The boys rushed down the nearest pathway toward the sound of their friend's voice as the cavern continued to rumble, causing rocks and small boulders to fall from the walls and ceiling.

Finally, Sebastian's face came into view.

"Come on, let's go!" Jonah told him.

"I can't," Sebastian replied.

"We have to go, now! The cavern is going to collapse." Jonah reached out and grabbed Sebastian's arm, tugging him forward. But it was like trying to drag a huge slab of cement.

Sebastian pulled his arm away. "I told you, I can't! The room is spelled."

"By who?" Chase asked.

Jonah smacked his brother on the back of the head and Sebastian gave him a snarky glare.

Chase's face reddened. "Oh…right."

Without wasting any time, Jonah headed for the doorway. "We'll be back," he promised. "We have to find a way to get Adeline to remove the barrier spell."

Sebastian shook his head without taking his eyes off his friends. "She won't do it. She'd rather see me die all over again than watch me walk out of her life. The shit she pulled with Avery proves that."

Jonah turned around; his face was more serious than Sebastian had ever seen before. "She'll do whatever we tell her to…or I'll kill her myself!" With that, Jonah and Chase ran out of the room.

~*~*~*~

The tremors from the Watchers' chanting continued to demolish the cavern and its infinite miles of tunnels. Most of the Cursed Ones had fled…or surrendered to save themselves from an untimely death by rock impalement. By the time Jonah and Chase returned to the main cavern where they had first entered, Adeline had transitioned into her Cursed Form. Two Watchers lay dead at her feet as she continued lunging, growling, and slashing at anyone who got too close to her. Thick, white foam dripped from her warped and misshapen mouth, making loud plunking sounds as it landed on the granite floor. She was acting like a rabid dog on the verge of an attack.

Eleven Watchers had carefully surrounded her, each of them holding a long, steel spear in their hand, slowly tightening their formation. Adeline lunged again, this time wrapping her large deformed paws around one of the spearheads. She pulled forward in one swift motion, jerking the spear away from its owner. The Watcher that had been holding onto the other end stumbled, nearly falling to the ground. Adeline then hurled the spear directly at his heart, sending it slicing straight through his body and exiting the other side. The Watcher landed hard on his knees and glanced down at his chest where the back end of the spear protruded. He coughed once, spraying blood out of his mouth, and then collapsed. That marked her third kill.

The remaining Watchers began chanting louder; ten of them aiming their spears high and thrusting toward Adeline, backing her into a corner. The cavern floor suddenly fractured. It dropped at least three feet and splintered, forming tiny spider-web-like cracks in every direction.

Jonah's voice echoed throughout the main cavern. "NOOOOOOOOOOOOOOO!"

Adeline's contorted face turned toward him just as her back hit the wall. She had nowhere else to go.

"DON'T KILL HER!" he shouted.

The Watchers weren't stopping; they were closing in. Soon Adeline would be dead, and Sebastian would be trapped in this dark cave-hell for the rest of eternity. There was no time to explain, not that anyone would be in the mood to listen anyway. Jonah did what his instincts told him to do. He dove in front of Adeline, blocking the path of all ten spearheads.

Everything after that seemed to be happening in slow motion. Jonah was soaring through the air before he had time to come to his senses. He could see Adeline bearing her teeth, snapping and growling at the Watchers as they continued pushing forward. His body came crashing down as he saw the flash of steel from his peripheral vision. Then the pain hit. A mind-numbing feeling that he had never experienced before. A spear had gone through his left shoulder, slicing straight through his muscles and tendons. The next spear hit his stomach. Jonah threw up. He couldn't help it. Another spear went through his upper thigh, severing his femoral artery. There was so much blood. And now there were loud screams and shouts erupting all around him. He could feel a gush of warm liquid shooting from his leg every time his heart would beat.

Sebastian was screaming into his mind, but Jonah was far too weak and lightheaded to focus on any of the words. Suddenly, he was lifted into the air. The scenery around him started to blur. His eyes opened and closed, each time his eyelids got heavier and heavier.

So, this is it, Jonah thought helplessly. *This is how I die.*

You're not going to die! Just hold on, J! Sebastian's words were barely a whisper in his mind, though the intensity behind them would suggest that he was shouting as loud as he could.

Sebastian was surprised to see Adeline's Cursed Form come barreling through the veiled doorway with Jonah clutched in her arms. She had a strange expression on her ferocious face, something between shock and sorrow. She transitioned back into her human form and placed Jonah on the floor at Sebastian's feet. The smell of blood filled the room as a puddle had already pooled beneath Jonah's butchered body. Sebastian's enraged gaze landed on her as he began putting pressure on the gaping hole in Jonah's thigh.

"He saved me," Adeline whispered. "I didn't do this! He jumped in front of me!"

Sebastian ignored her. He was too busy trying to shove his index finger into a severed artery to be bothered with her lies.

"He saved me," she repeated. "Why would he do that?" Adeline was beyond baffled…and if she would let herself admit it, she was feeling a little guilty.

"Why don't you shut the hell up and help me!?" Sebastian growled.

Surprisingly, Adeline dropped to her knees beside him. She put her hands on top of his and pressed down hard. "I can't heal him," she admitted. "The Watchers chanting…it's preventing me from…"

"Take off the ward," Sebastian ordered. "I'll tell them to stop so we can heal him together."

"And then what?"

Sebastian glared at her. "And then you will have saved the life of a boy who just saved yours! Isn't that enough?" *Cold-hearted bitch!*

Jonah's heart suddenly stopped beating.

Sebastian erupted, "REMOVE THE FUCKING WARD!"

Adeline's tough exterior crumbled as she closed her eyes and actually began to cry, but the magical veil disappeared.

Sebastian had not run so fast in all his life. He flew down the tunnel and into the main cavern, or what was left of it. He let out a roar so loud that it dropped every single Watcher and Cursed One to their knees.

"STOP THE CHANTING! JONAH IS DEAD!"

The cavern instantly fell silent.

Sebastian reached out to Adeline's mind as he raced back down the passageway. His heart was in his throat, and his entire body was shaking. *NOW! The chanting has stopped! Do it NOW!*

I need you, she told him. The tone of her voice sent a sickening feeling through his gut. *I need more power.*

As he entered the room, Sebastian practically jumped on top of her as he pulsed his red energy into her purple flames that were already covering Jonah's body.

A stampede of footsteps came running up the path. Isabelle and Elliot were in the front, with Chase close behind. No one said a word. Everyone watched as the precious moments ticked by.

Waiting.

Crying.

Hoping.

Praying.

Sebastian and Adeline connected into each other's minds...the power between them intensifying. *Healing thoughts. Healing words. Healing touch.*

Jonah's wounds slowly began to close. The flesh around each and every laceration began sealing right before everyone's eyes.

Healing thoughts. Healing words. Healing touch.

Bones crunched as they reset. Muscles and tendons stretched and reformed. Veins and arteries lengthened and reattached.

Sebastian and Adeline kept pushing. *Healing thoughts. Healing words. Healing touch.*

A few minutes later, to everyone's complete surprise, Jonah inhaled a small intake of air.

Healing thoughts. Healing words. Healing touch.

His blood began to circulate. His heart started beating steadily. His chest started rising and falling. And then his eyes fluttered open.

They had done it. Together. Jonah was alive!

Sebastian was so overcome with emotion that he mindlessly wrapped his arms around Adeline and squeezed her tight. *Thank you.* The embrace was quick and over not a moment too soon.

Jonah sat up and looked around.

Tear-filled eyes all stared back in his direction.

"What'd I miss?" he asked jokingly.

Isabelle, Elliot, and Chase rushed toward him. Their group-tackle-hug nearly knocked Jonah over.

Amidst the commotion, Adeline managed to slip out of the room and head back down the tunnel, but Sebastian was right on her heels.

"Going somewhere?"

She spun around in surprise.

"We still have unfinished business to attend to," he told her.

Adeline placed her hands on her hips. "And what business might that be?"

"The Pure Ones. Release the hold you have over them."

"Haven't I done enough?"

Sebastian held her gaze. "Not. Even. Close."

She sighed over-dramatically. "Dray…Hale…Kade…drain yourselves." She paused and sighed. "Leave enough blood to pump your hearts one final time."

The three Pure Ones instantly dropped to their knees in near perfect unison. Their white robes began turning a luscious shade of pink, then a deep crimson as blood quickly saturated the fabric. Dray's purple glow was the first to go out, Kade's followed shortly afterward, and Hale's was the last to fade away as all three of them simultaneously slumped to the floor. Blood continued seeping from every orifice on their bodies, quickly drenching the floor in a growing red puddle.

All eyes, both Cursed One and Watcher alike, landed on Adeline as if something had gone horribly wrong.

"Ivez is the key," she stated out loud, but she was looking directly at Sebastian. *The tainted blood has been extracted from all three of their bodies. I assume you know how the Purity Ritual works...but you'll need the three remaining Straps of Virtue to link them. They're hidden underneath Ivez's body.*

Sebastian immediately understood what he had to do. He nodded in her direction and then gathered a small group of Cursed Ones to help him clear the passageway leading to Ivez's secluded tomb...Adeline's Dark-Warrior was among them. Together they tossed the huge, heavy boulders away with ease. As they neared the end, Sebastian noticed the stone wall which led to Ivez's tomb had been broken in half from all the tremors, only the top part remained. He slipped inside and tore open the coffin's lid, carefully draping Ivez's stiff and motionless body over his shoulder. The Pure One was heavier than he expected. Even with his superhuman strength, he was struggling with the extra weight.

He pushed into Ivez's mind again. *I'm sorry it took so long, but everything is going to be alright.*

No reply.

Sebastian draped the leather straps over his other shoulder and stepped back through the broken opening. Motioning for the Cursed Ones to follow, he made his way back up the tunnel. They returned to the main cavern in time to see that the Watchers had finally managed to subdue Adeline. She was bound and locked in the same cell that Avery had been trapped in.

Sebastian pushed into her mind. *Ironic, isn't it?*

She scowled at him from the corner of her eye. *I guess you don't care what happens to me now that Jonah is alive again and the Pure Ones will be free.*

Sebastian sighed as he adjusted Ivez against his shoulder for a more comfortable position. *I won't allow the Watchers to harm you. I swear it.*

She didn't deserve his compassion or his mercy after

everything she had put him through, especially after all the torture and removing him from Avery's memory…but there he was, giving it to her anyway.

He walked over and handed the straps to Elliot, which were quickly bound to each of the Pure Ones' wrists, connecting them to each other until they formed three-fourths of a sphere.

Sebastian placed Ivez in the remaining spot beside his brothers, completing the circle. Three small groups of Watchers took their places at each strap. They laid their hands one on top of the other until their markings began to glow a deep, vibrant blue. Each of the groups took turns channeling their energy into the straps, causing them to glow brightly. The etchings on each one suddenly lit up, pulsing and fluctuating brighter and brighter with each passing minute. The Watchers' chanting started off as a distant whisper, slowly getting louder and louder, until their steady voices filled the cavern with their powerful words.

Dray was the first to suck in a deep, earth-shattering breath. Kade's was next. His body shuddered and shook as a gasp escaped his lips. Lastly, Hale took in a swift intake of air that was barely noticeable compared to his brothers.

Simultaneously, the etchings on the straps slowly began changing from the Watcher's brilliant blue to the Pure Ones' radiant purple glow. The three groups of Watchers released their hold on the straps and took a few steps back.

The purple glow was becoming so intense that everyone in the room had to shield their eyes from the burning light. When the brightness finally faded away, the Pure Ones were standing tall…all of them except Ivez. His body was lying perfectly still in the large puddle of blood from his brothers. Purple flames shot out of Dray, Kade, and Hale's eyes as they scanned the room, making eye contact with each and every soul in their presence. When their gaze landed on Sebastian, their powerful voices all spoke at the same time, somehow merging into one in his mind.

IT HAS BEEN A LONG TIME, YOUNG WARRIOR.

Sebastian suddenly felt the urge to bow out of respect.

Indeed, it has. He was instantly filled with fear. Fear that they were going to kill him and take his essence like they had tried to do weeks ago. He didn't dare project those thoughts, though they seemed to have heard him anyway.

YOUR NOBLE ACTIONS HAVE RESTORED THE PURITY IN OUR HEARTS, DRIVING THE TAINTED DARKNESS AWAY. THE WAYS-OF-OLD WILL NOW RETURN! WE SHALL REBUILD OUR EMPIRE TO THE WAY THE GODS INTENDED IT TO BE SO MANY MILLENNIA AGO.

Sebastian's head was still bowed. *I'm sorry I couldn't save Ivez.*

ALL IS NOT LOST, YOUNG WARRIOR! YOUR HEART IS PURE, AND YOUR INTENTIONS ARE TRUE. YOUR LIFE WAS NEVER IN DANGER. YOU WERE FORGIVEN THE MOMENT YOU LEFT US. OUR HORRENDOUS ACTIONS WERE NOT OUR OWN. Their gaze shifted toward Adeline. *THE LOST ONE WILL REMAIN WITH US, FOR OUR BROTHER'S ESSENCE STILL RESIDES INSIDE HER DARKENED HEART. DO NOT DESPAIR! WE WILL WAKE OUR BROTHER FROM HIS TORTURED SLUMBER.*

Sebastian locked eyes with Adeline.

She was shaking her head profusely, her eyes wide with fear of the unknown. *You can't leave me here with them! They will surely kill me for my transgressions!*

What choice did he have? He may not have wanted her dead, but her fate was out of his hands now.

I'm sorry, he told her. And he truly was. He turned his attention back to the Pure Ones. *What about Avery? Her mind has been altered by... the Lost One.*

The Pure Ones' purple flames grew brighter. *WE ARE AWARE OF THE MORTAL AND YOUR UNFAILING LOVE FOR HER.*

Sebastian flinched. Loving a mortal was still forbidden.

Dray's eyes softened, though his voice came through loud and clear. *WE WILL NOT INTERFERE WITH THE PREDETERMINED COURSE OF FATE! HOWEVER, YOUR DESTINY IS STILL YOUR OWN, YOUNG*

WARRIOR. LISTEN CLOSE, HEAR US! LIFE AS YOU KNOW IT IS GOING TO CHANGE. THE DARKNESS HAS COME TO AN END. THE LIGHT OF PURITY SHALL SHINE FOREVERMORE.

Sebastian bowed again, showing his loyalty and devotion, though his broken heart had just completely shattered. The Pure Ones were his last hope at restoring Avery's memories; now he had nowhere else to turn.

The atmosphere of the sanctuary had changed exponentially. The Cursed Ones that remained would be tested and taught the true ways of the Pure Ones. The rest would be searched for and brought 'home' to join their brethren. Hope had been restored for so many lost souls, yet Sebastian's soul was in tatters. The Watchers had gathered to say their goodbyes. The Pure Ones thanked them all, renewing their long-standing relationship and restoring their faith in one another. Their fallen comrades were given proper anointing to cleanse their bodies for the afterlife that awaited them. Things were definitely changing. A much brighter future lie ahead.

Jonah, Chase, Isabelle, and Elliot were the last of the Watchers to leave. They were waiting on Sebastian, who was nowhere to be found. As they stood on the edge of the mountain top, overlooking the beautiful, awe-inspiring scenery, a gut-wrenching cry echoed all around them. It sounded like a dying animal in distress, but they knew without a doubt that it was Sebastian.

His broken heart from losing Avery had become too much for him to bear. He refused to feel the pain that had latched itself deep inside to the core of his soul. A luminous flash appeared off in the distance…a tell-tale sign that he had shifted into his Cursed Form. His sorrow-filled cries repeated over and over, becoming further and further away until they died out completely.

CHAPTER 42

The End.

Just kidding…

CHAPTER 43

Four months later...

Night had fallen by the time Sebastian made it to the school parking lot. Tonight was supposed to be a special night for him and Avery. One that he wasn't exactly sure how he felt about. It had been over four months since his entire existence had been wiped from her mind and he still couldn't wrap his head around it all. He stood by his car and watched his fellow classmates entering the dimly lit entryway. They were all dressed up in tuxedos and long, elegant dresses. Music blared from inside the gymnasium where their prom was in full swing.

Sebastian looked down at his tattered and torn clothing and sighed. He was clearly under-dressed for such an occasion, but that is what happens when you travel the world at a moment's notice.

After losing Avery to Adeline's brain-wipe, his mind had been a swollen mess of sadness and betrayal. In a desperate attempt to dull his broken heart, he had turned off his humanity and transitioned to his Cursed Form. Blind fury was the only thing that had pushed him forward.

The entire time within his Cursed Form, he was unaware of the days and nights passing, right up until the moment he was forced back into his human form. The sudden and unexpected shift left him face down in the dirt, disoriented, dizzy, and slightly confused. The entire world felt as if it were spinning beneath him as he dug his fingers into the earth to steady himself.

Sebastian knew in that very moment that Ivez's essence had been restored. He felt the darkness of Moira's curse leave his body in such a rush that it momentarily left him in a paralytic state.

His fiery essence was fading away. The tainted blood running through his veins was slowly being purified. His power was being drained, taking away his gift of immortality. He was becoming human again. A mere mortal.

It was a strange and unsettling feeling to now be so defenseless and weak. He wasn't sure if he could actually live a normal life like he had always dreamed of...or if he would completely fail at re-entering human society. Only time would tell. But one thing was for sure; he needed to see Avery...at least one more time.

Sebastian entered through the side doors of the high school, heading down the familiar hallway, passing by small groups of people lingering in the corridor. Some of them stared at him, probably from his lack of attire, or perhaps because he looked as if he had just come from a war zone...which wasn't too far from the truth. Nevertheless, he ignored them. He honestly didn't care what they thought.

As he stood in the opened double doorway just out of sight, he scanned the crowded gymnasium for Avery. It was difficult without the ability to listen for her heartbeat, but eventually he spotted her dancing near the back corner with Valerie, Paige, and a few more of her friends. He smiled to himself as he watched her twirling in a beautiful, silver-sequined, floor-length gown. She and Valerie began jumping around, laughing and giggling.

She's finally happy, he thought to himself.

Jonah unexpectedly stepped out of the shadows on the other side of the doorway. "I wasn't sure if you were going to show up tonight. It's good to see you."

Sebastian acknowledged his friend's presence without taking his eyes off Avery. "How has she been since…?" His voice trailed off.

"She's been…normal, I guess," Jonah said quietly. He wasn't sure how else to respond.

Sebastian sighed. "And how exactly did you explain the sudden amnesia she has when it comes to me?"

Jonah crossed his arms. "Chase and I said you two had a bad falling out, and she's acting like she doesn't know you as a coping mechanism."

Sebastian's forehead wrinkled as he finally looked Jonah in the eye. "And everyone bought that?"

Jonah shrugged. "Yeah. So far."

Sebastian sighed again and rubbed his eyes. "Well, it'll be much easier to believe once I'm really gone. After a while, everyone will completely forget about me and move on. Then I'll just be a long-lost memory of good-ol-what's-his-name."

"Gone?" Jonah repeated. "Where are you going now? You just got back."

"I'm leaving…for good. There's nothing left for me here."

"How can you say that?" Jonah countered. His voice raised. "We're here! You may not need us as Watchers because you're not cursed anymore, but we're still your family!"

Sebastian shot his friend a heartfelt glance. "I know that…but I can't be this close to her and not have her in my life." He sighed again as he watched her continue to twirl and sway as the music played on.

Jonah knew that look all too well. "Why don't you ask her to dance? Introduce yourself and start over. Make her fall in love with you again."

"I didn't come here to dance, J. I came to say a final goodbye. Even if she doesn't remember me, I still owe her that much."

Jonah shook his head. "You're giving up way too easy."

"This is anything but easy," Sebastian snapped. "And I'm not giving up; I'm admitting defeat...there's a difference. I know when it's time to walk away. Besides, she only loved me because I was the boy who saved her. That was our bond. Now we have no starting point. I'd just be a regular guy in her eyes."

"But that's what you've always wanted," Jonah reminded him. Then he lowered his voice as a few students passed by. "To be just a regular guy. A human with no darkness inside."

At that exact moment, 'Thank You for Loving Me' by Jon Bon Jovi began to play. One by one, couples gathered on the dance floor. Avery had her eyes closed as she leaned her head against Kyle's shoulder. They were swaying in perfect sync as the melody played on. Kyle's hands were on her hips, holding her tight.

Sebastian's eyes began to glisten as he looked away. *Being human sucks.* He was unable to shut off his emotions. He was unable to hide his feelings. And because of that, he was an absolute vulnerable mess. "This is exactly why I have to go," he whispered sadly.

Jonah sighed quietly. "I know what you're thinking right now, but you should know that she didn't come here with anyone...and Kyle has been dancing with pretty much everyone."

"That doesn't change things."

Jonah placed his hand on his friend's shoulder. "I'm sorry, B."

Sebastian forced himself to look at her again. He wanted to remember each and every detail of her beautiful face. Then he said the one thing he had promised her that he would never say again. *Goodbye, Avery.* And with that, he turned to leave.

With each step that he took away from her, it felt like his broken heart was being smashed on the ground beneath his feet. As he pushed open the doors at the end of the hall, his heart seemed to flat line. He staggered across the parking lot, allowing the cool night air to caress his tear-stained face.

~*~*~*~

The moment Sebastian had turned to leave, Avery had barely caught the side view of his face before he disappeared into the shadows. All at once, a weird sensation came over her. She felt an uncontrollable urge to follow him.

Kyle leaned in closer. "Are you okay?"

"Yeah, I'm fine," she said quietly. "I just need to take a break for a minute and get some air. I'll be right back." She politely excused herself and headed for the doorway.

Jonah nodded a casual hello as he watched her curious expression.

Avery stood in the darkened hallway, only catching a glimpse of Sebastian's backside as he walked through the double doors at the end of the hall. Without any hesitation, she rushed to the doors, flinging them open. She scanned the parking lot until her eyes fell on the stranger who looked so familiar to her somehow. Suddenly, her head began to throb. She squeezed her eyes shut and clutched her head in her hands. This time, though, she heard a voice whispering to her. But the harder she strained to hear it, the worse her headache became. She stared after the boy who was now five-car rows away.

Sebastian slammed his fist on the hood of his car as he cried out in sadness and frustration. *I can't do this!* He slammed his fists three more times, but barely a dent was made. He thought about what would have happened had he done that when he still possessed his inhuman strength. The car would have easily become a compact. An emotional laugh slipped out without his permission as another tear rolled down his cheek.

Avery stumbled closer, still clutching her pounding head. The whispering in her mind was slowly getting louder and louder, though she still wasn't able to focus on the words. She watched as the boy slammed his fists against a car again and again. Then he covered his face with his hands. She could see his body trembling as his cries grew louder. As she staggered closer, her head felt like it was about to explode. *Is this what having an aneurysm feels like?*

She was only one-cars length away from him now. While she watched him pace back and forth, the whisper in her mind suddenly became clear.

I wish I could go back…back to seeing that scared little girl in the abandoned lot with those beautiful green eyes looking up at me. You never knew it, because I never told you, but I fell in love with you that day. I needed you in my life, but all I ever did was push you away. Oh, God, why did I push you away? I should have let you in sooner, then maybe we would have had more time. Time to let go. Time to just be us. But I can't go back. I can't make you love me again. The worst part of it all is that I never got to tell you how I felt. I didn't believe you when you said you'd never leave me. I'm so sorry for that. I wish I would have gotten to see the look on your face when I told you those three precious words that you so desperately wanted to hear…

As the voice talked about the past, memories came rushing back to Avery's mind in little flashes. She saw herself wrapping her arms around this stranger's neck and pulling him closer. She saw herself fighting with him. She saw herself crying over him. She saw herself in a darkened movie theater sitting by his side. As each small flashback played, emotions from each memory threatened to overtake her, causing more spikes of pain to shoot through her skull.

She took a step closer, angling herself so she could see the boy's face. She didn't know his name, she didn't know who he was, and she didn't know what was wrong…but something inside her was yearning to figure all those things out. She watched as his lips moved. That is when she realized it was *his* voice that she was somehow hearing inside her head.

Each word that he mouthed she could hear perfectly within her mind as if he was standing right beside her. The closer she got, the more memories flooded her thoughts, the more her heart began to race, the more her eyes filled with tears, and her head continued to pound. She was only a foot or so away from him now. Suddenly, his mouth stopped moving and the voice in her mind hushed.

Sebastian was not aware of Avery's close proximity to him without his ability to hear her heartbeat. So, when her voice promptly came from directly behind him, he was completely caught off guard.

"Hi…"

His breath caught in his throat as he stood there tense and unmoving. There was no time for him to compose himself. Hell, there was no time for him to run away either, not that he would have done that. So, he wiped his nose on his sleeve and let out a deep sigh; then he turned around. At first, he avoided making direct eye contact with her. "Uh, hi, Avery."

He knows me? "Is everything okay?" she asked softly.

He forced a smile and wiped his teary eyes. "Yeah. I'm fine. Just having a rough night."

Talking to her was harder than he ever could have imagined. Then he made the mistake of stealing a glance in her direction. The instant their eyes met, hers widened, and she gasped. For a split second he wondered if his eyes were glowing, then he remembered that wasn't possible anymore.

Avery managed to get out a small groan before she began to sway, nearly falling over. "I…feel…dizzy," she whispered.

Sebastian grabbed hold of her arm to help keep her steady just before she collapsed onto the ground. Without his lightning-fast reflexes, he was barely able to catch her in time.

"Hold onto me until it passes," he said quietly as he pulled her closer.

By this point, her head was throbbing so severely that she could barely move. She didn't even think twice about it as she nestled into his lap, sliding her arms around his waist.

Sebastian felt his already decimated heart crack just a little more. A million thoughts raced through his mind as he was holding her. *She doesn't know who I am anymore, but yet somehow, having her in my arms again feels like nothing has changed.* He wrapped his arms around her tighter, leaning his head against hers. *If only my curse hadn't taken you away from me, maybe then things could have ended differently. I always knew I'd lose you, but I never expected it to hurt this bad.*

Avery sniffled. And not even a second later, Sebastian heard two words that would change his life forever. Two words that he had heard countless times before, yet never expected to hear again.

"You're wrong," Avery whispered.

The ability to communicate telepathically should have been taken away when his curse was eliminated, but somehow their connection was still there. Sebastian loosened his grip and looked down at her, rather confused. "What? What did you just say?"

She looked up at him smiling, eyes glistening with unshed tears. "I said…you're wrong."

It was impossible, or at the very least it should have been, but there was that look of adoration she always gave him. The yearning in her eyes. The glimmer of hope that she always possessed.

Sebastian was so stunned that he had forgotten how to speak. The only thing he could say was her name, and even that came out as a pitiful whimper. "Avery…?"

Suddenly, she latched her arms around his neck and began sobbing into his shoulder. "I remember you…" she whispered. "I remember everything! I'm so sorry, Bastian." She squeezed him tighter.

Sebastian was so overcome with joy that he completely broke down. His mind, heart, and body were becoming highly overstimulated. He had forgotten how much emotional turmoil a mortal had to endure. He held onto her tight as he breathed her in. His body started shaking as tears blurred his vision. He was now crying so hard that he wasn't able to breathe anymore. He was gasping and choking on his own sobs, wishing that he could calm himself down.

His thoughts got lost in their last moments together. The final moments when she still remembered who he was…before her memories had been taken away…before his life had fallen apart…before they had been torn away from each other. He could clearly see himself lying in her lap on the cold dungeon floor, dying, fading into nothingness. He had been in the middle of showing her what their life would be like. He was about to tell her how much he loved her, but death took him first.

He pulled back for only a moment and stared into her

beautiful, glistening eyes and gasped.

"What is it?" she choked out. "What's wrong?"

Sebastian wasn't sure if he would be able to speak right then, but he opened his mouth and the words poured out. "I died before I could tell you…"

"Tell me what?"

With the worry of his curse no longer on his shoulders, Sebastian grinned from ear to ear as tears continued to fall. "I love you!" he suddenly cried out. He screamed it into her mind as he screamed it into the air. "A million times, *I LOVE YOU!*" Then he kissed her. Long and passionate.

Avery could not bring herself to close her eyes. *This has to be a dream*, she thought. She could feel his lips turn up into a smile while still pressed against hers.

It's not, he replied. *I can assure you, it's definitely not!*

She smiled too as she finally closed her eyes, running her fingers through his soft messy hair, pulling his tear-soaked face closer.

Years' worth of pent-up emotions continued to overflow, enveloping them in an invisible bubble of passion, wonderment, and love.

Neither of them were sure of how long they had been sitting there together…but it was long enough for Sebastian to finally regain some control over his emotional state. He still had tears rolling down his face, but at least he could breathe again. He stood, keeping his mouth against hers; pushing her gently against his car and wrapping his arms tighter around her.

He reached out to her mind. *I want to ask you something.*

Avery's body shivered even in his warm embrace. *Yes?*

Sebastian moved his hands down her arms until he found her hands, slowly intertwining their fingers together. *I may be somewhat underdressed for an event such as this, but…may I have the honor of the last dance?*

Avery grinned, pulling away from their kiss. *On one condition...*

~*~*~*~

Hand in hand they entered the gymnasium. Countless

strands of white and purple lights were twinkling overhead as Sebastian instantly broke out into one of their crazy dance sessions. Avery burst out laughing as a giddy feeling filled her heart. She didn't even hesitate as she joined right in, ignoring all the gawking stares. It was as if they had been transported back to her living room. Jumping around. Wiggling and laughing.

Sebastian eventually slowed his pace as he wrapped his arms around her waist. He pulled her toward him as he leaned down and kissed her forehead. For that moment, and the few that followed, it felt as though they were the only two people in the room. As their bodies began to sway perfectly together, 'Photograph' by Ed Sheeran started to play.

Avery spoke softly into his mind. *I love you.*

I love you more.

She pulled away and looked up at him, then she smiled. "What if you're wrong?"

He cupped her face in his hands as he leaned back down, hovering his mouth just centimeters from hers. "I'm never wrong," he whispered. Then he kissed her again.

THE END.

ABOUT THE AUTHOR

If you are interested to learn more about Dani Healy, visit:
Dani Healy: The Cursed One on Facebook
or
www.danihealyfiction.com

ABOUT THE COVER ARTIST

If you are interested to learn more about Kate Ford, visit:
www.katharine-ford.com

ACKNOWLEDGEMENTS

I want to say a HUGE thank you to all my family and friends who had a hand in the editing/publication process of my very first book, *The Cursed One.*

First and foremost, to my amazing mama, **Claudia**: There aren't enough words in the English language to convey how truly blessed I am to have you in my corner. Thank you for all the love, support, and encouragement you've always given me. I wouldn't be me without you! Forever my mother, always my friend. Jesus loves you and so do I! *muah*

My sweet Godmother, **Peggy**: *HA-HA* Here's to oversized Miami Dolphin slippers and trolls in your car...trips to the beach with Dunkin' Donuts in the early morning...and endless giggles after singing "This is the song that doesn't end..." Thank you for being the best Godmom a girl could ever ask for, and for supporting me in this dream. God bless! I love you more, I win (and since it's in writing, it must be true lol)!

Kate Ford: From 'dreams' to 'curses', you've literally been there for me every step of the way. Thank you for being my un-biological sister, for never allowing me to settle for less than my best, for knowing when to be blunt and when to let me down easy, for constantly making me laugh with your crazy-off-the-wall-ness lol...and also, thank you for the cool-as-hell cover. It took a while to figure out which direction to go, but you managed to create the most amazingly spectacular piece of art! You're the bestestest ever and I ruv joo bunches my loverpants!

Lynn Floyd: "I'm covered in beeeeeeees!" LOL Because of you, I finally realized that I was, in fact, a "Comma Queen" lol...C and J were actually twins (facepalm)...the bushes lining the road really did need more detail *FTB*...and what in the world is "crazing"???? lol Thank you for showing up in the middle of the night when I lacked inspiration, or just needed a hug. Twinnies 4 life + Cards Against Humanity = The Most Epic Nights Ever! I love you!

Frantz "The Tickle Monster" Jr.: You were one of the first to read the 'completed story' (which was how many drafts ago now? lol), and even back then, all the questions and ideas and feedback made my heart literally swell with joy. Being able to talk about my characters and have someone know who they are, that is the most amazing feeling ever! Also, thank you for helping me come up with the name for a certain "device" I ended up giving to Adeline, and for the gentle push that set a possible sequel in motion…let's see if I can actually get that done lol. I love you "Frantzypoo" hehe

Marthe: From strangers to friends, all because of a single book! Thank you for being the first person outside of my 'comfort circle' to share in this process! You have no idea how much your interest and positive feedback meant to me! I hope when you read this final version, you notice some changes and details that were added thanks to you. You are forever a part of my heart!

John Gerlach: *sounds foghorn* Well, here it is…the final moment we've been counting down to! I can hear you already, "Took ya long enough" lol. Thank you for pushing me even when I didn't want you to, and for listening to me vent when certain things just became too much (so many things fall into this category, eh?)…but most of all, thank you for being one of my dearest friends! Distance, schmistance…the 12-hour time difference didn't stand a chance against us lol I love you! See you in the current corner!

Ernie Aldama: The "Fuzzy-pawz-blanket-stealer-of-Crushbone" has arrived! lol Well, would ya lookie here, I finally published this thing! haha I wanted to thank you for being such a wonderful friend all these years and for supporting me and giving me your honest input on my story! Your words of encouragement really meant a lot to me! I hope to see you in the far-off lands of EQ2 for more of our awesome adventures. *super big tackle hugs*

Mohammed Al Mohammed Al Sibahi: Throughout this friendship of ours, I have learned that life isn't always sunshine and rainbows, and people aren't always who or what they seem...but if we keep our focus and hold onto our faith, we can get through anything. Thank you for always being honest... for being there for me (in so many ways)...and for being the final editor for my story! The ocean may separate us *for now*, but you still managed to be by my side. Always remember, "Not a day goes by..." and "Even if we can't find heaven, I'll walk through hell with you." بحبك I love you, bestie!

Randie Reigns: A quick shout-out to you, my dear friend, not only for teaching me about the whole frustrating template process, but also for jumping in at the last minute and giving me ideas that ended up adding some pretty important touches to my book! You rock, chick! Never forget, "Your crazy matches my crazy!" Thank you so much! Love and hugs!

Wa'el Jom'aa: My dear, Wa'el...my font-finding-partner haha. Thank you so much for all the help and support you've given me. The little tweaks and changes you offered were very much appreciated...even when my cussing drove you crazy lol. Your sweet words and positive opinions seriously made my day! P.S. those "creepy-bouncy-snowball-ghost-babies" are forever gonna remind me of you LOL (and when we read this in 50 years, we will probably look at each other and go, "What in the world were we talking about?" hahaha.) I love you!

And last, but certainly not least, to **YOU**, the person reading this right now...thank you too! I hope you enjoyed reading my story as much as I enjoyed writing it! And if there are any grammar mistakes or punctuation issues...blame those people above for not catching them! (just kidding...ish haha)